PROTÉGÉE

A NOVEL

C. C. AVRAM

Shields
Publishing

An Allen-Dobrin Book
Published by Shields Publishing
206 S. Fifth Ave.
Ann Arbor, MI 48104

Library Of Congress Catalog Number
93-83905

ISBN 1-883545-00-5

The characters and events portrayed in this book are fictitious. Any
similarities to real persons, living or dead, are purely coincidental and
not intended by the author.

ACKNOWLEDGMENTS

The privilege of friendships is what life is all about. If my heartfelt thanks could be written to all my wonderful friends, this book would span a thousand pages. To my unbelievable family who has always and will *forever* be the wind beneath my wings, I love you. My special thanks to my parents, Edley and Enid Moulton, my sisters and best friends Shirley F. Moulton (my "get-in-trouble" twin), Dawn C. Moulton-Tonico, Paulette Moulton-Levy, and to my Nana, Eliza Manderson for giving me the determination and the will to live my dream. To my most wonderful son Kenneth for his love and patience, my nieces, Natasha, Nonaine, Natalie and Megan and my brother-in-law H.George Levy for his vision and support of Protégée. To Darlene Dobrin, my editor: You are the best, the very best. Thanks for all the reading and rereading, but most of all for your continued support and your friendship. And Snookums, what can I say?

In memory of E.S.

Chapter 1

London

"Please remain seated until the aircraft has come to a complete stop." The British Airways flight attendant, immaculate in her navy blue suit and cocked bowler hat, had not completed her sentence before she saw that one passenger was already standing in the aisle, waiting impatiently for the doors to open. It was obvious that not only was this woman less than concerned with following directives, but that the startled attendant knew better than to say a word to her.

From the recent rash of print and television coverage, she had recognized the passenger as Andrea Jacobson, the New York-based business wizard whose worth was rumored to be fast approaching a billion dollars. Like so many others, the flight attendant was impressed—despite all the nasty gossip about her past touted by the splashy tabloids. This strikingly beautiful woman, the more respected journalists reported, had competed in a man's world and had come out on top of the heap as the sole owner of a giant computer conglomerate. Andrea Jacobson was certainly not someone with whom she was prepared to argue over fastening a seat belt! Behind her proper British facade, Andrea noticed that the flight attendant was awed, but she had become accustomed to that lately, and would have been mildly surprised had she not sensed it.

According to the media, Andrea Jacobson had revolutionized the computer industry. She was credited with moving Jacobson's Industry from a quite prosperous but neophyte business to that of a mature and efficient organization that had taken its place solidly among the Fortune 500 companies. Andrea, as those who knew her repeated, had always insisted that diversification was the key to the growth and longevity of her company and it came as no surprise to them when the prolific extent of her holdings was first revealed in the *Wall Street Journal*. She was reportedly involved in a kaleidoscope of industrial ventures in the United States as well as in countries around the world, and the dizzying growth of her company in the past eight years was unmatched by any other in recent history. To her dismay, because she had always carefully guarded her privacy, Andrea had become an overnight media sensation, a celebrity.

Giving the beaming flight attendant a casual nod of thanks, Andrea stepped briskly across the ramp of British Airways #532 and into Heathrow Airport. As she had intended, Andrea was the first passenger to deplane. She was followed closely by Melissa, lugging their lightweight carry-on bags. Much more than her personal attendant, Melissa was Andrea's oldest friend, who from her childhood memories had assumed the role of nurturing mother that Andrea had always wished hers to be. Having been with the Francis family since Andrea was two years old, their years of separation when Andrea left Jamaica for formal education in England had not for a moment affected this closeness. Every bit of the time apart was immediately erased when Melissa eventually came to New York to take charge of Andrea's own household. The pressures that followed the death of her husband, giving her the entire responsibility of directing the burgeoning Jacobson's Industry, had made Andrea's personal life nearly unmanageable, and she could think of no one better suited to take care of her than Melissa who knew Andrea like no other human being did—except perhaps her father.

As a child, it was into Melissa's bed that she would climb on nights when she had one of her spooky dreams.

"You shouldn't be scared to dream," Melissa would always say in her lilting, soothing voice, "dreams are your contact with the supernatural. They are there to protect and guide you if you would take the time to understand them. Andrea, I think that you have some special gift that you need to recognize. I can't explain it, child, but you do."

"What kind of gift, Melissa?" Andrea would press her to explain further.

"Do you remember the time when your sister Patricia was so very ill that the doctors thought she would die?"

"Yes," Andrea would always reply, knowing what was coming.

"I think it was you who saved her life."

"Oh Melissa, stop!" the girl would say, as usual.

"I mean it, you know. The moment the priest gave Pat her last rites I saw you fall to your knees under the big willow tree and start praying. You were only three years old at the time but you went into what seemed like a trance and just as you got up off your knees your sister, who had been unconscious for a week, opened her eyes and cried for your mother."

"Go on with you," Andrea would say, kissing the top of Melissa's forehead and snuggling up closer to her comfortable bosom. "You're as good at making up stories as father is."

She had finally gotten tired of listening to that story. It was repeated at Christmas, year after year, and as if on cue the entire family never failed to cry. Andrea had never believed a word of it, not really. When she was older she knew she often had what Melissa called "premonitions," but this was nothing she considered unusual. Anyway, how could she take Melissa seriously? After all, she was a member of one of those revivalist Christian congregations that spoke in tongues and believed God made miracles. As far as Andrea was concerned, people made their own miracles and she was sure that one day she would create hers.

Showing her passport, Andrea made her way quickly through customs while Melissa went on to the baggage claim area to identify their luggage. Melissa, leading a porter who was invisible behind a cart stacked high with Ginka luggage, soon joined Andrea in the main concourse of the airport. Clearing customs was simple. It had all been easily pre-arranged by a call from her New York office.

Looking about impatiently for her appointed driver, Andrea had quickly spotted the maroon Jacobson's insignia on his stylish navy jacket and moved swiftly towards the Bentley, briefly acknowledging the chauffeur's presence. Refusing to have her name held up on a piece of cardboard for everyone to see, she had her New York office arrange another way for her to identify her driver. Conferring with their office in Switzerland because she had no British holdings, they had decided on outfitting him in a custom-made Jacobson's Industry suit. It was the same uniform that was worn world-wide by everyone below middle management at Jacobson's Industry, expensive, understated, but easily recognizable.

As Andrea stepped into the limousine beside Melissa she checked her watch with a bemused expression and smiled. It had taken only fifteen minutes to be on her way into the city. Money had its advantages. Silently, Melissa pulled a Russian sable lap robe around Andrea's knees and then turned to the window, leaving

Andrea to her own thoughts. Andrea's wealth was something Melissa accepted without question because they both knew Andrea had been born to possess power.

Andrea had been aware of her unique strength very early in life, having had a way of getting what she wanted even as a child. Even though her father had succumbed to her expressive striped brown eyes much more often than her mother had, Andrea's ability to keep her mother feeling guilty for having abandoned her as a child had worked wonders in deepening her control over both parents. Indeed, Andrea's assertive personality had always served her well and she had no interest in altering it. In fact, she was not sure if she could change even if she tried, since she knew no other way of being.

"Andrea," her friend Linda Smith, head of Jacobson's Industry's public relations department, would often tell her, "You're always speeding along even when there's nothing to do. Why don't you take some instructions in relaxation and meditation? I know an excellent teacher."

"You're right, Linda," Andrea would say, just to appease her, not meaning one word of it. "Give me the name and phone number of your teacher and one day when I truly have nothing to do, I will surprise you and call for an appointment. But Linda," she would add sweetly, "never forget that this company was built on hard work, because I always found something to do when there was 'nothing to do'."

"You need to slow down"; "you have to be more patient"; and "you have to be less of a perfectionist," were phrases that Andrea heard often. As much as she appreciated this thoughtful advice from her well-meaning acquaintances, Andrea knew she couldn't possibly alter her frenetic style, positive it was a basic key to her success. And she liked it that way. In fact, she had been quite satisfied with her absorbing life, having deliberately perfected the art of getting what she wanted from early childhood. Andrea had viewed life as a difficult game she must win; she had learned well how to play it and was not about to change.

It had been nearly fourteen years since Andrea left England, and she looked around with undisguised interest as the limousine pulled away from Heathrow. Not much had changed in all those years, it seemed. Recalling the five years she had lived in this smoggy, gloomy country, Andrea felt they had been the best years of her life as memories of happier times flooded her mind. Yet, as the car sped quietly toward the hotel, the forbidding dark cloud again descended on her thoughts. She shuddered, trying to shake the fear, willing herself away from worrying about what tomorrow might bring, concentrating on the present as she had disciplined herself to do so well.

Although Andrea's Jamaican family were reasonably well off, the Francis' money had not afforded her excessive luxuries, nor when Alex died had she inherited enough from her husband's estate to make her the incredibly successful businesswoman she had since become. It was as sole owner of Jacobson's Industry in the five years since Alex's death that she had almost single-handedly achieved rock-solid financial independence and professional regard. Now, at thirty-five, she had become a woman of great power and social status, having fought her way to the top not only because she had focused almost exclusively on that goal, but because she was tough, charismatic and intelligent. Even though she was referred to by most of her employees as the "Dragon Lady," because she was volatile and difficult to please, they readily admitted that she was fair; their employer was a woman with a keen sense of decency along with an eye for the most profitable business deal. Obviously, everyone agreed, no one built a multibillion dollar corporation on fair play alone; but that was indeed Andrea Jacobson's greatest unspoken asset. She had left many casualties behind in her business dealings, but she always won fair and square.

Yet with all of her accomplishments, Andrea was still

burdened with one casualty that she could no longer pretend to ignore. The gnawing secret that had been submerged in her psyche all these years had finally begun to rob her of any tranquillity or peace of mind. Finally, courageously, Andrea had decided she must try to put the past to rest, a past that could only be laid to rest in England. She shivered again to think what was ahead, but knew she had to face it at last.

"Claridge's was it, ma'am?" the cockney voice interrupted her thoughts.

"Claridge's, yes, thank you," she said, the resignation in her voice causing Melissa to look at her with concern.

Having traveled for seven hours, Andrea was glad to have reached her destination. The luxurious Claridge's, one of the finest hotels in the world, would offer her the kind of pampering she so needed right now. In spite of her tiredness, she was suddenly amused at what the driver must have thought when he saw her. He must have been shocked to pick up a black woman who was neither an entertainer nor a movie star, yet if he was surprised, he was certainly diplomatic enough (or British enough, she chuckled inwardly) not to show it.

When the driver brought the car to a complete stop, Andrea was puzzled, wondering if he had misunderstood or had somehow changed the itinerary without her permission. She saw a uniformed doorman approaching them from the doorway of an inconspicuous building over which flags of various countries swayed gently in the breeze.

"This is Claridge's?"

"Yes ma'am, we are here."

How like the British, Andrea remembered, to be so elegantly unpretentious. She had heard that much of the history of England was reflected in this Mayfair establishment that had been the favorite haunt of royalty and other distinguished guests for more than a hundred years. It had grown old with dignity in a way that

7

only the Europeans seemed to appreciate.

"I will have a schedule of when I shall need you sent down in a hour or so, Peter," Andrea said, after checking the name neatly stitched on his lapel. "But," she continued, her proper English-educated words sparkling with the residue of a Jamaican lilt, "even when you are not scheduled, I want you to be available. And Peter," she said, already walking away, "Thank you."

Andrea, in her usual way, sailed from the car through the entrance of the hotel, Melissa hurrying in her wake, leaving the driver and a porter to struggle with her luggage.

Done in art deco, Claridge's lobby was almost as much a surprise to Andrea as she apparently was to it. As she strode purposefully toward the front desk all eyes turned toward this extremely tall slender woman with a *café au lait* complexion. Sheathed in a fashionably fitted Valentino suit, her expensive shoes showed merely a hint of heels but set off shapely long legs, and a tan cashmere coat was worn casually over her shoulders. She seemed oblivious to the appreciative stares of strangers. Whether they recognized her or were simply awed by Andrea's unique beauty, her audience was ignored.

Those stunning features had recently been splashed across the cover of every supermarket tabloid, her precious anonymity now gone. She wondered what prevarications the news magazines would write about her next. Had Andrea not been such a hot item for the press lately, she would have taken her private jet, but she had purposely made an exception for this trip, not wanting to appear as if she had something to hide which would make the hordes of paparazzi more curious than they already were. She had traveled from New York to London on a commercial airliner, on public display, the subject of whispered gossip and speculation.

Removing her gold-framed sunglasses, Andrea looked around the lobby and frowned, realizing only then to her utter dismay that the hotel was dimly lighted. Magnificent as it had proved to be,

Claridge's was far too somber for her. Andrea, too tired to deal with her dissatisfaction, made a mental note to find accommodations more suited to her aversion to darkness. She would have Melissa check them into another hotel in the morning where she was sure the lighting would be more to her liking. Andrea had hated darkness as a child, and even now slept with a night light on no matter who shared her bed. At the moment, however, she would be grateful just to sink into a warm bath and then to wrap herself in one of the immense and wonderfully thick terry-cloth robes that salved the conscience of luxury hotels for grossly overcharging their guests.

"Is everything satisfactory, madam?" the bell captain asked, walking toward her as if in a procession. He had been instructed by his superiors in no uncertain terms to make sure she wanted for nothing. She was certainly an outstanding example of female pulchritude, he could see that. Why, even the crease in her brow when she frowned added a certain mystique to this Andrea Jacobson. Yes, he could see she was a most magnificent woman, most magnificent indeed! Her face was exquisite, unblemished by time or weather; the tone contrasted gloriously with almost translucent striped brown eyes, a characteristic possessed, he thought, only by tigers. Her ancestry declared itself again in thick jet-black hair worn swept back into a French twist. A style that would have given most women a severe look only served to accentuate Andrea's high cheek bones and gave her an exotic air of sophistication. One of God's more perfect creations, the captain decided, his haughty demeanor masking his thoughts.

"Everything is fine, thank you."

"Welcome to Claridge's, Ms. Jacobson," the concierge said politely from behind the counter. "Your travel cases are being delivered to your suite. I have several messages waiting for you, madam, would you like them now?" he continued.

"No, thank you, John, I'll call for them later."

Andrea had years ago learned the art of memorizing name tags whenever possible. The personal touch tended to reinforce their admiration and stimulate the alacrity of their response to her needs.

"If you follow the porter, he will direct you to your suite," the concierge said, with a smile acknowledging her thoughtfulness. Melissa was already being led away, accepted as one of Andrea's exclusive "insiders," a companion rather than servant, and therefore a person to handle most courteously.

Contrary to what she had expected, the rooms were light and airy and their high sculptured ceilings made them appear bigger than they really were. Numerous pieces of luggage were already neatly placed in one corner of the sitting room, ready to be sorted out by the maids. Andrea decided to look around the suite, intrigued as always by the decor of a hotel new to her. Although the furniture was a dark mahogany, the fabrics and accessories were in beautiful pastels. There were a variety of green, blue and peach pillows on the flowered chaise longue. Andrea was delighted. She would not need to check out of the hotel after all. And she loved the color peach.

Flowers flanked the room, but a particular floral arrangement on the highly polished cocktail table especially caught her attention. Long graceful birds of paradise were interwoven with orchids and roses in a most unusual arrangement. There was a note attached. Andrea opened the scented envelope and smiled as she read the inscription: "I dare you not to notice. *J.*" She laid the card next to the bouquet and tossed her coat over a chair on the way to her bedroom where she found a splendid canopied bed draped with sheer peach curtains and covered with a down comforter in a floral design that matched the chaise longue in the sitting room. Heavy brocade with tassels and ties covered an expanse of windows. Andrea pulled them open, fastening the tassels to the gold window hooks, and absorbed bustling London for a long moment before turning away.

On a small table she discovered a huge basket of fruit, and a nearby silver tray held a bottle of her favorite wine, Château d'Yquem, two gold-rimmed hand-cut tulip glasses and a very sinful box of Neahaus chocolates. A discreetly placed card let her know these gifts were from the hotel, not a secret admirer. Andrea opened the chocolates. She would have to do thirty extra jumps in her morning aerobics routine just for this indulgence, but what the hell, she thought, why not?

Pouring herself a glass of wine, momentarily savoring the electric sweetness, she carried it with her to yet another room which proved to be a study complete with an ornate Chippendale desk, leather chairs, an Impressionist painting above a fireplace, Claridge's engraved stationery and some bound books. She wondered idly if the painting was a duplication. Since the rooms were beautifully appointed and cheerfully decorated, with every imaginable convenience at her fingertips, Andrea began to make herself at home.

She was beginning to unwind after her long journey when the flashing red light on the phone reminded her that she had messages. There were two, one from her office in New York which she decided to ignore until morning and one from Jacques asking her to meet him for dinner at seven. Andrea looked at her watch. It was two o'clock British time, enough time to take a long hot bath and to get at least three hours of needed sleep before meeting him. Her mind lingered on Jacques momentarily, but she quickly pushed him out of her thoughts as the buzzer rang and Melissa entered the room.

"Everything is all taken care of. I am just down the hall from your sitting room. And here is my extension and the phone number to the car," she said.

"Melissa, have you arranged for the luggage to be unpacked?"

"Yes, the maid will be here momentarily."

"Good, then after you've drawn my bath please feel free to do whatever you wish," Andrea said. "I will be going to dinner at seven with Jacques, so do come back to help me dress at six will you? I'll take a nap until then. What do you think I should wear?"

"Maybe you are too tired to go out," Melissa suggested obliquely. "Why not just sleep for the rest of the day?"

"Ah! And maybe you are just too protective, Melissa," Andrea teased as Melissa headed toward the bathroom.

Abandoning her clothes, Andrea put on the soft heated robe that Melissa brought from the spacious bathroom. Humid lavender-smelling steam from the bath clouded the mirror and Andrea could not tell if she looked as tired as she felt. When the deep tub was full, Melissa disappeared and Andrea stepped into the hot bubbly water. Resting her head against an air pillow, she sank slowly and deliciously into the warmth and closed her eyes, feeling light-headed and dreamy as the heat permeated her body. How dramatically her life had changed over the years, Andrea reflected as she began to relax. As if needing the reality of her past to face an uncertain future, Andrea willed a montage of images from her childhood to come tumbling into her mind.

Chapter 2

Jamaica

"Andrea, come inside at once!" her mother was screaming. She had done it again, Andrea thought. She had a knack for doing just the opposite of what her mother wanted. Now her beautiful piqué dress was covered in mud, but what did her mother expect, she was only four. She was not a bad child by any means, but she was stubborn.

At the age of seven or perhaps even before, Andrea recognized that she was different from her three sisters. For one thing, she always had to have an explanation while Stephanie, Patricia and Charmaine would just accept events as they came. Andrea was always mistakenly taken as the eldest because she was very mature both physically and mentally for her age.

Lila Francis, Andrea's mother, thought her third daughter an especially difficult child and she hoped and prayed that Andrea would one day learn to conform to the traditional behaviors and values expected of all four of the Francis girls. Lila was concerned about Andrea's present, not her *future*. She knew this daughter was destined to be successful. On occasion, however, Lila had to question how that destiny would ever become a reality when she found herself agonizing over the unnecessary complications that Andrea's stubbornness continued to cause her. This tendency had already resulted in so much disruption in the family, especially between herself and Andrea, to say nothing of the many summonses to Andrea's school for conferences and the numerous threats of suspension. Lila was not a woman who took public embarrassment easily and she was at her wit's end with Andrea's escapades.

At its best, her mother/daughter relationship with Andrea was cordial. The girl never let Lila forget that she had left Jamaica to study nursing in England when Andrea was only a year old, even though it was Andrew's encouragement that had ultimately persuaded her to go. Andrew Francis had insisted that his young wife be further educated, a luxury he assumed she missed by marrying and becoming a mother at such an early age. But Lila felt that those five years spent away from her youngest child had caused an emotional instability in her daughter and she knew it had damaged their relationship. Andrea seemed unable to forgive her for this desertion. In any case, Lila had certainly not been old enough to question her husband's authority or his decisions at that time, much as she might have been inclined to disagree. Never, though, had she regretted choosing Andrew as her husband and the father of her children. All of the girls adored him, but Andrea had a special, almost reverential regard for her father. Their third and intended last child, she was named for Andrew because there was no son.

Andrew Francis had never seen a good reason to discipline or reprimand any of the children harshly, least of all Andrea, having what his wife termed a soft spot for his namesake daughter. He had never quite understood or shared her concern over the girl. In fact, Lila suspected that he silently applauded Andrea's spirited demonstrations of independence. Andrew seemed to understand that like Lila herself, Andrea could be cold and caustic to anyone she disliked while carefully hidden deep inside her was a passionate, loving, generous heart. But that quality was evident only to people to whom she was deeply committed. When Andrea determined that someone was worthy of her love, she was utterly and totally dedicated.

Until she met Adam Stern, Andrew Francis was the only recipient of Andrea's absolute and unconditional love. And after his death, a devastating loss that happened just before her twenty-sixth birthday, her father remained one of Andrea's strongest and most positive influences. When she was growing up it seemed he rather than her mother had always been there for his daughters. It was Andrew who had responded to the children's middle of the night requests for a drink of water or a toilet trip, their early morning hot cocoa and their Friday evening outings to the movies. Without question, there was a place inside Andrea that was forever vulnerable to her father.

The party was given at the country home of one of her childhood friends. For thirteen-year-old girls in Andrea's family the thought of boys, and, God forbid, older men, was taboo. But there was something about the man across the room that stirred every fiber of her being. Andrea gazed at him, thinking he was the handsomest man she had ever seen in her life, staring openly at him as he circulated about the room chatting with people who greeted him. He seemed to be an honored guest. Having just returned to Jamaica after living in the United States for ten years, she heard, he had only come back after his stepfather's death to manage the family estates. No wonder she had never seen the man before.

As he stood there, clearly the most attractive man in the room, she felt a magnetic pull and could not control the hypnotic impulse that forced her to move closer to him. Though she was just a child, Andrea knew that she wanted this man. Embarrassed about the awful thoughts running through her mind, not all of which she understood, she looked around nervously to see if anyone could tell what she had been thinking. These strange new feelings were overwhelming! Worried that her thoughts might be exposed, she moved hastily toward the door to get away from the obsession that was about to have her make a fool of herself. As Andrea reached the doorway and was about to make her escape, someone caught her by the arm.

"May I have this dance?"

Andrea jerked her arm away abruptly, turning sharply to decline, her face flushed with resentment at having her private thoughts intruded upon and came face to face with the man who had dominated her mind for the last three hours. She gasped at how much more handsome he was up close and wondered if her attraction to him was obvious. Without waiting for an answer, he guided her onto the dance floor. Her heart pounded in her chest as he pulled her closely into a waltz. He was at least six feet two, a good ten inches taller than she was. His skin was dark and flawless; his eyes were a molten brown. Other than a pencil thin mustache, he was clean shaven. Andrea noticed that his white cotton shirt was opened almost to his waist revealing a mat of black hair and she liked the way his khaki pants hugged his narrow hips. Catching the clean, sharp scent of his cologne mixed with the exotic smell of Jamaican rum on his breath, she was totally captivated. She knew from that moment on she was going to belong to this man, and that somehow he was going to change her life. Finally she relaxed in his arms, molding her young child's body to his.

"What is your name?" he asked, looking down at her. "Andrea Francis," she answered almost inaudibly. His deep voice and steady gaze brought a flood of emotions that she had never experienced before.

"Well, Andrea Francis, it's wonderful to meet you. I am sure we will meet again," he said.

When? she wanted to ask him—after all this man did not hang out at the playground—but she was speechless.

As if reading her mind he said, "I will see you tomorrow."

With that, he lowered his head and kissed her full on the lips. Before Andrea realized what had happened he was gone. She touched her lips and her body tingled with a longing she had never felt before. Having often been told she had an overactive imagination and knowing she was prone to fantasies, Andrea pinched her arm hard to make sure she was not daydreaming again. It was real. She had just been kissed by Prince Charming! Torn between her desire for this man and her parents' orthodox values, she quickly made her escape to the garden.

Finally in the open air, Andrea gave in to the weakness in her knees and as her legs buckled under her she sank to the ground. It was a cool and breezy evening and the sun was just going down. When the bright blue sky turned to deep shades of orange and purple, she decided that the bruised look of the heavens reflected the turmoil in her mind. Andrea saw there were some stars already hanging up there to illuminate the sky. Melissa had said they were there to end the evening fight between the moon and the sun, bringing harmony. The night was beautiful, one of the most beautiful she had ever seen. But then, she would not have noticed before. Love had a way of making the ordinary extraordinary. Andrea vowed at that moment never to forget the consuming love she felt for this stranger whose name she did not even know. She had only just met him, but she could not shake the feeling that this love was not new. Somehow, somewhere, she sensed she had known this man before.

Trying to find a rational explanation for her behavior, Andrea lay back on the grass. There, resting her head against the soft turf, she closed her eyes and was lost in thought when she was startled by a light touch on her shoulder. She jumped to her feet, stumbled, and again found herself looking into the face of the man who had her hypnotized. Transfixed by the piercing brown eyes, Andrea felt a passion as natural to her as breathing.

"I am sorry, Andrea," he said, holding her, "I did not mean to startle you. I just wanted to apologize for kissing you earlier. I don't know what came over me. To be quite honest I feel as though I've know you for a long time. How old are you anyway?"

For a second Andrea panicked, considering lying about her age because she felt there was no way he would ever speak to her again if he knew she was only thirteen. But it did not seem right to lie to a friend. Already she thought of him as a friend.

"I will see you tomorrow," he said emphatically, and again he was walking away, leaving her alone with her confusion. Neither his expression nor voice betrayed any concern about her age and Andrea was sure he did not care. She watched him walk away, confident and self-assured. Only then did she realize she still did not even know his name.

Andrea beamed at her family and friends as she walked across the stage to receive her high school diploma. Holding it, she moved the blue and yellow tassel across to the other side of her cap. She had officially graduated from the convent school even after the anguish she had caused the nuns. Even though it had been a wonderful seven years at St. Auberstein, Andrea was glad to be graduating. What made the event so memorable was the promise Adam had made to her five years before.

But she had waited patiently after her graduation party for Adam to fulfill his promise and the fulfillment never came. Miserably disappointed, she had spent the rest of the night crying into her pillow. What should have been the happiest time of her life turned into a painful never-ending night.

Weeks went by and still Adam did not seem to notice that she had graduated and that he had not kept his promise. Nothing had changed between them at all. She was still the prized little virgin he had reared from the age of thirteen and apparently that was just the way he wanted her to remain. Yes, Adam Stern had groomed Andrea. She was his protégée. What could she do but wait? At eighteen, Andrea was a beautiful woman with a fairy tale childhood, and she was a woman in love—but without a lover. Wasn't five years of waiting enough for him? What else could she do to prove her love? Andrea was having a difficult time restraining the hormonal urges that overtook her body every time she was near Adam and she prayed that he would soon make love to her. Yes, she affirmed, she would wait, but not much longer.

Both of them loved the ocean. They spent much of their time together lying on the cool white sands of Negril beach, reading, talking or just simply being. They had always been able to discuss anything under the sun, but now, frustration finally getting the better of her, Andrea was quiet and uncommunicative. It did not seem to matter to Adam, he continued to talk about everything—except what Andrea most wanted to hear.

Six weeks after her graduation, Andrea decided she had to try a new approach to get Adam to fulfill his promise to make love to her. He was lying on his back, half buried in the pure white sand, a book propped over his face. Andrea lifted the book and kissed him on the tip of his nose, allowing her body to press very close to his. Her full breasts pulsed against him as she moved her lips slowly downward until she felt his mouth warm beneath hers.

"Adam," she began, kissing him gently between words, "I've been wondering...." Just then a mosquito buried its stinger into her arm. Reflexively, Andrea jerked back, jumping to her feet. The bite was already beginning to swell.

"Damn!" she said, rubbing the red spot that was now itching mercilessly. Adam sat up from his sandy bed taking Andrea's arm between his hands.

"Honey, you need to go and get some medicated cream from the cabin. Quickly now! You can't afford to have that arm swollen tonight."

"Tonight?" Andrea said, perking up, not wanting a little thing like a mosquito bite to stand in the way.

"Tonight we are going to a party at Henry Fischer's. He is announcing his engagement to Barbara. I think it will be exciting since she doesn't expect it, don't you?".

Andrea's spirits sank. She was annoyed that he seemed so happy for Henry and Barbara, yet he had not even given a thought to the promise she longed for. For chrissake, she thought, shrugging free of his hands, she was not asking him for marriage, she simply wanted to be in his arms and finally experience the consummation of their love. He had promised!

"What time is the party?" she asked, thinking fast.

"Nine or so, I imagine."

"I probably won't be able to leave home until ten. My parents are having out-of-town guests to dinner."

"Well, I'll pick you up at ten then. And darling, wear something terribly sexy," he grinned, getting to his feet.

"Quickly now," he ordered, kissing her reddened arm, "go and get something for that bite."

Andrea turned toward the cabin. She was fighting back tears and refused to let him see her cry. Noticing her mood, he caught her by the waist. Holding her in his arms, he gently kissed the nape of her neck.

"I love you Andrea. Why do you doubt that?"

"I don't know."

With Melissa's help that night Andrea donned her favorite evening dress, a Gianfranco Ferre. She had always loved the way the graceful gold chinon hugged her tiny waist, accentuating her shapely hips and long legs. Having grown six inches over the past five years, she could almost look Adam straight in the eyes. The low cut exposed enough of her cleavage to entice even the most modest man and the exotic off-the-shoulder effect of the neckline embroidered with gold frill she knew was seductive. Andrea's hair was coiffed in a half-rounded chignon, a timeless style of the French revolution, and was held by a sapphire and diamond Royal Pave hair clasp. She wore a matching sapphire and diamond choker, earrings and bracelet. Her fingers she left bare, hoping he would notice. Dressed to the nines, examining her reflection in the mirror, Andrea smiled. She was going to show Adam Stern what he was missing. She would flirt with every good looking man in the room tonight. It would serve him right!

Adam was speechless as Andrea moved gracefully into his view, walking toward the car with an amazingly seductive swing to her hips. She was magnificent! She was no longer his little protégée; she was a woman. His woman. He was glad that he had made her wait for him. His control over her was now complete and tonight he would finally make her his.

"Andrea," he said, wanting so badly to take her at that very moment, "you are. . . sensational."

"Thank you, darling," she said, her eyes not leaving his face. She sat in the car, crossing her long legs deliberately to show the suggestive slit up the side of her dress. Her look at Adam held the most daring expression of wanton passion.

Adam desired her. The insistent pressure in his pants pushing against his zipper told him his lust was fast becoming obvious, but he firmly regained his control and quietly drove away before she could see that he was mad with desire. This was not the time or place. He would not change what he had planned so carefully.

21

The party was in full swing when they arrived.

"Hello darlings," Barbara greeted them, her face beaming with excitement. "Just look, Andrea," her friend said, holding her ringed finger up for speculation. "Isn't it divine? It must have cost him a fortune, don't you think? I just love my Henry so much," she turned toward her fiancé. "Darling, I am going to make you the happiest man in the world," she said, kissing him lightly on the cheek as she ran off to greet yet another group of arrivals. Barbara darted around the room showing off her five-carat pear-shaped canary diamond to anyone who cared to look, even to those who were green with envy. After all, besides Adam, Henry was one of the most desirable bachelors in the community. Andrea had mixed emotions, happy for Barbara, but jealous of her friend's bliss.

"Adam," Henry said, slapping his long-time friend, who was to be his best man, on the shoulder, "you are next in line. Little old Andrea here is perfect for you, man. Don't you think?"

"Yes, I suppose you're right," Adam said, shifting uneasily, wishing Henry would shut his fucking mouth. He pulled at Andrea. "Let's dance," he said, leading her to the dance floor. He was grateful to get away from Henry and his rambling on about marriage.

"Isn't that a sparkler on Barbara's finger? I think they will be very happy," he said, encircling her slim waist as he pulled her into a slow dance. Andrea nodded and lowered her head, too upset to speak and too close to tears to trust looking into Adam's eyes directly. He held her close, nestling his lips against her neck and again she was overwhelmed with the burning need to be everything to this man, knowing she was his love captive. She relaxed against his broad shoulders and as usual her anger faded. She was happy at least to have him in her arms, even if she had yet to become his lover or his wife. She rested her cheek against Adam's, snuggling up against his warm body. She loved the way he smelled. God how she loved him.

"Come with me," he whispered, as his lips brushed her ears. "Tonight I am going to make you a woman. The woman you have wanted to be for the last five years." The touch of their bodies no matter how slight was always enough to send Andrea's repressed emotions soaring, and tonight she was consumed with passion.

So this was to be the night he had prepared her for all these years. She had waited for this moment for so long. A flush of intense excitement at the thought of finally belonging to him made her feel faint. It seemed to Andrea that she had loved him for a lifetime, and as much as she had wanted him during the past five years, he had insisted that she was too young. She looked up at Adam and her heart felt as though it would burst. She gently kissed his lips. Holding her hand, Adam led her through the crowded room and into the garden. An aromatic smell of blooming flowers filled the night air.

Adam pulled Andrea close against him and kissed her softly on the forehead, eyelids, earlobes and finally covered her eager lips. The kiss was tender at first, but as their years of pent up desire for each other grew it became more and more demanding, until the passion consumed them both. He slipped his hand inside her dress and began caressing her breasts with their already swollen nipples. She could feel the urgency building in her loins as warm moisture flowed from between her legs. Andrea, having rehearsed this scene millions of times in her mind, reached down and caressed the throbbing bulge, forcing open the zipper of Adam's pants. His penis was fully erect.

"Oh God", she moaned, as he slipped his hand under her skirt and explored her body. His breath was coming fast and the intensity of his passion matched hers in every way. Andrea tried to unbuckle his belt as she pulled him to the ground, wanting to commit herself to him for life.

"My darling, not here," he whispered, "tonight is going to be very special."

"But Adam," she cried, "I can't wait! Not another moment! Please," she begged, "Now."

"Andrea, we have waited for five years. A half hour more cannot kill you my darling and I promise it will be worth it."

He pulled her to her feet.

"Well if I have to wait, then you had better kiss me again," she said, smoothing her dress over her hips, "and make me feel what tonight promises to bring."

As he covered her lips again, she closed her eyes, dreaming about what was to come. When he finally let her go she was ready to follow him to the end of the earth. She looked up at the sky and thanked God she had met her love so early in life. A love so true, so pure, had to have been ordained from the heavens. The moon was full and in its white glow she was sure she saw the "man in the moon" smile. The stars seemed to dance. This evening was as beautiful as the night they had first met.

Chapter 3

"Andrea jumped as the telephone on the bedside table rang loudly. She looked at the gold and leather travel clock on the bathroom counter and realized that she had been so lost in thought that an hour had passed since she stepped into the bath. Standing on the thick mat, she wrapped herself hastily in one of Claridge's huge towels and answered the phone on the fourth ring.

"Andrea Jacobson," she said irritably, "What is it?"

"*Dahling*, don't be cross, I just wanted to know if dinner at seven was on."

Her voice softened, "Yes, Jacques, dinner at seven will be perfect."

"I will pick you up," he said in his most enchanting French accent. "We have reservations at the Savoy."

"That will be fine. I'll be ready." Her voice was cool, yet kind.

"Until seven then," he said, and after a slight pause, "*ma chérie*, I love you." Before Andrea could respond he had hung up. Andrea was annoyed. She did not want him to love her. In fact, the sound of the word love made her feel ill. Love, to her meant only another heartbreak and more pain and dear God just how much more pain would she have to endure before this ordeal was over?

A frown on her face, Andrea made her way back to the bathroom. She caught a glimpse of her naked body in the mirror, firm breasts, smooth skin, alluring cherry lips, and she could understand the effect she had on men. Andrea stared back at the face in the mirror. As young as she appeared, she recognized evidence of too many years of hard work and psychological torment beginning to gather around her eyes. She quickly looked away and began toweling her hair vigorously. Dressing in a simple white silk shift, she climbed between the satin sheets and pulled the down coverlet up to her shoulders. Reaching for the telephone, she requested a wake up call for six o'clock and soon drifted off to sleep.

She was already awake when Melissa arrived to help her dress, a red chiffon dress in hand, another Valentino.

"Melissa," Andrea reprimanded, "How can you give me a Valentino to wear when you know I am going out with Jacques? You are terribly naughty."

"I thought red would brighten you up a bit. Anyway, you don't have to wear something St. Pierre created just because you are going out with him."

Ignoring her, Andrea went to the closet to choose a different attire and picked out a raw silk drop-waist dress that had been designed for her by Jacques. Dressing took some effort and she decided she was still quite tired from her trip. She would return to the hotel right after dinner.

The ring of the door bell was insistent. She wished Jacques weren't so damned impatient. And she hated the fact that he was always early.

"I'll get it, Melissa," she said. As she hobbled over to the door trying to put on her other shoe she snagged her nylons.

"Hell!" she said angrily as she pulled the door open.

"Jacques, must you always be so damned impatient?"

"Only when I haven't seen you for so long, *dahling*," he said good-naturedly, kissing her on both cheeks.

"Melissa," Andrea called over her shoulder, "I need a new pair of stockings, I just snagged these."

Melissa entered immediately with another pair of nylons.

"Darling," Andrea said more casually than seductively, "pour us a drink, will you, while I change these nylons? I won't be but a minute."

Jacques St. Pierre had not taken his eyes off Andrea since he had walked into the room. He had nearly forgotten how beautiful she was, and that she always took his breath away. She was the most desirable woman he had ever known. He sighed heavily.

"Jacques, are you all right?" Andrea turned to look at him.

"Fine 'dahling,' just fine," he said, exaggerating the rolling letter 'r' in darling, "will you have brandy?"

"Yes, thank you."

Melissa watched Jacques as Andrea disappeared into the dressing room. She did not like this man and never had. She was sure that he was just a bit unscrupulous and that Scott Preston was much better for Andrea in every way. Yes, she thought, even though she was trying to avoid him, Scott was the kind of man Andrea needed. Melissa knew too, that Andrea was frightened of falling in love.

Jacques was so absorbed in his thoughts that he had not even noticed Melissa. He wanted so badly to kiss Andrea's moist ruby lips, wanted to walk over to her and take her in his arms and make passionate love to her, wanted to feel her warm body clinging to him, begging him not to stop as he released his passion deep within her. Wanting her from the first time he had laid eyes on her in Paris and again when he saw her the last time in New York, he was patient, difficult as it was for a man who had never been known for that virtue.

Their affair had been torrid and short-lived. He realized he had been no more important to her than any of the other men in her life. Andrea, he knew, was not ready for a serious relationship, and so he waited. And he would have continued waiting had it not been for Scott Preston entering the scene, damn him. He knew all along that Andrea's attraction to the man was different from the others, yet he had no idea what she saw in him. For God's sake, he was so, well, so bloody boring. It would not last, he consoled himself, Andrea needed more in a man. He wondered if their lovemaking was as good as his and Andrea's had been, and at the thought of Andrea with Scott, the hairs on his back stiffened with anger. He was not sure how much longer he could play the 'good friend' role. What he did know, however, was that he was going to have her again, soon.

Jacques St. Pierre was the epitome of masculinity and as handsome as any man could ever be. He was not only recognized everywhere he went but he wielded his power as only a man born to wealth could. At an early age Jacques had developed a distinct taste in fashion. He would sit on the staircase on nights his mother gave one of her famous soirées and watch all the delicate and not so delicate women in their one-of-a-kind dresses. He had felt a certain passion as he watched these women parade themselves. In fact, he had gotten so turned on at the nearly bare breasts of one guest that he had masturbated himself to an orgasm right on the stairs. As he got older, Jacques' sense of style became evident. He would tell women how to make themselves more attractive, and better yet, he would make each of them feel as though she were the most beautiful woman who had ever lived. Such debonair charm had gotten him seduced at fourteen by a woman twice his age, and since then almost daily by unhappily married women whom he treated like royalty. Thank God he had been indoctrinated early into an appreciation of women, for in the fashion industry men were most often more attracted to other men.

Many women would kill to be seen escorted by Jacques St. Pierre. Andrea Jacobson was not one of them. Jacques had become well-established as a fashion designer in his early twenties. The boy wonder had taken the world by storm and he had establishments in Milan, Paris, Tokyo, New York and London, having gained an early reputation as the designer for the rich and famous. St. Pierre clothes were twice as expensive as those of most of his contemporaries, but he wanted only the distinguished to wear his designs. He did not want his clothes to be on every starving model or minor starlet.

Jacques had first seen Andrea on a street in Paris when he was beginning to be known as an up and coming designer. At twenty, her delicate but suggestive beauty had made him feel instant desire, which of course compelled him to introduce himself. She told him she might learn to be a model when he asked if she happened to be one. He was sure then that she could become the high fashion model that would make St. Pierre a household name, but he could never find her again.

When he saw her years later at a major haute couture gala in New York he recognized her instantly. He would never have forgotten such a face. He took bets with himself as he approached her whether or not she would remember him. Why, he wondered, if she had so obviously become such a successful model had he not heard of her? Jacques moved toward Andrea who was chatting gaily with a small group of people, her head thrown back, her soft laughter filling the space between them.

She was such a stunning woman. Even though she was not wearing one of his designs but his competitor's, an Ungaro, she looked marvelous in the pale pink skintight slipper-satin gown caught at the waist with intricate satin bows. The plunging neckline revealed the firmness of her breasts and accentuated the ruby and gold necklace that encircled her graceful neck.

Andrea turned as he approached her.

"Ah, I see you called another designer," he said, extending his hand.

"I beg your pardon," Andrea said, confusion crossing her face.

"You do not even remember me, eh? Ah, *ma chère*, I am devastated. Have I such a forgettable face?"

The face seemed familiar but Andrea could not quite place it.

"Give me a hint," she said, beginning to enjoy the mystery.

"Springtime in Paris on the Rue l'Opéra, ten years ago."

Andrea had brightened at the memory, "Ah yes, you wanted to know if I was a model. Later you took me on a tour of Paris. Please forgive me, but it has been a long time. And all these years I had no idea that you were the famous Jacques St. Pierre. I always thought I recognized something familiar about you from your pictures but..." she allowed the sentence to trail off. "Well it is good to see you again," she extended her hand again.

"At your service," he brought her hand to his lips, catching the scent of Joy De Patou. Marvelous, he thought.

"And you have become a famous model after all."

"No, as a matter of fact I have not."

"Well then, what have you being doing with yourself all these years?"

"I am Andrea Jacobson."

"*The* Andrea Jacobson?" his eyes widened.

"The one and only," Andrea said, her smile broadening at his surprise. She had never allowed herself to be photographed by the press and she loved the way people's mouths fell open when they finally associated her face with her name.

"Well, I am glad then for your sake that you did not take me up on the offer to be my model in Paris," he retorted, smiling, hiding the fact that he was impressed. "I say we should get away from here and catch up on the last sixteen years. What do you say, *chérie?"*

"Just ask that tall gray-haired gentleman over there if he minds. He is my husband."

Not to be put off, Jacques said, "Well, how about lunch?"

"Why not?" Andrea smiled, walking over to join Alex. "Call me. I am sure you will find Jacobson's Industry in the book."

From then on he had designed most of her wardrobe. He had also felt the need to give up his philandering because for the first time in his life he was in love. But she was already married! Until Alex Jacobson's death a year later they had remained just friends, but within another year he became Andrea's lover. When Andrea ended the brief affair he had remained her good friend only so he could be near her, knowing she was not ready for marriage. Not yet.

Tonight over dinner they would discuss her fall wardrobe and if he had his way, her future as Madame St. Pierre. Jacques had a game plan and he did not intend to lose this time.

"I'm ready, darling," Andrea said as she downed the last of her drink. The brandy warmed her insides and seemed to go more quickly than usual to her head. She had been so uptight about this trip that she had forgotten to eat all day. She knew better than to have alcohol on an empty stomach, but what the hell, she was safe with Jacques.

They arrived at the Savoy within minutes. The sleek black Daimler pulled to a halt and Jacques, giving the keys to the valet, encircled her waist with his arm as they moved toward the door.

"Good evening, madam, M. St. Pierre," the maître d' greeted them warmly as they entered the dining room.

"Your table is ready, sir. Shall I bring you the usual?"

"No, tonight madam will choose."

"Very well, sir. I will be back momentarily with the menu and the wine steward will bring you the wine list."

"I think we will have champagne. The Jouët," Andrea said,

31

"and some fresh strawberries, please."

"Jacques," Andrea said finally, "it is so good to see you." She leaned over and gave him one of her usual quick meaningless kisses. She smelled wonderful. He had always liked the scent of Joy on her. He could not say that for most of the women he dated. The perfume was only to be worn by those who could live up to its reputation.

"I am sorry I was such a grouch tonight, but I have very little patience these days and the long flight wore me out."

"Andrea, you have been working too hard." He had noticed the new creases around her eyes. "By the way, congratulations. I would wager that deal you just concluded in Hong Kong took a lot of out of you."

"It was a difficult negotiation, and yes, indeed, I'm glad it is over."

"I am not sure whether your latest addition was an acquisition, merger, or takeover."

"Jacques, do I look like a shark? A merger of course. Jacobson's Industry holds fifty-one percent controlling interest in Hanoi Industries. In fact, over the next two years very little will change for either company."

"Well Mrs. Jacobson, you are one clever lady and I just want you to know how very much I admire you."

"Thank you, darling, I'm pleased with the outcome."

"I still think you need a vacation though, Andrea," Jacques said with genuine concern. "Let me take you away to Gstaad, the fresh air will do you good."

"God, skiing sounds like just the thing to clear my mind, but I am afraid I can't. I'd been planning a trip to Monaco, but I've had some unexpected changes and must postpone my plans. But never mind about my problems. How are things with you?"

"Ah, *chèrie*, they are marvelous. Life could only be better if you promise to stay here with me."

"Why do you always ask for the impossible, Jacques? If things work out I will be here for less than a week."

"Actually, I can't believe you are even here. Your business in London must be of the utmost importance. What has happened?"

"You do jump to conclusions, darling. How do you know I am not here just to see you about my fall wardrobe?"

"I would like to think it was because you missed me rather than my designs, but apart from your fall wardrobe Andrea, what is your business in London?" Jacques asked curiously.

Andrea, he knew, had lived in England several years earlier, but for some reason she would never discuss that period of her life and had not been back since. He was surprised she had made the trip. She had made so many objections to coming to England every time he had mentioned it to her before.

"Jacques, my visit is personal and I don't want to discuss it." Her tone softened at his expression, "Let's just say I am trying to find myself. Maybe I'll be as lucky as Shirley MacLaine. Spaceships, spirits and all," she quipped.

They both laughed and the mood lightened.

"A toast to—whatever," Jacques said clinking his champagne glass against hers.

A voice interrupted them. "Good evening. Madame Jacobson, is it not?"

"Good evening," Andrea said hesitantly, not knowing to whom she was talking. She wished the man would move into the light but there was not much of that in the restaurant.

"I can see you do not remember me," he said, shaking his head. "Ah, it has been many years, *ma Chocolát*, but surely—"

It could not be! But who else would dare to call her "*ma Chocolát*!" And that voice, how could she ever forget it!

"Ralph? Oh, Ralph!" she said rising from her chair to hug him. "How good it is to see you. Of all the people to run into on my first night in London! I could not think of a better person," she rambled on.

Jacques looked from one to the other. He certainly recognized Ralph deHavalon, but how did he, of all people, know Andrea? Ralph deHavalon, Jacques knew, was a Parisian expatriate who had made his home in London for at least eighteen years. A nobody in terms of his background, he had made a name for himself as one of Britain's best polo players. It was rumored that he was the envy of most players, far better at polo than Charles. Prince Charles, if one must use the title. No fan of British royalty, Jacques found them stodgy and dull.

"Ralph," Andrea beamed, "meet my good friend, Jacques St. Pierre. Jacques, this is Ralph deHavalon."

"We need no introduction. M. St. Pierre's fame precedes him," Ralph said, extending his hand, "My pleasure, Monsieur."

"How do you do," Jacques said, grudgingly.

Jacques wished that Ralph would go away and he certainly wished he would stop calling Andrea his "*Chocolát.*" Recognizing Jacques' discomfort, and taking his cue, Ralph lifted Andrea's hand to his lips and kissed it tenderly.

"Tell me where you are staying and I will call on you. Maybe we can go riding and then have a picnic. What do you say, my *Chocolát?*" He winked at her.

"I would love to Ralph. I'm staying at Claridge's." For a moment they stood gazing at each other, finally jolted back to the present as Jacques cleared his throat.

"Until tomorrow then, my *Chocolát.* M. St. Pierre," Ralph nodded and turned away from the table.

Andrea watched Ralph walk away and knew immediately that she had made a mistake in encouraging him to call her. She wanted to stop him but he was already out of sight.

Outside the Savoy Ralph felt chilled. The night air was damp and foggy. He pulled his coat collar up and tucked his cashmere scarf closer to his neck, then stood for a moment leaning against the hotel wall. He felt weak. He could not believe he had actually met Andrea Francis again. Why was his heart beating this fast? he asked himself, knowing the answer. It had taken him a long time to get over her and tonight all those old emotions came flooding back. Nearly fourteen years, he counted them, and she had changed so little. She was even more beautiful than he remembered.

The same old feelings he had for her were surfacing again. He could tell by his phallus that swelled shamelessly in his trousers. Thank God he had his coat on. But he had acted calmly, he told himself. Even if his penis had a mind of its own, his emotions had been under control and he had left without betraying his weakness.

Back at Claridge's, Andrea lightly kissed Jacques goodnight in front of her door and quickly entered her suite, not inviting him in, promising to call him in a day or so. Disgruntled, Jacques was acting like a jealous lover, and she was certainly not going to entertain any questions from him about Ralph. Under normal circumstances she would have asked him in for coffee and liqueur, but not tonight. Tonight she was too shaken and too vulnerable to be alone with Jacques. Usually she rather enjoyed flirting with him because he had always made her feel so special, but tonight, though she was not in the least interested in rekindling their old affair, she was not sure she had the strength to resist him.

Andrea had not wanted the past to return so soon. She wanted to be free for at least two more days before confronting what she had left behind. She had enough problems to deal with without Ralph. Seeing him had brought back in full force the nostalgia of a time in her life she had tried desperately to banish, embedding it so deeply in her subconscious at times it seemed as though she had dreamed the whole experience.

First thing in the morning she would call and cancel their date, Andrea decided, but just as quickly she realized she had not asked for his number. She dialed the operator who said the number was unlisted. He would telephone tomorrow and she would tell him then.

Andrea headed straight for the bottle of brandy to calm her nerves and her shaking hands. Above all, a good night's rest was what she really needed, she knew, but since she was already slightly tipsy, she thought she might as well have another drink. Downing the warm brandy quickly, Andrea slipped into a silk nightgown Melissa had laid out for her on the bed. Sitting at the dressing table, she removed her makeup carefully with cotton and cleansing cream, again noticing the faint lines around her eyes. Tomorrow she would put cucumber slices on them.

Getting into bed, she dialed the front desk and asked for her calls to be held. Ensconced in bed under her canopy she felt safe. Out there was a brutal world, was her last thought before tiredness took over and Andrea slipped into a deep sleep. It was not long, however, before she was twisting and turning fitfully. She awoke damp with perspiration and in tears. Unable now to go back to sleep, Andrea curled her body into a fetal position, waiting for the dawn, unable to remember the nightmare.

At seven o'clock Andrea got wearily out of bed, pulled the curtains halfway open and peered out the window, glad that it was finally morning. Again she tried to remember the dream that had made her cry but she couldn't. She climbed back into bed and silently stared at the ceiling.

Chapter 4

"Good morning, Andrea," Melissa said opening the curtains all the way. "Did you sleep well?"

"Not very well."

"What about a strong cup of coffee?"

"Yes, that would be wonderful."

"Would you like your cottage cheese and fruit?"

"Just some toast and marmalade this morning," Andrea said. Toast, that had been a habit she had picked up from Scott. For a moment her mind lingered on Scott, back in New York. She missed his gentle hands, his quick smile and his candid disregard for her neuroses.

"Melissa, I'm going shopping today. Do you want to come along?"

"Not unless you need me to. I have a cousin here and I would like to visit her, if that's all right with you."

"I didn't know you had a relative in England. That's just wonderful!" Melissa never ceased to surprise her just when Andrea thought she knew everything about her. "Take the car. I won't need it at all today. I'll let the driver know on my way out," she said.

Andrea nodded to the doorman as she passed through the entrance.

"Madam, your driver is waiting over to the right."

"Thank you. Please tell him to be ready in an hour or so to take my companion wherever she wishes to go.

"Where is the closest bus stop to Bond street?" she asked, on a sudden whim.

Unruffled, he hid his amazement and replied, "Just across the street, madam. Take the number six."

Andrea climbed onto a double decker red bus and made her way to the top deck. She loosened her cashmere coat and removed her Hermès scarf, tucking it into her coat pocket. Face pressed against the window, she allowed herself to recall the London she had once known so well.

The beauty of this venerable city still amazed her. Even the bleak weather could not hide the enchantment of its quaint buildings or the radiance of its parks and typical English gardens. So many familiar sights, Andrea thought, as the bus screeched to a halt near Hyde Park; how could she have allowed herself to forget London?

She could hear music in the park where she had spent so many afternoons with Maria. She smiled as she saw the red uniforms of a British band entertaining a crowd of appreciative shoppers. On foot in the eddying crowd, just like any other tourist, Andrea passed by the imposing statue of Lord Nelson in Trafalgar Square, having looked again at Buckingham Palace, Whitehall, the Thames and its bridges, the British Museum, the Tate; each was still there, solidly withstanding the centuries.

Instead of Simpson's on the Strand as she had originally planned, Andrea decided to have lunch at The Crown and Anchor in Sutton Street. That would be just like old times with Maria. Suddenly, with a pang, she missed Maria deeply. They had spent most of their free time at school finding some mischief or other to get into. It was Maria who had insisted that Andrea should see as much of the Continent as she could, and the girls had spent many a vacation traveling throughout Europe.

The shops on Bond Street were buzzing as usual. Although Andrea in recent years had never found time to shop, today she found window shopping fun. She darted in and out of boutiques picking up a gift here and there for her friends and family at home. Linda would be pleased with the Hermès scarf, and she would no doubt wear it to work on the day after she received it. Lately she had taken to wearing scarves in a variety of very becoming styles. "It adds pizzazz to a tired outfit," she would insist.

As Andrea passed a jeweler's window she noticed a small but exquisite sapphire and diamond butterfly brooch. A perfect gift for Helen. At the thought of Helen her heart raced and perspiration beaded her forehead. Realizing she was having an anxiety attack, Andrea took a deep breath and rang the buzzer at the door.

"Madam," the doorman greeted her.

Andrea remembered having impulsively purchased an ostentatious fifteen-carat emerald pendant flanked by ten-carat diamond baguettes for herself in Milan. Such a waste of money. She never wore the thing. But this brooch was so delicate.

"Would one give that brooch to a fourteen-year-old?" she asked the saleswoman while dabbing at her brow.

"Why, yes, the design of the brooch makes it appropriate for any age."

"Very well then, I'll take it."

The woman eyed Andrea suspiciously. Her face seemed familiar but she could not place it.

"That will be eight thousand pounds, madam. Converted to American currency, it is thirteen thousand dollars," she replied in a supercilious voice.

"Thank you." Andrea handed her an American Express credit card. "Would you gift wrap it for me?"

Andrea Jacobson, the woman read the charge plate. Of course. She should have known. Her smile broadened instantly.

It was almost four o'clock by the time Andrea arrived back at the hotel.

"There are six calls for you, Ms. Jacobson," said the desk clerk. Andrea knew instinctively that they were all from Ralph.

For two hours Andrea kept herself occupied by ordering tea and trying to concentrate on the Times and some glossy fashion magazines, until she could no longer put off calling Ralph. At six o'clock she dialed the number he had left. Ralph answered on the first ring, as though he had been waiting beside the telephone.

"Ah! *Chocolát*, you have been a naughty girl," he reprimanded. "I have been trying to reach you all day. In fact, I called very early this morning and found you had already left the hotel. I thought we were going to spend the day together. I feel ashamed to admit it, but I have not left home all day hoping you would call. Are you trying to avoid me, Andrea?"

"Oh Ralph, I'm sorry. But I didn't think we had made a firm plan."

"In my mind we had."

"Anyway, I couldn't call since you didn't give me your number. I found out you are unlisted."

"Well, the problem is now solved. I want to see you Andrea."

"The truth, Ralph, is that I'm hesitant to bring back memories of the time we had together."

"*Chocolát*, I am disappointed. Memories cannot hurt you. Anyway, *Chocolát*, the memories we share are wonderful. They should please you, no?"

"That's the problem, Ralph, they please me too much," Andrea said sadly.

"Good, then let me come and fetch you."

"Ralph," Andrea pleaded, "we can't go back to the way it was. We should leave things the way they are." She was sure she had not misread the look in his eyes the night before.

Ignoring the tremor in her voice, Ralph said cheerfully, "Very well, let's just go forward then. How about a quiet night together at my place? I will even bring the picnic basket this time."

"This time?" Andrea questioned, "I believe you also brought it the last time."

"Oh what a memory you have, my child," he joked.

"All the more reason to stay away from you, you big bad wolf," Andrea smiled. Andrea's better judgment said she should say no to the invitation but her heart told her to say yes.

"Very well, I'll be ready at eight o'clock."

"Then I will collect you at eight o'clock."

"Good. I will meet you in the lobby."

Andrea dressed casually but carefully. A crew-neck white sweater, tan suede pants and snug boots made her feel protected. At eight o'clock sharp she arrived in the lobby where Ralph stood waiting beside the lift. He moved toward her quickly, kissing her lightly and it seemed like only yesterday that they had parted, a sad but necessary parting. He took her by the elbow and guided her to his car. She glanced at the sleek gray Jaguar Vanden Plas with it's plush black leather interior and laughed aloud.

"Who would think, Ralph, that our lives would have gone in the direction they have. Some of our tastes seem to be parallel. I have the exact duplicate of this car at home."

"I always said we were destined for great things: to be together and to own the same cars continents apart."

Andrea chuckled at his attempt at humor, yet she shifted uneasily at the comment on togetherness.

41

"And where are we off to?"

"Not far. About a half hour's drive, depending on traffic."

Ralph pulled the car expertly into the flow of traffic and they sped silently away from the city. Soon they were in the midst of traffic.

"So," Ralph was saying, "are you about to purchase Great Britain?"

"Not entirely," Andrea said, "just bits and pieces of it."

"It is so good to see you, Andrea," Ralph said, squeezing her hand.

"And it's good to see you again, Ralph." Conversation faded into a silence broken only by soft classical music from the tape console.

"Well here we are," Ralph announced exactly thirty minutes later, as he pulled the car into the circular driveway of a handsome Kensington Tudor mansion.

"I would pull into the garage," he said, "but after you see dinner, you might decide that you would rather go out."

Andrea was impressed. The red brick and white plaster, dark-beamed, very British house stood in the center of at least five acres of trees, lawns and manicured gardens. Its interior, however, reflected all the French in Ralph.

"Such a lovely home," Andrea said as she looked around. The long passageway opened into a dramatic foyer complete with a winding staircase and lined with pictures of Ralph's polo activities. He had, it seemed, played with celebrities throughout the world. The man had indeed done well for himself. She wondered how he had managed to remain single all these years.

"Let me hang your coat. I gave the servants the night off. Can I get you a drink or are you terribly hungry? We can begin our picnic right away if you like."

"I'm famished, but a drink would be nice. But where are we having this picnic, Ralph? It's far too cold to set it up outside,"

Andrea said. "My dear, you have no faith. Do you think I would risk your getting pneumonia? Anyway, you underestimate my creativity. Follow me and I will show you." He led her upstairs and into what appeared to be his bedroom.

"My, this is definitely the picnic spot of choice," Andrea laughed, enjoying the fantasy. "In fact I love the tree over there, so big and shady."

"Sit a moment, my dear, under this beautiful weeping willow," he said, motioning to the bed, "while I change into my picnic attire."

As Ralph disappeared into the bathroom, Andrea walked over to the tall uncovered windows that ran the width of the room. The view was incredibly beautiful. From the bedroom were stairs that wound down to a glass-enclosed gazebo. Light from lamps in the garden reflected off the glass panes to glitter and dance on the Thames beyond. In the far distance she could hear Big Ben ringing out nine o'clock. Andrea took a deep breath and closed her eyes. Ah, she thought, her shoulders slumping, England, so silent and so majestic, had always enchanted her heart. There was a sense of peace about it that she had always found comforting; it was hard to believe that this country could hold such bitter memories for her. So much of her young life had been spent here, carefree, until—deliberately she shifted her thoughts to the present and turned to admire Ralph's very masculine bedroom.

A massive four-poster mahogany bed stood centered opposite the windows. The walls and cornices were in muted shades of white and cream. An antique chest of drawers, a huge armoire and a closed cabinet, presumably an entertainment center, were its only other furnishings. The large area rug was a thick hand-woven Persian carpet in peacock blues and light tan. Not a room necessarily for fun and frolic.

"Penny for your thoughts," Ralph whispered as he brushed her ear lightly with his lips.

"You are still cheap," she smiled turning around to look at him. "Today, my dear Ralph, I am worth a million dollars a thought."

"I will gladly pay for two thoughts, madam," he said playfully, "after which I will be completely bankrupt and dependent on you for my protection. Not a bad idea, eh!"

"Not at all, if you want to be totally controlled by a heartless woman. Would you care to begin by rendering to me all your worldly possessions?"

They both laughed as he picked her up and unceremoniously dumped her on the luxurious featherbed.

"I may be poor, Madame, but I am still very much a man," Ralph said, as he bent over her. She stared at him, realizing he had dressed as he had the first time they had gone on a picnic, riding boots and all, so many years before. Surprised, Andrea felt a pang of uneasiness wondering how this game would end.

"You are a hopeless romantic," she said cheerfully, jumping to her feet, not wanting to be serious.

"Romantic, you say, Madame? No, just a man who has been in love with you for as far back as he can remember." Ralph's voice was low, urgent. Then, as if sensing her concern, he playfully took her hand and led her onto the enclosed patio and down the stairs to the heated gazebo.

"Here, my dear, is the picnic site," he said, spreading a checkered cloth on the table. They both laughed, relaxing again, as he poured them each a glass of Pouilly Fuissé.

"Oh Ralph, I can't believe this. What a coincidence that we met at the restaurant! And now all the years seem to have evaporated. To friendship," Andrea raised her glass to his.

Ralph took a step closer and tilted Andrea's face to his. "And to everlasting love. "I have missed you so, my darling," he whispered. This is no coincidence, it is destiny." Lightening his tone when she lowered her eyes, he continued, "When I read of your arrival in London I easily found out where you were staying. Amazing what information a few pounds to the right people will buy! Then I telephoned Claridge's and literally forced your maid to tell me where you were dining last evening. Actually, I was my usual charming self and I think she really liked me."

"Horrible spy," Andrea said playfully, taking a sip of her wine. "And Melissa is not my maid, she's an old friend who's taken care of me since I was a baby. She knows about you. Otherwise she'd never have told you anything." She hesitated, softening her voice, "I'm glad that you went to the trouble of finding me. Dear Ralph," she touched his cheek, "I can think of no better welcome to England than spending an evening with you. I'm having a wonderful time." Andrea looked up at Ralph and smiled, raising her glass to him.

"To coincidence."

"To possibilities," he said, looking directly into the tiger-striped eyes of the only woman he had ever truly loved.

"My God, Andrea, you are beautiful," he said, kissing her cheek, feeling abruptly out of control at the touch of her soft skin under his lips.

A thrill went through Andrea and she turned to meet his lips with her own, and when he kissed her, a long, deep burning kiss, she responded without restraint, matching his desire with her own.

"Andrea, Andrea," Ralph repeated her name as he slid a hand under her sweater. She could feel his hardness against her. Slowly he moved his hand back and forth across her nipples, massaging them between his fingers until they grew taut. She put her hand on the back of his neck pulling him to her, returning his kisses passionately, not wanting him to stop. When Ralph finally released her, they were both breathless, hot with desire. Ralph's tensed muscles trembled, his pupils dilated with excitement, yet his tenderness was heartbreaking.

"I need you," he murmured, "I want you."

"Yes, yes, my darling, I want you too. But Ralph," Andrea pleaded, "please just let tonight be tonight. I couldn't suffer through hurting you again."

"Andrea, you know I am not a man who is afraid to take a chance," he said between kisses. "After all, I have done well for myself by taking chances—but I think it was knowing you once loved me that gave me the courage to gamble on myself," he whispered against her ear, "I remembered the tears in your eyes when you left me at the train station. Those tears gave me the strength to carry on. They proved you loved me then, and so my darling, if I can't have you forever, tonight will be enough."

He lifted her sweater and she closed her eyes as he gently kissed her breasts. She knew it was dishonorable to give Ralph a hope that could never come true, but she needed this man tonight. She wouldn't, she couldn't, think about tomorrow. Of all the people in her past to whom she wanted to make restitution, Ralph was one of them. Yes, she wanted to complete the circle, to end what she had started fourteen years ago. Such pain, she shuddered when his only guilt was loving her too much.

"What about the picnic," she murmured, pliant in his arms.

"It will keep," he said between covering her face with little kisses.

"Ralph, I— " Her lips parted as he kissed her deeply.

"Touch me," he said, "feel what you do to me".

His hand guided her as she unzipped his twill riding pants letting the throbbing head of his penis spring free. Ralph was sucking hard on her nipples, his other hand freeing the suede pants from her hips. Andrea could feel dampness on her thighs as his finger found its way deep inside of her. She moaned, falling to her knees and devouring him with her eager, hungry mouth.

The patio was hidden by a thicket of trees and the idea of making love under the stars with only a glass roof between the two of them and the world served to heighten her passion. Andrea slid her mouth back and forth over the purple head of his engorged penis, her lips moving faster and faster. He withdrew before she drove him beyond ecstasy and led her into the hot tub. Gazing at her naked body, he saw again how beautiful she was. Andrea could feel his warm breath on her bare skin as his mouth and tongue caressed every inch of her body. His face, damp from the steam, came to rest between her breasts. She gripped the taut muscles of his back, pulling him closer to her as he moved up to her, kissing her parted lips. With his knee he spread her legs apart allowing the warm water to caressing her clitoris. Andrea moved rhythmically against him, wanting to pull him inside her, wanting the riptide of their passion to carry her far away. Involuntary cries of pleasure escaped her as he plunged deeply inside. Begging him not to stop, her hands clasped around his buttocks, she moved in a wild frenzy as waves of her orgasm began to sweep through her body.

Ralph pulled back, postponing the climax. He wanted this to be an unforgettable night for Andrea. He wanted to make her realize that their love was true and wonderful and worth considering. Tonight he was going to savor every moment of this experience, an experience he had waited over a decade for. He would take her without haste, would make her want him. He wanted this night to remain forever etched in both his memory and hers.

"Ralph," Andrea whispered, quivering, gasping for breath, "don't stop. Don't punish me. I did love you. Please, darling, you must believe that." It was as though she had read his mind. She pulled him back inside her, moving with him, holding him captive to her need. They were lying on the soft rug now, both glistening from the soothing water. He teased her nipples. She begged, he touched her, she opened up to the sudden rush. He teased some more until finally Ralph poised his body high above hers, and with a thrust pushed deeper inside again and again. Andrea clasped her legs around his waist holding him, rising to meet every thrust, moving towards the edge of rapture. As she felt Ralph's body stiffen she contracted every muscle in her pelvis trying to prolong the pleasure she was feeling. With a final plunge he collapsed on her, spent, his breathing uneven. Her own orgasm was powerful and when it was over her body quivered, exhausted. Andrea stroked Ralph's damp jet black hair, holding him until he was still.

"Andrea," he whispered, "I can't live without you."

Andrea looked at him sadly, knowing she had done the wrong thing, but for what she thought was the right reason.

"Let's not talk about it Ralph. Tonight you have made me a happy, satisfied woman and I hope I've made you a happy man. That's all that matters now. I said so from the beginning and you agreed," she tried to explain.

But Ralph could not imagine why Andrea did not *know*, as he did, that they belonged together? How was he expected to love so completely again when Andrea was the only woman who had ever taken complete possession of his mind, his soul, and now his body? He loved her and nothing could change that. Not now, not tomorrow, not ever. Yet something had always stood between them. Years ago, long before she had become this powerful and famous woman, he had spent many nights in her bed just holding her when she had one of her nightmares and was too frightened to sleep. But as close as they were, she always remained a mystery. A mystery that became more tantalizing with every glimpse of herself she revealed to him. What had tormented her throughout the time she had been with him, remained a quandary. He never found out. Yet he knew she had loved him once.

"I cried for a week after you left England," he said. "That was the first time in my life I had ever cried. It took me years to try to get my life back together. How can I go back to one night stands and superficial relationships after this?"

"Now Ralph, there must be someone special in your life after all these years."

"No. They could never compare to you. Ah, *Chocolát*, yes there are many women in my life, a special one, no."

"Oh Ralph, I'm so sorry. I wish it could have been different for us."

Ralph rested his head between her breasts. With one hand he began stroking her smooth flat stomach. The other hand crept inside her thighs, still moist from their love-making. Andrea found herself stirring again with excitement.

"I won't lose hope," Ralph said. "After all, you did come back."

With a feeling of utter love, he kissed her passionately, stopping her reply. Andrea felt her body come to life again, needing this man as urgently as before, her regrets forgotten as he gathered her into his arms and carried her up to his bed. Lovemaking was not just a drug she needed tonight. She needed closeness, she needed this to be a special night. Tomorrow she would try to put things in perspective. One thing at a time.

Chapter 5

Stougborough, England

"**N**ext stop, Stougborough," said the short stubby conductor, repeating the same thing from car to car while the train slowed and finally glided to a smooth stop. Andrea, on her own and feeling quite grown up at nineteen, quickly gathered her baggage and made her way to the exit. She had brought more suitcases it seemed than all the other passengers put together. A porter helped her take the luggage to the platform.

"Have a good stay in England, lass," he said good naturedly.

"Thank you," Andrea beamed, pleased to have arrived at her destination at last.

New York and her family seemed light years away and Andrea was relieved to be away from her mother's constant nagging. She looked at the unfamiliar place and realized that this, the Midlands, was where she would spend the next five years, a lifetime. Maybe she should not have been in such a hurry to leave her family, she thought, with a sinking feeling. Still, she had to admit that she was excited about beginning life on her own.

"A cab for you, Miss?" a man in a checked flannel shirt asked her.

"Yes, please, my luggage is over there."

"Blimey, lass, where are you going, to the royal palace?" the cabby drawled in a thick accent. His English did not sound like the British she had heard in the movies, Andrea thought, amused. He sounded downright low class.

"I would like to be taken to the Stougborough Infirmary please," she replied with authority.

" 'op in then, duckie," he continued, "we'll be there in a minute." A minute was indeed all the ride took.

"That will be eighty pence," the cabby said, holding out his hand. Andrea gave him a five pound note and told him to keep the change.

He looked at her curiously. "You must be some sort of African princess," he grinned, as she dashed off to find help with her luggage. It was weeks later before she realized how much she had overtipped him, not having taken time in the beginning to learn the exchange rate. Headstrong as usual, Andrea had refused to take money from her parents when she left New York, determined to make it on her own; but she soon realized that it was going to be next to impossible to do it on the measly student salary the infirmary paid. Andrea looked around the gray stone building that seemed to go on for miles. Not sure where she was to go, she climbed the stairs to the entrance of the hospital.

"One of the new girls, are you?" a pretty brunette in a white heavily starched nurse's uniform said as she approached the doorway.

"Yes, as a matter of fact, I am," Andrea replied cheerfully. "I'm Andrea Francis."

"Well, welcome to SNU," she said, "and where are you from?"

"New York," Andrea answered.

"A Yank, eh? Well we don't like Americans much here, but ah reckon we'll get along jes' fine," the girl grinned, mimicking her idea of an American drawl. "I'm Laura Bradberry," she continued, dropping the accent. "I'm a first year student nurse, as I have been marked here for all to see." She pointed to the lone purple stripe on the sleeve of her uniform.

"And what do you get on your sleeve after the first year?" Andrea asked.

"For each year of training until your fourth, a new purple stripe. Then you become an acting staff nurse and you get a light blue stripe on the cap. After that you get two stripes if you become a sister and a dark blue stripe if you become a matron," she giggled. "Come, I'll fetch you to Matron Perry. We call her the 'horned lady' and I am sure you will find out why very soon." Andrea found herself liking Laura immensely. The English girl was about five feet six and had a healthy glow. Her thick shoulder length brown hair was cut in a page boy style and her sea green eyes framed with long dark lashes lit up when she smiled. As they walked down the corridors Laura talked gaily about all she knew of life as a student nurse, until they stopped abruptly at a door that was marked Matron. Laura tapped lightly and a stern voice on the other side ordered her in.

"Good afternoon, Matron. This is Andrea Francis. She just arrived," Laura introduced her and fled.

Matron Perry was a middle-aged woman with graying hair pulled back in a severe knot. Her words were more like the British voices Andrea was used to from the movies and television. She motioned for Andrea to sit. Andrea immediately understood Laura's dislike for this woman. Hidden behind every word Matron uttered was the implied threat of what would happen if one were to break any of her rules—yet there was a certain kindness behind the squinting gray eyes.

"Nurse Francis, I am Matron Perry. Welcome to Stougborough. I knew your mother. I hope you will prove to be as good a student as she was. I am sure she has told you about SNU."

"Some, but I daresay it was not enough," Andrea answered, awed.

"As a new recruit you will be living in the nurses' dormitory," the Matron continued. "If your behavior and academic performance is up to standards, you will move into the flats by your sixth month. If not, you will remain in the hostel with the other new recruits. Where is your luggage?"

Andrea was so taken with being called Nurse Francis, that Matron Perry had to repeat the question.

"Nurse Francis, do you have a hearing problem? I said where is your luggage?" Andrea cringed. She had left her luggage in front of the hospital right where the cabby had placed them on the sidewalk. In her excitement and the chatter with Laura she had forgotten it.

"I am afraid I left it outside," Andrea said shyly. "I hope that was all right."

"Of course it is not all right. We do allow, however, for a few stupid actions, and you have just committed one," Matron Perry said. "I will have the porter bring your luggage to your room. Follow me," she ordered, as she turned abruptly on her heel.

"She does have horns," Andrea thought, following obediently behind Matron Perry. They went out the front door of the hospital where she spoke quickly to a porter and then continued on to a building at the far end of the hospital. Matron Perry stopped in front of a door and let herself in with a key that hung from a chain on her belt. "This is the nurses' dorm." They went up three flights of stairs, stopping at the third door on the right of a long corridor. "Well here we are, Nurse Francis," she said, opening the door with another key from the same chain on her belt. "You should wash and take a nap before tea. The bathrooms are down the hall to the left. You have two hours."

"Thank you, Matron," Andrea said, dutifully.

The room was clean and airy, the furniture sparse but practical. On one end of the room was a sink and on the other a wardrobe. A single bed stood in the middle of the room, covered by what Andrea later found out to be the trademark bedspread of the hostel. They came in orange, blue, or green. Hers was orange.

Andrea found her toiletries and made her way to the bathroom. For a moment she thought she had left England since all the nurses seemed to be speaking in foreign languages. Before she left the washroom she had met several new students from all over the world. Andrea noticed that there were many Indian and Malaysian nurses in the new batch of recruits.

Back in her room Andrea was glad to climb into the short single bed. Wondering how she was going to fit in it, since as far back as she could remember she had always had an extra long big bed, were her last thoughts before falling asleep.

Andrea awoke to a loud knock on her door. "Nurse Francis, it is time to dress for tea." A ruddy face peaked around the door. Apparently this was the housemother.

"You must be exhausted after your trip. Is there anything I can do to help you?"

"No thank you, but could you just check back in a few minutes to be sure that I'm up?"

"I am leaving your room key on the dresser," she said promising to be back.

She seemed pleasant enough, thought Andrea, at least more so than Matron Perry.

Dinner was served promptly at seven. The student nurses all ate in the same dinning area, seated at the tables by order of their rank. Dinner was awful, some unknown cut of tough roast beef, Yorkshire pudding, boiled potatoes, and some sort of raisin concoction called mince pie. The food in England seemed just generally bad, she soon discovered. There were always potatoes, fried potatoes, mashed potatoes, potatoes of any sort with kidney or shepherd pies and usually trifle with custard. The only thing that Andrea found palatable were fish and chips with a dash of vinegar, wrapped in old newspaper. Sometimes, she swore she could actually read the news off the side of the fish. It took only a month for her to drop ten pounds.

"We've not had many Americans here before," a first year student was saying to Andrea.

"I'm not really American. I only lived there for a year. I am from Jamaica."

"That explains it then."

"Explains what?" Andrea asked.

"We British are very loyal to our colonies. I think it is wonderful to be able to help people less fortunate than ourselves."

"I don't consider myself less fortunate than you, my dear," Andrea said, acidly, "in fact, I consider anyone who makes such a statement to be a perfect ass. But I suppose you have never left Stougborough, so I will forgive you your ignorance."

The girl glared at Andrea, but apparently was uninterested in taking up the challenge.

"You told that trifling idiot," Laura laughed, as the girls walked back to the hostel. "She's really a stupid cow and I doubt if she will last a full year here. Her parents are potters or something in Stoke-On-Trent. You know. That's where they make Royal Doulton and Wedgwood. I wouldn't worry about her, she's just obnoxious. I think she suffers from an inferiority complex. I haven't taken Psych yet so I don't know all the proper medical terminology to describe her."

"No wonder my mother brought back trunks of that stuff when she came home."

"What? Psych terminology?"

"No stupid, Royal Doulton."
The girls had already forgotten the incident at dinner.

Andrea and Laura became inseparable over the next three months. Every evening they would walk up to the flats on Crooked Bridge Road where their new homes would be after the probationary period in the dorms.

"Well, back to the hostel we go, old girl," Laura said, as they trekked back from their evening walk. "It won't be long now before I move over to the flats. I'll be so glad to see the last of that bloody hostel."

"Laura, I am going to skip dinner tonight," Andrea interrupted, "I'm having prelims tomorrow and there's some material that I need to review. Do come up after and tell me all about the poison they served."

"Shall I bring you something back?"

"Not unless you want me to have nightmares about the potato that ate my exam."

"You are disgusting and terribly critical. I'll see you later then. I'm famished."

Two weeks later Andrea got the results of her exam. She had passed with honors.

That evening when Andrea went to Laura's room to meet her for their evening walk, she announced her entrance with a primal scream.

"Whatever's the matter with you?" Laura said, looking up from the newspaper.

"You know, Laura, one day your brain is going to fall right out into one of those newspapers, but don't say I didn't warn you. Why you fill your head with all that junk is beyond me. Haven't you heard that no news is good news? Anyway, put away that damn paper, my dear, because no news could be more interesting than mine. You are looking at a three-month graduate of this hell hole."

"Congrats, Andrea!" Laura said, hugging her, "I'm surprised—since you barely even read your textbooks."

"My dear, there is little a true genius can do to improve her talent. God, I'm so happy! How long before you transfer to the flats?" Andrea asked, as she moved out of Laura's embrace, uncomfortable with Laura's need to show affection, never quite at ease with her friend's hugs and kisses.

"I'll be moving soon but you have another three months before they let you defect," Laura said, misinterpreting Andrea's discomfort.

"We'll see about that," Andrea said. "I am not staying here without you. Those damn girls from India and Malaysia never speak a word of English if they can avoid it."

Laura was right, she seldom studied. She didn't need to. The work was simply not challenging enough for her. She learned quickly and soon earned the reputation as the star pupil who always asked too many questions. Gossip had it that the only reason she scored so high was because Mr. Killiston, the head lecturer, was lusting for her body. Although Andrea was sure he did have the hots for her, she also knew that she was a first-rate student, liked by all her teachers. What's more, she had decided she would utilize her innate intelligence and personality to get them to let her move to the flats early.

"Laura," Andrea said, one evening as they made their way to the dorm after working in the hospital, "do you think they will let me go next week when you do since I did so well on prelims?"

"I doubt it, but it is worth a try," Laura said.

"Let's request that we share the same quarters—if they allow it," Andrea said.

Laura said, thrilled by the idea. "Let's ask tonight at the newcomers dance. By the way, what are you wearing?"

"I've no idea," Andrea said, not having given even a thought to the dance. She knew she would have no problem finding something appropriate. "What about you?"

"I wanted to buy something new," Laura said, "but I can't afford it. I don't have a closet full of gorgeous clothes like you do, so I suppose I'll wear my only party dress."

"Wear something of mine," Andrea offered. "We're about the same size. Why don't you come with me to my room now and find something you like?"

"Do you mean it?" Laura said, hugging Andrea.

"Of course I do," Andrea said, smiling, getting more used to Laura's displays of affection.

Laura looked stunning in one of Andrea's evening dresses with her shining brunette hair piled becomingly on top of her head. As Laura and Andrea entered the ballroom at Presley Hall all eyes turned to them and conversation stopped. Used to being the center of attention, Andrea swept into the room with her usual air of confidence, Laura closely following in her regal wake. Then the girls separated and mingled with the others.

"You must be an American," a voice behind her said.

Andrea turned to see that it was coming from a square-looking bloke whom she had seen watching her.

"As a matter of fact I am not," Andrea said pleasantly.

"I thought only women from New York could carry off such a look," he continued, almost breathing down her neck.

"I did come from New York, but—" Andrea was beginning to explain.

"I knew it," he said, interrupting her before she could finish. "I can always spot a class act from America. Most Brits do not like Americans, you know," he stated, "but I absolutely adore them."

Andrea thought she had never met anyone quite so rude before and she wished he would simply bugger off. She stifled a yawn as his monologue became even more boring. Abruptly excusing herself, she made her way over to where Laura was chatting with a beautiful dark-haired woman she didn't know.

"There you are, duckie," Laura greeted her warmly, "I was wondering when you would escape from Victor. He's a reporter with the local paper and no doubt will be reporting on the ball. I wouldn't be surprised if your name is all over the front page. He is a trifle boring, isn't he?"

"To say the least." Andrea was barely listening to Laura, her attention drawn to the interesting-looking woman at Laura's side. She was wearing a simple, sophisticated, obviously expensive dress.

"Andrea, this is Maya," Laura said, smiling at both of them.

"Hello, Andrea," Maya said, looking directly into her eyes. "You are very beautiful."

"Thank you," Andrea said, flushing slightly. "Do you work here?"

"Yes," she answered, as she continued to hold Andrea's gaze. "I am a third-year student, but I have been on night duty for the last three months, so we've never met." She extended her hand. It was warm.

At the contact Andrea felt an electric shock go through her body. Wondering why the woman was having such an extraordinary effect on her, Andrea's eyes were again caught by Maya's piercing blue gaze. She shuddered. Puzzled, she felt a strange sense of recognition. Something dark. Something sinister. But that was impossible. This Maya was a stranger. "You live in one of the flats then, do you?" Andrea said still holding Maya's steady gaze. A determination and strength behind the crystal blue eyes seemed to hold a private message for her. Bewildered, Andrea lowered her eyes, not knowing the exact cause of her nervousness.

But it was not long before she was again drawn to the lucid eyes where for a brief moment Andrea saw a picture. It was only a flash and it was hazy but it was definitely there, and Andrea knew it had something to do with her. She blinked, trying to avoid the surrealistic effect. Why did she feel as though she knew this woman? And why did Maya's eyes seem to express something that she wanted to burn into Andrea's consciousness? She felt as though she were being put under a spell by a sorceress.

"Would you care to dance?" A foreign accent broke her connection with Maya and a hand took hold of her elbow, pulling her toward the dance floor. Andrea pulled her arm away, and turned to see a very handsome Arab behind her.

"You should at least wait for an answer to your question," she said sharply as she allowed him to lead her into a waltz. Although annoyed, a bit of her anger was dissipated by his good looks. "I was in the middle of a conversation, sir, and I am not a camel to be led. Is that what you do in the desert?"

"A temper! Ah, I love that in a woman," he said in a teasing voice. "But I am sorry to have been so rude," he continued. "I will of course return you to your friends if that is your wish."

"Now you sound like a goddamn genie. Your wish is my command," she mimicked.

He threw his head back and laughed, an attractive laugh. They danced well together and when Andrea allowed herself to relax in his arms she realized that the entire situation was indeed funny. She was annoyed because she had wanted to talk with Maya, yet she was also relieved that he had interrupted them. This Maya woman seemed to be—quite strange.

"I am sorry," Andrea said, "I did not mean the bit about your camels."

"To be quite honest I wouldn't mind showing you my camels sometime. I am Saleem Shaheed, and you are, no doubt, one of the new nurses."

"And why could I not be one of the new doctors?" she said indignantly.

"Because I would have met you before in the doctors' lounge. What is your name?"

"Andrea Francis," she said, "And I am truly sorry about being a little rude just now."

"I will forgive you if you have dinner with me next week."

"I shall have to think about that," Andrea said, "but how will I reach you to tell you what I've decided?"

"I am in pediatrics. I pick up my messages at noon. I also tie my camels beside the doctors' bungalow, number 243." He smiled broadly and Andrea was shocked to see that at that moment he looked a lot like Adam.

"*Salaam Alaeikum,*" he said, returning her to where Laura was standing with a group of nurses. He moved away to mingle with the others at the party. Maya was nowhere in sight.

That night Andrea could not sleep. It was not the thought of Saleem that kept her awake; it was the image of Maya. Andrea felt a shiver go down her spine as she remembered the penetrating blue of the woman's eyes. What was it that she had seen in those eyes? She drifted off trying to piece the picture together in her mind.

Maya felt relieved. She had finally been able to make her first contact with Andrea. Even in a crowded room Andrea had felt the connection between them although Maya knew that the girl did not fully understand it. It was just as well. The vibration of her own psychic power was almost painfully acute in the presence of Andrea and Maya now *knew*. Yes, Maya was satisfied that the daughter possessed the same powers Lila Francis had. And she knew that so far Andrea was unaware of her latent abilities.

"You have got to get up," Laura was shaking Andrea.

"Damn it, Laura, do you have to jump on the bed when I'm sleeping?"

"I have good news! I just thought you'd like to hear it."

"What the hell is it then? What time is it anyway?"

"Eight-twenty," Laura said brightly.

"Ah hell, it's Saturday morning and anything you have to tell me can wait until later."

"Very well," Laura said, "I guess I'll just go and pack my things."

"Pack your things for what?" Andrea asked, popping her head out from under the pillow.

"I will tell you later if you wish but you will have to come to see me at my new flat."

Andrea leaned her head up on her hand and wondered what on earth Laura was rambling on about. "I don't get it," she said, rolling over.

"Sometimes you are so dumb, Andrea! We are moving to the flats."

"I know that, so what's all the excitement?"

"We, stupid, I did not say me. *We* are moving. Today. I asked the housemother at breakfast if there was any way that you could move over to the flats earlier. I literally made you sound like the only responsible person in Stougborough. I also told her that since you had no other friends from your own country I felt you would be lonely among the other girls."

"You *are* wonderful," Andrea said, touching her friend's arm lightly, "I owe you one."

"I told her that since we were both starting our rotations on Monday, we'd like to be settled in before tomorrow. She told me she would check into it and let me know. I met her in the hall later and she said we could move in today. We even get to share the same flat!"

"Oh my God," Andrea said, jumping to her feet. "I can't believe we are getting out of here. I'm so thrilled! Oh Laura I really do owe you one. Well what are we waiting for? Let's start packing."

The two spent most of the day packing and moving their belongings to the flats, and by the time they had unloaded the last of their possessions, they were exhausted.

"Let's just leave these things here and have some tea," Andrea said, falling onto her bed. "We can unpack later."

"Who the hell left all these damn bags in the hallway?" a voice screamed from the corridor. "I think I've broken my bloody neck!"

Andrea and Laura ran to the door of the bedroom to see a girl sprawled on the floor.

"I *am* sorry," Andrea said, looking down at the girl, sprawled ungracefully on top of their luggage. "We've just moved in. We've been doing it all day and we just had to rest for a bit."

"Well, you could at least have moved the damn bags to one side. It's stupid to just leave them in the hall. I see you rookies have a lot to learn."

The girl rose to her feet and smoothed her dress. She looked at one and then the other of the bumbling new nurses. "I live here too. And I don't expect to fall on my face every time I walk into this flat. Damn idiots!" She breezed past them and slammed the door to her room.

The girls hurriedly moved the pile of luggage to their respective rooms.

"What a bitch," Andrea said. "I think we'd better request either a new roommate or a different flat."

"She is a witch," Laura agreed. "Ah well, let's have that tea. It's a good idea to stay out of her way tonight."

They were on their way to the kitchen as the door opened and a beautiful girl came into the flat.

"Hello girls," she said good-naturedly. I'm Jennifer, one of your new roommates."

"Thank God," Andrea said.

"I see you must have met Maria," Jennifer smiled. "She *is* an absolute ogre, isn't she? Not to worry, she's all bark, not a bite in her. Isn't that so, Maria?" she shouted into Maria's room.

"I would prefer it if you tried not to damage my reputation," Maria said, coming out of the bedroom. "And I have a right to be mad. These dimwits left all their bags spread out in the hall and I fell over them when I came in."

"I'm glad you didn't bruise more than your ego," Jennifer said, smiling at Maria who in turn gave her a scornful but tamed look. The girls laughed, relieved.

"Why don't we walk over to the cafeteria and have some dinner?" Jennifer asked.

"Wait. I'll get my jacket," said Maria.

Dinner was fun. Andrea thought of the contrast between her two new roommates. Jennifer was tall, dark haired. She was not beautiful, but with her warm personality she outshone Maria, who was a stunning tiny blond. Maria had a forcefulness about her that made her seem bigger than her five feet two inches. Andrea decided that God had made a mistake and forgotten to give her red hair to match her temper.

"I suppose that you are really a redhead," Andrea blurted out.

"Why the hell is that?"

"Your foul temper of course."

"A smart ass are you? God, why do we always have to get them." Maria snorted.

"*You* are the one who's been acting like the ultimate bitch," Andrea said, "and you don't scare me one bit, so if I were you I would get that temper of yours under control and just relax."

Over the next few months, despite their differences, Maria and Andrea became as inseparable as Siamese twins, leaving Laura feeling betrayed and angry.

"Let's go to the pub tonight," Laura suggested as she and Andrea walked from the hospital to the flats after work on Wednesday night.

"I can't Laura, I already have plans to go to the movies with Maria."

"Well I suppose that's an exclusive outing as always," Laura said indignantly. "Andrea, I really don't understand you."

"Don't start that again," Andrea said angrily, "I see nothing wrong with going to the movies with Maria."

"Then why was I not invited along?" Laura said, looking hurt.

They were still arguing when they reached the flats. "Laura, you've got to find some other friends to do things with. I can't fill all your needs. I cannot be what you want me to be."

With that she went to her room and shut the door.

Tears drenched Laura's face. She had loved Andrea, but she had known for some time that she could not compete with Maria for Andrea's friendship. Maria and Andrea were so much alike, both volatile, aggressive, quick witted and outspoken. Their insensitivity to others genuinely amazed them when it was pointed out. Laura began to realize that she had been a bridge, a transitional phase for Andrea, a person to be close to while she was new at school and friendless, but to leave by the wayside when someone better came along. Andrea had a mean streak. Laura had seen that some time ago, but she was always ready to give her the benefit of the doubt because she loved her.

Laura decided to take a walk and clear the fog in her mind. Was she really such a clinging vine or were her feelings about

Andrea having used and discarded her correct? She jumped as someone appeared before her in the dark.

"Laura, it is Maya."

"Maya, you startled me! I suppose you can't sleep either?"

"I usually take a walk before bedtime. It clears my head," Maya said.

Laura hated the way Maya always seemed to be watching Andrea and her, and especially the way she looked at Andrea. It unnerved her, as though Maya knew something about them that she herself did not know. Andrea had always said there was something eerie about Maya and tonight Laura felt she was absolutely right. She had seen the woman several times walking past their flat at night as if she had been watching them. It was weird.

"Why have you been crying?" she said, looking intently at Laura.

"I'm just upset about something," Laura said, shrugging her shoulders.

"Come inside for a while, won't you? I will make some tea. A good cup of hot tea always soothes the nerves," she said. Laura felt she could not refuse without appearing rude.

"Did you have a fight with Andrea?" she asked as she poured hot water into the teapot.

"How did you know?" Laura asked.

"Because I know Andrea," Maya said without further explanation.

Andrea wondered if she had been too cruel to Laura, who was so easily hurt. But she hated the way Laura always had to be at her heels, more demanding and possessive every day. She was trying to put more distance between them, but Laura refused to understand and continued to be invasive. Lately Andrea was beginning to feel more and more, of the old familiar instinct to strike out. It always took over when she felt pressured. She knew she could easily crush Laura and she knew she would if Laura continued to push—it was as if she were fighting for her own survival. Why, she wondered, was the need so strong to protect herself from certain people who insisted on having her undivided attention? She hated to be possessed, caged. She had to be free from the stifling shackles of love. Being with Maria was different. Like Andrea, she was independent. She could take care of herself.

Chapter 6

The day had finally arrived for the new student nurses to do their practical experience on the wards and Andrea was excited about it. Sleep the night before was fitful, but she awoke early Monday morning and dressed in her new white uniform with the lone purple stripe. Appraising herself in the mirror, she thought she looked better in this white pinafore with the lone purple stripe and the thick belt encircling her tiny waist than she did in some of her so-called designer dresses. She pinned on her fob watch and chained her scissors to her pocket, having already removed her jewelry and trimmed her nails. They had warned the nurses about that in orientation. Finally she clipped the starched white cap to her head and again took a long look at herself in the full length mirror. She was pleased with what she saw.

"Let's go," she shouted to Laura. Both girls grabbed their navy capes and headed for the door.

"My God, Andrea," Laura exclaimed, "you look as though you are off to a fashion show. How could anyone look that good in a simple white uniform? Why are we in such a hurry anyway? Let's have a cup of tea."

"I'm so excited about my first day on the wards," Andrea said, "I'm afraid if I swallow anything I might just throw up!"

"I was excited too on my first day, but I am *not* looking forward to the OR on this rotation. I heard Sister Pratt is a real bear."

"Well I think Pediatrics was a good first choice for me," Andrea said, "I've never worked with children before, but I think I'll enjoy it."

"Well then, let's be off," Laura chimed, walking out the door.

The ward smelled of antiseptic. Andrea was totally unprepared for the wave of nausea that came over her. She straightened and took a deep breath. She was not going to succumb to weakness.

Andrea stood at the far corner of the cramped reporting office. It did not seem large enough for all the day staff as they trickled in to receive the night duty nurse's report. During the report, Andrea was totally confused.

"Baby Lasher slept well until about four-thirty," the night nurse was saying, "then suddenly she began gurgling loudly. She had a pulmonary collapse and was successfully tapped. We transferred her to pediatric ICU. If you remember, she had thrown an embolism after surgery and we believe it may have been the cause of the lung collapse."

Andrea was mesmerized. She recognized the medical terms being used from her classroom studies but she would be damned if she could remember what they meant. Andrea had become so focused on trying to understand what had just been said that she was completely unaware of the rest of the report.

"And we would like to welcome our new trainee," the Sister was saying, referring to Andrea. "Welcome to our staff, Nurse

Francis, I hope you will enjoy your stay here."

Andrea started at hearing her name. She had been trying to figure out how she was going to cope with her first day.

"Thank you, Sister," she said simply.

"Today I will assign you to Nurse Brown. You will both be responsible for baby Jones who has spinabifida, and baby Owens, who is here for mitral stenosis after a bout with rheumatic fever." As far as Andrea could tell the nurse was talking Greek.

However, by the end of the day much of her fears and anxieties had disappeared. She had made baby formulas, changed diapers, given her first injection, taken rectal temperatures and had even attempted passing a naso-gastric tube. Andrea decided she liked her work, but above all she positively adored the taste of the baby formula, and in the weeks to come would often duck into the feed room and spoon some formula powder into her hand to enjoy.

At the end of the shift that first day Andrea was emotionally and physically exhausted. She decided to go to the staff lounge to have some tea before heading home.

"Your work was outstanding today, Nurse Francis," Sister Pashby said, just outside the lounge, "We are going to enjoy having such a good worker."

"Thank you, Sister. I was just about to have some tea before leaving, is that all right?"

"Of course it is. I would join you but I must go and check on one of my little tykes."

Sister Pashby was one of the most compassionate women Andrea had ever met. Totally in tune with all the children on the ward, she seemed to understand their sounds.

"If a child's cry is shrill and loud," she often said, "it is because they are hungry, if it is piercing but dull it is because they are in pain and if it's just whiney their diapers need changing." She wept openly for the loss of a new life and often attended her tiny patients' funerals, constantly reminding both herself and the students that the children were in a better place.

Andrea filled the kettle and was about to pour a cup of tea when Saleem entered the room.

"May I?" he asked, taking the teapot from her. Andrea was annoyed. She wished he would grow accustomed to Western ways and wait for indications before he assumed that his attention was welcomed. She tried to understand his behavior in light of his Middle Eastern culture, but she still found him rude.

"I have been observing you all day," he said, "you are going to be an excellent nurse, but I do believe you have the talent and the brains to be a wonderful doctor."

"You are a wonderful doctor yourself," Andrea replied. She looked at his long hands. "You have the hands of a surgeon."

"But I did not operate today," he said curiously, "How did you arrive at that conclusion?"

"You did do a cut down, did you not?" she said. "It was on baby Jefferies. You could not find a ready vein so you had to cut down into the ankle to put in the IV."

"Quite," he said. Then, looking directly into her eyes, he changed the subject. "Why have I not heard from you, Andrea?" he said. "I have checked my mail box for the last month and not a word from you."

"I've been extremely busy," Andrea said. "I have had to study a great deal for this rotation." Saleem ignored the lie.

"I would like to take you to dinner on Friday night—or would you rather learn how to play a good game of table tennis? I happen to have been the table tennis champion of Cairo," he joked.

"Dinner sounds better," Andrea said, trying not to laugh and failing. The dinner date was set for Saturday.

She had five days to come up with a plan to get out of it, but by Friday she had dug herself deeper and deeper into the commitment by not deciding how to decline gracefully.

Saleem was prompt. His perfect white teeth gleamed at her as he smiled.

"I have brought you something," he said, handing her a bouquet of white roses.

"Oh, these are lovely," Andrea exclaimed, surprised. "I know what red and yellow and pink roses signify but what does white mean?"

"Purity and innocence."

"Well I am glad that you think that of me. Come in while I arrange them in a vase? Would you like a drink?" she said, then flushed, remembering having heard Arabs did not drink alcohol.

"No thank you, I think we should get along. The restaurant will only hold our reservations for ten minutes, so we should not be late."

"Done this before, have you, with new students?" she said, and was sorry the moment the words left her mouth. He did not answer.

The eclectic Raj decor of the Indian restaurant was beautiful. It smelled strongly of spices.

"Mmm curry! I love it," Andrea said, "We always had it at home."

"You have an Indian influence then," he said.

"I guess that's why they call it Jamaica, West Indies," Andrea replied, making what was for her a new discovery.

"This is a very good Indian restaurant, I think you will enjoy it."

Dinner was superb, and to Andrea's surprise she found herself having a wonderful time. Saleem was interesting and easy to talk to. He had a sense of humor that Andrea appreciated.

"Tell me," he said, "what really brought you to England?"

"My mother studied at this hospital and is a qualified nurse because my father thought every woman should have a professional education whether she used it or not. One of my sisters is a doctor. They've all been educated in the States, but I could not take being that close to my mother for another second."

"Typical adolescent discontent," Saleem smiled.

"Not so typical. I was having a particular crisis that I felt she could not understand."

"What was that?"

"I really don't want to discuss it," Andrea replied, wanting to get off the topic. "What about you? Why are you here?"

"I studied medicine in Cairo," he began, "I wanted to specialize in pediatric surgery, so I came here to study under Mr. Bridgeton who is world-renowned."

"And who did you leave behind?" Andrea asked sheepishly.

"Three wives and eight children," he said, waiting for the inevitable response.

Andrea's head jerked up from the paratha and curry chicken that she was enjoying.

"I beg your pardon?"

"You heard me right. It is not unusual where I am from to have more than one wife."

"So exactly what is it that you want from *me*?" Andrea said, coming directly to the point in her usual way.

Saleem studied her face for a moment before he answered. He was not used to this kind of bluntness in a women, not used to spirited, questioning, feisty women, but strangely he found himself enjoying these qualities in this Andrea Francis.

"I want to get to know you better, maybe very much better," he said, sure of himself.

"If you play with fire Saleem, you may get burnt. That's an

English saying. I'm certain that Western women are very different from the women you are used to, and you would be taking a chance."

"Perhaps, but I am willing to risk it."

Subdued, Andrea finished her meal.

"Do you want me to fetch a cab or shall we walk?" Saleem asked when dinner was over.

"I think we should walk," Andrea said," it's such a lovely night. You know, the stars just are not the same here or in America as they are in Jamaica. There they seem to light up the sky."

"In Cairo they are very luminous too," he said. "Let's walk back to my place," Saleem suggested, "We can have coffee and continue our conversation."

Andrea started to decline but changed her mind, not ready to go back to the flats, wanting her first real evening out to go on for a while longer. "Why not?" she said. Besides, the handsome Saleem intrigued her, wives, children, camels and all.

The flat was not large, but it was exquisitely decorated with artifacts and furnishings from the Middle East.

"You have beautiful things Saleem," Andrea said, looking around.

"I do," he said, beaming with pride. "Will you have brandy?"

"I thought we were going to have coffee," Andrea replied, "I thought Arabs did not drink alcohol."

"Then there are surprises in store for you. All Arabs are not the same." He opened a cabinet which housed his television and a well-stocked bar. All the comforts of home and designed for good living, Andrea thought. He handed her a snifter half filled with Grand Marnier.

"I would like to change out of these clothes," he said

disappearing into the bedroom. When he returned he was wearing what appeared to be a long loincloth wrapped around his waist. His chest was bare except for a silky mat of black hair. "We relax in these at home. Would you like to change into one?"

"Oh no! I would rather have my chest covered. I don't have any black chest hairs to show off. And even Jane wore more clothes than Tarzan," she said flippantly, and was sorry she had.

"Well I will give you one that covers your entire body, just like Jane," he said. "Be daring."

Loving the challenge, she too disappeared into the room and returned wrapped from shoulders to toes in the beautiful silk sarong-like dress he had given her. She briefly wondered how many women had worn it before her.

"Better," he said, "is that not more comfortable?"

"Yes," she admitted, "it certainly is." Andrea slid down to the floor beside him on the rich carpet.

"Would you like to smoke?" he said, reaching for a silver cigarette box inset with mother of pearl.

"Yes, please," Andrea said, watching him as he presented her with a slim brightly colored cigarette that automatically popped out of the container at the flick of a button.

"I hate the taste of English cigarettes. These are from Egypt." Saleem lit her cigarette before handing it to her. Andrea inhaled deeply and choked on the pungent smoke.

"These are strong," she said, coughing. He smiled and nodded, puffing on his own cigarette.

Andrea looked at Saleem through the sweet-smelling smoke. He was truly a very good-looking man, she thought. And he looked so much like Adam that it was eerie. Still she could not really decide whether he actually looked like him or whether she imagined the resemblance. She continued to stare at him and decided that it was his smile that was like Adam's. Andrea carefully pushed the image of Adam out of her mind and concentrated on the handsome man sitting beside her.

"Andrea," he said, a smile crossing his face, "you can take off your shoes. A sarong is usually worn without them,"

"I guess I look pretty silly," she said, laughing and looking down at her feet. She felt ridiculous being half-naked and still wearing her high heels.

"Let me." He reached over to pull off her shoes, gently stroking each foot as he removed first one shoe and then the other.

"That feels marvelous," Andrea said, snuggling up against his broad shoulder. "Tell me, Saleem, are you always this rehearsed in your seduction?" She was feeling the full effect of the brandy.

"What seduction?" he said, arching his too-perfectly shaped eyebrows, pretending not to understand her inference. "Do you think I am seducing you?"

"Of course not! How mistaken I am. This, of course, is just normal Arabic hospitality."

"Or maybe you have cast a Western spell on me. Another drink?"

"Why not? I'm already half drunk and it will make it much easier for you to take advantage of me if I'm completely intoxicated."

"Andrea, that's unfair! First you call me uncultured and now you attack my integrity."

"I don't mean to insult you Saleem, but do you know what you're getting yourself into?"

"I have an idea," he answered ruefully, "yet I don't seem to want to stop trying. But good Lord, are you always this direct?"

"Yes. Always."

He got up and poured each of them more brandy.

"I guess I will have to get used to your candidness then, won't I?" he stated, lowering himself back beside her on the floor.

The alcohol had made Andrea drowsy. To keep her head from bobbing up and down, she again rested against his shoulder.

"You want to make love to me, don't you?" Andrea said, sipping her brandy. She knew she should stop drinking. She knew she was getting tipsy. "It could be difficult to get me into your bed, Saleem. I never sleep with men I don't know."

In truth, Andrea had slept with only one man, but he had made her thoroughly familiar with seduction and lovemaking. Adam had taught her everything. "There are no barriers between lovers," she could hear him saying, "With body and soul totally merged, one experiences completeness."

Adam had indoctrinated her to his way of thinking, of being. She had learned to believe in him the way Christians believed in Jesus Christ. That the process of any indoctrination was much the same had not mattered, because more than anything in her life, she wanted to belong to Adam. She was his protégée. She missed him so much, his boyishness, his freedom from conformity, his ability to express love. She had always thought that Adam's touch was the only one in the world that could make her feel like a woman; but God, how she needed the embrace of a man tonight. But, she wondered, would just any man do?

She looked up at Saleem who was smiling at her. It had been eighteen months since she had seen Adam and now here was this man beside her with Adam's smile. What harm could there be in pretending?

"I do want to make love to you, Andrea" he said, "but I am a patient man. I will wait until your are ready to be mine."

"Saleem," Andrea cautioned, "don't try to possess me. Don't try to make me your central focus. I'm not capable of loving another man. I'm warning you, I'm not good for you," she said, suddenly feeling very tired. Before he could ask her to explain the other man, Andrea had suddenly gotten heavy against him. He looked down at her and realized she had fallen asleep.

Saleem lifted her in his arms, carried her to his bedroom and laid her gently on the bed. As he removed the sarong he saw that she had a beautiful body. Lying there motionless, she seemed so young, so innocent; but he knew better than to think Andrea Francis was innocent or naive. What was it about this girl, he wondered, that had him so spellbound? Why he wanted to get himself involved with this mere child was a mystery. She was at least fifteen years younger than he, and he had always preferred mature women, women who knew how to please a man.

Saleem knew instinctively that Andrea's age was only due to chronology, not experience, but looking at the sleeping young girl on the bed, Saleem was suddenly moved by a rush of love. Those black lashes appeared to caress her cheeks, contrasting with the perfect bronze skin. How could anyone, he wondered, have escaped adolescence without a single blemish? Andrea's firm breasts with the dark ruby nipples moved up and down with each breath. Saleem felt a surge of excitement, but he carefully pulled the quilt up to cover her bare body. With his face so close to hers, he kissed her lips softly. She stirred long enough to return his kiss and then fell promptly back to sleep. She smelled of brandy, not a drink for a mere nineteen-year-old. He should not have allowed her to drink so much.

Saleem kissed her again, cradling his face in the curve of her neck. Again she stirred sleepily, this time locking her arms around his neck and seeking his lips hungrily. He wanted her. He considered taking her right then, but he knew he could not. He wanted her awake and consenting voluntarily. Yes, he smiled, he wanted her to know where he tied his camel.

Taking a blanket and pillow from the closet, Saleem went to sleep on the couch in the living room. Something deep in his psyche told him that he was initiating a dangerous liaison, but the ache deep in his loins told him he was not going to be able to stop it.

When Andrea awoke it was already light outside. She sat up, leaning on her elbows and looked slowly around the room, wondering where on earth she was. Suddenly she remembered. She looked down at her naked body and quickly pulled the covers up to her bare breasts. The silk sarong that she had worn the night before was spread out beneath her like a sheet.

"My God!" she said, softly, "I must have slept with him! I can't remember any of it," she thought wracking her brain to recollect her actions. In the kitchen Saleem was clinking dishes and singing an Egyptian song. His jovial mood did not give her much hope for her virtue. The song was absolutely dreadful and she wished he would shut up and not add to the pounding in her head.

Andrea swung her feet over the side of the bed pulling the sarong along to cover herself. She would leave before he came in. In her haste, she stood up too suddenly and the pounding in her temples intensified.

"Good morning," Saleem whispered, coming into the room and handing her a cup of coffee. "Sorry I have no tomato juice."

"Why are you whispering?"

"Because I imagine you have an awful hangover. Coffee? It is better than tea for a hangover, you know."

Andrea nodded and took the steaming cup of coffee gratefully.

"Cigarette?"

Andrea accepted the lighted cigarette, pulling hard on it. Inhaling the smoke deep into her lungs she sat back and looked at Saleem. His chiseled nose and fine features could belong to an androgynous person. Those jet black eyes were lined with long curling lashes, too long for a man. He was very handsome, though he was not as tall as she had thought, probably under six feet. Like Adam, he had a pencil thin mustache. That and his smile, she was sure, were the reasons for her attraction. Andrea continued to survey him. He had long fingers with perfectly manicured nails, the hands of a surgeon. Andrea brought her eyes to the mat of curly black hair on his chest and her gaze continued steadily down his body to his crotch. Maybe sleeping with him hadn't been so bad, she thought. If only she could remember!

"I guess I was a little drunk last night," she said, frowning, disgusted that he would have taken advantage of her in such a state.

"That you were," he said. "You passed out right in the middle of a sentence. How is your head?"

"Pounding. Anyway, I had better go," Andrea said, downing the coffee quickly. She pulled the sarong from around her waist and threw it on the bed, only then did she remember that she was wearing nothing but her panties. Andrea reached down to retrieve the sarong but his hand caught hers and forced her to stop.

"Never cover anything as magnificent as your body." His hand brushed her nipples.

"You have such beautiful breasts," he said, moving so close to her that she could feel his breath on her cheek. Andrea allowed the sarong to fall slowly to the floor and silently, as though the movement was choreographed, she took a small step forward until her body was against his. Saleem ran a hand down her spine and held her buttock. Andrea leaned closer into the embrace pressing her breasts into his chest. He moved his other hand to cover her right breast, rubbing her nipple between his fingers as he brought his mouth down firmly on hers, his tongue tracing the inside of her lips. Andrea parted her legs slightly as he guided a hand between her thighs, his fingers exploring.

"Let's finish what we started last night," he breathed into her ear.

"Finish, you mean—"

"I told you Andrea, I have integrity."

"Saleem," Andrea said, looking up at him, finding it difficult to resist his caresses, "I have no idea why you want to be involved with me, but I must be honest with you. I'm not capable of giving you what you desire. You want to make love to me and I want you as well, but I caution you not to start fantasizing about anything else beyond this moment." Andrea pulled away from his embrace and look deeply into the jet black eyes. "Do we understand each other Saleem?"

"Perfectly."

Andrea moved back against the bed. She reached over and unfastened the edge of his waist-high sarong, allowing it to fall on the floor between them. She laid back on the bed, placing her hands between her thighs and slowly pushed them apart. Saleem fell to his knees his tongue tracing delicate kisses over her exposed vulva.

"I don't think I can honor your wish," he murmured, between kisses, "loving you will be the only thing to do."

"Then love at your own risk," she said, raising her hips to meet his eager mouth.

Saleem should have been shocked, but instead he was impressed with her candor. If an Arabic woman had spoken to her man in such a manner, she would have been thrashed in public. Western women, he decided, were much more of a challenge to one's ego, and he was unequivocally ready for the challenge. Saleem raised his head and looked directly into Andrea's eyes. She met his gaze without so much as a smile. He saw something disturbing in her stripped brown eyes and again felt the earlier caution nagging in his guts.

"Don't be so sure of yourself, Andrea," he said, kissing her behind her ear, "you may very well fall in love with me. I actually think you are the one who is afraid of what might happen," he whispered, sinking his teeth painfully into her breast. She twinged at the unexpected pain. Oh...yes...ohhhh, Andrea heard herself moaning with pleasure as his fingers parted the two soft lips and found the point of her pleasure. His touch to her clitoris now altering her reality. "It feels so good when you touch me...so very good," she kissed his hand.

Still calculating about whether he should or should not do this, knowing it was against his better judgment, Saleem kissed the impetuous lips already parted from passion. Andrea instantly responded, needing him urgently. Involuntarily she arched her back, straining to be closer to him as he ran his hand over her breasts and down her belly. His hand moved again down the smooth curve of her stomach rested momentarily on her thigh, then slipped between her legs, his fingers disappearing into her moist center.

"I won't hurt you," he said, easing his body against hers. "I will never hurt you."

As he said the words, he knew he was pleading with her not to hurt him.

Saleem pulled her buttocks to him, and in an urgent thrust, buried himself deep within her, forcing the breath out of her lungs. Andrea wrapped her legs around his body and rolled them both over until she straddled him. In this dominant position, she contracted her abdominal muscles tightly, holding him captive inside her, teasing him until she felt his urgency. She quickened her pace, moving rapidly, matching his movements boldly and with abandon. Saleem gripped the soft flesh of her buttocks, letting himself be sucked into her until he felt the familiar viscous liquid rising in him. She was in control. Rolling back on top of her, he tried to regain dominance but it was too late, he was in the grip of sexual inferno. With a final thrust he collapsed, spent. Her body trembled from the throes of its own climax.

Close to tears, half conscious and emotionally famished, Andrea yearned for the man she loved. The salty tears dampened her cheeks as she clung to Saleem and whispered, "I love you, Adam."

Andrea showered and dressed quickly.

"I have no surgery scheduled for today," Saleem informed her as she brushed her hair into a ponytail. "What would you like to do?" he asked, feeling better than he had in years and taking for granted that he would spend the day with his wonderfully adept young lover.

"Saleem," Andrea said, seriously "what happened between us was a mistake. I should not have allowed it and it won't happen again."

"I enjoyed every moment of our lovemaking and I cannot agree with you that it was a mistake."

"You won't take me seriously, Saleem. I'm sorry, but I am not ever going to be what you want. I'm spending today with Maria. And now I must go."

Andrea stepped out into the hot midday sun, furious with herself for having lost control. As much as she liked Saleem, she had no interest in becoming his lover. At any rate, not on a permanent basis. She already had the only man she would ever need. Adam had made sure of that. The pain she had felt leaving him was a pain she would never forget. Why was it that love was so painful? She walked out the door and did not look back.

Saleem stared after Andrea until she was completely out of sight. "*Salaam Alaeikum,*" he said softly. He knew he had already fallen in love with her. Again he asked himself why he wanted to pursue such an enigmatic, restless girl. And who the hell was Adam? She had clung to him in tears as she reached her orgasm and called him Adam, apparently not even aware that he, Saleem, was there. He was sure she considered him just another man, an illusion that served her purpose. He could have been any man, it would not have mattered, because to her he had been Adam.

Not a day went by that Saleem did not think of Andrea. He found himself urgently wanting to be close to her even though she had been distant and aloof since their lovemaking and had refused to take his calls. The thought of their union a week ago had kept him in an almost constant state of erection and he had made up his mind that he wanted her at any cost.

Andrea did all she could to avoid contact with Saleem. He had telephoned her, sent her flowers, chocolates and expensive perfumes. He had even come to her flat but she had refused to see him. It was obvious to her that Saleem wanted to be more to her than just her lover. Andrea thought of the night she had spent with him. He was a good lover. He knew how to please a woman using all the tricks of the trade plus a few Middle Eastern ones of his own. She had enjoyed making love with him and she would not mind having him as her lover on a casual basis. As long as good sex was all he wanted, then she could handle that; but she was concerned that he could not accept this proposal.

Her resolve weakened with every new gift Saleem sent her and the flowers that arrived daily, until finally two weeks after their night together she accepted one of his calls and agreed to meet him on Friday night at his bungalow.

"Hello, Andrea," he greeted her, kissing both cheeks.

"Saleem. How are you?"

"Not good until now. I have missed you."

"I guessed that from all the flowers, chocolates and perfume. You're good for the retail businesses in Stougborough, but very dangerous to my figure. You do know how to woo a woman, though. Thank you for the gifts."

"Can I get you a drink? Or are you too scared to drink with me?"

"Let's walk down to the pub and have a drink there, shall we?" Andrea said as she entered his flat.

"No, I want to have you all to myself. I do not want to share you with all those people. Not right now."

"I think you're getting into something that you will be very sorry about, Saleem. Or could it be that you are just plain horny?" she teased, running her hand up the obvious bulge in his pants. "What will it be, Saleem?" she said as she squeezed, "Goodbye or good fun?"

"All right, Andrea. You win. I promise that I will not fall in love with you. Is that what you want? I promise that you will be simply my personal little Jamaican concubine."

"Then I will have a brandy."

Andrea took a sip of the brandy and rested the glass on the coffee table. She slipped her dress over her head, smoothed her hair, unsnapped the fasteners of her brassiere and stepped out of her panties, spread her legs and allowed Saleem his desire.

"You are my love slave," she whispered, crooking her finger and beckoning Saleem to take her on a journey of pure animal passion. It was only moments later before they were again making carnal forays on each other's bodies, writhing together on the floor.

"I love you, Andrea."

She pretended not to hear.

Six months had gone by since Andrea and Saleem had begun playing love captives. Their erotic games and fantasies were fun for a while, but Andrea was becoming bored as Saleem became more and more demanding. He wanted Andrea to make a commitment to be his permanent lover. Andrea liked Saleem and was satisfied with the way things were; but their relationship was changing. Saleem wanted to know about her childhood, her past and especially about Adam. It was not part of the bargain and a dangerous sign, Things started to change when Saleem began telling her how much he loved her. For her, all there was between them was sex and she had no wish to share her private life with him. She did not care about Saleem in a special way. He was only there to fulfill her physical needs and that was all. Now after their lovemaking, Andrea wanted to leave immediately. She was tired of his demands for communication. For chrissake, she said to herself, she was fucking him almost daily—what the hell more communicating could he want?

"I don't understand Andrea. Why is it that you tell me nothing about yourself? And why is it that you are always in a hurry to leave?"

"Saleem, I am a very private person. My past has nothing to do with the present. Don't ask me again. Anyway," she continued hurriedly, we have been spending so much time together that I've been neglecting my school work. I must see you less. I have to go now," she kissed him lightly, "I'll call tomorrow."

The truth was they were spending so much of their free time together that she was feeling suffocated. Saleem was becoming too possessive and they were arguing about even the most trifling matters. Andrea was growing resentful of these demands.

"You can be very cold, Andrea. Or is it that you are scared of what you are feeling for me?"

Ignoring his statement, Andrea would say, "I'm leaving now, Saleem. I'll call you." There was no point in Saleem arguing and he knew it.

On Friday nights, Andrea would almost always pack an overnight case and trot off to spend the weekend with Saleem. But after work on this Friday she decided not to go to him.

"Same plans tonight?" Maria asked as the girls gathered their coats to leave work.

"No, not tonight. I've been thinking of calling it quits with Saleem. He is beginning to get on my nerves. I must do it slowly though. He says he's in love with me."

"Well, if you're not going to play house this weekend, how about a night on the town?" Maria suggested as they walked home to the flats. "We haven't seen that much of you since you've been dating Saleem. One night without you won't kill him. Besides, it's necessary to get to know other people if you intend to make the break. What do you say? It will be fun."

"God, I'd love to," Andrea said, jumping at Maria's suggestion.

"I'm indeed suffering from overexposure to Saleem. What time?"
"Nine?"
"Wonderful."

Chapter 7

The room was dark as they entered and it took a few minutes before Andrea's eyes adjusted to the dimness. A circular ceiling light was busily spinning, flashing its different colored beams everywhere, outlining silhouettes of people Andrea did not recognize. She began moving her feet to the disco music and was glad she was not with Saleem.

"Hey duckie, what brought you to town? We've not seen much of you lately," Laura said too loudly as she approached Andrea. "Busy riding camels, are you?"

"Oh shut up, Laura," Andrea said, sticking her tongue out at her roommate. "Are we jealous by any chance?"

"Sure. Who'd not be? You have the most handsome doctor in this entire hell hole spellbound and pussy whipped," Laura replied drunkenly.

"Then you can have him. Come on, let's find some nice men and dance," Andrea said, changing the subject.

Andrea headed in the direction of the bar.

"What are you drinking, pretty lady?" a masculine voice asked.

"Brandy," she said, turning. She recognized him from the hospital, a surgery resident. Quite good looking, Andrea thought, sizing him up, shorter than the men she was usually attracted to, but his hazel eyes and snub nose gave him a boyish, mischievous, appealing look.

"Brandy? I hope you've had dinner. I'm James," he said, extending his hand, "and I already know who you are."

"Good," Andrea said, "then let's skip the formalities, shall we, and have a dance?"

"What about your drink?"

"It will keep. If not it will just turn to vinegar. It would still have some use. We can pour it over our greasy fish and chips. Anyway, dancing with you will be more fun. You look like a great dancer."

"Mmmmm, that's a great compliment. Shall we?" he repeated taking her hand and moving towards the dance floor.

David pulled her close to him as they danced.

"*If only for one night* ..." Andrea began singing the words to the song, moving in perfect unison with David.

"You sing well, Andrea. Have you ever sung professionally?"

"If singing in the bathtub is professional."

"And do you mean what you are singing?"

"Maybe, but we will have to wait and see won't we," she said as the waltz came to an end. "Thanks a bunch." She smiled as she walked off to find Maria.

"What about that drink?" David said after her.

"Maybe later." Entirely too presumptuous she thought as she moved in the direction of a lively looking group.

She found Maria chatting with a group of residents. Andrea had spent so much time with Saleem that although she recognized most of them by sight she had never really met them.

"Hello," she said, joining the group.

"Oh hello, duckie," Maria said. "Guys, I would like you to meet my dear friend Andrea."

"What are you drinking, Andrea?" a tall, nice looking resident asked, looking her over her with interest.

"Brandy."

She could tell from his accent that he was from somewhere in Africa.

"Where are you from?" Andrea asked, meeting his stare boldly, definitely attracted to him. He had penetrating black eyes that seemed to undress her. His wavy black hair was cut neatly and he was clean shaven. His deep tan coloring made him absolutely irresistible.

Andrea could tell from his expensive clothes and the easy way he wore them that he had to be financially solvent. It must be family money, she thought, because no one could dress that lavishly on the measly salary of a resident. His gray and yellow argyle sweater matched his socks and the gray in his socks and sweater appeared to be the identical shade of the gray of his pants. The Baume Mercier watch he wore did not go unnoticed either. His speech and attitude was that of a self-confident, well-bred man.

"Tunisia. I am Stefan," he extended his hand. Their handshake held for a moment longer than was necessary.

"Would you care to dance, Andrea?" His stare seemed to burn through her.

"I would love to if you can tell me what color they are?"

"What color is what?" he looked puzzled.

"My panties of course. From the way your eyes are undressing me I'm sure you would know."

"Touché."

The party went on for hours. Andrea and Stefan spent most of the night dancing and making idle conversation together. Stefan was a splendid dancer. His rhythm was exactly coordinated with Andrea's own style. She was enjoying his company immensely, and the brandies never stopped coming. She also enjoyed feeling the swelling in his pants deliberately brushing against her. Tonight definitely had possibilities.

Deciding she was feeling very sexy and in need of a man other than Saleem, she could think of no better way to spend the night than with Stefan. His wild and exotic spirit had already piqued her interest. When she left the party he was with her.

"I have a flat across town," he offered as they got into his Fiat convertible. "Do you want to come over for a bite to eat?"

Andrea nodded. What he was going to eat, she giggled, was the real question, knowing what was to happen between them was completely understood.

Stefan was a gracious host. First he fed her, then wooed her and then made love to her passionately.

It was always the same, first the passion, then the oblivion and finally the illusion. As Andrea felt the familiar rise of her lust, she closed her eyes and as she climaxed, whispered softly, "I love you, Adam."

The next morning Andrea rose early and left the apartment quietly. She had looked over at Stefan who was still asleep, and thought what a magnificent man and a wonderful lover he was. Her body shuddered as she remembered his hot tongue darting, probing, demanding her surrender. She had the urge to lower herself on his stiff morning erection, his morning glory, already making a tent in the satin sheet, but she resisted. She hoped that she would see him again.

When Stefan awoke he felt completely alive and refreshed. Andrea Francis was his kind of woman, fiery and expressive. He wondered, however, who was Adam?

The phone was ringing as Andrea entered the flat.

"Where the hell have you been all night?" Saleem was shouting. "I was expecting you."

"Where I have been is none of your business, Saleem. I don't have to call and ask for your permission to go out," Andrea retorted angrily.

"But a call, Andrea—"

"Saleem, you are suffocating me," Andrea brutally interrupted him. "I told you not to get stuck on me because I had nothing permanent to offer. I'm tired of your possessiveness and I think it's time we stop seeing each other."

"The hell you do," he continued, "I am in love with you Andrea, can't you see that."

"Yes," she said softly, "I know. That is why it is best that we stop now. Anyway, Saleem, you are a married man three times over, do grow up and accept what we had for what it was. A good time and that's all."

"But Andrea—"

"Goodbye, Saleem."

Andrea hung up the phone and went to her room. The tears lingered on her lashes but did not fall. She knew that Saleem was hurting badly, but what could she do? She had not promised him anything and he had promised not to love her. But why had she continued with him, knowing how he felt, when there could be no future for them? That night sleep did not come easily.

Andrea was glad that her rotation on peds had ended. It would be easier for her to avoid seeing Saleem. At times she felt guilty for abandoning him; but it was not because she loved him. Doubts of her stability plagued her. Why was it so easy for her to keep her body separate from her heart? It was a trait so unlike a woman, one usually reserved for men. As time went on, however, it became easier and easier for her to dissociate love from sex. And now that she was fooling around with Stefan, Saleem was fast becoming a distant memory.

After a few dates with Stefan, Andrea sensed that she was far too enthralled with him to maintain an exclusive or even a constant relationship. She realized that the thought of becoming emotionally involved frightened her. She could not allow herself to fall in love with Stefan, not because she was incapable of loving him, but because she could never betray Adam's love. The solution, Andrea decided, was to have at least four lovers at a time. If she had many lovers, she rationalized, she would not have to spend too much time with any of them. A week here and a week there was all she wanted to invest. And she had to admit she had no complaints about the variety of sex.

Chapter 8

Laura had learned to be cautious around Andrea. Every so often over the months they had lived together she had seen a ruthless side to her friend's personality that threatened her. Andrea became especially defensive when her "space" was being invaded. Laura was disturbed about Andrea's fear of intimacy; it was apparently why she was sleeping around. What could she hope to find in such wantonly promiscuous behavior? Although the answer was obvious, Laura was never able to broach the subject with her, and whenever she tried, Andrea would always go into one of her reprimanding outbursts.

"Laura, I am a grown woman. I left home to be away from my mother and I assure you I did not come here looking for a substitute mother, so for chrissake, back off."

Maria was definitely more Andrea's speed. She never seemed in need of becoming enveloped in a friendship, and she subscribed to the philosophy of live and let live. Every day when their shifts ended the two would go to the cafeteria for a cup of tea before heading home.

"Maria," Andrea began, "I had another tiff with Laura. I'm thinking of moving to a new flat so she won't be so aware of everything I do."

"What was the fight about this time?"

"The usual. She is very concerned about my bedroom behavior."

"Speaking of which, I asked Nick to get us prescriptions for the pill. We don't want any little bastards running around now do we? Although I must admit that sometimes I fantasize about having Nick's children."

"They'll all be drug addicts," Andrea said, not caring much for Nick.

"Never mind the shitty comments, at least he'll save your bloody uterus from bulging. Or do you want to have Stefan's baby or maybe David's or maybe Christian's? How about Saleem's?"

"Shut up, Maria," Andrea snapped. "I can't imagine why you think you're so fucking pure. Damn you to hell, you bitch."

"I wish you would stop the profanity. I never said I was pure, but my dear, I use common sense. If I sleep around, it is only with Jewish men. They would never think of banging up a nice Christian girl. They all wear condoms. It's their custom."

"And I suppose you don't mind eating matzo balls either?!"

Both girls convulsed in laughter.

"By the way, Andy, I saw Saleem today."

"I don't care. And I don't want to discuss it."

"He told me to ask you to return his calls."

"Did I or did I not just say I don't want to discuss him? Sometimes I think you're deaf. Now," she added firmly, "I have to get going. I'm meeting Laura for a shopping spree at Marks and Sparks." Andrea made a face. "Can you imagine any well-bred woman shopping at Marks and Spencers?"

"They have good underwear there," Maria said, "although I

can't imagine what you would want with underwear. After all Andrea, you don't keep them on very long."

"If you are trying to piss me off, Maria, you're not going to succeed. I will not give you the pleasure and neither am I going to give you another minute of my time. I'm surprised at you but I really don't know why your behavior should surprise me. I knew all along that you are just as low class as the plebeians on the street, and far worse, I might add, than anyone who shops at Marks and Spencers. If you were not so stuck on silly Nick, you too might be having some fun. For God's sake, Maria, this is our youth! We're supposed to have these lewd memories, panties or no panties. And you want to know something else?" Andrea said, putting on her cape, "Sometimes I actually keep my panties on. It's more fun that way." Andrea walked towards the door. "Well, see you later, stupid," she said, reaching back to pull Maria's ponytail. They laughed.

The girls loved bantering with each other. Andrea admitted that if she considered anyone a friend, it was Maria.

"Happy panty hunting then, oh Queen of the Lingerie."

"What shall we do for our vacation," Laura asked, as she and Andrea lay across the bed, exhausted from their shopping expedition.

"How about a trip to France? I've never been and I think it should be interesting," Andrea responded. "Maria said Paris is a lot of fun and my parents always said the same. Let's see if Maria can schedule her time then as well. She'll be a great tour guide."

Laura knew better than to be annoyed. Although she had hoped to spend sometime with Andrea alone, she was well aware that the friendship existing between Maria and Andrea was much more then theirs could ever be.

"Helloooo duckies," Maria said, as she came floating into the room, flopping down on the bed. "And what luxurious purchases have you made today?" she continued, winking at Andrea. The girls moved over to make room for her on the narrow single bed. Andrea flashed a warning look in Maria's direction. "I have great news," Maria said, quickly changing the subject, "but let me run to the loo before I tell you."

"Why exactly do the British call the bathroom loo?" Andrea asked Laura.

"I really don't know. That's just the way it's always been. I think it's from the song, skip to my loo."

"I seriously doubt that. Then again, maybe. Usually if one wants to pee badly enough they do kind of skip around. I think, my dear Watson, that is a good enough explanation," she replied as Maria returned.

"What's the news, Maria?" both girls asked at the same time.

"I am going to Morocco with Nick for my vacation. He asked me today."

"Oh goodie," Andrea said, elated. She knew how much Maria cared for Nick, and as much as she personally disliked him, she was happy for her friend's sake. Laura quietly sighed, relieved.

"We were just about to invite you to come along to France with us, but I guess you have better things to do," Andrea said.

"I may be able to join you for a few days, but I'll have to let you know. Wild horses couldn't stop me from going to Morocco. Do you think Nick will ask me to marry him?"

"Not a chance in hell. He's going there to get drugged up."

"Andrea, you have the charm of a mongoose and the tongue of a boa constrictor. I can't understand why I even like you."

"Thank you, sweetie. Anyway we leave on Saturday, so let us know by Friday. By the way, did we get the prescription?"

"God Andrea! You don't plan to get laid in France, do you?"

"Who knows. They say France is for lovers, and after all a relationship can begin anywhere, can't it?"

Andrea and Laura awoke early Saturday morning, impatient to begin their trip, caught the early train from Stougborough to London and then to Dover. Now Andrea understood why all the hoopla about the white cliffs of Dover. She was fascinated with them.

"Take a picture of me," she said, handing her camera to Laura. "Say cheese."

"Now your turn, Laura. Smile, smile," her voice echoed.

The girls took the hovercraft across the Channel to Calais and then caught the train into the Paris Gar du Nord, where with the help of an English couple, they learned how to obtain a taxi. Paris was nothing like New York and getting a cab was a different routine. They had to go to a taxi stand rather that flag a cab down in the middle of the street.

Andrea soon regretted not having taken French in high school.

"Andrea, I am telling you," she could hear her mother emphasize, "every cultured young lady should at least speak conversational French." Of course Andrea had not listened. She had taken Spanish instead. Now here she was in France and her nine years of Spanish did not help one bit.

The hotel, a bed and breakfast, was not even close to Andrea's idea of comfort, let alone exquisite accommodations. One day she would return to France, she thought, looking around the well worn room, and then she would stay at the Plaza Athénée or the George V. However, she soon perked up; they were in Paris and that was all that mattered.

It was springtime and Paris was beautiful. The sun shone, its glorious light giving life and color to millions of flowers that were just beginning to bloom in order, Andrea decided, to provide clothing for the nude Greek statues in the Tuileries Jardin. Although Andrea felt Paris pulsating and loved it, she could not imagine living there.

They did the usual touristy things, visited the cathedral of Notre Dame and the Eiffel Tower, wandered around in the Louvre. Andrea loved the daily fashion shows in the Louvre courtyards and daydreamed of the day when she could wear such fashionable clothes. Although they could not afford to shop on the Avenue Montaigne or the Champs Elysées they enjoyed sightseeing in the designer shops.

"I think you have an admirer," Laura said one day as an absolutely gorgeous man in a most expensively tailored suit approached them near the Opéra.

"Good thing I got the pill," Andrea whispered.

"Who do you model for?" He spoke directly to Andrea—in French.

"Pardon, *non parle Français.*"

"Who is your agent? the man repeated in heavily accented English?"

"Agent for what?" Andrea asked, puzzled.

"You are a model, *non*?"

"No!" Andrea said, smiling at the Frenchman.

"I think you must be. A woman who looks like you is crazy not to be. I am Jacques St. Pierre," he said, holding out his hand. "I am a designer here in Paris and I would like to see my clothes on you."

"You want me to model your clothes," Andrea repeated in disbelief.

"Here is my card. Call me and we can discuss your terms, but regardless of modeling, call me if you really want to see Paris."

Andrea felt incredibly complemented as she carefully tucked the card in her handbag.

"And what do you think of that?" Laura asked as the girls made their way into more shops, a little envious that she was not even noticed.

"I have no interest in being a starving model, but by God, I would love to see that man again."

Andrea was surprised that more Parisians did not speak English. In fact they acted quite insulted if one should even ask. The girls' attempts at asking "*parle vouz Englaise*" only brought a lifted eyebrow and a hostile *non, Madame*! Madame? Who the hell did they think was married anyway?

Like New York and London, the Paris traffic was horrendous. But even more horrendous than the traffic was the endless mounds of dog excrement. The streets and sidewalks were always crowded and it could take up to an hour to be seated at a café.

"Are you ready for another culinary experience?" Laura asked, as the girls made their way to a little corner café on the Avenue Pierre de Ler Serbie. When they were finally seated, Laura took out her English to French dictionary and began ordering lunch. As usual they expertly ordered two little cups of *café noir*, and then they would end up pointing to the menu, infuriating the waiter with their attempts at speaking French. When the food arrived it was never anything like it had sounded.

"Who ever heard of a pizza with an egg in the middle? What the hell is this?" Andrea said loudly, earning her a scornful look from several patrons.

"I think it may be some of the dog poo," Laura said, laughing as Andrea covered her mouth as if she was about to throw up.

"I think I'll stick to pastries while I'm here. Adding a few pounds is better than sure death." Andrea said, pushing her plate aside and ordering a tart and more coffee.

"Let's take another look into the shops. I want to buy something terribly expensive," Andrea announced. "Come on Laura, let's spend our lunch money on a good bottle of French perfume. It will probably save our lives since the food is so horrible. And a lack of cash will keep the pounds off our hips."

Laura was glad that Maria was not with them. She had enjoyed the old carefree Andrea she had not seen since their first months together in the nurses' hostel. Their last night in Paris was to have been a big bang, but instead of celebrating, the girls decided to stay in and get ready for their early departure back to England.

"Andrea, I've had a wonderful time. I'm glad we came to Paris together. I hope we can be as close when we return to England."

"I've had a wonderful time too, Laura, and I'm sorry if I have been bitchy with you at times. I really do like you a lot and I know we'll always be friends."

"You're a different person in England, though, Andrea," Laura said, now intending to introduce the subject she knew was taboo. "What exactly are you doing to yourself? Is it necessary for you to sleep with so many different men? You have been quite free with your affections, you know."

Andrea felt the blood rise to her cheeks. "To be perfectly frank, Laura, what I do is none of your damn business. Why are you so concerned about my bedroom habits anyway?"

"Because I care about you and I just don't know what you're hoping to find by doing what you're doing," Laura said.

"You probably won't understand this Laura," Andrea said quietly, "but I don't really want to find anything. Maybe I am trying to stay away from this thing called love. If you date only one man dependency creeps up on you and before you know it, the whole thing gets out of control. But to be honest with you, sometimes when I'm alone even I question the way I behave.

"I know you think I am mean and evil at times and I guess I am. Something crazy takes hold of me when I'm with people who demand things from me that I just can't give. It drives me mad when people, men or women, act dependent. People should learn to stand on their own two feet.

"Most of the men I know try to camouflage it, but Laura, men always want to possess you, to own you. They think they can control you and make you into the clinging type. They take so much and give so very little in return, yet they expect you to be at their beck and call. If you allow it they'll even try to convince you that you were the one who started it all in the first place! If a woman resists this machismo, then the man becomes the dependent one, almost parasitic. You see, I refuse to be controlled so I always end up with dependent men. I won't let my heart become a victim of this thing called love, but why should I deny myself physical pleasure?

"One day I am going to do wonderful things with my life and I don't want to be tied to a kitchen and dirty diapers. Anyway, men are more interested when you keep then at arm's distance and that's just fine with me."

What she was saying, Andrea knew, was only partly true. She could not risk falling in love again. And even if she wanted to, the thought of Adam loomed over her, making it impossible. There could never be anyone to match him. She was a victim of emotional bondage, of ultimate control. Adam had made her his love slave. But, much as she loved him, she also resented the effect he was having on her life. She remembered vividly the ache in her heart when she had to leave him and she could never again risk such a loss. Not for a moment did the pain of leaving Adam go away. She would never be free to love another man. The love of a protégée never dies.

Andrea became restless after her talk with Laura, not wanting to think of the implications of what she had said. Did Adam really love her, or was she just a toy that he could wind up whenever he felt like it? If he did love her, then why did he need to have all those other women in his life? Why had he let her go? She had never been able to acknowledge her anger at Adam and she was not going to now. The conversation was over and for the rest of the evening Andrea was silent. Laura wished she had not brought up the subject.

After an hour or so of edgy silence, Andrea went over to the phone on the bedside table.

PROTÉGÉE

"I think I'll call that man Jacques," she said, looking at his card. "It's only seven o'clock and I feel like going dancing." Andrea dialed the number.

The phone ring was insistent. Jacques finally tore himself away from—God, he couldn't remember her name! Things were really getting bad when he couldn't remember the name of the woman in his bed. Jacques shook his head, pulled on his silk robe and answered the telephone.

"*Allô?*"

"This is Andrea Francis. We met earlier near the Opéra. If you are free, I would like to see Paris."

"Ah, hello. I am glad you decided to call. I will pick you up in an hour. Give me your address."

Back in the bedroom, Jacques hastily got rid of Gizelle, thanking God he had finally remembered her name. He was beginning to worry about the blur that most of the women in his life were becoming. He had stopped writing their names in his black book after he had gotten to book number eight. To be honest, he was getting very tired of these doting women and wished that his princess would appear soon.

Jacques showered, dressed quickly, and was on his way to pick up Andrea within thirty minutes. For some reason he felt anxious, like a man going on his first date. He was glad she had called. By morning he had been anxious to see her again, but when he dialed the number she had already left. Unexplainably, he had felt very sad.

Chapter 9

Jamaica

The tall man in the mirror was almost a stranger to himself. He peered closely at his reflection before slamming his fist into the mirror, shattering it. What had he done to himself? He used to be a handsome man. He walked into the darkened room and sat in the wing chair where he had been for the last four hours before he had to go to the bathroom.

"Oh Andrea," he said softly. "I need you now."

Andrea had been on his mind constantly in the past few weeks, although not a day had gone by in two years that he had not thought of her. He wished tonight that she was with him. He needed to hear her soft voice telling him that he would be just fine. She had such a great attitude towards life. Everything was always going to be fine. Of all the countless women in his life, only Andrea could possibly understand what he was feeling.

Damn! Adam swore under his breath. He had made such a botch of his life. At thirty-five he was washed up—divorced, the father of two, and a millionaire with nothing to do and no place to go. Here he was with all the trappings of life and none of it could make him happy. God, how he missed Andrea. He sighed heavily. There was no one else. He tried to recall what his ex-wife looked like and failed. He thought of his two children, but they were like figments of his imagination. They had been so young when he left the States that he doubted if they remembered him. He had let them down too. But most of all, he missed Andrea. No one but Andrea had ever understood him or loved him unconditionally. Was he dying, he wondered? He had heard that when people sensed their own death they saw their lives flash in front of them. And his life was definitely coming into focus.

Andrea had never known of his marriage or his children. Very few people in Jamaica knew. He had wanted to tell her many times, those times when he had felt so much love for her that he wanted her to know everything about him. But he never did. Even though he knew she would have understood, he could never allow her to see him as the coward he really was. And the way he had abandoned his wife and children was nothing short of cowardice. At that moment, Adam realized he had kept quiet about the truth because of his own need to deny his behavior. He had to admit that he had handled his denial well, even if it had been self-destructive. He had drowned his sorrow in the bottle.

If only he had been as strong as Andrea. He had never known anyone as determined and self-assured as she was. She always took responsibility for her own behavior and it seemed she gave in to her emotions no matter which one she was experiencing at any given moment. Sometimes she had gotten furious with him because he refused to acknowledge pain. No matter how angry she had gotten though, it was not long before her rage was replaced with acceptance, forgiveness and love. Adam knew unequivocally that while Andrea was more often kind and loving, she could also be ruthless and vengeful when she felt used or deceived, and he feared those feelings might one day be aimed at him.

Andrea had been thirteen years old when he met her. Just a child. Her youthful beauty and innocence had made him feel alive. Her quick smile came effortlessly and her sharp mind was always ready to offer advice with wisdom far beyond the experiences of age. She had loved him without questions, expectations or demands. She had given herself to him totally, trustingly, and he had let her down.

Where had he found the courage to give her the freedom that was necessary for her growth? It was his greatest sacrifice. He had not wanted her to leave, but the man she had come to adore had nothing more to offer her. He knew that Andrea Francis was destined for great things. He had felt that deeply as he watched her grow from a child into a woman. She had such visions of their future together. Yet, as much as he loved her and wanted her, he could not interfere with a life so destined.

How he wanted to tell her to stay as she clung to him, tears streaming down her face, begging him not to let her go. His own tears threatened to surface as he watched her walk the short distance to the plane. In a few months, he consoled himself, she would get over him. But two years later her letters still arrived twice a week without fail. The letters were always filled with the reminiscence of happy times they had shared and the hope of their reunion.

She never mentioned her life in England. It was as though the present did not exist for her.

Adam got up to close the window shade all the way. He could not stand the streak of light peeping in. He retied the belt to his blue and white silk robe that had come undone as he moved towards the window and stood momentarily looking into the distance. He could barely tolerate the poignant beauty of the sunset. It reminded him of the night he had met Andrea. Slowly he moved back to resume his position in the chair. His life might have turned out differently if he had known when he was young what it was like to be loved—like Andrea loved him.

He could still hear his mother's words, "Adam Stern, I have no choice but to send you away to boarding school. Neither I nor your teachers can do anything with you. Maybe a good strict boarding school in Luzein will do you some good."

"Will Raymond come too, Mother?"

"No, Raymond does not need to be disciplined. Every mother in town is blaming your father and me because you will not leave their daughters alone. They're threatening to sue! Raymond has a steady girlfriend and he has not gotten himself expelled from every school on the island. For identical twins, you are each so completely different."

At that moment, fourteen-year-old Adam Stern thought his life had come to an end. His twin brother Raymond, only minutes younger than Adam, was his only friend and companion. A social butterfly, their mother had been too busy to bother with her children or even her husband for that matter. And his father was too busy making money and being drunk to even know he had children. Adam put his trust in no one but Raymond, not even his nannies who came closest to loving him. For some odd reason or the other, the nannies he liked were soon dismissed. Later he found out it was because his father always made them his mistresses. Finally his mother found a nanny so old and arthritic that she could never begin to keep up with him or his two siblings. Josephine, the third child, was years younger than he and Raymond and was no trouble at all.

After his mother's pronouncement Adam stormed out of the house and went straight to his father's office. He took the elevator to the twelfth floor which opened into the reception area of his father's suite.

"I want to speak with my father," he informed the secretary.

"Your father is in a very important meeting, Adam, and cannot be disturbed."

"The hell he can't," he said, pushing past her and bursting through his father's office door.

"I must speak with you, Father."

His father rose from the chair behind his huge oak desk, pushing aside the woman who was on his lap.

"Can't it wait, son? Christ, which one are you, Adam or Raymond?" he said, zipping up the fly of his pants.

Adam looked at his father in disgust, turned on his heels and went home to pack for his trip to Luzein.

At seventeen Adam graduated from boarding school. His entire family was there for his graduation, but to him it made no difference. He barely spoke to anyone except Raymond and Josephine. As far as he was concerned he had no family except for them. Three hours after the final graduation sermon, he boarded a plane and was on his way to the United States where he had been accepted at Columbia University in New York.

Adjusting to college life in a an entirely foreign culture was hard at first, but he managed. He was so handsome that most of the guys hated him and most of the girls loved him. He began to enjoy school tremendously, especially the girls. He loved the freedom of the women on American campuses and gained such a reputation for his sexual expertise that he was nicknamed "Prickadilly" for his prowess and his cute British accent. If he had doubts about his academic abilities, which he did not, the girls joked that he would certainly graduate with a B.S., a Bachelor of Sexology. But he went on to receive his Masters Degree in Finance.

At twenty-five Adam became a professor at the prestigious Georgetown University in Washington, D.C. Because as an academician it seemed to be the thing to do, and because he had been drunk at the time, he married the pretty pre-law student from a good family with whom he had been sleeping for the past year. Within three years he had become the father of two children, a boy and a girl. He had made his life exemplary, as American as apple pie. And as boring. After enduring three years of marriage and respectability with its confinement and responsibility, Adam felt completely trapped.

When his stepfather died it was his opportunity to escape. He returned to Jamaica to oversee the family's vast holdings to which the last will and testament had named him manager and chief executive. Adam, the former hellion and problem child, was the only one of the siblings with enough knowledge of business to take charge. He did not return to the United States to his American family. He simply vanquished the thought of that phase of his life. It was as if it never existed.

As much as he hated to admit it after all his years of denial, Adam finally accepted the fact that he was no different from his father. He was an alcoholic and a womanizer who used his power and money to ensnare people.

But when he met Andrea he had changed—for a time. Andrea. From her he learned the true meaning of trust, respect and love. Yet when he finally made himself realize how little he had to offer her, he denigrated their relationship by seeing other women and diluted his feelings with alcohol. If he had been able to love himself as much as she had loved him, the world could have been theirs, but that was impossible.

A wry smile crossed Adam's lips as he remembered vividly the time Andrea arrived unexpectedly at his house and found him with Michelle. Betrayed and hurt as he knew she was, her pride did not allow the tears that glistened in her eyes to fall. She had trusted him implicitly. The thought of other women in his life had never even occurred to her. First she had given him a stinging slap in the face and then had waited stolidly by the door while Michelle fled to the bathroom to dress. When Michelle emerged from the bathroom, Andrea had turned to her and said in a gentle voice, "Michelle, I'm not angry that you love Adam. I can understand that. It's so easy to love this man even if he is such a bastard. It's Adam who should be ashamed of himself for having taken advantage of you. I am so sorry my dear, but he does belong to me."

She was always so sure of her territory, her turf, that even Adam Stern could not reduce her to begging for his love. Either love her for herself or she would eradicate him from her life permanently, she had informed him; and he firmly believed she was capable of doing just that. He had promised never to betray her again. The incident was never referred to after that, and their love had grown stronger in the face of that adversity. Yes, Adam sighed, Andrea Francis was one of a kind. After a firm lecture on responsibility, monogamy and control, she had made him feel completely forgiven and he loved her for that.

Adam suddenly gasped as the sharp stabbing pain in his stomach knifed mercilessly through his thoughts. He shut his eyes and held his breath for a moment in terror over what was happening to his body. When he was able to focus again, he saw that the room was quite dark. The illuminated dial on the clock signaled eight o'clock. Another wasted day. Maybe tomorrow, he consoled himself, surely tomorrow things would improve. Today had definitely not been one of his better days. The only thing, he concluded, that could possibly make staying alive worthwhile was to see Andrea again.

The telephone rang but he did not answer it, wanting to be alone tonight with the memories of his only love. Even as the pain raged in his stomach, he took a drink from the stale glass of rum and Coke he'd been sipping. Thinking of the things he and Andrea had done together would make him feel better.

Two years ago he had consummated his promise to make her a woman. He could still remember the pleading look in her eyes day after day begging him to take her. But he had insisted that she was too young, still a schoolgirl.

He remembered how eager she was to give herself to him the night of her graduation and her disappointment when he did not. She had looked at him every day for weeks after that with the obvious question in her eyes that she was too proud to ask. He had used every ounce of self-control and many other women in order to keep his hands off Andrea through all those years of her growing up, and he had sometimes almost gone crazy with wanting her. He was obsessed with her but he knew he had to be patient. The timing was all important. He had to be sure she was ready, and that she would never as long as she lived forget him. He was to be the first man to make love to her, and the power of such a thought made him ache with desire. But he would make certain that when it happened, the bond would never break. Andrea would be his protégée. She would belong to him forever.

It was a beautiful night when he finally fulfilled his promise. The stars seemed to cling firmly to the sky with such certainty and possessiveness he knew that love was what kept them there. There was nothing more romantic, he thought, than a tropical night under the stars. The garden had been in full bloom and shadows of the sweet smelling flowers danced in the moonlight.

The drive with Andrea to his house in the country seemed longer than usual. Nestled behind overgrown sugarcane fields, the house was almost concealed from view. Andrea had squeaked with excitement at her first sight of the old Victorian mansion. She was torn between her childish eagerness to explore the house and her desire to be in his arms. It took only a prod from him to send her flying gaily up the winding staircase, looking back to make sure he was following. At the top she waited for him. As he climbed the last step, Andrea wound her arms around his neck and kissed him blissfully.

"Oh, my darling Adam, I'm so happy, are you?"

"Andrea, I have never been happier," he said, and he had meant every word. "In here," he said, pulling her into a large bedroom.

The room was dimly lighted and the heavenly scent of fresh cut flowers permeated the air. The massive walnut four poster bed was covered with an exquisite peach colored hand-made coverlet. Under the windows was a chaise longue and across from the bed was a fireplace. On a round antique table flanked by chairs covered in a delicate satin fabric, sat a silver tray with two champagne glasses. In the huge adjoining bathroom was a sunken Roman tub surrounded by French windows that looked over a forest of trees, so thick that there was no need for curtains.

"Oh Adam, this is a beautiful room! I love it! It makes me want to sink right into the tub and stay there."

"You belong in this house," he said, pulling her close to him and circling her slim waist. He tilted her face upward so he could look into her translucent brown eyes, finding there a mixture of wild excitement, eagerness, happiness and fear. For a moment their gaze met and held.

"Oh Adam, I love you so much it scares me. Please darling, never let this moment end." She closed her eyes as he lowered his head and kissed her lips.

"Why don't you take that bath?" he said, turning on the tap, dimming the lights, and filling the water with foaming liquid. On the wide side of the tub was a china plate of chocolate-covered strawberries. He told her he had them flown in from France especially for the occasion. Andrea was pleased that he had arranged things so exquisitely. She bit into one of the plump berries and fed the other half to Adam.

He unzipped her gold dress, allowing it to fall to the floor, then stood mesmerized as he watched Andrea get into the bathtub.

She was ravishing. His penis ramrod hard and begging for attention, Adam undressed and got into the tub with her.

"Dear Andrea," he whispered, taking her face between his hands, "I am so much in love with you. I promise to take care of you and to love you like no other man will ever be able to do. My dearest," he continued, "remember that love has no barriers or restrictions. Whatever we do tonight will be the ultimate experience in fulfilling our love."

Not knowing whether it was the warm temperature of the water or the excitement of the moment, Andrea was feeling faint.

"I still can't believe you love me."

"And why not?"

"Because I just can't."

Adam kissed her again, slowly, longingly, his desire for this girl greater than anything he had ever felt. Andrea wrapped her legs around him, moving so her body was perfectly contoured to him. The warm water buoyed them as their arms and legs entwined. Again Adam kissed Andrea's soft moist lips and they parted to receive his tongue. She felt a piercing passion and began trembling with desire. Slowly he soaped her body. His hand caressing every inch of her. Their close embrace was not enough. He wanted to be inside of her, fused forever with her, never to let her go, knowing she felt the same way. He touched a hand to her cheek and kissed her closed eyelids. Andrea's entire body convulsed against him. She wound her arms tightly around his neck and moved her body in slow motion against him, the water buoying them, both of them floating in a sea of eroticism. The seductiveness of it all threatened Adam's tight control and the throbbing in his groin could wait no longer. None of his many women had excited him this way, the thought flickered briefly: with them he had total control and their adoration; yet this pulsating adolescent, as innocent and trusting as a child, was about to make him lose all of his restraint. The intensity of his hunger, his need for her, frightened him so much that he instinctively pushed her away.

Adam," she whispered, "what am I doing wrong? I want so much to please you," she said with tears in her eyes.

Shhhhh," he said, kissing her again, "you are pleasing me beyond words. It is just overwhelming to feel so close to another human being."

Gently he lifted her out of the tub and after toweling her dry, carried her to the large bed. Her lithe, young body looked lost in it.

"You are beautiful," he murmured, staring down at her. Andrea's quick intake of breath pushed her firm breasts up and Adam covered one of her stiffening nipples with his mouth, tracing the areola with his tongue. His hand slid down over her. For a moment it rested on the triangle of moist black hair between her legs and then his fingers crept deeper and deeper inside of her. Oh Adam...Adam...oh...please, please. Andrea screamed, but only once, as her hymen was penetrated.

"Don't move," he said, pulling his hand away, leaving a void that Andrea wanted filled again. She was opened to him, her body pleading, begging for him to enter her. His hand moved back and forth over her, now lubricated with a mixture of her pleasure and her womanhood and he stroked her. When his thumb found the virgin mound, he gently caressed her until her body shuddered. Involuntary cries escaped her lips, her eyes burned with desire. All modesty gone, her legs spontaneously opened wider and his tongue warm and soft, commanded her body. Virginity be damned, Andrea pulled his hand, guiding it back inside her. She was electrified by an overpowering hot rush of rapture, the widening center of it emanating from between her legs.

"Now," she whispered, "please do it now."

And Adam buried himself deep inside her, shuddering at her scream of both pain and pleasure as the last vestige of her membrane tore, confirming her womanhood. She raised her hips and pushed upward at him, her body gyrating out of control. For a moment he felt humbled by Andrea's purity as he was bathed in her warm blood. Andrea screamed once more, her body covered in perspiration, tears streaking her glowing cheeks, then she was limp, barely conscious but immensely happy. He waited a few moments before withdrawing, kissing her again and again until she responded.

Bewitched by this child under him, so innocent, so giving and so guileless, he found himself wanting her again. Adam positioned himself over her and entered her slowly. She gasped, clung to him and then gave him full access to her body. Her vagina tightened on him, teasing him, caressing him, and he felt the power of a passion he had never known before. She held him mercilessly in a vice-like grip, rotating, pulsating, moving up and down, each time her hips rising higher with him. He felt every move, every quiver, every unleashed involuntary contraction. He pushed further inside her, thrusting deeper and deeper. When he heard her call out, "Adam, Adam, Adam!" he felt himself coming rapidly, and losing all restraint, he plunged again and again with uncontrollable lust. Exhausted, her body convulsed and then was limp, but Adam was now engulfed in his own passion and there was no turning back from the abyss. Consumed, he rose for a final thrust. He called her name before they passed into Nirvana.

Returning from oblivion, drained, he became aware that Andrea was crying softly against his chest, telling him over and over how much she loved him, that he was her destiny, her only purpose for living, that she would love him for the rest of her life. She was his forever, marked and branded.

"Are you all right, my darling?" he stroked her hair, concern on his face.

"I'm fine Adam. Just so wonderfully fine."

They lay entwined for a long time before he said, "Well, I think we have something to celebrate then, don't you?"

"Oh yes," she answered emphatically.

He disappeared into the sitting room, returning with a bottle of champagne in a silver ice bucket and two flute glasses.

"To womanhood," he said raising his glass.

"And to forever," Andrea said, sipping the cool dry champagne.

Adam knew that his life had changed. It was no ordinary night. Their souls as well as their bodies had merged and united. Andrea was his one and only true love for eternity. From the first time they had met, when she was only thirteen years old, he had recognized that she would be an important part of his life.

Yes indeed, he loved Andrea Francis, of that he was positive. He had never been quite certain of much in his life but of her he was sure. And because he loved her so much, he had let her go.

The pain in his stomach caught him off guard like an unexpected knife in the gut. He stumbled to the kitchen to get some antacid. It would help for awhile although its effectiveness was getting shorter and shorter. He *had* to stop drinking. He knew that. All the doctors had told him so and he had agreed, but it was more difficult than he had thought. He was an alcoholic, a drunk. For the first time in his life he had faced that fact head on. He had to change his habits. Just one more drink, he thought, and he would stop altogether. He leaned over the kitchen table to reach for the bottle of rum and saw the letter that had arrived from Andrea that morning. It simply read:

"Dear Adam,

I am coming home soon. I love you.

Forever and always.

The love of your life."

He had always called her that, the love of his life and he had meant every word. Because he loved her, he would write to her and tell her not to come.

Chapter 10

Stougborough

"Graham," Andrea announced a week before Christmas, "I've been thinking about going to New York for the holidays. I have a month off and I want to go home. I'm tired of England and I miss my family."

"What a wonderful idea!" Graham said, feeling happy for her. He had been aware of Andrea's underlying depression and moods of intermittent sadness and thought they happened because she was homesick. "Let me see if I can arrange to come with you."

"That would be nice," Andrea interrupted, "but you can't break your engagements, besides, the fellows need the money for Christmas. And I've not seen my family in a couple of years and I need to mend some broken fences, so I think my first trip home should be alone. Maybe next time," she said quickly, trying to lessen his disappointment. She put her arms around him and kissed the tip of his nose.

"Okay, luv, if that's what you want," he said, "I'll meet them later then." He was obviously feeling let down, but he had learned there was no use arguing with Andrea; once her mind was made up that was it.

"Anyway," he continued cheerfully, "it will give me time to have your surprise ready for you when you return. It will almost be your birthday by then."

"I feel like going to the movies," Andrea said, changing the subject. " There's a good film at the Odeon. Come on," she said, pulling him to his feet, "let's go."

They seated themselves at the back of the nearly empty theater. Halfway though the movie Andrea slipped her hand over Graham's leg and felt him stiffen. She was in a peculiar mood, wanting to make love to him right then and there, Knowing he would be furious, she reached her hand inside his pants and squeezed gently. She kissed him sensuously and moved her body closer, teasing him.

"How much of a risk taker are you?" she whispered running her hand over the bulge in his trousers.

"Andrea, I am not going to...Oh God, don't." It was too late.

Andrea sat smugly back in her seat a triumphant smile lingered on her lips. He had to admit making love in the darkened movie house had turned him on tremendously. He had bitten his lower lip to muffle the groans that escaped. Andrea was in total control. She had not made the slightest sound. Afterwards, without uttering a word, she gave him a look that had satisfaction and conquest written all over her face. Her eyes were unnaturally bright. She was so wild it scared him. She might even have looked a little mad; he dismissed that idea. No! she reminded him of a tiger after devouring its prey.

Andrea had been seeing Graham for six months, quite a departure from her usual brief relationships. He was a musician, entirely different from the men she usually dated. She had met him at a nightclub called The Willow in Birmingham where she had gone for the first time with a friend, Jane, from the flats.

The disco was crowded with patrons. Andrea and Jane literally had to push their way to the bar to get a drink. Andrea finally decided after spilling most of her drink just to sit beside the stage and listen to the band. That was when she noticed him. Tall, *sensual*. His narrow hips swinging to the beat of the reggae music, perspiration drenching his face making his ebony skin glisten in the night.

"My God," she turned to Jane, "look at that gorgeous hunk playing the guitar. Would I like to meet him!" Andrea caught him looking at her at that moment and she winked.

He found her during the intermission.

"Hi, tell me quickly before I die that you are the woman of my dreams."

"My friend, I think you are about to die," Andrea said, jokingly.

"You play that guitar very well. I've always had a vicarious wish to be a singer but I settled on being a nurse instead. I did take voice lessons once," she rambled on.

"Care to sing a song with us on stage?" he asked as they forced their way to the bar. "I'm Graham, by the way."

"I'm Andrea Francis," she laughed, "and I can't sing that well. I've always wanted to try though. Thanks anyway."

"Well then this could be your audition."

"Funny," she said, leaving him standing, disappearing into the crowd.

By the time the band came back on stage, Andrea had made herself inconspicuous, knowing she had made her mark.

"Ladies and Gentlemen, tonight we have a brand new talent to introduce to you. We have not heard her sing either but from the way she looks, she has to be goooood! Let's welcome Andrea Francis!" The way he dragged out the word good, insinuated that her talents were more than just singing. Andrea was mortified. She was furious that Graham had taken the joke so far. Well she would show him! She had taken voice in high school and sung in the choir. She *did* have a good voice and she would definitely show him!

The audience roared with good humor as Andrea took the stage. She was not nervous, it was all a joke. She whispered to Graham and when the band started playing, Andrea closed her eyes and began softly singing the Roberta Flack song:

"The first time ever I saw your face..."

She had sung this song silently to Adam every night for the past two years and tonight she knew he would hear her. When she was through, the silence in the audience lingered a moment and then they began to applaud her. Andrea left the stage fighting back tears. She had forgotten that she could cry.

A few days later Graham called and they had been seeing each other since. Andrea never quite understood why she had treated him differently from the rest. She was kinder to him, more considerate. Maybe, she thought, it was because he had allowed her to sing, to express in public the anguish of her lost love.

She was not emotionally involved with him. Their lovemaking was deeply satisfying and he was thoughtful. The more of himself he gave to her, however, the more Andrea began to withdraw. Graham, who had once been so independent and funny, was becoming impatient with her lack of commitment and his dependency was showing. Andrea wanted to keep the relationship superficial because she had nothing more to give him. Her heart was already committed.

She would have to end the relationship when she returned from vacation. Men! she thought. They were supposed to just want sex for its own sake!

Surprising himself, Graham had fallen in love with Andrea. He loved the spirit and the sparkle she had brought to his life, her spontaneity. He was going to ask her to marry him, but he would wait now until she returned from her trip.

Chapter 11

New York

Stephanie was waving madly in Andrea's direction as she entered the waiting area at Kennedy Airport. Andrea spotted her sister and they began running toward each other.

"Oh, I can't believe you're actually here!" said Stephanie, hugging her so tightly that Andrea almost stopped breathing. "I have so much to tell you and I am dying to see your English wardrobe! Speak!" Stephanie ordered, "Let me hear your British accent."

"The rain in Spain falls mainly on the plain," Andrea exaggerated, playing Eliza Doolittle in *My Fair Lady*.

"By Jove, she's got it," Stephanie said in her best British imitation of Henry Higgins, "I think she's got it!" The girls broke into laughter. It was as if they had never parted.

Stephanie, two years older, had been Andrea's best childhood friend and both sisters had cherished that close friendship; they had shared their secrets and had sworn never to snitch on each other.

They had laughed together, cried together and even lied for each other when necessary. Stephanie had even covered for her the night Andrea had slept with Adam for the first time.

"I missed you, poops," Stephanie said, linking her arm securely through her sister's.

"I missed you too," Andrea said as they ran arm in arm to where their parents stood waiting.

"Hello, Mother," Andrea said. Her quick kiss was slightly restrained.

"You look well, Andrea, welcome home," Lila said, returning her daughter's tentative hug and kiss.

Andrea then turned to her father and embraced him warmly, saying simply, "Oh, Daddy." She rested her head on his shoulder, wanting to stay in his arms.

"I've missed you so much, Daddy," she whispered, close to tears.

"And I you," he ruffled the top of her head just like he used to do when she was a little girl. "I have really missed you, ratbat." He held his daughter at arm's length to look at her. She had grown beautiful as he had known she would. "Ratbat" was the nickname he had always called her. It was a term of endearment, as much a verbal expression of love as Andrew Francis was capable of, not being an outwardly emotional man. He showed his love in other ways. He was the one, for instance, who got up to see his daughters off after a holiday at home, when in the wee hours of the morning the driver would pick them up for the long four hour drive back to school. He was the one who was there for them when they were sick and had even come home one day from work when her sister Stephanie had suffered severe menstrual cramps. That was the biggest difference, Andrea thought, between the way her mother and father treated their daughters: they heard the words of love and caring from one and saw them in action from the other.

To the surprise of everyone who knew him as a confirmed

bachelor, at age forty, Andrew Francis met, fell in love with and married twenty-year-old Lila Daniels.

A brilliant young man, he had received the much-sought-after Wheatherby Scholarship which enabled him to be educated at Oxford. Studying in England had kept him occupied; but when he graduated with honors and was given his first position as accountant at a British firm headquartered in Jamaica, he soon made up for the scholarly years. With wine, women and song, Andrew had created what he considered an enviable and permanent lifestyle.

When he was introduced to Lila Daniels at a company Christmas party, everything in his life changed. By that time through diligence and hard work, he had become chief financial officer of the largest sugar producing corporation on the island, an important position. Andrew Francis liked his life and his bachelor status, but from the moment he laid eyes on Lila, the petite and poised girl had evoked a passion in him that he had never before experienced or envisioned.

"Robert, who is that woman talking to Butch?"

"Forget it, Andy," his best friend whispered, "Apart from the fact that she is the daughter of the *big* chief, she is not yet twenty. And that, my friend, is half your age in case you have forgotten."

"Never mind the lecture, old chap, I am going to marry that girl. I can feel it in my bones."

A year later he had indeed married "that girl."

Once considered notorious with women, Andrew became a devoted and faithful husband. Even after he was elevated to C.E.O of the company and the family was transferred to New York where opportunities to be unfaithful were even more available than in Jamaica, he had never entertained the thought of cheating on his wife. Lila Francis was as much woman as he could handle. As if she had cast a spell on him, Andrew was still in love with his wife after thirty years of marriage.

"Where are Patricia and Charmaine?" Andrea asked her father. "I thought they would be here."

"Pat is driving in from Michigan," Andrew replied. "and she will no doubt be late since her final year in medical school consumes most of her time these days."

"And Charmaine is in school today, or so we hope," her mother added, "She is having pre-adolescent blues."

Andrea again embraced her mother, this time more at ease.

"It's good to see you, Mother," she said softly, meaning it. At that moment the differences that had existed between them seemed far away and unimportant.

Andrea was grateful for New York City's noisy intrusion into her thoughts. The traffic jams, imposing skyscrapers, hurrying crowds and littered streets were the same as she remembered them, but this time the city was festooned with the season's decorations and people seemed to be in a holiday mood. The Francis family had moved to their house in Roslyn on Long Island soon after Andrea graduated from high school in Jamaica, and to her New York was still the most exciting city in the world. As their car sped forward on the Van Wyck and then the Long Island Expressway toward Roslyn, an hour from the city, Andrea felt a sense of peace, something she had not known in a very long time. She was back in the safe haven of her family.

Grandma Daniels and Andrea's young sister, Charmaine, were on the front steps as they pulled into the driveway. Colorful Christmas lights twinkled on two giant pine trees in front of the sprawling ranch-style brick house.

"Welcome home, stinker," her grandmother said, embracing her tightly.

"Hi, Nana!" Andrea said, kissing the beaming, still unlined face of her grandmother.

This woman had been everything that a grandmother could have been and more, helping take care of the girls when they were children while Lila was away at nursing school in England, then moving with the family to New York after Grandpa Daniels died. She would never forget the time Sheila Daniels pretended she was dead to get the rowdy girls to quiet down. Terrified, the four-year-old Andrea decided that feeding Nana her hot soup would surely revive her. Clumsily she spilled steaming soup all over her grandmother, who immediately jumped up spluttering, back from the dead. Grandma's joke had backfired, but Andrea had squealed in delight that her ingenious solution had worked.

"And how are *you?"* Andrea said, pinching her little sister's chubby cheek.

"Too old to have my cheeks pinched," Charmaine said, hugging her. "I missed you lots, Andy. Are you home to stay now?"

"No, Charmaine, I can't stay. But I'm certainly glad to be here. I've missed you too."

Lila and Grandma Daniels immediately disappeared to the kitchen to supervise preparations for Andrea's special dinner while Andrew and the girls brought in the luggage.

"Oh! Here comes Patricia!" Charmaine yelled, jumping up and down with excitement. They flocked back to the driveway to meet the eldest of the sisters.

"Great timing, kiddo," Andrew Francis hugged his daughter, "we just pulled in ourselves."

"Hi, Daddy!" Patricia kissed him and turned to her sisters, "hello, girls."

"Girls? Come on, Pat, you're not a big shot doctor yet, so greet us properly," said Stephanie with mock disdain.

The giggling trio descended on Pat, wrestling her to the ground until she acknowledged each one of them suitably by name. Still laughing, the four walked with their father to the house.

That evening the candlelit dinner table was elegant. Red and white roses arranged as a holiday centerpiece on pine branches added their fresh scent to the glorious aroma of poached salmon, roast duck, and all the trimmings.

"We are dying to hear about England, Andrea," her mother said during a lull in the chatter. "We could only assume that you were fine since you did not write," she added wryly.

"Mother, you know I hate writing letters. If I ever write that will be the time to worry."

"I think a toast is in order," Andrew said, raising his wine glass. "To a wonderful family."

"To the family I took for granted all these years," Andrea murmured, as they all touched glasses.

After dinner and much reminiscing and re-telling of the old family tales, the four girls retired to Andrea's bedroom to catch up on their own stories.

Nothing had been changed in Andrea's room. Even the childhood dolls she had brought from Jamaica were where she had arranged them. The peach and white floral wallpaper looked as new as it did when she chose it nearly three years before, as did the curtains and the coverlet on her white canopy bed which boasted the same colors.

"Mother thought you needed to have a sense of familiarity," Stephanie said. "She had everything cleaned and put back exactly the same way just for you." And Mother was right this time, thought Andrea, pleased at Lila's consideration.

The girls were so happy to be reunited after two years that they were unable to sleep so they stayed in Andrea's room most of the night talking. One of the reasons she needed her family, Andrea soon realized, was that when she was with them she felt grounded. This sense of belonging could never be duplicated.

"Tell me, Patricia," Andrea asked, "where is this doctor guy you are so in love with?"

"Back in Michigan studying for boards, but he'll be here early next week so we can drive back together, and you'll meet him then.

He's gorgeous," she sighed.

"He is not," Stephanie chimed in, "Andrea, believe me, this is truly one of those cases where beauty is in the eyes of the beholder."

"Shut up, Stephanie," Patricia warned.

"He's really short," ten-year-old Charmaine spoke up from her half-doze.

"Get out of here," Patricia scolded, "this is grownup talk. Go to your room."

"I'm going to tell daddy," Charmaine cried as she left. But as much as she loved her sisters, this talk about men was boring and she was ready for bed.

"Well, as long as you love him," Andrea said, "that's all that matters."

"You sound a little undecided about that," Stephanie said, winking at Patricia.

"What about your boyfriends, Steph?" Andrea asked.

"Oh, I have one here and one there, you know me. I don't think I'll ever get married. In fact I don't like the idea of even going steady. Anyway, I'm only twenty-two and I can't worry about men. I actually find them quite mediocre." Stephanie turned to Andrea and said, "Now tell us about you."

"There's not much to tell. England is a fun place."

"Silly, we don't care about England," said Patricia, "What about the men?"

"Oh God!" Stephanie said, surprised by the pensive look on her sister's face, "You aren't still pining over that Adam guy are you? Dear God," she repeated, "and I suppose you're still singing that 'first time' song every night too. Andrea, quite frankly, I think you should have your head examined."

"Steph," Patricia said, "it is not our fault if you're a born bitch. I believe that Andrea's love is very real. True love is a gift that only a few ever experience. Adam must be her soul mate."

"Oh please—don't start that hokey true love, soul mate stuff again, Pat. I believe they're feeding you too much corn in Kansas or Nebraska or wherever the hell it is."

"Michigan. And it is possible to love someone more than you love yourself, you know," Patricia continued, unruffled.

"Then that person would have to be God as far as I'm concerned. Anyway, loving someone more than you love yourself is asking for trouble," Stephanie said.

"I'm going to Jamaica next week," Andrea announced out of the blue. "I know Mother will be furious, but I must see Adam again or I'll go mad. I've already booked my flight and I'll tell her tomorrow and get it over with."

Stunned, neither of her sisters seemed able to utter a word, so Andrea went on, "In the two years that I've been in England I must have slept with at least a couple of dozen men trying to find Adam in them. All I found was a lot of animalistic behavior and wild parties and I left a great deal of anger and some broken hearts back there. I need to remember how it feels when making love is meaningful."

"I can't let you go, Andrea," her mother was shouting. "I thought you would have gotten over that man by now! I just cannot imagine why you want to waste your life on a drunk who is twice your age when your future looks so bright. Andrea, please, for your own sake, I want you to reconsider your decision."

"Mother," Andrea said, "I don't expect you to understand, but I'm sure your love for Daddy was the same if you could only try to remember. And Daddy is twenty years older than you are."

"It is not the same at all, Andrea. Your father is from a good family and he was never addicted to the bottle."

"Adam's family is one of the wealthiest in Jamaica, and I know he drinks more than he should, but what has any of that got to do with love?" Andrea's hostility was beginning to surface.

"Wealthy families are not necessarily good families, Andrea!"

Ignoring her, Andrea went on, "And Daddy himself was no stranger to the bottle when you married him, Mother. Drinking in Jamaica is a social disorder more than anything else, you know that. Please try not to be so critical."

"But we have not seen you in two years," her mother protested, changing her tactics. How well she knew that harping on Adam's shortcomings would only make her stubborn daughter more determined. A fight with Andrea was the last thing she wanted. It would only make matters worse.

Calming herself, she went on, "Well dear, if you insist on going to Jamaica we must let Melissa know so she can have the driver pick you up and make sure the house is staffed."

"That won't be necessary, Mother. I'm going to rent a car and I am perfectly capable of taking care of myself."

Worriedly, Lila began to protest again, "But Andrea, you know how dangerous it is to drive in Jamaica—"

"Mother, please. I've been on my own for two years now and I've managed just fine."

"All right, Andrea, but you know I don't approve—"

There was no point in continuing the conversation and Lila knew that she would get no support from her husband as far as Andrea was concerned. Fighting with Andrea was not the way to handle this. She knew what had to be done. First she would write to Adam and plead with him to end the relationship once and for all, and if that did not work, there was always the other recourse. Well, she thought, I just hope the first option works. Adam could offer her daughter nothing but a lifetime of unhappiness. Nothing in the world could prevent the inevitable pain of such a destructive relationship. She was acutely aware of the fact that she would do whatever she had to do. She hoped she was not going to be forced to use her influence, but if it meant protecting her child from Adam

Stern, a fate she considered worse than death, there was no question about what Lila would do.

Chapter 12

Jamaica

The heat was stifling. Andrea had forgotten how hot it got in Jamaica. After living in countries with cold winters, the January heat was almost unbearable.

"Do you have anything to declare?" the customs officer asked.

"No, nothing at all." Customs was such a chore. One of Andrea's fondest fantasies was that she would one day be able to walk through customs without being stopped. Andrea made her way to Avis and rented a sturdy Rover. She had never driven in Jamaica and she had to admit it was a challenge. The roads were narrow and winding and she had to share them with buses, taxis, pushcarts and donkeys. Still, she was glad to be back. Jamaica would always be part of her. It was her real home, the place where she had been born and raised, and the place where Adam lived. The familiar smell of roasting corn and sugar cane filled her nostrils as she drove through the town of Wearing on her way to Seaport.

"Buy mi corn," the vendors by the side of the road shouted.

Andrea pulled the car over and bought sugar cane. Although Seaport, her hometown, was only eighteen miles from the airport, the winding roads made the trip an hour long. With the house finally in view, Andrea heaved a sigh of relief. Driving in Jamaica, she concluded, was for the bravest and most daring. She should have listened to her mother. Andrea had a fleeting thought that perhaps she should listen to her mother more often. Pulling the car up to the big iron gates of her family home, she hopped out, unlatched them, and drove up the familiar driveway to the front door. The old faithful Tamarind tree under whose branches she and Adam had spent many an evening was still there. Whimsically, she thought it was holding memories of them. Yes, indeed, she was home.

"I thought I heard a car come in," said Melissa, coming to the door. "Andrea, darling, I had no idea you were coming home. I thought you were all staying in New York for the holidays this year. The house is not staffed."

"I'm here on my own, Melissa. It was a spur of the moment decision. Don't worry about staffing the place just for me."

"It sure is good to have you back," Melissa said in her musical Jamaican patois. "Come over here and let me look at you. Good gracious, you are far too skinny. Are you hungry, child? I'll make you some lunch."

"Dear, dear Melissa, I'm fine. But I must admit that I am a little hungry." Melissa vanished into the kitchen, returning shortly with a light lunch of chicken salad.

"Melissa, I'm so happy to see you. And the house is still so beautiful and well kept. All this hard work and you haven't aged a bit." Andrea put her plate on the side table and put her arms around Melissa, "How glad I am to be home."

Melissa was as permanent as the fixtures in the house, and had been the one she went to for comforting for as far back as Andrea could remember.

133

"Child, it sure is good to have you home. We so look forward to when the family comes home for holidays, but it just never felt right without you here too. Now," Melissa ordered, "get some rest and we will chat later." Andrea smiled. Nothing had changed, not even Melissa still treating her like a child at twenty!

Andrea wondered what Adam would think when he saw her. She had sent him a note that she was coming, but had not told him when. Andrea closed her eyes and tried to imagine his face when he saw her. Maybe she should have told him the time of her arrival but that would have spoiled the surprise.

Stepping into the shower, she shivered luxuriously as the chilly water nipped at her body, making it tingle. The cold shower felt wonderful, opposed to the stifling heat of the island. The temperature had to be over a hundred degrees.

After her shower, she slipped into a short cotton nightgown and climbed between fresh cool cotton sheets. A nap was definitely in order after her trip. Later in the evening she planned to go to the Coconut Grove, the nightclub Adam owned and where he would probably be. Her impatience threatened to get the better of her. She wanted to call him immediately but restrained the impulse. She would wait.

At seven Andrea began dressing for her reunion with Adam. She looked at her naked body in the wardrobe mirror and realized how much her figure had blossomed since she had last seen him. She was no longer a lanky eighteen-year-old. Putting on a white halter top linen dress, Andrea surveyed her reflection and was pleased with her appearance.

She arrived at the club at eight-thirty, swinging the yellow Rover into a narrow parking space with precision. Her heart began to do a tap dance in her chest as she made her way up the narrow steps to the entrance.

He was sitting at the bar, his back to her, holding a glass of what was probably rum and coke in his hand. Andrea stopped to regain her composure. The sight of Adam had unnerved her. She could not believe she was actually here looking at her love, her happiness. No one seemed to have recognized her as she moved to stand behind Adam. She placed her hands over his eyes and said, "Guess who?"

"Oh Andrea," he whispered without turning around, "you have come home. Love of my life," he continued, turning slowly to her, "I knew you would be here tonight. I felt your presence all day."

He stood and took her face between his hands. Looking deep into her eyes he said, "Welcome home, little one. Welcome home." Both in tears, they held each other, forgetting everything and everyone. Time stood still when Adam lowered his head and kissed her tenderly. Locked in an endless embrace they were startled back into reality when everyone in the club started clapping.

"Look who is home!" Adam said. "I told you she would be here, did I not? Let's have a toast and let's strike up the band!"

When the band began to play Adam surprised her by climbing onto the stage, a guitar in his hand. He strummed the instrument and a happy tune escaped his lips. Andrea had not known that he was musically talented, and he was not. One after the other the guitar strings snapped and went flying until soon there was only one string left.

It was a night of laughter and music and dancing. Andrea could not remember ever being so relaxed and happy. She had felt her heart stop and start a thousand times that night looking at Adam, touching him, knowing that this was the only love she would ever need in her life. As merriment turned to longing, Andrea leaned over to Adam.

"Let's go home," she whispered.

"Let's," he replied.

"I'll drive," Andrea said excitedly, jumping in behind the wheel of the Rover. "You've never seen me drive, have you, Adam?"

"I have not," he said unable to take his eyes off this beautiful woman. His beautiful woman. He reached over and squeezed her hand.

Andrea looked at him and felt a jolt of pure joy course through her veins. She thought of the hearts that she had broken and wished that she could take away their pain. If they had loved her as much as she loved Adam, she could understand why they had clung to her so desperately. When she left them, they had each been furious with her, very often to the point of sheer hatred. A calculating cold heartless bitch was what she had been called. Deep in her heart she knew she was not. Her love for Adam proved that.

Andrea entered the hallway of her family's home with Adam. He stopped inside the doorway, admiring the huge airy living room with its cathedral ceiling and skylights. He had driven past this house hundreds of times in the past seven years, but he had never been inside. Andrea's mother would have killed him for sure if he had tried to visit her daughter at home.

"A drink, my darling?"

"I would love one. Do you remember what I drink?

"How could anyone ever forget?"

Andrea, moved past him and opened the door to the liquor cabinet. She poured them both a drink, knowing how to fix his rum and coke perfectly. Adam looked at her as she moved gracefully across the room, thinking how grown up she had become.

She took a sip of her brandy and lit a cigarette, blowing the smoke out in rings. He glanced at her through the smoke and knew she was no longer the little girl that had gone away two years ago. The rounding of her hips and the fullness of her breasts had all happened since she had been away. Smoking and drinking were new habits she had learned. She had become quite a sophisticated woman, it seemed. He wondered what other habits she had learned and was seized with irrational jealousy, even anger, knowing that she must have given herself to others. He knew it was crazy to expect her to be faithful to him when he could offer her nothing, but he could not help the way he was feeling. He had literally forced her away from him when the Francis family moved to New York, making her understand that she had to leave Jamaica to further her education. But because he had raised Andrea to be his protégée, the thought of another man touching her made him physically ill. Part of Adam wanted to know about other men she might have been with, but he knew he could not stand hearing it.

Andrea stubbed out her cigarette. She could tell that Adam disapproved.

Coming up behind her and kissing the lobe of her ear, he asked, "Have you missed me?"

She turned and looked into his luminous brown eyes. If only she could put into words how she had felt during the lonely nights, or tell him of the pain, the tears, the anguish and the sense of hopelessness she felt without him, the memories of him that were forever etched in her mind, of the many men she had called Adam in her weakest moments of passion, of how she felt right now being with him. She wanted to tell him everything, but those feelings could never be adequately described in words.

"I've missed you more than you will ever know," she said almost inaudibly, leaning against his chest. "I can't live without you, Adam, please don't make me go back."

"No matter what happens or where we find ourselves, Andrea, we will always be together. Our souls are one."

"I have to believe that, Adam. My life depends on it."

Andrea abruptly left his embrace to switch on the stereo and began slowly, seductively moving to the haunting music.

"The first time ever I lay with you, I felt the earth move in my hands—" It was their song.

Andrea released the button at her neck that held the simple

halter dress, letting it slide in folds to the floor, revealing her glowing body as she turned to him. Adam held his breath as she moved toward him, a bronze-tinted goddess.

In a fluid movement, he picked her up and carried her effortlessly to the wide couch. Andrea rested her head against his shoulder, her face buried in his neck. Adam laid her down, and for a moment stood above her transfixed, absorbing her satin smooth flesh, firm breasts and the look of desire on her face. As she waited for him to touch her, Andrea felt exactly as she had the first time with him, as shy and self-conscious as a virgin.

"Andrea," he said, kneeling beside her, "the love I feel for you could not be of this world. I have never felt it with anyone else. This love is bigger than just you and me, it is divine, it is a gift from God."

She did not fully comprehend what he was saying nor did she care at that moment. All she wanted was to be held in his arms with their bodies joined together as one. Her nipples grew hard on her firm, full breasts and her whole body trembled with hot desire. She was moist and ready when he stroked her belly and covered her lips with his. Finally, Andrea could bear it no more. She had waited for such a long time.

"Now," she demanded, "oh please, now." He entered her, and with each movement buried himself deeper and deeper inside her until he was lost in his passion. Tonight Andrea had returned to her real world, where the fusion of two bodies was a true joining of souls. Their bodies surged together and merged, becoming one, and the intensity of her orgasm consumed them both. As Adam's hot ejaculation filled her, she cried out, "I love you, Adam." And it really *was* Adam.

For a long time they lay breathless in each other's arms. Neither one could speak. Words were not necessary.

On the last day together the sun did not shine. Like a bad omen, the weather was bleak and it rained heavily. The heavens cried for her, Andrea thought, because she could not. She was beyond tears. Parting again after three idyllic weeks was too painful to think about. That night as Adam helped her pack for her return to England they hardly spoke, knowing that they would both say the wrong things.

"I can't leave you," Andrea said, breaking the silence.

"Shhhh, my dearest," he said, sounding strangely older to her ears. "Sometimes, to love is to let go. You know you must finish your schooling. After that we will talk about a future."

"Why do I have to finish my schooling? I only went to England because I could no longer remain in the same house as Mother. She threatened to send me to a psychiatrist in New York, then a psychologist and finally to a psychic to help me get over you. There's no need for me to work. Between your family and mine we have enough money to buy an island."

"Come now, Andrea, you know money has nothing to do with it. Work gives meaning to life and I just know one day you will be famous because of your work."

"Sure, another Florence Nightingale."

"No, I think that you are going to be a businesswoman."

"I think that it is time that you stop drinking. You're hallucinating."

"Okay then, let's change the subject. Tell me all about your time in England. What did you do?"

"I did a lot of searching," Andrea replied, "but I found nothing."

"You found something. You have become quite an experienced lover," he said, in an off-hand way. "How many?" some demon prodded him to ask.

"I don't know," Andrea said, lowering her eyes, "fifteen, maybe twenty. It was so meaningless half the time I couldn't even remember their names."

Adam was visibly agitated. One or two he could understand.

But fifteen or twenty? It was enough to make him want to kill her. Something seemed to snap in his brain. He tried to block out the images of other men making love to Andrea but the green tentacles of jealousy and the effect of too many rum and cokes rendered his self-control useless.

He pulled her roughly to him and forced her backward onto the floor, then ripped her blouse open and viciously sank his teeth into her breast.

Andrea screamed as she felt pain go through her like a steel blade. Adam had gone mad. The pain was excruciating but it was nothing compared to the humiliation. She felt cheapened and violated, but no matter how she fought or pleaded he continued to force himself on her. He yanked her skirt above her waist and ruthlessly tore through her panties, kissing her so hard it bruised her mouth. In spite of herself she began to respond. The thought of Adam taking her forcibly seemed to heighten her desire.

His breath reeked of alcohol. For the first time, she realized he was drunk. His pupils were dilated and his breathing was raspy.

"Did they do it like this? Or this? What about this?" he said as he continued to violate her.

Andrea began sobbing uncontrollably, her passion gone. She wanted to get away from this drunken madman, as far away as possible.

"Adam," she cried, "you're hurting me! Why, why are you doing this? I was looking for you in those men. I just kept on looking and looking. Please, oh please, Adam you're hurting me."

Her sobbing cries seemed to bring him back to reality and he jumped to his feet, a look of disbelief on his face.

Andrea remained crumpled on the floor, tears spilling silently down her face.

"Oh God," he said, "I am so very sorry. Oh Andrea, please forgive me. I don't know what came over me. I just went crazy at the thought of you being with other men. Andrea, please forgive me." He covered his face with both hands and turned away in shame.

Andrea had never seen him so emotionally distraught. Though his behavior was unbelievable, it had been triggered by jealousy, and she still loved him, she would always love him. She got to her feet and held his bowed head against her breasts.

"I'm sorry too, my darling, for the pain I've caused you. I had no idea—oh, Adam, believe me," she said quietly, "no one will ever take your place. Even if we can never be together again, there is no man who can ever take your place in my heart, not ever."

Adam wept for the love that was bigger than he was, for the love that could have given him a new life, and for the love that he would never again share with Andrea in this way. He knew that everything was ending and he did not know how to stop it.

That night, after she left for England, he prayed: "Dear God, why? Why did you give her to me for such a short time?"

Chapter 13

Stougborough

Heathrow was swarming with people from all over the world. As much as Andrea always found people-watching fun, the airport was far too chaotic, and today of all days she had no interest in it. Andrea followed the disembarking crowd aimlessly. Vaguely she hoped they were headed for baggage claim. She stood lost in thought and angry at herself for not insisting that Adam find a way for them to stay together. She was surprised when someone kissed her on the cheek.

"Well hello, my Yankee girl."

"Graham," she said, turning to him, her voice sounding detached and distant to her ears, "how good to see you." She smiled mechanically.

Graham was happy to have Andrea back. He collected her luggage and ushered her quickly to the car. He was chatting away gaily as they drove out of London on the M1 highway. "Andrea," he said excitedly as they approached Stougborough, "I want to take you to see our new home." Andrea stared at him blankly.

"Andrea, Andrea," he repeated. "did you hear what I just said?"

"I'm sorry, Graham. What did you say?"

"I said we should drive by our new home."

"Our new home? What new home?"

"The one we shall live in after we are married."

"Married? Graham, what are you talking about?"

He swerved the car over to the side of the road.

"Look, my darling, this is what I mean." He pulled something from his jacket pocket.

"For you," he said proudly.

Andrea opened the little velvet box and saw a beautiful diamond and sapphire engagement ring.

"Will you marry me, Andrea?" he said, simply.

Speechless, she stared at the road ahead.

"You're not happy?"

"Oh yes, of course Graham, but it's such a surprise, I can't give you an answer right away. Graham, this is all happening too soon."

"I thought we should get married on your twenty-first birthday," he said, "that's still two months away.

"A wonderful idea, but darling, could we talk about it more later?" Andrea touched his hand lingeringly. "The trip has worn me out."

"Of course, darling. You must be exhausted." Graham seemed content with that explanation and drove on while Andrea closed her eyes and rested her head against the seat cushion. She needed to block out the reality of the situation and the rising panic that was engulfing her.

Graham pulled the car into the familiar parking lot of the flats not a minute too soon for Andrea. She quickly got out, leaving him to get the luggage.

"Do you have your key, Graham?" she asked as he

approached the door, "I can't seem to find mine."

"Let's see," he put the luggage down, and searched around in his pants pocket, shortly producing a single key. He handed it to her so she could unlock the door while he gathered up her luggage.

"Graham, I am so very tired." She kissed him lightly, ushering him out, "What I need to do most of all right now, is get into the tub and then into bed. I also need some time to think. Your proposal is so sudden, darling, it took me by surprise. I'll call you first thing in the morning and we'll talk about our wedding plans."

"But Andrea—"

"Please, darling," she said kissing him again, "just be patient. Until tomorrow," she blew him another kiss. "We can see the house then. And Graham," she said, as he put her bags down and started to leave, "thank you for everything."

"You know I can't deny you anything, Andrea," he said warmly kissing her goodnight.

"I'll see you bright and early tomorrow."

Andrea shut the door and leaned against it. She gasped for breath. Any moment now she expected to fall to the floor convulsed by the agony of her own hardening heart. She felt sick about what she had to do. But it had to be done.

Graham was puzzled. He had been sure Andrea would be happy about his surprise. There was so much about her he could not fathom. But what did he really know about her? Now that he thought about it, he knew very little at all. She never spoke of her past or her family except for mentioning having had some problems with her mother. And tonight she was unusually subdued, not his bubbling Andrea. Well maybe, he consoled himself, things did not go well in New York. By tomorrow, he was convinced she would be fine. And, considering he would be spending the rest of his life with her, he could wait one more night. Nevertheless, the whole situation was puzzling. Had she missed him at all? Why did she not want to make love to him? They had been apart for a whole month and he wanted her so badly.

Days turned into weeks and weeks turned into months and Graham never heard from or saw Andrea. He had tried calling, writing and coming to the flat, but she was always out, according to her roommates. Finally, two months later, almost to the date he had hoped they would be married, he received a small package from her containing the diamond and sapphire engagement ring he had given her along with a note that said, "I am so sorry. Please forgive me."

The emergency room was hectic. Although she was working hard, Andrea had not been sleeping or eating well for weeks and she felt weak and tired. And the smell of sickness and medicine was making her stomach queasy. A sudden wave of nausea sent Andrea running off in the direction of the washroom. That was the last thing she remembered. When she came to she was moving her head away from the pungent smell of ammonia under her nose. She opened her eyes and saw several nurses standing over her.

"Nurse Francis, how do you feel?"

"What happened?" she asked from her prone position on the floor.

"You fainted," one of the nurses replied. "I found you lying here on the floor. Dr. Shaheed is on call today, covering for Dr. Petel. I called him and he's on his way down to see you."

Andrea raised herself to a sitting position.

"I am really all right now, Nurse Barnard." She tried to stand but felt so weak she could hardly move.

"Here, let me help you onto the trolley," the nurse offered as the porter pulled up with a gurney.

Andrea was grateful to be lying down again, still insisting that she was fine. Under no circumstance did she want to see Saleem. Nurse Barnard ignored her protests, insisting that she had to be examined.

"I am going to leave the curtains slightly open so I can see you while I work," she said, wheeling her into a cubicle. " And I will be back soon to check on you."

"Yes, Jan," Andrea replied, accepting the inevitable.

"Hello, Andrea," a familiar voice said, as Saleem pulled the curtains around them. "What seems to be the matter?"

Andrea opened her eyes to see him staring at her. "Saleem," she rose to a sitting position, "thank you for coming. I tried to tell the nurses not to disturb you, but I'm afraid I lost the battle. I hope you weren't sleeping."

"No. I rarely sleep when I am on call. Now lie back down, and tell me what happened."

"Nothing really. I didn't have breakfast this morning and we were so busy in the ER that I didn't have time for lunch or dinner. I also worked a double shift for one of the nurses who called in sick, and I guess I was tired and my blood sugar was low. I just fainted that's all, they should not have made a big deal out of it. I've just been working too hard."

"You should take better care of yourself, Andrea. Now unzip that uniform so I can listen to your heartbeat."

Saleem was a perfect gentleman. He betrayed no sign of familiarity even with the stethoscope under her exposed breasts. Saleem was glad to have been on call. He'd been unable to forget her even though they had not been together in over a year. The familiar breasts made him want to bend over and take them into his mouth.

"You are going to be fine," he said returning the stethoscope to the pocket of his starched white lab coat. "I will get the nurses to bring you some dinner, and I think we will keep you under observation for tonight."

"Saleem, that can't be necessary. I would rather go home. Maria will be there to watch out for me."

"Very well then, get dressed and I will drive you over to the flats." Andrea began to protest. "It is either that, Andrea, or I will send you to the medical ward for the night."

"Fine, I will be out in a few minutes."

When they arrived at the flats, Saleem turned to look at her.

"Andrea," he said, "I am glad I had an opportunity to see you. I was going to send you a card but I feel a lot better being able to say goodbye in person."

"You're leaving?"

"Yes, in two weeks. I have decided to take a position in Cairo. I just wanted to let you know that I have no regrets about us. In fact the time with you will be a memory I shall always cherish. I have never quite understood what happened between us," he said, "but now it does not seem so important."

"Saleem," Andrea said taking his hand, "I wish I could explain my behavior to you, but most of the time I don't understand my dark evil side. You were very good to me and I would like to ask you to forgive me for my insensitivity."

"Andrea, of course I forgive you. I forgave you a long time ago. After all, I was to blame. You told me what to expect on our first date and I chose to ignore your wishes. Will you show me that you have accepted my apology by having dinner with me before I leave?" He grinned, "Besides, someone has to make sure you eat."

"I would like that," Andrea said. "I have next Tuesday off. Is that good for you?"

"I will fetch you at seven on Tuesday. And I promise to leave my camels at home." Saleem smiled at the old joke, but he felt sad. Andrea Francis was the reason he could no longer stay in

Stougborough. But as far away as he might go, he knew that he would always carry his love for this woman in his heart.

Still feeling weak, Andrea spent the next day in bed slowly regaining her strength, but the queasiness in her stomach remained. She knew something was seriously wrong because she seemed to be gaining weight even though she could eat very little. Her clothes were getting tighter day by day and her nipples were unusually tender. Suddenly it dawned on her that she had not had a period since she returned from Jamaica. She had been so depressed over leaving Adam, then upset at Graham's surprising marriage proposal, that she had not paid any attention to her menstrual periods. They had always been irregular anyway.

"Maria," Andrea confided a few weeks later, "I've not had a period in two months, maybe three. I've gained eight pounds and this morning I threw up. I think I may be pregnant."

"But you've been taking the pill, how can that be?"

"I stopped taking those wretched things just before I went home. I didn't want my mother to find them. Oh shit, Maria, what am I going to do? I wouldn't even know for sure who the father is."

"For one thing, you could calm down. So far everything is just speculation. You don't know for sure that you're pregnant."

"And how do you propose I find out without causing a major scandal? This infirmary is the only health facility for miles."

"Well, I can ask Nick if he could suggest something."

"Meaning an abortion?" Andrea exclaimed.

"Who's talking about abortion?" You can't have an abortion until you know whether you are pregnant or not. I was talking about getting a test. Now, tomorrow I'll bring home a urine specimen container. We'll have Nick write up a lab report request with a bogus name. I will deliver it personally to the lab and have him call down for the results the following morning. How is that for ingenuity? Sometimes I'm so clever it scares me."

"And if I am pregnant, then what?" Andrea was not in the mood for humor.

"Then I can ask Nick to suggest the name of a doctor that does—"

"No! Never. I could never do that, Maria. Not an abortion! Listen, I must go, but please don't mention this to anyone."

"Not even Nick?"

"Not even Nick. Tell him the test is for a friend, but don't let him know that the friend is me. And for God's sake, don't tell Laura anything."

"Not to worry. Miss Prim and Proper would faint dead away. Just be glad you two are on different shifts."

A few days later Andrea's suspicion was confirmed. She had no idea where to turn or what to do. There was no one except Maria that she could talk to. Certainly not her family. She shuddered at the thought. Lila Francis would kill her rather than stand disgrace by a bastard child. To her mother, defiling the family name and reputation would be a worse fate than death.

Andrea had stopped wearing her uniform belt to avoid drawing attention to her rounding tummy. She was now four months pregnant, but her height concealed it.

"Hello, Andrea."

"Maya," Andrea said, as she passed her on her way into the flats. "How are you?"

"Fine. And you?"

"Wonderful," Andrea said, making a gallant effort to sound cheerful.

"Would you care to join me for some tea?"

"I'd like to," Andrea lied, "but I have to get some letters to the post."

"They can wait, can't they?" Maya said, staring directly at her middle. Andrea shifted uneasily, bringing her hand down to cover her stomach. She had never liked Maya. Ever since they had met at the dance in Presley Hall, Andrea knew there was something weird about her. After a few meetings, Andrea had tried to avoid Maya at all costs since it seemed every time they were in each other's presence, something strange would happen to Andrea. As much as Andrea tried to keep away from her, however, Maya had continued to materialize, almost as if she were watching her. Maya's piercing blue eyes seemed to burn a hole directly into Andrea's very soul and completely unnerved her.

Andrea was sure there had been some kind of message for her in Maya's eyes on the night they met; and tonight she had a feeling that she was finally going to find out what it had been.

"It is time," Maya was saying, "We must talk."

"What do you mean?" Andrea asked, curious, "Talk about what?"

"About the baby."

Andrea was shocked. It had not been verified until a week ago that she was pregnant. The only other person who knew was Maria and Maria would not have told anyone.

"How did you know?" Andrea sank into a hallway chair, acutely aware of the futility of denying what Maya obviously already knew.

"Come inside, my dear." Maya sounded very much older than her two years seniority to Andrea. "and we will discuss this," she said, opening the door to her flat. "How about that tea now?" Maya said, plugging in the electric tea kettle.

"I think I need something stronger," Andrea replied.

"That is not a good idea," Maya responded, "You cannot corrupt your body, not at a time like this. You must think of the baby."

"Who *are* you?" Andrea pleaded.

"I am a friend, Andrea. You must trust me. Don't be frightened. I will never do anything to hurt you. I am only here to guide you.

"Andrea, you were born a special child and you are destined for great things. Your mother is also a special person, but she had no interest in using her powers. Her husband and children altered her destined path, but you are here to take over where she left off. Your life has reached the point now where I must guide you. You see, you have a responsibility to the world. In time it will all be revealed to you.

"You must have this baby; but you will tell no one of it, no one, not even your parents. I will arrange everything. You will have to graduate a few months late but no one will ever suspect why. You will work until you are six months pregnant. Your height and clothes will conceal it. After that we will go to a safe place in Surrey where you will give birth. The baby will remain with my friends in England. After you graduate, you are to go back to America. You are not to worry about the baby because the child will be well cared for. You are going to have many other things to do."

"And what will I tell Matron Perry is the reason I have to leave?"

"An illness in the family would be logical since you know nursing."

Andrea did as Maya told her to without question, complying with her directions, relieved that the problem had been taken out of her hands.

Chapter 14

The pain was unbearable. Andrea screamed as the contractions became worse.

"I want it out!" she cried, "Take this thing out of me!" She was drenched in sweat and the cotton sheet that was once white was red with her blood.

Lila Francis awoke suddenly from a deep sleep and her thoughts went immediately to Andrea. She had to call Andrea! She was perspiring and having severe cramping in her lower abdomen, exactly, she realized, like the pain of childbirth. The pain subsided as quickly as it had come. Andrea was all right. She would not call her daughter. It would only alarm her unnecessarily, she thought, settling back to sleep.

"Push, Andrea," someone was telling her.

"The baby is breech," said someone else.

Yet another voice said, "I have to try to turn it with forceps."

The unending pain was getting worse and worse.

"Episiotomy," someone ordered.

Andrea felt cold steel against her body. She screamed once more as the knife cut into her flesh and then everything went black.

Suddenly the lights came on again. Act Two must have begun, she thought groggily. The pain was gone. Andrea rose up from the bed but her body stayed there. Curious, she wondered what was going on. It was as if she were watching a movie from the best seat in the theater, or an opera from the king's box. She looked down and recognized herself on the bed, her legs up in stirrups, an awkward position. She felt sorry for the Andrea on the bed who was crying out in pain, begging for help. When help was not forthcoming, Andrea tried to go to her own aid. The shrill screaming made her come closer. She saw a tiny head emerging from between her legs and heard Andrea pleading for the white-clad people surrounding her to stop the pain. Maya was standing at the head of the bed wiping away the sweat as it poured off her forehead. Finally the entire body of a baby came out of her and immediately announced its entrance into the world with a piercing squall, its arms and legs waving madly. Andrea smiled at the robust child. Someone was lifting her onto a clean bed and others were taking the baby away. The pain had ceased.

"It's all right," she heard Maya say, "You have a beautiful daughter."

"Let me see her," she heard herself beg, but they ignored her and kept walking away with her baby while Andrea sobbed.

A thin silver cord kept her attached to her body on the bed while she floated higher above it. Up and up she went into another time and another dimension. It dawned on Andrea that she might be dead. She remembered having heard that just before they crossed over to the other side, people who came back had related going through the same thing. But shouldn't her entire life be flashing before her eyes now? Maybe she was not dead after all. Perhaps she was having an out of body experience. Whatever it was, it was pleasant, and seemed not at all out of the ordinary.

Andrea's thoughts were distracted by a white glow, the brightest light she had ever seen, and she closed her eyes from the glare. When she opened them again she saw that she was in a beautiful garden. It must be Heaven, she decided, since there were no horned creatures, or, she grinned at her pun, horny ones either, so the place couldn't be Hell. Andrea stifled a grin at the naughty thoughts she was having even up here in Heaven. She looked around in awe at the beauty of the lush garden: the trees were the greenest she had ever seen, the flowers were the most colorful, and the radiant light bathed her in it's warm glow. Suddenly she noticed a narrow beam of an even more brilliant light moving toward her. She faced it without hesitation.

And then in a flash it all came back to her. Her baby! Who would take care of her baby if she died? Not Adam. Not Graham. If the child was Adam's, it would be her love child and their eternity, but if it was Graham's it would always remind her of her guilt. She was condemned to eternal love or eternal guilt.

But why was Maya letting those strangers take her baby away? She had to hurry now, to catch them before they got too far with her precious and beautiful daughter. She panicked. They could not take her little girl away. She would not let them. Adam's or Graham's, that child was living proof of her everlasting love or her everlasting guilt. And she was prepared to accept either. She refused to die. Not now. If she was going to catch up with them, she had to hurry. Then the bright light disappeared and everything was black.

When Andrea awoke she was in a room she did not recognize.

Maya was by her side.

"Thank God," she heard her say, "we almost lost you."

"My baby, Maya, where is she?"

"She is fine, Andrea, I promise you. But now you must go back to sleep. This was a very hard delivery for you. Rest, child. I will take care of you and soon everything will be back to normal."

Andrea returned to Stougborough by train. She had been isolated with Maya at the house in Surrey for nearly four months. Her memory of childbirth was now only a pervasive feeling of terrible loss. Maya had not allowed her to see her baby, not even for a moment. She had begged and pleaded but Maya insisted that it was for the best. Once, after listening to her desolate crying, Andrea thought Maya was going to break down and let her see her daughter, but she had merely explained that the baby had been taken to a place far from Surrey. At this, Andrea stopped speaking and would not even listen any more. She longed for her child. If the baby was Adam's, then it was the child of the man who was her very life. Surely Maya should understand that this child was the only one who could comfort her. Refusing to eat even broth until Maya finally threatened her with intravenous feeding, Andrea lost twenty pounds. By the time Maya put her on the train at Surrey she looked emaciated.

"What will happen to my daughter now, Maya?" Andrea had asked forlornly as Maya found her a first class compartment on the train.

"Andrea, I meant what I said. We will take very good care of her. She is a special child, just like you and your mother were and we will train her to use her powers for the good of mankind. But you must tell no one about this. Believe me, it is for the sake of your daughter's future and your own."

She had no choice but to comply. Maya did not return with

her to school.

Back in Stougborough, Andrea was unable to cope with the loss of her child and because she could tell no one about the birth, she sometimes felt as though she were losing her sanity. She rarely attended classes and finally became such a recluse that one day Maria threatened to call the doctor.

"I have to help you, Andrea," she pleaded, "I can't see you like this. What happened to you? What did they do to you? My God," she wailed, "what has happened to the vibrant, carefree person you once were?"

Tears flowed silently down Andrea's face. Maria had never seen the tiger striped eyes so dull. She stroked Andrea's hair and watched the tears fall from her lashes, making a wet spot on the sheets. Never before had Maria seen Andrea Francis cry and at the sight she felt so sad, so at a loss and so helpless. Maria knelt beside her friend, holding her tightly, and cried with her.

"I don't remember what happened. I don't even know where I was," Andrea lied, suddenly aware of Maya's firm admonitions about mentioning the baby. Suddenly stricken with fear, Andrea stopped talking.

There were still eight months to go before she would finish her training. Andrea had not gone out with anyone in England since her return from Jamaica fourteen months before, when her entire life had come crashing down around her. First the pregnancy, then the loss of her baby, and then the news when she returned that Graham had taken his own life. She had been devastated at hearing of his suicide. It had driven her into an even deeper depression. She felt responsible for his death. Had she not been so selfish she would have thought about the suffering she had caused him and she would somehow have been kinder. She had never intentionally meant to hurt him, but what was she supposed to do? Her love would always be only for Adam. How could she have married someone else, loving Adam the way she did? She wished she could ask for Graham's forgiveness. She wished she could explain her agony. But it was too late. She could not even attend the funeral because he had died while she was in Surrey, when everyone thought she had gone away to New York.

Sleep became a stranger to Andrea. At night the montage of her fears rose before her like an angry god. She began having terrible nightmares and as evening came she dreaded the hours ahead. Guilt and fear were her only companions. She kept to herself. Most of her associates left her alone, not understanding why she was so uncommunicative. There were rumors going around that she had left school because she had had a nervous breakdown.

Maria was her only friend, the only person she ever spoke with anymore. Dear Maria, she had always given so unselfishly of herself, thought Andrea. She was the only one who knew she had been pregnant, but Maria would never hound her with questions to which Andrea could give no answers.

Laura no longer knew who Andrea was. She had no idea what had happened to make her adored friend stop caring about anyone and anything, including herself. Since Maria seemed to be the only one Andrea would talk to, Laura had eventually stopped trying. She hated the heartache of her unrequited love, but she refused to continue looking for Andrea's friendship. Even though she had been selfish and caustic with her at times, Laura knew she would always be Andrea's friend; and hurtful as Andrea's example often had been, Laura realized that from her she had learned to be more independent, assertive, and charming, no matter how she might feel inside. Yes, she had gained so much by knowing Andrea Francis; and it was terrible to see her friend in such anguish. She vowed to do all she could for her, even if it meant letting her alone as Andrea requested.

When she was not listlessly attending classes, Andrea spent most of her time alone just listening to old familiar songs. Music was the only connection with the past that she dared to allow herself; the music touched something deep in her soul.

Stretched out on the floor in the living room of the empty flat one evening with the stereo on loud, she sang the words to herself: *"Stay with me baby...remember you said you would never leave me..."* and let the tears spill down her face. She had cried so much in the past few months.

"Excuse me," a voice broke into her solitude. Andrea blinked, as the lights went on.

"I am sorry to disturb you, mademoiselle, but I have a great attachment to my lighter."

As Andrea's eyes adjusted to the light, she saw that the unfamiliar voice was coming from a rather dashing looking man. From his accent, she gathered that he was French.

"What the hell were you doing in here?" Andrea shouted, "This is a women's flat and men are not permitted here."

"As I said, I am looking for my lighter. I left it here when I was visiting Laura this afternoon. May I look around?"

"Just make it snappy." Andrea turned her face away so he could not see that she had been crying.

"You should not cry," he said. "Although tears are good for cleansing the eyes, after a while it is bad on the complexion, and you are far too beautiful to entertain the thought of a bad complexion."

Andrea could have killed him. Couldn't he tell she was not in a conversational mood?

"What are you, some kind of half-baked dermatologist that smokes your lungs out? Maybe you should have gone into pulmonary diseases. Lung cancer is a good specialty," she lashed out.

"I am neither," he began, "I am——"

"Spare me the intro, okay? Frankly, I don't give a damn. Why don't you just look around for your lighter, and make it fast," she said in a hostile voice.

Ralph stood for a moment watching Andrea. He was going to enjoy this. Laura had warned him about Andrea, but to be quite honest he was looking for a new challenge in his life. Most of his women were so pleasing—and oh so stifling.

"Well, are you going to look around or what?" Andrea said when Ralph made no attempt to move, "Or are you faking the lighter bit as much as you are faking that phony French accent?"

"I am Ralph deHavalon," he said ignoring her outburst. "You may question the authenticity of my heritage, mademoiselle, but please never my accent. As I was going to tell you before, I am a French teacher at the University."

"Good for you." Andrea turned, signaling the end of the conversation.

"Ah, here it is." Ralph said after a few moments. "Thank you for your hospitality and I hope to see you again, very soon." He knew she would not answer.

A week later Ralph was again at the flats, this time as Laura's dinner guest. Throughout the entire meal of roast beef and Yorkshire pudding, Andrea barely spoke to any of them. After desert of apple pie and custard, Andrea quickly got up and offered to wash the dishes. She definitely did not want to join Ralph and her other roommates in the sitting room for coffee or idle chatter. She would feign a headache and escape to bed.

"Let me help with the dishes," Ralph offered, standing up to clear the table.

"Oh no, I can manage, thank you. Besides, it's rude to have a guest wash his own dinner plate."

"I know that you can manage, but I would still like to help."

Even up to her elbows in suds, Andrea looked to him like quite a novice housekeeper, a role he was convinced she would never play. She was far too exotic a woman to be tied to an apron, much less a husband and children.

"I really don't need any help, ah..."

"Ralph," he volunteered.

"Ralph. You are very kind, but I do insist that you join the others." Andrea was trying hard not to lose her temper at this persistent man.

"Have you ever done dishes before? You look quite new at it and to be honest you have too much detergent in the water."

"What does that have to do with anything? I'll rinse them well. What is it with you, anyway?" Andrea said, stopping her chore momentarily and facing Ralph. "Can't you see I am not interested in idle chatter?"

"I was only trying to make conversation."

"Why don't you take your monologue elsewhere?" Andrea snorted. "Can't you take a hint? I'm sure there are multitudes of small talk about to take place among your hosts in the living room."

"Hint?" he repeated with a quizzical look on his face. "No speakie English. *Parle vous Français?*"

Andrea could not help laughing. She looked at Ralph from the corner of her eye. Handsome, she thought, looking away. Ralph deHavalon was well built and his dark complexion, jet black hair and sharp nose made him look more Mediterranean than French. Tonight he was casually dressed in cuffed navy blue linen pants with a white cotton shirt unbuttoned enough to expose his hairy chest.

"Listen Ralph, I don't want you to take this the wrong way, but I really would like to be alone."

Ralph made a face and went on with his no speakie English routine.

"Vamoose! Do you understand that word?"

"Okay, okay, but first let me apologize to you."

"What for?"

"For invading your privacy the other day. I think you are still punishing me for that, but are you not being a little hard on me? Allow me to take you out and I will show you what a gentleman I can be."

"You're very charming and if my instincts are right, you are also a wonderful man, but I am not interested in finding out. I am a loner and I want to be alone. I really don't want to be rude, but you leave me no choice."

Now he understood what Laura had meant about Andrea Francis. Laura was being kind about her friend, but Ralph was quickly coming to the conclusion that this girl was crazy. He was interested in challenging women yes, but a psychotic one, not a chance. He ought to leave her alone, of that he was sure, but he was curious to find out what had made her so frightened and so angry. He wanted to get to know her. But she was putting up quite a fight. How much more of her insults he could take was questionable. He decided to try a new approach.

"Now listen to me, you little brat. I do not care if you are a loner or a whiner or just plain stupid, good manners are something you must become acquainted with. Now move over and let me help you with these damn dishes."

Andrea was so surprised at the sudden outburst that she found herself automatically moving over.

"Now," he said, with satisfaction, "was that not easier than fighting?"

"I suppose, but you left far too much soap on the dishes," she could not resist saying.

"So tell me, are you good at riding?"

"What?" Andrea looked startled.

"Goodness," he said, from the look on her face realizing what she thought, "I mean horses of course. These slangs of today with their double meanings are making the English language very difficult to interpret."

"Why do you ask if I ride?"

"It is that your body looks built for riding," he said. "Your long legs would be good on a horse. May I take you riding on Sunday?" he asked.

Andrea started to decline, but stopped. It was time to pull herself together. She had to put the past behind her somehow. She knew she needed to go out, but she had been such a recluse over the past few months she was not sure she remembered how to socialize. She rather liked this wacky Frenchman called Ralph. He seemed to be patient, he had a sense of humor, and he was definitely self-assured.

"I would love to," she finally replied, "if you promise to teach me to ride English style."

"A good old Western saddle is not for you, eh?"

"Not at all."

On Sunday the weather was perfect and Andrea donned her newly-purchased riding habit and boots. The fashionable cut of the black jodhpurs inside her knee-high maroon leather riding boots made her legs seem longer than ever, and the maroon and black tweed jacket hugged her narrow waist as though it had been cut and stitched on her body. Andrea twirled around and around in front of the mirror. Even though she was ten pounds too light she looked well in her suit. She had lost a lot of things over the last year, but her vanity was not one of them. If she was going to make a fool of herself on top of a horse, she might as well do it in style.

"Beep beep!" She heard a car horn and looked out to see

Ralph in a white Volkswagen convertible.

"I'll be right there," she shouted, "just let me get a scarf if you intend to keep the top down."

Maria came out of her room and nodded her approval at Andrea's attire.

"What do you think?"

"Smashing, darling. I'm so glad you decided to go out with Ralph," Maria said, putting her arms around her friend, "I think this is what you need." Maria closed the last button on Andrea's riding jacket and sighed. "I will never understand why I was not born tall," she said, enviously. "You look divine. Have fun, duckie, and don't be an ogre. Ralph is really a swell bloke."

Laura had been right, she thought, if anyone can get Andrea out of this slump, it would be Ralph.

"Ready," Andrea said, getting into the VW and tying the scarf around her hair. The white bug roared down the narrow streets of Stougborough and headed in the direction of Birmingham.

Ralph chatted away, "It will take over an hour to get to the stables. We will turn off just before we get to Birmingham and head north." He talked for most of the hour, filling Andrea in on all the landmarks and points of interest on the way.

"So?" he said after a while, "tell me about yourself."

"There is nothing to tell," Andrea said, abruptly. "Why are you so awfully pushy? If I wanted to tell you about myself I would have."

"I had no idea asking someone about herself was pushy," Ralph replied. "I call it conversation, but if you do not want to tell me about yourself I will just make up something. And for your information, from what I have seen, you are very defensive and rude."

"Listen, I—" Andrea said, feeling the need to apologize.

"No need to explain, Andrea, you are entitled to be and do whatever you want." They rode in silence the rest of the way.

"We have arrived," he said pulling the car into a long driveway. A sign read, Brighton Stables.

"Good morning, Mr. deHavalon, Miss," a stable hand greeted them. "It's a lovely morning for riding."

"It certainly is, Jeff," Ralph responded. "This is Miss Francis. She tells me she does not ride, so I think Princess will be about her speed."

"Very well, sir."

Jeff returned shortly with two horses, a high-spirited black stallion and a quieter brown mare with a tan mane and tail.

"Your mount is Princess," Ralph said, proudly indicating the brown mare. "I own her."

"You must come here often then," Andrea said, tentatively stroking the horse's velvety nose.

"Every chance I get. I love riding. It clears my head."

"You'll need a clear head," Andrea cautioned, "because as soon as I get on this horse I am going to have a major coronary."

"Nonsense, Princess will be gentle and you are going to love riding. It is the closest thing to flying that one can do on the ground. Do you fly?"

"Not in the sense you mean," Andrea said, steadily looking at the horse, not intending to explain. She had flown at the birth of her child, right over the entire delivery.

"I will hold the reins as you mount. Up you go," he said, cupping his hand under her foot and helping her into the saddle. Andrea swung a leg up over the horse.

"Not bad," he said, sounding impressed, "you have a natural knack for this."

"Now just hold the bridle steady and guide her by nudging her gently with your knee," he said, handing her the reins. "If she starts getting stubborn, nudge her with your heel."

"Right," Andrea said, enjoying herself more than she thought she would. Seated on Princess, she waited as Ralph mounted the stallion, which he did with graceful precision.

"Let's go, Princess!" she shouted, as they headed for the path leading to the pond.

"Hold the reins firmly but not too tight," he called after her as her horse galloped off. "Remember, use your knees to direct the horse, and for God's sake try not to end up in the pond, would you?"

"Stop being so protective," Andrea yelled back. "I thought you said I had a natural ability for this!"

"You are doing marvelously," he said loudly, following closely behind her.

Andrea was actually enjoying herself. She had not had this much fun since she had returned from—but she was not going to think about—anything. When they stopped at the pond, she jumped off the mare and waited for Ralph to dismount. He tied both horses to a big oak tree.

"Thank you," Andrea said earnestly, "Riding *is* as wonderful as you said it would be. And this is such a beautiful place."

"I love it here," Ralph said, breathing deeply, filling his lungs with the clean fresh air. "My family always used to come here for the summer. I think my father came only to please my mother. She was English and this was a childhood memory for her. We shall rest for awhile and then we will head back. I am getting terribly hungry."

Ralph felt uneasy with this mixed-up girl. He was not in the least bit hungry, but he did not want to be alone for too long with Andrea. There was something strangely mysterious, almost sinister, about her, and he had to admit he felt the first stirring of sexual arousal. Andrea, while keeping herself an enigma, was able to elicit talk from him, and before long Ralph found himself discussing both his childhood and family. As far back as he could remember, Ralph had made a habit of never discussing his private life or his family with any of his women friends. Somehow doing so seemed to create in them a hope of deeper intimacy, one he was not interested in fostering. He glanced quickly at Andrea, who was now sitting on the grass, her long legs stretched out before her like a never-ending road.

"Ralph, are you terribly hungry or can we stay here for awhile?"

"We can stay if that is your wish. I can survive starvation for a bit longer."

"Oh I wish I could stay here forever. It's so peaceful, and so..."

"So calming," Ralph finished her sentence.

She echoed his words, "So calming. I wish I had brought some bread to feed the ducks," Andrea said, turning her attention to the ducks leading their ducklings across the pond. They were so protective of their young, often swimming back to collect the slowpoke young ones. Andrea felt a stab of pain knock her jovial mood to the ground: she had not been allowed to protect and nurture her offspring.

"They don't look hungry to me," Ralph said, lying on the grass a few feet from Andrea. He went on, "I come here because it reminds me of a place back in Chamonix where my parents used to take my sister and me riding. My mother was an equestrienne competitor. Outside of her family, riding was her life. And I think she chose the stables in Chamonix because it reminded her of this place."

"Are they still in France?"

"My father and sister, yes. My mother died three years ago in a riding accident."

"I'm so sorry, Ralph. I know how painful losses can be."

"Thank you, Andrea," he said, touched by her concern. "I have often found it ironic that the very sport my mother loved so much took her life."

"And you still love to ride?"

166

"Yes, very much. As a tribute to my mother perhaps, and because it is also my life. For what I want, I must continue to perfect my riding skills."

"And what is that?"

"To be the best polo player in England."

"Now I understand why you are so unrelenting. I don't think you'll ever have to worry, Ralph, your dream will come true."

Andrea closed her eyes momentarily, soothed by the sounds of nature. The willows stirring in the breeze, the birds chirping overhead, the horses chewing on dried grass, all added to the tranquillity, and before long Andrea drifted into her first peaceful sleep in many months.

Andrea stirred, glanced at her watch and then looked at Ralph who sat looking down at her. "I can't believe I slept for three hours. I'm so sorry! Why didn't you wake me? Goodness, Ralph, you must be starving."

"Famished. But it is obvious, *ma chère,* that you needed the sleep." Ralph untied their horses and they rode side by side back to the stables.

"You are very good at riding, Andrea," Ralph said as they approached the stalls. "Are you sure you have not done this before?"

"I have ridden on the backs of donkeys," she answered. "The concept is the same, isn't it?"

"Most definitely, but I daresay not as graceful."

Ralph got off his horse and came over to help Andrea. He had been attentive and considerate throughout the day and Andrea was grateful for his kindness.

"Down you come," he said. "Now concede, Miss Francis, aren't you glad you came?"

"I most certainly am. Could we do this again?"

"Certainly," he replied, "just say when."

"So how hungry are you, sir?"

"Starving, let's have lunch."

"I don't see a restaurant," Andrea said, looking around at the fields and forests. "Where are we dining?"

"We could graze right there," he pointed off in the distance, "under that big willow. It will shade us from the sun as we eat to our heart's content. The grass looks delicious, does it not?"

"Funny," Andrea said, reaching up to pull his riding cap over his eyes.

"I should have packed a lunch," she said apologetically, "Forgive me for being so thoughtless." She had never sought penance from anyone before, not even God, as she had been instructed to do by Father Hill after her childhood confessions. Hail Mary, full of grace—. She had never believed in it.

"Ah, not to worry. I am not as neglectful of our health as you are, my dear," he said, basking in her repentant mood as he walked toward the car, "I shall return shortly."

He reappeared moments later with a wicker hamper, complete with checkered tablecloth, flowers, two wine glasses and a bottle of chilled wine in its own insulated bag, among other goodies.

"If you choke on all this food," Andrea said, "I can offer some assistance. Sir, I just want you to be aware that you are in the hands of the best nurse in Stougborough."

"If that is so, then I pray I do not choke," he grinned.

Ralph was kind, funny and easy to talk to. Andrea liked him. Exactly what he wanted from her, she did not know. She should stop all this immediately, before he got hurt, just like all the others had been. Yet Ralph had not done anything inappropriate or suggestive.

"Let me help," Andrea said. He handed her a sharp knife and she began slicing the bread and cutting the cheese, while Ralph opened and poured the wine. Andrea found that food tasted delicious again and ate ravenously, suddenly starved.

When they had finished lunch, Ralph stood up, and pulling Andrea to her feet, said, "Let's take a walk by the pond so we can burn off all the calories we have just consumed."

Andrea covered her ears, "I don't want to remember my indulgent ways. Have you ever heard of denial?"

"I do not deal in denial," he said, sounding serious. Andrea lowered her eyes from his gaze.

Quickly changing his tone, he said, "Come. I will race you to the willow!"

"Okay. Let's see if you are as good at running as you are at having those horses run for you." Andrea did not want to lose the playful, bantering mood they had been enjoying all day.

"Ready, set—" before Andrea could say go, Ralph was halfway to the tree. Andrea reached the tree moments later and flopped down beside him, convulsing in laughter. "You are a cheat and a rascal," Andrea said, pounding on his chest in mock anger. "I must tell you sir, you are no gentleman."

"Ahhhh," he pretended to double over in pain, "you are killing me, madam. A lady of good breeding you are not." He grabbed her hands and they fell back together onto the soft turf. The moment their bodies touched, Andrea stiffened. She jumped quickly to her feet.

"It is time we head back," she said, soberly, "I have the early shift tomorrow and I must get some studying done before finals."

"Did I do something wrong, Andrea?"

"No," she replied, "I'm just tired."

They packed the hamper with the litter from lunch, walked to the car, waved at Jeff and the horses, and drove away. Ralph turned the radio on and they listened to music while he maneuvered the car back to Stougborough. When they arrived at the flats Andrea reached over and kissed him softly on the cheek.

"What was that for?" he asked, surprised.

"For a wonderful day—and for not giving up on me."

Chapter 15

Ralph and Andrea saw each other frequently in the next few weeks. She was surprised at how much she missed him when he left for France to attend a two-week long academic conference.

On Thursday, the day he was due back, Andrea awoke more cheerful than she had been since he had gone. She did not want to acknowledge his return as the only reason for her happy disposition, but all day she puttered around the flat, not wanting to leave for a moment. At four in the afternoon the telephone finally rang. She knew it would be Ralph.

"Hello," Andrea said, jumping to pick it up on the first ring.

"Bon jour, ma'mselle," Ralph's voice greeted her. "I will be right over if that is all right," he continued, "and I will bring fish and chips. Are the roommates going to be there? Do you want Coke and Cadbury's?"

"No one is here but me, kind sir, and I'm starving so bring plenty, especially the chocolate! See you shortly then," Andrea said happily, hanging up the phone.

She went to the bathroom, fixed her hair, powered her nose and put on lipstick. Her feet felt as light as air. She changed into a comfortable apricot-colored sweat suit and waited impatiently for Ralph to arrive. It seemed like ages, but within fifteen minutes he was knocking at the door.

"Come in," Andrea said, opening the door wide and giving Ralph a big bearhug, "I'm so glad to see you."

"I am happy to see you too," he said, amazed at her enthusiastic greeting. Without thinking, he kissed her full on the lips. Andrea pulled away suddenly.

"I am sorry."

"You shouldn't have done that, Ralph. You know how much I care about you, but as a friend. Let's not spoil things," she said in a reprimanding voice. "I'm starving. What goodies did you bring?" she went on more cheerfully.

"*Oh là là!*" Ralph smacked his forehead, "I have forgotten the *vinegaire*!"

"We have gallons of vinegar. Come along, let's find some." Andrea led the way to the kitchen.

After dinner Andrea and Ralph spent the evening catching up on the news from their two-week separation.

"I did my first major scrub last week with Mr. Patterson. He is an excellent surgeon and he has a very funny way of giving orders. He uses sign language. This means close the door and this means a tea break," Andrea demonstrated the gestures. I'm not sure I want the responsibility of surgery. I think I'll do pediatrics. What did you do in France?"

"I sat in on some dull lectures and had several meeting with my boring colleagues, but I did have a wonderful time with my sister and father in Paris. They joined me for two days. They are wonderful, and my sister is getting married in May. Can you come with me to the wedding?"

"I will be leaving England in January."

"Right, I forgot."

"I missed you terribly," Andrea said, moving to sit next to Ralph. "Two weeks seemed so long."

"Listen Andrea, I think we should talk about us. Why is it that if we missed each other so much, you hesitate to move this relationship forward?

"We have discussed this before, Ralph. Why do you always insist on bringing this topic up?"

"Because I want more now. I want to define our commitment."

"I know this is hard for you to understand, but Ralph, I don't want to hurt you and I don't want to be hurt anymore either."

"Andrea," he said, taking her hand in his and looking deep into her eyes. "What hurt? Please, darling, talk to me," he whispered.

Andrea got up and walked over to the window, her back to Ralph. After a few minutes she turned and her eyes met his. Ralph had never seen such a wild and terrified look in anyone's eyes before.

"Andrea, what is it?" Ralph said, getting up to stand beside her. Andrea hesitated, staring down at her hands. When Ralph took her hands, they were as cold as ice and her palms were damp.

"Please, *Chocolát*. I must know."

"Yes," she said, "I owe you that much."

"I was thirteen when I met him. Our meeting was dramatic and extraordinary and I believed he was my soul mate, as if it were predestined. He always knew what I was thinking before the thoughts even formulated in my head. I loved him beyond words. From the time we first met, he groomed me to love him and only him. My love for him was complete and profound and it was consummated when I was eighteen. I did not realize my dedication to him was so ingrained until I was forced to leave him. I knew then that I would never be able to love another man.

"When my mother found out about the relationship, she

173

moved our entire family to the United States six months before we were scheduled to go. My father had been sent there by his company and my mother decided it was time for us to join him. For a year I was tormented by his memory day and night. I spent the entire year in tears. I blamed my mother for my unhappiness and she became very concerned for my health. She encouraged me to come to England to school. I needed to get away from her and to try and make a new start.

"When I first arrived here, I tried to recapture what I had felt for him with dozens of men but none of them could ever measure up and I've left a trail of broken hearts behind me. My last lover committed suicide. He shocked me when he asked me to marry him, and I wasn't even considerate enough to refuse him in person; I sent his ring back in the mail. He killed himself in the house he had bought for us to live in after we were married. It's been seven months since he died, but I've given up on men. I like you so much, Ralph, and that's why I don't want to hurt you, but pain just seems to follow me. I'll be leaving for New York in four months and I would like to be able to call you just to say hello. That's why I don't want you to love me. Can you understand this?"

"Andrea," he gently squeezed her hands, "I know I love you, no matter what we do about it. I also know," Ralph went on, "you have set yourself up for disappointment. No one can control another human being unless they allow it. I have no doubt that you love this man, but you were young and impressionable and the illusion that you may never find someone as worthwhile is simply ridiculous. You must bring your feelings for him into a more realistic light. You need to put the ghost of the past behind you."

"Don't think I haven't tried." Andrea released her hand from his grip. "I knew you wouldn't be able to understand; I don't quite understand it myself, but Ralph, it's just not possible to forget. Every time I'm with someone I'm attracted to I feel as though I am betraying him. I always find a way to sabotage the relationship,

174

most often leaving the other person emotionally damaged. You see, Ralph, I can't find peace away from this man and I cannot betray his love. And now, with—oh Ralph," Andrea pleaded, "please believe me, I have no choice and I am so unhappy."

Ralph pulled Andrea's trembling body close to him, as if protecting her from the gloom that seemed to frighten her so.

"Now with—what, *Chocolát?*" he said quietly. "Whatever could it be that makes you so frightened?"

"It's not important now, Ralph," She gazed sadly at him, "There is nothing I can do about it."

"But there is, my darling. Just let me comfort you, Andrea," he said unbuttoning her sweater, "believe me I do understand how you must feel, because I love you as much as you love him. *Chocolát*, let me show you that I can heal your broken heart, that I can help you forget." He eased her sweater over her shoulders. "I am," he said, "capable of making you forget him, if only for one night."

"Oh Ralph," she clung to him, "there is no way out and I could not bear the grief if I were to hurt you."

"Darling, there is a way, let me show you. I need you Andrea," he said softly, "and I am hurting now more than you will ever know." Andrea allowed him to undress her.

Lowering her to the bed, he kissed her still trembling lips. At first she recoiled at the feel of his hand on her and she had to struggle with herself not to push him away. Andrea closed her eyes and allowed him to slowly explore her body. He sensed rather than felt Andrea's resistance and brought his hand up to caress her hair until she became more familiar with his touch. When he saw that the tension had left her body, he slowly moved his hand over the curve of her buttock continuing until he reached the parting of her legs and felt the moistness there.

"Andrea, my Andrea," he whispered as his tongue flickered hungrily over her breast. Andrea felt panic rising in her chest and when Ralph knelt on the floor beside the bed, her body stiffened; but by then Ralph was attuned to the erotic rising of his manhood. Carefully, yet so hungrily, he was ready to finally taste the exotic fruit of his passion. He wedged his body between her legs forcing them apart; but as he began to enter, her vagina seemed to close against him like a wall.

"I can't," she whimpered, as the recollection of her daughter's birth tearing her body apart came flooding into her consciousness, blotting out pleasure with the memory of horribly excruciating pain.

Ralph, eased himself away from Andrea, studying her naked body now shinny with perspiration, her long legs now curling into a fetal position, and he knew he would be left lost in his own unfulfilled longing.

"I love you," he said softly, gently stroking her hair, now wet with perspiration. "Do you not want me to love you, Andrea?" he pleaded.

"I'm not sure that word exists for me anymore," she answered, a new stream of tears, pain, and shame contorting her face.

"Very well, my darling, only when you are sure."

Andrea buried her face in her hands, humiliated. Ralph reached out to her, embracing her quivering body, holding her secure, forgiving her frailty and comforting her anguish. Something was unquestionably wrong with her, and it had to be more than the story she had told him.

Grateful for Ralph's compassion, for the first time in her life Andrea felt a man appreciated her as a friend and not just an instrument of desire. The friendship she felt with Ralph was new and fulfilling. Other men could not compare with Adam because in her mind he was separate from them all, yet her friendship with Ralph had a quality that she had never experienced with Adam, much as she adored him. To her, Adam was a kind of god; she knew he was her friend, but her friendship with Ralph had somehow been more equal, more real.

Ralph had fallen in love with Andrea the night he had first seen her. From the moment he found her crying in the dark living room of her flat, he had wanted to comfort her. He recognized her frail vulnerability even then and he had wanted more than anything to share all of her sorrow. He knew there was something she was holding back.

Since the night of their aborted lovemaking, Ralph never again pressured her into a physical relationship, yet they continued to share every experience, every idea, everything except sex. He slept with her each night, wanting her sometimes more than he could bear. She slept fitfully, often thrashing around as though she were trying to get away from some evil spirit. Many times she awoke crying and he would soothe her back to sleep.

Ralph respected Andrea, and ever since the night of their "understanding" as he called it, she had grown to respect him even more than before. At times, however, even in their intimate times of sharing, he had to prod her into talking about her feelings. Sometimes she would retreat into her defensive behavior, lashing out at him relentlessly, unleashing the quick temper and the acid tongue he considered her trademark. She had gotten so angry when he had asked her about the reason she was graduating late, that he had abandoned the questioning. Ralph knew there was so much more than she was telling, but no matter how close they became, she never learned to trust him quite enough to share it.

Chapter 16

"**W**hat shall we do today, *Chocolát*?" Ralph asked as Andrea toweled her hair.

"Anything you would like, but I must make time this morning to get some gifts to take home. Why don't you come with me? We could have lunch, and afterwards you could buy me Cadbury chocolate and Coke."

"You want me to help you keep up your denial?"

"Yes."

Ralph had ferreted out Andrea's secret destructive behavior. Every night when she thought he was asleep, she would creep out of bed and head for the kitchen. One night he followed her and soon found out the reason for her nightly disappearance, by catching her in the act of devouring an entire bar of Cadbury chocolate and a bottle of Coke. She looked so entirely guilty with chocolate all over her face and hands that he erupted into helpless laughter. From then on Ralph's nickname for her was "*Chocolát*."

"For goodness sake, Ralph, are you trying to get me expelled?

It's midnight! You're not even supposed to be in this flat—"

"Shame on you, Andrea, you scoundrel! So this is your secret passion is it? And all the time I thought you were meeting a mysterious lover. I am surprised that you are not two stones overweight."

Andrea chuckled, caught in the act. "Please don't scold me. I hide it under the cupboard," she confessed, licking her fingers, "I simply can't give it up. I adore chocolate. The night keeps my secret and by morning I can pretend that it never happened."

Just like his Andrea, he thought, always denying.

That night after their shopping expedition, Andrea and Ralph lay in bed, each of them thinking of her impending departure. "It does not seem possible that eight months have gone by so quickly. I am going to miss you," Ralph said, massaging her tense muscles into relaxation as he did every night. Andrea propped the pillows under her head as she rolled over to face him.

"And I can't tell you how much I'm going to miss you..." she began but stopped, choked with emotion. How was she going to go on without Ralph's comforting friendship? With him she had experienced the freedom to be herself. He loved her in a way that was both supportive and genuine. But she had graduated and it was time to go home to New York.

"I will write to you every day," she continued.

"For how long? Until you meet someone else or go back to Adam? What will I mean to you then?"

"You will always mean everything good to me."

From the corner of her eye she looked at the beautiful man beside her with whom she had spent some of the best moments in life, and her heart felt heavy. Ralph deHavalon was one of a kind, and yes, she would miss him terribly.

How she wanted to be able to grant him his desire to make love to her, to make their relationship complete. She decided she needed to try just one more time.

"You know," she said, "I would like very, very much to kiss you."

"Are you patronizing me, Andrea? It is awfully cruel."

"Only if you want it to be," she said reaching over to kiss him.

"Yum," Ralph grinned, licking his lips, "You taste good. Do that again, *Chocolát*." Then he noticed the sadness in her eyes. "Is something wrong, Andrea?"

"No," she said becoming solemn. "I was just thinking of what a great comfort you've been to me over the past eight months. God, I wish I had met you sooner. Maybe then I wouldn't have experienced so much anger and hurt. I want you to know that you're my dearest friend."

She cupped his face in her hands and kissed him again full on the lips, forcing her mind to surrender its rigid control over her body.

"I want you to make love to me tonight," she whispered. "I want this more than anything in the world."

Hiding his surprise, Ralph kissed her softly and she responded. He held her firmly as one hand slid over her shoulders releasing the terrycloth robe she wore every night to keep her body separated from his.

"Are you sure, Andrea?"

"Yes," she said with certainty, "I'm sure."

Ralph began stroking her back as he had done so many times before, the only way he could get her to go back to sleep when she had one of her nightmares. He hoped it would relax her now. Finally he allowed his hand to come to rest on her breast.

"You are shivering, my love," he said, holding her close against his chest. "Are you cold?"

"No," she whispered, "I'm not cold, I just don't want anything to go wrong." Andrea rested her head in the cradle of his neck, willing her body to relax and her mind to obey her body's signals.

Ralph closed his eyes and allowed the pent-up feeling of desire to engulf him. Before him was his Goddess of Beauty. Easing himself on top of her, he moved so they were fully aligned, nose touching nose, mouth touching mouth, breasts touching breasts and hearts beating as one. For a moment he was completely still.

"If I were to just melt into your body now," he said, "in this position, you would absorb me without a trace. I would become you, Andrea, my mirror image."

"You are so philosophical," Andrea smiled, "I had no idea. Is that a subject you teach at the university as well?"

"No. It is only that I can think of no better way of joining forever with you; to love with mind, body, and soul is the apogee of God's intent. Oh Andrea, I don't want you to go."

"Please Ralph," Andrea pleaded, "don't."

"Forgive me," he said, "but after all it is not every day that a man loses the only woman he will ever love."

"Don't think of it as the end. I may be away from you but you will never be forgotten. This is only the beginning. Darling, make love to me."

"Oh yes. I want more than anything to be inside of you and to be one with you."

Ralph moved down the length of her body, kissing every inch of her, his tongue darting over places Andrea had forgotten existed. Slowly he moved his hand down her body, stroking her until he felt the smooth black hair between her legs. Andrea arched her back toward him and his hand began probing inside her. Involuntarily she caught his hand, forcing it to stop. He could feel her closing up again.

"Relax, Andrea," he coaxed, "I am not going to hurt you. Darling, I love you." She released his hand and he continued stroking inside and found that she was dry.

Andrea's eyes had snapped shut as the memories of her daughter's birth began streaming into her consciousness. The pain, the blackness and the emptiness began closing in. She tried to fight it, but she was slowly losing the battle. Go away, she pleaded silently to the images, as tears welled up in her eyes.

Ralph again tried to enter her. It was no use. He stopped and sat staring into the darkness.

"I'm so sorry. Ralph, please don't hate me."

"I could never hate you, my darling. Not now, not ever." He took her into his arms and held her close until her sobs became quieter and she drifted off into a fitful sleep. He kissed her gently over and over again, knowing that their time together had ended.

Ralph said goodbye to Andrea the following day. "I love you," he shouted, running along beside the train as it pulled out of the Stougborough station. She was crying inside, but she did not allow the tears to fall.

"Andrea," he pleaded, "tell me just once that you love me." The engine of the train was so loud that all she could see was Ralph's lips moving. She did not hear him but she knew what he had said. As the train pulled away from the station, her tears now flowing freely, she placed her face against the window and pressed her lips to the cold glass. "I love you," she whispered.

Chapter 17

New York

Andrea sat behind the colossal mahogany desk and signed the last of a stack of papers. Leaning back in the leather chair and propping her feet up against the corner of the desk, she lit a cigarette and inhaled deeply, happy with the outcome of her latest deal. Jacobson's Industry was now a world-wide conglomerate and she, Andrea Jacobson, had orchestrated it all. She wished there were others she could share her triumph with, but as usual it was home to an empty apartment.

Alex would have been proud of her, she knew. "Your vision is infinity, Andrea," he had often reminded her. "You, my dear, are going to become a superpower in the business world." And he had backed her in every decision regarding the direction and future of the company he had founded. Yet now, with all her business acumen and ultimate power, she was alone.

Maybe, she thought, she should call one of her lovers. But she could not think of a single one of her bedmates who might be intelligent enough or even sincere enough to appreciate her triumph. Most of the men she met were so stupid, either wealthy and stupid or poor and stupid. She had a very low opinion of New York men, having chosen those she could get rid of easily once she tired of their company, usually with a few expensive gifts. To Andrea, they served one purpose and one purpose only: sexual satisfaction. After all, a woman of thirty-five still had certain needs.

Alex's death after they had been married for only two years had left a void in her life and Andrea had chosen not to become involved again; personal loss was too painful to be endured. It was not for a lack of suitors that she was alone, but sometimes she questioned her decision to stay single.

Andrea got up and went to the window to look down at the Fifth Avenue side of Central Park. The sidewalks and the park were alive as usual. Today, she wanted to be a part of the hubbub of New York, wanted to feel the vibrations of the most lively city in the world pulsing through her veins. After all, she was responsible for a good part of this city's revenues.

In her years with Alex, Andrea had never enjoyed being part of New York's "in" crowd; and she had chosen to stay out of society's limelight after his death. As Alex Jacobson's wife there had been many social obligations and invitations, yet Andrea had insisted on keeping a very low profile, attending only the most important or worthwhile events. "Publicity is dangerous if you want a private life," Andrea had always said, convincing Alex to pay his public relations people handsome retainers to guard their privacy. Thus, the Jacobsons had never been photographed and their financial status was never publicized.

But today she wanted desperately to feel life around her, so she decided to walk down to the corner deli and have something terribly fattening. She glanced at her diamond and emerald studded watch, noticing that it was already three o'clock. The phone on her desk buzzed as she was about to get her coat.

"What is it, Janice?" she said into the intercom.

"It's time for you to get ready for the taping of the Rachel Hersey show," Janice replied. "The work crew are here setting up right now."

"Good Lord! I had completely forgotten about it," Andrea said, "tell them I'll be ready in about half an hour."

Damn, thought Andrea, wishing she had never consented to do this interview. The show was being taped in her office since she could not find the time to go to Los Angeles. It was her first television appearance and she had to face the fact that her precious anonymity would soon be history. She had agreed to do the show only because Jacobson's Industry was about to take its rightful position among America's top corporations, and it seemed only fitting that the chief executive officer should make the announcement herself.

She looked around at her plush surroundings. The sacrifice was worth it, she thought. Andrea had devoted herself completely to Jacobson's Industry in the five years since Alex's death, practically living in her office, working long arduous hours, and sacrificing everything else in her life. She had a work-out gym and jacuzzi installed as well as a bedroom, sitting room and kitchen, which along with her office suite took an entire floor. Huge mahogany double doors on which the gold Jacobson's Industry logo was carved led into her office. Unlike her home, the handsome office was done in solid mahogany paneling with bright tapestry fabrics covering the antique furniture which lessened the masculine effect. As a central focus, a priceless hand-woven Aubusson carpet was indirectly lighted over its JB insignia. Floor to ceiling glass made up two walls of the corner office high above Central Park. Her hard work and dedication to the success of Jacobson's Industry had paid off. "Thank you for believing in me, Alex," she whispered.

Andrea quickly slipped into her coat and going through her sitting room took the private elevator down to the Park Avenue exit. She would have a pastrami on rye with Swiss cheese if it killed her, maybe even some chopped liver. With her belted coat pulled closely around her, a Hermès scarf over her head, and eyes hidden behind dark glasses, she was just another New York woman. Walking hastily to the deli, Andrea reflected on the events in her life that had led to a triumph like today's.

Chapter 18

At twenty-six, a recent graduate of the Wharton School of Business with no work experience to qualify her for the position she wanted, except for a short stint as an office girl, Andrea decided to interview for a job with Jacobson's Industry. Her youth and enthusiasm for the growing computer business, she felt to this day, had been a major asset and part of the reason Alex Jacobson had hired her.

He had briefly glanced at her resume after she had arrived in his office from Personnel.

"Well, Miss Francis, and what do you think you can contribute to Jacobson's?"

"Infinity," she heard herself answer.

He had nodded, and the interview was over. The following Monday she was no longer an unemployed graduate, but a mid-level marketing executive at Jacobson's, which was becoming a heavy player in the industry.

By 1980 the computer industry had made a quantum leap,

bringing personal computers to almost every desk in America. Andrea Francis had made some innovative judgments about Jacobson's role in this area and her decisions had positioned the company high in the marketplace. Andrea was promoted to Marketing Director later that year. And then married its founder and chief executive officer, her boss, Alex Jacobson.

Alex had changed the course of her life. He had begun by valuing her quick mind, then learned to appreciate and rely on her sound decisions. He was sixty, so much older than she that a relationship between them had never occurred to Andrea, yet they had spent so much time together in the past two years and had become such friends that it had not come as a complete surprise when he proposed marriage.

"Andrea, I'm not getting any younger and I can't imagine spending the rest of my life without you. My dear, I want you to marry me."

"Alex, that's impossible. I'm not in love with you. Of course I care about you, we're friends, but—"

"Who said anything about being in love? I want you to be my wife, my companion, my friend, for life, and I want to give you a good life."

Alex Jacobson was a gentle and good man. Andrea liked and respected him. During the years at Jacobson's, Alex had become her closest friend. She married him because she genuinely cared for him, and she had been true to her marriage vows. Alex was an interesting and cultured man who spoiled his young bride beyond reason, introducing her to the advantages of real wealth. The Jacobson name appeared on the "A" list in New York and Alex had insisted that it was proper to make appearances at certain functions, "if only," he said, his blue eyes laughing, "to solicit some of the largest accounts in the world."

Unknown to Andrea, who was blind to color, he also made it known in certain circles that society would accept his wife or do without him. As a Jew, Alex Jacobson had frequently encountered prejudice and he was damned if he would subject his adored wife to a hint of sarcasm or innuendo. There had been no need for him to worry, as it turned out. On her own, beautiful and witty Andrea was an immediate social success possibly because of her explosive intolerance of ignorance. If occasional social commentary about Andrea's ethnic origin was heard, it was always behind closed door. It was at the annual Jacobson's holiday celebration that Andrea, who had been in the bathroom stall heard:

"What could have possessed him to marry her?" the slightly too over-dressed Elena Brockman asked.

"*Black* Magic," Christina Goldberg answered. Their laughter quickly fading as Andrea opened the stall door.

"Good evening ladies," she walked passed the two women whose true breeding was more than evident in their overdone couture. The nerve of them; both were second wives about to be discarded.

Two years after their marriage Alex died of a massive cardiac arrest in the office where Andrea now worked.

In those two years Andrea had grown accustomed to living in style. The house in the Hamptons and the apartment that covered three floors in the Trump Towers became settings for lavish entertaining. Their guest lists were carefully scrutinized to include only the socially prominent and read like "Who's Who." These were people who took for granted things like the Château Petrus wine and Beluga which were trademarks of the Jacobson parties. Power, money, limousines, private jets and haute couture became normal accouterments of Andrea's life.

But after Alex's death Andrea became a social recluse. She sold the house in Southampton, keeping only the East Side apartment. The parties ceased entirely. Without Alex at her side, she simply refused to be part of the *nouveaux riches* who had little time for everyday reality or even human feelings; their cocooned world was as complex as figuring out why they were left off an approved list and how to rectify it. To Andrea, after the initial glitter and fuss, social events had become a complete waste of time, and she immersed herself in work. She found that she too had little time for human feelings, although she justified herself by saying she had a reason for not caring.

"I'll never love anyone again," Andrea had vowed at Alex's funeral. Alex was the third man she had loved deeply in her thirty-five years of living, and she had lost him too.

It was well over a year after Alex died that Andrea found herself needing a man, and Jacques St. Pierre became her lover. But she soon replaced him with another, then another temporary male for her physical needs. In this aspect of her life she was an artist. When a romance was over, it was done, *kaput*, no remember whens. She concealed this part of her life quite well, as she had learned to do with certain areas of her past, so well in fact that in her mind these men simply did not exist. In her own way she had loved Alex Jacobson. She missed him very much. Marriage or involvement, she decided, would never again be an option.

Within five years Andrea had quadrupled Jacobson's revenues, beginning by diversifying the product line, and then taking Jacobson's Industry public, which made her an instant multimillionaire after the closing of the stock offering. Yes, tonight Alex would have been so very proud of her.

Rachel Hersey was excited about doing the show, the first media person ever to interview Andrea Jacobson. Such an interview would be the coup of anyone's career and Rachel Hersey had gotten where she was because she was a very shrewd and calculating reporter. She interviewed only those people or did only those stories that furthered her television career by boosting ratings. She had deliberately cultivated all the right people and had developed a repertoire of proper responses for every imaginable situation: she could cry, laugh, look surprised or empathetic at the drop of a hat. Her audiences were so captivated by the unfolding drama that they would never believe she faked any of her reactions. A mere five feet two, she possessed the air of someone much taller. Her petite frame had often worked to her advantage; she was usually considered harmless because she was tiny. Not only had Rachel Hersey been in the right places at the right times with the right people, but she had a knack of making even the most insignificant story a media event. As many unsuspecting targets had discovered, this green-eyed little brunette reporter was far from harmless.

A graduate of Columbia's School of Journalism, where she had gone by the grace of a scholarship, she had always felt like a social outcast. To be a five-foot-two-inch Jewish charity case was humiliating, and she had vowed to show all the snobs just who was who in journalism and to make her mark on the world.

Rachel had found out about the pending merger in Southeast Asia months before it actually happened, although it was a top company secret. Seducing and sleeping with Jonathan Buckley, Jacobson's director of sales had paid off. Rachel straightened her mike, tugged at the sleeve of her Lacroix suit, and prepared to meet this fabled female entrepreneur. She intended to get the real scoop on Andrea Jacobson. The merger between two companies was of little interest to Rachel; she was interested in Andrea Jacobson herself, and so was the rest of the world.

Andrea hated pandemonium. While she had been an executive at Jacobson's Industry and even when she took over the company after Alex died, she had managed to keep a low profile. Reporters clamored to find out about the reclusive millionaire who had made Jacobson's a household name and lined the pockets of Wall Street brokers, but she had declined to be interviewed or photographed. Andrea was particularly concerned about media exposure because she knew that reporters had a way of digging up dirt and adding a few lumps of their own to make a story. She could not afford a scandal about her past. That was the reason Andrea had convinced Alex to create a public relations screen to keep the Jacobsons out of the public eye. Their main function was to make sure that no unnecessary attention ever fell on her.

She thought of how coincidental it was that the deal had been signed so close to her first public appearance. Only now was Rachel Hersey being briefed on the merger, or so she assumed. Andrea was going to announce that Jacobson's had just become the single largest computer company in the world. It had been a tedious and rigorous negotiation, but as far as Andrea was concerned she still did not know what there was to talk about besides the announcement. It was all so simple. The bright lighting felt hot and there were lots of people buzzing around her.

"Five minutes to air," someone called. "Take that shine off her nose, fix her hair, straighten her collar, attach the mike." There was a brouhaha as people shouted orders. Andrea could not wait until they all cleared out of her office where she was seated at her desk with the Hersey woman across from her.

"Ready?" Rachel said to her while looking into the camera. Andrea nodded.

"Today we are going to introduce to you one of the richest females of this decade, Andrea Jacobson. She is the owner of Jacobson's Industry, a technology company headquartered here in New York. Ms. Jacobson is going to share with us the secrets of her success, the drive behind her ever-growing empire, and the future directions of her company, which we understand in light of its recent activities is the largest of its kind in the world.

"And later we will be joined by Dr. Scott Preston who is a well-known psychiatrist and expert on the personalities and psyches of the rich and famous. Dr. Preston is also a leading specialist on the subconscious mind and contends that most successful people have significant deficiencies in their personal lives which motivates them to external success, and," Rachel smiled at the camera as if sharing a secret with the viewers, "are usually a little more than normally mad."

She continued, "Dr. Preston has written numerous books on the subject. His latest, "Rich Me, Poor Me," is on the *New York Times* best seller list. Stay with us."

"Five seconds," the cameraman cued. Andrea was sweating under the hot studio light. A woman in a smock quickly darted over to powder her face.

"Standby to air."

"Five, four, three, two, we are on."

Rachel turned to Andrea and in her direct and forceful tone she said. "Tell us Ms. Jacobson, how does one get to be so wealthy in such a short time? "

"With a great deal of hard work and singlemindedness toward a goal," Andrea responded. "I suppose for Jacobson's Industry that our timing was also right. The need for our technology was a key factor in our success. The United States was clamoring for new technological information and there was a great need for what we have to offer. In other words, we solved a national problem."

"Has the fact that you are black caused you any setback?"

"If it has, I've never noticed. My company had the technology and the expertise to solve the problems and that was what mattered. I have never felt it a handicap to be black."

"Most people cannot even put a face to your name. Why is that?"

"Publicity is not necessary for success, in fact sometimes it is a hindrance."

"What do you think has been the biggest motivation for your success?"

"A strong need to be in control of my own destiny."

"Is there a special person in your life who has contributed to your success since your husband died?"

"Not to my knowledge."

"It is said that you have not dated since Alex Jacobson died. Is that all made up publicity from news-starved media people?"

"I suppose it could be. I have been widowed for five years. I don't think that is a lifetime."

"Do you date?"

"Occasionally."

"How do men respond to a woman of your position and wealth?"

"I really don't know. I suppose some men might find me competitive and intimidating, but I have not asked."

"Do you think you will ever find a man that is not intimidated by you?"

"I don't know that they are, but when I've conducted a formal survey, I promise to come back on your show and tell you the results." Andrea was beginning to dislike the line of questioning.

"Have you ever been passionately in love?"

"Yes I have, Miss Hersey, but I loved my husband in a way that was greater than passion."

"Then when did you first feel passionate love?"

"Twenty-two years ago." Andrea said, immediately realizing the fatal error she had made. The sneaky bitch had tricked her!

"But you would only have been thirteen?"

Andrea's eyes flashed at her.

Rachel turned to the camera. "We are talking with Andrea Jacobson of Jacobson's Industry and we will be right back after these words from our sponsor."

Rachel knew when to take a commercial break. She had opened a can of worms and she needed to regroup. She could tell from the twitch of the perfectly arched eyebrows that she had offended Andrea Jacobson, but she was too much of a newshound not to have realized that she had stumbled onto something big. She would get the story if it killed her.

Andrea pulled at the mike, clipped to her lapel. She was enraged. She had told her public relations people to authorize no questions about her personal life. They were to make sure that all questions were confined to her immediate work with Southeast Asia. She knew that Rachel Hersey had not submitted the questions she had asked. This was completely unprofessional and Andrea would make sure this woman felt the full wrath of her anger. However, she would wait. Too drastic a move could instantly incriminate her and add fuel to a smoldering fire.

"I will not answer any more personal questions, Miss Hersey," Andrea informed her interviewer during the break. "I suggest you stick to those that were approved," Andrea said too sweetly, "because if you insist on deviating from the approved questions, I will stop the interview. And, Miss Hersey, as you know, my only reason for agreeing to be interviewed was to deliver the details of our merger to the public, so you will avoid any other questions about Jacobson's Industry as well."

Rachel did not want to make an enemy of Andrea Jacobson or alienate her most prized guest in front of millions of viewers. She had just opened Pandora's Box! It had been a risk to do what she had done, but, she reasoned, the greater the gamble the greater the payoff, and gambling was her forte. All her reporter's instincts told her she was on the edge of a wonderful scandal and that eventually she would uncover the skeletons in Andrea Jacobson's closet. But she had to wait until the time was right. For now she would smooth the ruffled feathers. She was not going to push her luck.

By the time Rachel Hersey and her crew left Andrea's office

the entire company was swamped with calls from people all over the country, and mobs of reporters with minicams were gathering in the lobby to get a glimpse of Andrea Jacobson. Many people were only interested in the fact that she was black; the office had already received some threat calls from racists and neo-Nazis. In her naïveté, she had always assumed that most people were civilized, a mistake she could no longer afford to make. Andrea took refuge in her office that night because of the crowds milling outside her building. Never again would she give a live interview, she promised herself.

The following afternoon in her office Andrea forced herself to watch a videotape of the show. Although she had been furious with Rachel Hersey's tactics, she had to admit that she was very good at what she did, presenting Andrea as a no-nonsense businesswoman while maximizing her own charismatic aura. All things considered, Andrea felt the show was a positive one for Jacobson's.

The segment with Dr. Scott Preston had been taped by remote, and as Andrea watched him, she was glad she had not been present for that because never in her life had she seen such an arrogant, self-inflated, pompous ass. He commented about her psyche, her workaholic tendencies and her possible inability to maintain a close and trusting relationship.

"Ms. Jacobson," he had stated in a slight drawl, "typifies the obsessive compulsive behavior of most workaholics. I would say she is running away from something she does not want to face on a personal level. Perhaps she is still grieving over the death of her husband. Five years is a long time to grieve, but many people in a pervasive depression indulge in overactivity to prevent themselves from having time to resolve their feelings."

Yes, had she been there she would surely have punched him in the face. Mad enough to spit, she intended to have the last word. She buzzed her secretary.

"Get Dr. Preston on the phone, Janice."

A minute later Janice buzzed back, "Ms. Jacobson, Dr. Preston is on line three."

"This is Andrea Jacobson," she said flatly.

"Who? Please speak up," he said, "I am in the middle of a very noisy office party."

"This is Andrea Jacobson!" she shouted into the receiver.

"Not so loud! I'm not deaf."

Andrea felt the blood rush to her head. She was shaking; the contraction in her chest suggested she was either having a major coronary attack or about to pass out from sheer anger.

"You may not be deaf, Dr. Preston," she said, "but you *are* entirely out of line making such statements about people you don't even know. I want to talk to you!"

"Ah!" he said, finally registering who she was. "I'm glad you called, but listen," he continued, "I'm in the middle of a going away party. However, I'm free this evening. Let's say seven o'clock for dinner at Un Deux Trois, the French bistro in the Theater District. It means one-two-three." He hung up.

The colossal nerve, Andrea thought, now thoroughly irritated. She slammed the receiver down so hard that it broke. She was not used to such cavalier treatment. A French bistro! What about dining at Le Cirque or Lutece? Taking her to an appropriate restaurant was the least he could do after insulting her publicly. She was furious. She had not felt this much emotion in a very long time. Andrea paced up and down her office.

She would certainly not show up for dinner. That would teach Dr. Scott Preston to be so presumptuous. And so condescending. One-two-three, indeed! Whatever happened to good manners? She poured herself a snifter of Grand Marnier. The country was filled with too many idiots trying desperately to make an impression when they really had nothing to say. Scott Preston was no exception.

As it approached six-thirty, Andrea's curiosity and the brandy got the better of her. She wanted to meet this bastard in person. She lit a cigarette before dialing Janice's extension from her private phone since the other telephone was broken.

"Janice, I need to get out of the building without being seen. I suppose there are still some reporters lurking around. Call down and have David bring the car into the garage. I'll meet him there instead of at the Fifth Avenue entrance. I'll see you here tomorrow before I leave for Hong Kong. Is everything set for Hong Kong?"

"Of course, Ms. Jacobson. But are you sure you want to fly commercial with this media hype still at a peak?"

"I'm positive, thanks."

Andrea took the elevator from her suite directly to the garage where David was waiting and climbed into the long blue Mercedes. Until tonight she had always hated its tinted windows because they made her feel like a Mafia moll. But she much preferred that feeling than being a media puppet.

Chapter 19

Andrea did not notice Scott Preston when the car pulled up to the entrance of Un Deux Trois until David opened her door.

"Andrea!" He greeted her with a kiss on her cheek when she got out of the car, as though they were long-time friends. "How good to see you."

Andrea stepped back from his embrace and extended her hand. His grip was firm. He was much taller than she had expected from seeing him on television and he had broad shoulders. He leaned toward her as they walked to the restaurant.

"I am glad you called," he drawled, "I can call you Andrea, can't I?" he said, more as a statement than a question. His enunciation was deliberate and calculating. Andrea decided he had gone through speech therapy as a child.

"Hungry?" he asked, reaching to open the door to the restaurant, but Andrea opened it herself.

"Even if bistros weren't so noisy I would not have an appetite tonight."

He eyed her with renewed curiosity as she moved quickly to a table and pulled out her own chair.

"Not a dependent person are you?" he said, observing her behavior.

"Not in the least," she said acidly, pulling herself closer to the table.

"Would you like a cocktail before dinner?" the waiter offered, looking at Andrea questioningly.

"Chivis and soda," she said, lighting a cigarette.

"Tomato juice," Preston ordered, studying her. She wished his eyes would fall out of his head and bounce on the table.

He took a sip of his juice and adjusted his position in the chair, not once shifting his gaze from her face. She found his open stare offensive.

"You should try to stop smoking," he said, "it's bad for everyone's health."

"I'm not concerned with everyone's health," she said. Yet her hand went involuntarily to the ashtray and she stubbed out the cigarette, annoyed that she had been so obedient.

"Now," he continued, leaning back in his chair, "what is it that you want to talk about?"

Andrea was speechless that he was so direct, so abrupt and so rude. She wondered how soon he would drop this routine and retreat into subservience like all the rest of her male conquests. But she didn't want to conquer him because he was far too boring for her taste. His behavior confused her though, and now that he was sitting before her big as life, she felt silly that she had even requested the meeting.

"I wanted to tell you," she said curtly, "not to make such rash statements about a person you don't know, especially on national television. It's the kind of irresponsible nonsense that creates damaging gossip."

He smiled at her, flashing a perfect set of white teeth. The smile transformed his face and unnerved her even more. She felt in her bag for a cigarette but restrained herself from lighting it. What's the matter with me? she wondered.

"First, let me apologize if what I implied offended you. I'm an expert on overachievement. I was not picking on you personally, just making an observation about people with your drive and ambition. My theory is backed by many years of research and it has been proven correct. What exactly did you take exception to?"

"I'm sure," Andrea began, "that everyone has certain problems they have to cope with, but do they all have to be bonkers to be successful? And does success always mean that they haven't addressed their problems and that they're incapable of loving?"

"Not always. Some people are successful because they've reached a spiritual maturity that allows them to be multidimensional. Money, to these people, is a by-product of their contentment as well as their commitment to life. They're not flamboyant or obvious with their wealth. These people live simple lives and try to help others attain spiritual maturity."

"Aren't you being terribly metaphysical?" she asked.

"Yes, I am," he said, without further explanation.

"I knew someone who was clairvoyant. She seemed to be quite interested in me, but I didn't like her." She nearly blurted out that she didn't like him either.

"She might have been your spiritual guide," he said. Andrea realized now that he was quite crazy. She had heard of these weird metaphysical types, but she had not actually met one—other than Maya.

"Are you ready to order or do you need some more time?" Scott inquired.

"I'm not really hungry," she said.

Scott ordered cold foie gras garnished with caviar and medallions of veal in lemon beurre blanc for both of them. Andrea found herself admiring his masterful manner. She still didn't like him.

"What of flamboyant wealthy people?" she asked, assuming he placed her in this category.

"These people," he began, "are rooted in the material world. In many cases they have had crises in their lives that they were unable to reconcile. These problems have a multitude of origins. It could be some sort of abuse, perceived or real, the fear of poverty, childhood trauma, a broken love affair or emotional abandonment of some sort.

"For example," he went on, "a child separated from its mother for an extended period of time might develop an unconscious fear of rejection. Usually the perceived problems are distorted. With therapy, many of these people can reconcile their problems."

Andrea shifted nervously in her chair. "This is all very interesting," she said, "but it's speculation and has no scientific basis."

"Neither does Christianity," he said, "it is based on faith. Andrea, I really did not mean to offend you, but I would bet that your drive toward success is an escape from something you don't want to face. And look what you have achieved as a result of it. The end results are sometimes not bad, but if you had all of yourself in alignment, think how much more you could achieve."

"Well, Dr. Preston," Andrea said, "I must get home. I'm flying to Hong Kong tomorrow. My driver is waiting. Thank you for dinner and a most interesting conversation."

"My pleasure," he said, "Shall we continue our discussion of the spiritual dimension when you return from your trip?"

"I would like that," Andrea replied politely, not meaning it.

Scott Preston smiled as he made his way to his car. He liked Andrea Jacobson. She was spirited and beautiful, a far cry from the somber women he usually saw. Behind her emotional armor was a passionate woman starving for love, he decided. He wanted to be the man to penetrate that wall.

Scott Preston was an inconspicuous man even though his books were well-known. No one would notice him in a crowd; he had no flair. His picture was not on the books he had written, but neither had he shied away from publicity. He had simply never felt the need to show off the masculine ego that drove so many men. Self-approving and self-accepting, he had created a fulfilling, successful life, considering where he had come from. Even today he preferred not to think of his painful youth, hating his childhood. He had been a victim of a stern, unforgiving father, whose idea of love was to control his wife and two children. The only son, Scott became the target of his father's wrath, an anger that he never understood. He had tried to win his father's approval but the man had neither a conscience nor a heart the boy could appeal to. His mother had given him love, but she was too weak to disagree openly with her husband. Scott wished she had been a stronger woman.

By the time Scott was fifteen he had become a loner, lacking the emotional skills to help him survive in the world of his peers. Much as he had fantasized about sex, he could never bring himself to approach a girl in high school. Finally, on graduation night, he mustered the courage and Susan Atterbury had let him make love to her in the back of her father's car. Yet even months later, when he thought of himself as an accomplished lover, he was still very shy.

His wife had changed all that. He met her in his third year of residency at Johns Hopkins. She was a woman who knew what she wanted and would stop at nothing to get it. A psychiatric resident, two years his junior, she was already a very confident and competent doctor. She was from a completely different world; and he had been impressed with the affection and candor her family displayed. Angela was a strong woman, vivacious, loving and kind, the opposite of his mother. Within a year of their courtship they were married. Angela had taught Scott to be emotionally secure. She made him feel omnipotent and capable of doing anything, even helping him accept and put his feelings for his father in perspective.

"Scott you can't blame yourself for your father's behavior. You may never know what made him so bitter, but it was not your fault. Do you have any idea why he was such an angry person?"

"My mother always said he wanted to be a doctor but when she got pregnant with me he had to leave school and find a job to support his family. I think he blamed us for robbing him of his chance to do what he wanted to do."

"His own father was probably just as controlling as he was," Angela replied, "but that's behind you now—and we just have to accept what we cannot change."

Angela was the best thing that had ever happened to Scott. She had believed in him so fiercely that all his doubts seemed to evaporate, working with him night after night until his first book on New Age theories was published. When he felt stifled by their relationship, Angela had understood his fear that his life was being controlled by her and moved into the background, allowing him to develop at his own pace. He had loved her dearly.

Scott's shoulders slumped as he thought about Angela. There was something about this Andrea Jacobson that reminded him of her.

Andrea was lost in thought as her car pulled up to the brass facade of Trump Towers.

"Ms. Jacobson," the driver turned to look at her, "we are here, madam. Did you want to go elsewhere?"

"Oh no, thank you, David."

Inside the building, Andrea took her keys from her bag, let herself into the private elevator and pushed the button to the twenty-fifth floor. She leaned against the wall as it silently slid upwards, her mind turned to Scott Preston. And she felt a warm sensation. The elevator came to a stop and the doors opened into the marble foyer of her apartment. Pushing the double doors open, Andrea kicked off her shoes in the hallway and went to the kitchen to fix a brandy, carrying it to the sitting room off her bedroom. She sat down and leaned back on the chaise longue.

Scott Preston was indeed an interesting character, she decided. She was intrigued at how easily he had defused her anger and that she had found herself talking to him as she had not talked with anyone in years. She had even mentioned Maya! She was impressed with his openness about spirituality since admitting to being spiritual seemed so contrary to the accepted idea of masculinity. Andrea was annoyed and embarrassed at the effect he had on her. How silly she must have sounded to him.

Andrea finished her brandy and removed her navy blue Louis Féraud suit. She ran her hands over her stomach moving them up to her breasts, aware of the beginning of desire as she had not felt in years—too many years. She quickly stepped into the shower, repressing the feeling for Scott Preston. She was attracted to him, and because of that, she was sure she would do everything in her power never to see him again.

Andrea dialed the phone to Melissa's suite.

"Hi, I'm home. Want to have coffee?"

"May I ask what is the occasion?" A smile was in her warm Jamaican lilt.

"Melissa, I met a man tonight that made me feel like a woman."

"Dear, I will be right down."

Melissa took the elevator from her suite that opened directly into Andrea's foyer.

"In here," Andrea called.

"I am all ears," Melissa said.

"Actually, he's the psychiatrist that was on the Rachel Hersey show."

"Well, my dear, you certainly like a challenge."

Chapter 20

The flight to Hong Kong was one Andrea hated. The thirteen hour time change always gave her severe jet lag no matter how much fluid she drank. She would have sent Jonathan, her Vice President of Sales, but this was a matter she had to attend to herself. She had worked personally on the deal and it was only proper that she attend the celebration of the merger.

Air Cathay touched down on the runway precisely at ten in the morning, Tokyo time. Narita airport was as stoic as the Japanese. Even the snack bars were boring. Seaweed candy indeed. Andrea handed her passport to a Japanese official who barely looked up from his work. She wondered what would happen if he smiled. Maybe his face would crack. The man looked from the passport picture to Andrea and his slanted eyes widened.

"Ah so, Ms. Jacobson," he said, hurrying from behind the desk, "Welcome to Japan! I show you special waiting area if you follow me please. I bring you tea, yes?"

"Yes," Andrea replied.

He bowed politely and left the room backwards, soon returning with a steaming cup of tea in the airport's best china.

"Only forty-five minutes for connecting flight to Hong Kong. I come and get you when time to board," he said, in very halting English, again leaving the room backwards.

Andrea opened her briefcase and studied the documents she was carrying with her. The signing of those documents had made her not only one of the wealthiest women in America but indeed in the world. She wanted to remember all the details when she gave her speech.

The Hong Kong airport was crowded as usual with immigrants from various Asian countries, especially Viet Nam. Andrea moved quickly to the executive line trying to avoid the scurrying tourists who would step on your toes and then flash their shiny gold-capped teeth as acknowledgment to be excused.

Hong Kong was no longer the shopping haven it had been, but tourists still flocked to it looking for the inevitable bargain, trying to get the last bit of free trade before Great Britain was to turn it back over to Chinese rule in 1997. Hong Kong had always been fascinating to Andrea, not a place she would visit too often, but fascinating. There was a great cultural difference between Hong Kong and the United States; but it was not unlike her own country, Jamaica, that until 1962 had also been a British colony, where the contrived peddling of goods under the guise of tourist attraction was subtle but effective. The Cantonese philosophy of working together for the good of the entire country appeared to obliterate their own private aspirations. They seemed contented and outwardly prosperous. Away from the tourist glitter, there was much to learn from the local people, whose customs and beliefs were so linked with spirituality and destiny that Andrea decided they had developed as a way of coping with poverty. They seemed obsessed with death and wealth, but of course to them death was the beginning of a better life and "*gong xi fa chai*," or wealth, was what everyone strived for. The vast difference between the rich and the poor in this country was to Andrea the epitome of capitalism.

Everywhere one walked in Hong Kong there was some image of Buddha, of prosperity or happiness or whatever one wanted to pray for, whether health, wealth, or just a good plot of land on which to be buried. Amused, Andrea had burned incense and prayed to various Buddhas many times but she had never believed in their power. What she had prayed for she could not even remember.

On the few occasions that Andrea had visited the Orient, it had never ever crossed her mind to visit a spiritual gathering, but after her conversation with Scott she was more than a little curious about the origin of this spiritual concept that was a way of life in the Far East.

"Chan," Andrea said to her bilingual Chinese assistant, "I would like to visit an authentic spiritual meeting of your people. Do you think that you could arrange it?"

"Aii-ya, Missy Jacobson, are you sure?"

"I'm sure."

"Then I make possible. I make a call and I ring you at two o'clock."

Andrea visited an assembly of Zen Buddhists in a monastery the following afternoon. Listening to their chants, although she did not understand what was being said, she felt a resonance and familiarity in herself that responded to the vibrations of the mantras. After the chanting was finished, Andrea went to have her fortune told by the leader of the gathering who seemed to be all things: a healer of romantic and physical illness, a giver of wealth and fortune, and a spiritual guru.

"You," the fortune teller had told her, "will experience much turmoil in the next few months. Do not despair, however, because only good will come out of it. You, my child, are a chosen one. It is necessary for you to experience this coming turmoil so that you can clear the way for your contribution to the world. Right now you are blocking the realization of your powers by occupying your time with many activities and you have lacked the courage to find your destiny."

"What do you mean?" Andrea asked.

"Do not be impatient, you will know when the time is right."

"And when will that be?"

"Soon. Very soon. But be careful my child of those professing friendship and loyalty."

There was so much peace and love in the room that even though Andrea had wanted to laugh at the hocus pocus gathering and the nonsensical fortune reading, she realized in her soul a recognition of the truth of this religion. What could possibly go wrong? Her life was at its zenith. Andrea returned twice more to visit with this fortune teller.

She asked questions about the way of Zen. From what she could gather her soul was eternal and she was here to work on areas in her life that needed adjusting before she could continue on her spiral to perfection, which was, he said, to be realized in this lifetime. But she was not convinced.

Andrea delivered her speech at nine on Wednesday morning at a final reception in her honor which was over by noon. Matters of business concluded to Andrea's satisfaction, she made her way to the shopping district before her scheduled departure from Hong Kong.

The abundance of imitation haute couture in Hong Kong never ceased to amaze her. There were so many fakes that legitimate merchandisers had to have a license of authenticity displayed in their shop windows. Any designer imitation to be found was here in the shopping district of Kowloon. There was also exquisite shopping that could be done in Hong Kong if one wanted to expend the time and energy. Andrea much preferred the ambiance of Paris or Milan shops.

Finally, tired of the noise and confusion, she made her way back to the Peninsula Hotel which contained over sixty exclusive shops. She enjoyed walking through the five levels of shops in the hotel where she picked out a silk scarf for Janice, a Chanel purse for Linda and a silk kimono for Melissa, and was very tempted to buy a fat pompous-looking silver Buddha for Scott, but resisted the impulse.

She regretted that she did not have time to purchase more porcelain. On her last visit she had acquired several prized pieces of Oriental porcelain that were among the favorite items in her apartment. She wished she had time to add to that collection. At two o'clock she left the hotel for the airport.

Andrea always arrived at the airport an hour earlier than necessary. She liked browsing in the airport bookstores for in-flight reading material. It was relaxing for her to read the latest celebrity gossip magazines and trashy tabloids. She made a point never to do business while flying, and though she always carried her laptop computer with her, it was more a psychological crutch than anything else, useful for carrying her exotic reading material..

As she strolled into the bookstore to purchase every tabloid in sight, she glimpsed the latest metaphysical book by Shirley MacLaine. In light of her talks with Scott and the Oriental fortune teller, she was curious and decided to buy the book. She was surprised at how often the thought of Scott drifted into her mind. Why was she thinking of him? She was never going to see him again, and now that her fleeting desire for him had quenched itself, she was back to hating the pompous, self- centered ass.

Chapter 21

It was well past seven o'clock the following evening when Andrea finally took the elevator to her apartment. She was back on familiar turf. Suddenly lonely, she found herself wishing there was a man to come home to, but a woman of her status had to be careful of the people she trusted, and Andrea trusted no one. Strangely, she wanted to call Scott. Instead she called Melissa.

Andrea's home in the Trump Towers was magnificent. Alex had bought three apartments on the twenty-fifth floor and had them converted into one huge apartment, complete with a spa, gourmet kitchen, beauty salon. Andrea's personal fitness trainer came every morning at five-thirty and her beautician came three mornings a week following her workouts. The maids came in daily because Melissa was the only person Andrea wanted close by after Alex died. Andrea had purchased an apartment for Melissa one level up and had an intercom system installed so they could talk when Melissa was not downstairs.

The spacious apartment reflected every aspect of Andrea's

personality. Her private elevator opened into a large foyer inlaid with black and white Italian marble. A Van Gogh, three Picassos and two Matisse paintings lined the long hallway which opened onto a spectacular living room with one of the most breathtaking views in New York. Two walls of the living room were glass, and at night when the curtains were pulled back Andrea felt she could walk straight into the sky over the majestic city. The vaulted room was light and airy, decorated with all white furniture. Oriental rugs in peach, gray, blues and green, were accented with accessories of the same shades of pastel. It was a fairytale living room. Several of Dali's numbered lithographs, top-lighted original Impressionist oil paintings and other objets d'art from all over the world enhanced the oyster walls, each looking as if they belonged there.

Andrea's eyes went involuntarily to the painting over the fireplace. For a moment she stood staring into the familiar face. Money, fame, success, he had told her she would have it all. But she would have given everything up to be with him. Life had no meaning without someone to share it with. Oh how true were the words spoken in *Les Miserables*: "To love another person is to see the face of God." And to her he had always had the face of God. As much as she loved him she knew their destiny had been sealed.

Andrea shifted her gaze to the empty silver frame on the mantel and unexpected tears ran silently down her cheeks. "Oh my darling," she whispered, holding the frame close to her heart "please, please forgive me."

Dropping her purse on a velvet chair in the hall, Andrea kicked off her shoes and walked into the kitchen. The oak floors felt cool under her feet. Cabinets of the same golden oak as the floor gleamed under the recessed ceiling lights illuminating the room. She opened a corner breakfront and removed a balloon snifter which she proceeded to fill half full of amber Grand Marnier. Brandy in hand she moved to the expanse of glass, a floor to ceiling kitchen wall framed in polished oak, to watch the colors of the setting sun reflected in the windows of Manhattan's East Side buildings and on the East River. It was a panoramic view. The teeming city lay beneath her, its noisy chaos silenced by the glass walls of her apartment. My own glass menagerie, she thought, I'm living in a make-believe world. Shrugging off the oppressive thought, she poured herself another generous amount of brandy. Sipping it, she closed her eyes as the liquid warmed her insides. Suddenly she felt so isolated that she wanted to cry. When Alex was alive she had someone to come home to, and if anyone could understand what she was feeling, he could. It was true that at times during her marriage she had yearned for the touch of a man she could love wildly, but she had always welcomed Alex's solid, considerate friendship, remembering that passion, lust and wild abandon destroyed lives more often than it had created happiness. And of all people, what right did she have to deserve passion?

Andrea tried to shake the emptiness she was feeling. She rationalized that in addition to the anticlimax of the trip to Hong Kong where she had finalized the biggest business deal in Jacobson's history, she was probably having a bad case of mid-life crisis. Andrea picked up the phone and dialed Melissa to tell her she was home and then phoned Boston to talk to her sister Stephanie. Stephanie with her "in your face!" attitude would soon cheer her up. The phone rang several times before the answering device clicked on.

"Dammit, Steph, where are you?" she said loudly to the tape, "I'm practically having a nervous breakdown and you're not there to listen to me whine. It's unforgivable. Actually I just got in and I probably just have the blahs from jet lag. Oh yes, I must tell you about a man I had dinner with before I left, but don't call me tonight because I'm going straight to bed."

Andrea poured herself another brandy and made her way back to living room, pressed the button on her answering machine and flopped down on the exquisite Henredon couch to listen to her messages. She heard a voice that snapped her back to reality.

"Hello Andrea, this is Scott Preston, I'm hoping you're back in town and wondered if you would care to be my guest at a party I'm giving on Friday. I know you're wondering how I got your telephone number, but that was the easy part. Don't be too annoyed."

Andrea was not in the least bit annoyed; she was elated. This was the first time in years that anyone besides her family or her secretary had called her private number. Certainly no man did. Her lovers did not have her home number; she called them when their services were needed, and maintained an apartment on Central Park West for that purpose only.

"Please call me at home or at the office and let me know if you can make it," the soothing voice continued. He had a wonderful voice, she thought, strong, deliberate and comforting. Andrea involuntarily brought her hand up to her firm breast. Her body was hot, her nipples tingled under her touch and she felt a warm glow that was not from the brandy; it was either passion, lust, desire or simply madness. Andrea decided it was madness. She must try to forget him. She would not call Scott Preston.

There was a long pause, and as she was about to reset the tape another voice began speaking.

"Andrea this is Maya." Andrea stiffened. "I wonder if you would call me. I would like to speak with you." As the eerie voice went on to give her a phone number in England, Andrea panicked. Shaking, she dropped the glass of brandy on the carpet leaving a large brown stain on the rug. She played the message over and over again trying to determine from the tone of Maya's voice, what could possibly have happened, yet she could detect nothing. Maya sounded calm and matter-of-fact. There was no sense of urgency in her voice. But something must be wrong because Maya had not called her once in the twelve years since she had left England, nor in the thirteen years since she had given birth to the child Maya told her had been named Helen.

Andrea felt ill. If something had happened to her daughter, she wouldn't be able to stand it. Her secret dream was of encountering the girl one day. It had taken years to control her desire to find Helen; she had done everything in her power to forget the horrible night she lost her daughter to the mystical unexplainable Maya.

She had received occasional brief notes from Maya mailed from London concerning Helen's growing up and her progress in school, but there were no photographs and no return address. She had no idea what Helen looked like or where she was, but she pictured her to be lithe and graceful with dark olive skin, jet black hair, long dark lashes framing dark brown eyes, and high smooth cheeks. She visualized Helen's wavy hair blowing in the wind or tied in a bun with lace, as she gracefully danced as a prodigy ballerina. She could see the widening of her expressive eyes as she tried to remember her lines in her first school play; but she could also see those large sad brown eyes staring at her accusingly, hating her for what she had done.

Andrea felt the sting of salty tears on her cheeks. She had never told anyone of Helen's existence, not even Melissa. What would she do now if something were wrong with Helen? There would be a scandal if the truth about her illegitimate child were to come out. What would the world think of Andrea Jacobson, the cowardly mother who they would assume had abandoned her child in favor of fortune and fame? The public would never forgive her and Jacobson's Industry would be forever tainted.

Maya had said when the mysterious people had taken her baby away, "In time you will be able to accept and understand this, Andrea. This child is special. Allow us to take care of her. She must develop her powers for the good of mankind and we are the only ones who can help her do that."

"Oh Helen," Andrea whispered, now standing in front of the empty silver frame. "Please be all right."

Just then Melissa came into the room. She hurried over to Andrea who looked as if she had seen a ghost. "What is it, Andrea?" she asked, noticing the brandy glass that lay on the carpet, its spilled contents making a widening stain.

"Nothing Mel, I'm sorry I disturbed you. All of a sudden I feel very tired. We'll talk tomorrow."

Once she had persuaded Melissa to leave, Andrea paced back and forth for an hour. She looked at her watch. It was already ten o'clock. It would be three in the morning in England. She would try to get some sleep and call when she woke up. What was it the Buddhist fortune teller had said? Turmoil very soon. Andrea shuddered.

Tired, depressed, and quite tipsy, she left her Chanel suit in a heap on the floor and sat at her dressing table methodically removing her makeup, cleansing her face with a Clinique scrub and applying clarifying lotion. She refused to give in to superstition or Buddhist hocus pocus! She glanced briefly at the red puffy circles under her eyes. Then, exhausted, she climbed between the cool satin sheets and prayed that sleep would come quickly. But the long hours of travel and the brandies did not dull her anxiety. She dozed fitfully. It was a long night.

In the morning Andrea had a severe headache, but she crawled out of bed at five o'clock and pulled on a leotard to get ready for her exercise routine thinking it might help, although she was not sure if she could stand Paul's ruthless routine this morning. His deep voice echoed in her pounding head, "Come on, Andrea, bend, no not like that, like this. Stretch and hold. Further, further. The key to life is taut muscles and flat abs," Paul would shout as she strenuously willed her body into shape.

At thirty-five she still had the body of an eighteen-year-old. This morning, however, Andrea looked at herself in the mirror and gasped. She looked forty! She made her way to the kitchen and poured herself a glass of tomato juice, then returned with it to the bathroom and examined the puffiness and the lines at the corners of her eyes. She skillfully applied makeup which covered the lines, but did little else to improve her appearance or the way she felt.

Andrea sat wearily on the side of her bed. She was tempted to get back in bed but she knew that would make only matters worse. She had to go to the office where she would have something to occupy her time. In bed she would only have nightmares. Andrea looked at her watch: five twenty-five. Her heart pounding, she dialed the number in England. There was no answer. The intercom in her bedroom buzzed.

"Andrea, I forgot to tell you last night, Paul called to say he could not come in this morning because his wife went into premature labor last evening. Do you want me to get a substitute?"

"No Mel, that's all right. I'm actually glad he can't make it today. I'm exhausted. I think I'll go back to bed for an hour or two. Call Janice, would you, and let her know that I won't get to the office until around nine."

For years, seven-fifteen was the latest Andrea had ever gotten to her office and in those years she had never missed a day unless she was traveling on business. For the last four years, however, she had curtailed most of her traveling, preferring to send one of her senior associates.

"So how was the trip?" Melissa continued on the other end of the line.

"Too long, but interesting. I went to a psychic. Darling, come down at seven-thirty and have breakfast with me, will you? I'll tell you all about the trip then."

"Very well, dear, I will see you then."

Melissa let herself into the apartment at seven and going directly to the kitchen, made a light breakfast of toast, poached eggs, orange juice and coffee for herself and Andrea. She put the breakfast on a rolling table and wheeled it into Andrea's bedroom.

"Good morning, child. You look positively awful," she said, drawing the curtains back to let the daylight in.

"Good morning," Andrea said, kissing Melissa's wrinkled cheek. "Thank you so much for that comment. That was all I needed to hear, and do let me assure you that I feel as badly as you think I look."

"This black coffee should perk you up a bit."

Andrea nodded and winced. The pain in her head was brutal.

Melissa knew better than to pry into Andrea's affairs, yet she knew something was very wrong. She had known Andrea far too long not to be able to read her like a book. She handed Andrea a steaming cup of black coffee.

"I have made you a healthy breakfast that you will eat," she ordered, "Enough of that cottage cheese stuff, what you need are some good old fashioned eggs."

Andrea nearly gagged. "I couldn't eat a thing."

"Some toast might help that hangover, Andrea," Melissa cautioned, "Please dear, if something is wrong, you know that I will always be there for you when you are ready to talk about it, but I cannot stand by and see you kill yourself with work and alcohol. Andy, it is time to confront what has been ailing you all these years.

"Well now," she said, dropping the lecturing tone, "tell me what happened with the psychic."

"I was curious about this New Age religion Scott Preston talked about during dinner. He said it has its origin in Eastern culture, so I went to a Buddhist temple in Hong Kong. My Chinese assistant took me there and translated. This spiritual teacher, the high priest of the gathering, told my future. It was quite an elaborate ritual, Melissa, I couldn't enter the temple until I removed my shoes and washed my hands."

"I can understand the shoes, but what does washing the hands have to do with anything?"

"It signifies you are cleansing yourself of your worldly impurities. Once inside, we burned incense and chanted mantras. It was a wonderful experience, really. I felt completely at one with everything around me. Anyway, after the gathering, he told me that I was some sort of special person and I'm destined to be a master, but like my mother, I've been resisting the calling." Andrea laughed aloud, "I didn't tell him that I was already master of a billion dollar empire and that as far as I knew my mother's only calling was her AT&T calling card."

Melissa could see that Andrea's eyes were not laughing and sadness hung like a black cloud in the room.

"He told me that my life will soon be in turmoil," Andrea continued. "Well, it appears he was right. I can't explain it now, Mel, but one day I will."

Melissa listened but she did not say a word. It did not surprise her. She knew that Andrea had always been a special child. Even the magnitude of her accomplishments was being orchestrated by divine intervention, Melissa was convinced.

"At least your life will not be boring. Everyone needs challenges now and then and I am sure, Andrea, you will rise to any that is presented. I have never yet seen you fail to do so."

"Thank you, darling," Andrea squeezed her friend's hand. "You always make me feel so much better. Now," she said biting into her toast, "I am going to get ready for work."

Andrea changed into her swimsuit and swam six laps in the heated pool off the workout room, then showered quickly and dressed in an cream Adolfo suit. She could not possibly wear anything dark today, not with the circles beneath her bloodshot eyes. Had she not been so late already, she would have walked the ten blocks to her office hoping the crisp winter air would do her some good. Instead she hopped into the back of her waiting limousine, glad she did not have to negotiate the Manhattan traffic herself.

At nine o'clock, she stepped hurriedly from the elevator and marched down the marbled corridor, her heels making an awful clicking noise that was an insult to the pounding in her head. She had never noticed the sound before, but it was not every day that she came to work hung over and wearing dark glasses to hide her eyes. She would have the corridor carpeted. Inside her office Andrea took off her dark glasses and squeezed two drops of Murine in each eye, feeling like an addict trying to conceal the evidence of a binge. She poured herself another cup of steaming black coffee from the silver thermos pitcher on her desk and again dialed the number that Maya had left. Still there was no answer. Something had to be wrong.

The shrillness of the telephone ring made Andrea cringe in pain. She reached over and turned down the intrusive bell. Finally she picked up the receiver holding it as far away as possible from her ear.

"Yes Janice?"

"Dr. Preston is on the line for you Mrs. Jacobson, he has been calling for two days now," Janice announced.

"Please tell Dr. Preston that I am not available. Tell him I am still in Hong Kong. If you can't lie, then tell him I died. That wouldn't be lying because today I am absolutely dead. Janice, I can't deal with Dr. Preston right now."

"Very well, Mrs. Jacobson." Janice was perplexed. Andrea Jacobson was not in the habit of avoiding anyone. Not this way.

Andrea sat staring at the walls of her office. She had not accomplished anything all day. She simply could not concentrate. She wished to God that this introspective period of her life would pass quickly so she could go back to living the way she always had, uncomplicated. Well, if not uncomplicated, she retracted, she had certainly been capable of denial. Either way, it was just the way she liked it.

It seemed all of her misbegotten past was catching up with her. What had happened to her in thirty-five years of living did not happen to most people in a lifetime. She had fallen in love, had a child, broken many hearts, and killed a lover, all before she had turned twenty-two. She was never quite sure if she had ever really been happy. Her happiness had been so short-lived that it seemed more like a dream rather than a real part of her life. Why, she wondered, did people have to fall in love? Love, Andrea finally concluded, was the root of all evil. All her love had done for her was cause pain and entangle her in the lives of too many people. She was like a black widow spider: she mated and then killed.

Andrea slammed her fist on the desk. She was never going to let Scott Preston into her life, and that was final. His presence was the last thing she needed right now.

Andrea dialed her sister Stephanie and hung up when the machine came on. She walked around her office trying to block out the sense of doom. Andrea's gloomy feeling that her world was about to collapse persisted. In fact, she was sure her glass menagerie, make-believe life was about to shatter into millions of little pieces. "*Humpty Dumpty sat on a wall, Humpty Dumpty had a great fall...*" the childhood nursery rhyme kept running through her mind.

Why did she have to do that damned television interview? It was the first bad omen. Had she not gone against her intuition, she would never have met the provocative Scott Preston who kept surfacing in her mind—nor blurted out her past to Rachel Hersey. Her world would have remained emotionally dormant and predictable, just as she had arranged it.

Andrea pulled a leather-bound notebook from her desk drawer, determined to write the long overdue speech to the employees of Jacobson's Industry explaining the merger. Try as she might, she could neither focus nor concentrate. She closed the notebook and rocked back in her chair, chewing mercilessly on the end of a perfectly good fountain pen. She bit harder and harder into it until the expensive Mont Blanc pen was ruined.

Why, continued her hysterical thoughts, had she been so stupid? She should have known that Maya would surface again. She had been such a naive fool. But when she thought about it, it all made sense. "Oh God, dear God," she said aloud, "if I have to pay the price of my own negligence, I am willing to do so, but why now," she argued, "when I am at the peak of my career?" Immediately Andrea realized how silly she must sound praying and pleading to a God she had turned her back on nineteen years before. Her pleading turned to anger at everything and everyone who came to mind: she was angry at Scott Preston for making her feel physical desire again; angry at Maya for forcing her to have a child she couldn't keep and who after all these years was about to disrupt her life; angry for having consented to an interview and furious with that Hersey bitch for tricking her; and she was angry that she had been so silly as to mention her passionate love at thirteen. And Adam. She was truly angry at Adam. In fact she blamed him for everything. Adam, the one and only love of her lifetime; her love for him had been the best thing that ever happened to her and now that love was about to destroy her. Why had he ever come into her life? Why did he take away her childhood?

She had been a happy child, carefree, headstrong, inquisitive and bright. She had every reason to succeed, and in spite of Scott Preston's theory, she did not need trauma to motivate her. She had a loving family, an absolutely wonderful family. "Then why is all this happening to me?" Andrea screamed, becoming hysterical. She was losing control; even more than that, she was losing her sanity. She felt so alone, but worse, so horribly lonely. She needed to talk with someone she could trust, someone who would not expect her to be the Rock of Gibraltar, someone she loved. There was only one person. She had to call Adam. He was her very life, he would not expect her to be more than she was. With him she could be the child again who needed only his love to be happy.

She had been happy with Adam. It was he and not the abundance of her accomplishments that had brought the rare moments of happiness into her life. Her heart softened at the thought of Adam. How could she ever be angry with him? She had never stopped loving Adam, not for one day, not for one moment. If life had worked out for them, their marriage would have been as passionate as it would have been chaotic, as alterable as it would have been committed.

Even after her marriage to Alex, she wrote to Adam, but he never answered any of her letters. For months during her pregnancy she had been tempted to tell him about the baby. She had fantasized that he would marry her and take her away from the insanity she was enduring; but she knew in her heart that nothing would change. She knew it would never be possible for them to be man and wife because Adam was already married—to the bottle. Maybe Scott Preston was right after all. Her success might have originated from an attempt to bury the past.

For once Andrea Jacobson, the tower of strength, felt helpless because she was not in control of whatever was about to happen in her life. Yes, she would call Adam and she would tell him about Helen. With her resolve to call Adam she felt better. Her peace did not last very long, her mind continued racing anxiously.

"You will experience much turmoil," she could hear the wizened psychic saying, "but it will all be for the best." She bloody well hoped so after all the torment she was feeling. But of course, Andrea consoled herself, that silly fortune teller back in Hong Kong could not be right about her impending disasters. After all, she was Andrea Jacobson, untouchable. In spite of the turn her life had taken, she argued, what was happening to her was merely coincidental and nothing was going to get her involved in metaphysical theory. She, Andrea Jacobson, was too smart a woman to get involved with all that weird New Age hocus pocus.

Chapter 22

Jamaica

He hated the hospital. His father had died here. They had told him his father had succumbed to a heart condition, but even at fourteen, he knew better: his father drank himself to death, just as he was doing.

Though he felt betrayed by him, Adam had loved his father deeply and there had been some good times with him. His mother had remarried barely six months after she divorced his father, and Adam was so angry, that had it not been for his twin brother Raymond, his childhood would have been unbearable. Isabelle had become so wrapped up in her new husband and her new life that she had forgotten her children existed. All Adam could remember of family life were the vacations in Europe where he saw more of his nanny than his mother or stepfather. Adam and his brother had become inseparable not just because they were twins but because they were each other's strength. They were attuned to one another that they could always tell what the other was thinking even when

Adam was in boarding school in Switzerland.

Even weak and debilitated, Adam Stern was a handsome man. He flirted with all the nurses, who were happy to get any attention from him. It appeared to nearly everyone that he had everything to live for, yet he had wasted his life on women and alcohol. His life, people said, read like the adventures of Don Juan. Of the numerous stories about him, that part was true. As far back as Adam could recall, he enjoyed women; he loved their passion, their submissiveness and even their anger once they found out he was a scoundrel.

Although he had messed up most of his life, he had done one thing right: He loved Andrea Francis. The rest of his life, he had to admit, was not a pretty picture. By twenty-eight his overt addiction to women and alcohol had caused the failure of his marriage, trashed his academic career, and alienated him from the two children that he had left as infants. He had not seen his children in the nineteen years since he had deserted his family in the States and gone back to Jamaica. He was a wealthy man, but he had given up on finding happiness. And all of his problems he blamed on his mother for not loving him and his father for dying.

Then he had met Andrea Francis, no more than a child and yet she had made him want to love again. As if it were predestined, it was not a love he could control, but how he could be so captured by a mere child nearly twenty years his junior was a question he had never answered to his own satisfaction. After Andrea left Jamaica the last time, he nursed his wounds with the bottle and as many women as he could handle. Now here he was with tubes in his arm and down his nose. Helpless as a babe.

He wished he had lived his life differently. He wished he had had the courage to accept responsibilities instead of pretending they never existed. Life was cruel; it had a way of evening the score and never letting you get away with much. He wished Andrea were there with him. He had done an unselfish thing when he made her go and of that he was proud. He had tried so hard not to interfere with her life. As many times as he had wanted to contact her, he had exercised restrain. He had never answered any of her letters; he never knew what to say.

Well, Adam Stern, he thought, your time is running out and you have to stop being a coward. He had been drinking heavily again, he knew, to hide what he had suspected all along, that he was a coward. He was proud of Andrea. She had become everything he thought she would. A tear escaped, ran down his face and onto his silk pajamas. He did not bother to hide his grief when the nurse came into the room. He was crying for all the things he should have done and hadn't.

"It is time for your medication, Mr. Stern," the nurse said rolling him over on his side.

"You are going to poke me with that needle again?" he said as light-heartedly as he could.

"Just a tiny prick," she replied sweetly as the needle disappeared into his leg. "Now that did not hurt, did it?"

"Not much, but I could think of better things you could do to me," he said touching her hand lightly.

"You are an incurably dirty man," she laughed as she turned away. Adam tried to get back to a sitting position. Just then a wave of coughing erupted and blood spewed from his mouth as though a tap had burst. He felt faint and it dawned on him that he was going to die.

The nurse rang the emergency buzzer and within minutes the room was full of doctors and nurses.

He had to see Andrea once more. He had to see her soon or it would be too late. At fifty-five he was dying, and the only pleasure he had ever known were the times he spent with Andrea.

"Send for her," he whispered.

"Who, Mr. Stern?"

"Andrea."

"Ms. Jacobson," Janice came into her office with a worried look on her face, "an urgent telegram has arrived for you. The mailman will only deliver it to you personally."

Andrea's knuckles were bloodless as she gripped the desk for support. She was visibly shaken as she walked across the room to sign for the telegram. Back at her desk she sat looking at the envelope for what seemed like hours. She could not bring herself to open it. Oh God! she thought, if something has happened to Helen she would never be able to live with the guilt of not seeing her child just once.

Finally, unable to put off the inevitable any longer, Andrea tore the envelope open with trembling hands. She had not noticed that the envelope was from Jamaica and not England.

"COME AT ONCE STOP ADAM CRITICAL STOP NOT EXPECTED TO LIVE STOP RAYMOND"

Andrea covered her face with her hands and sobbed uncontrollably. Janice, hearing crying coming from Andrea's office hurried in. She had never seen Andrea Jacobson give in to any emotions and she was horrified by the sight of this powerhouse of a woman reduced to tears. Janice poured Andrea some brandy, made her take a sip and held her until she was quiet. When Andrea had regained some control, she told Janice to make arrangements for her private jet to fly to Jamaica immediately. She would not go home to pack, she would buy whatever she needed there.

Within an hour Andrea boarded the Boeing 747. The plush charcoal gray carpet with the interwoven JI logo felt soft under her feet. The attendant fixed his boss her usual brandy. Andrea buckled her seat belt and instructed the attendant to tell the pilot to take off as soon as he was cleared. She removed her dark glasses and dug in her purse for a cigarette.

"Is there anything else I can do for you, Miss Jacobson?" the flight attendant asked.

"No thank you," Andrea answered, "I'll be fine." As tired as Andrea was, however, she could not relax. She closed her eyes but her thoughts were coming a mile a minute. If only she had never left him she chided herself, they could have been happy. She should never have listened to him about the wonderful life that was awaiting her, about her destiny. Look where his wisdom had gotten him. He had wanted her to reach for the sky, but now she had everything and was she miserable. She would trade it all for the sight of a man she loved and trusted coming through her door. She had fantasized about what life with another human being might have been like, where emotions were mutual, someone who was always nearby. Andrea had been thankful she had her work because by morning the loneliness was replaced with another million dollar deal that gave her temporary satisfaction.

Four hours later the plane landed in Montego Bay. As usual it took Andrea just fifteen minutes to clear customs and be on her way. Andrea dialed Raymond's office number. Identical twins, Raymond and Adam had played tricks on her for months after she had started dating Adam because she had difficulty telling them apart.

"Andrea!" Raymond said sounding exactly like his brother, "I am so glad you got my telegram. When are you arriving?"

"I am at the Montego Bay airport, I flew down as soon as I could."

"I will be right over to pick you up."

"Never mind, Raymond, I have a cottage at the Half Moon and I'll take a cab there. Why don't you meet me there in an hour? How is Adam?" she said, bracing herself and trying to remain calm.

"He is holding his own—but why don't I tell you about it when I see you."

In the lobby of the hotel, Andrea asked to have someone from the boutique sent to her room with clothing in her size. Realizing she had to keep up her strength, Andrea also ordered and tried to eat some food, but pushed her plate away. She waited nervously for Raymond. Then Andrea remembered that she had not placed the call to England and knew she was not going to because she could not take another emotional beating right now.

Scott Preston was certain he would have heard from Andrea by now, but Andrea Jacobson had proved to be totally unpredictable. Every time he called her office, her secretary said she was unavailable. He assumed she was trying to avoid him. Well, he was not giving up so easily. He wanted to get to know this woman and he would—in time.

"Janice, is Ms. Jacobson in her office?" Jonathan asked, distraught, looking at the paper in front of him.

"No Mr. Buckley, she asked me to give you this."

Jonathan glanced hastily over the flight log then hurried back to his office. Impatiently he punched out a number on the keypad and spoke quietly and hurriedly to the party on the other line.

Chapter 23

"My God, Andrea," Raymond said, hugging her, "you look wonderful. How long has it been?"

"Fifteen years, Raymond, and you have not changed a bit. You look wonderful yourself. Would you like a drink?"

He released her and looked down at her, "I don't drink. I can't believe what drinking has done to my brother. If only I had been able to get him to stop."

Andrea put a hand on his shoulder. "You can't blame yourself for Adam's behavior. We each attract to us experiences in our lives that we must learn from in order to continue to grow." Andrea wondered where all that bullshit she was talking was coming from. "Raymond," she continued softly, "Is he going to die?"

"I think so. He has an esophageal varices that has been bleeding for the last forty-two hours. They have been transfusing into him as much blood as he has been losing. If the bleeding does not stop—but over the last few hours he seems to have stabilized a bit."

"I'd like to see him now."

They climbed into the olive green Range Rover and headed toward the hospital. Andrea had not been in a hospital in twelve years and her past experience as a nurse seemed so much like a dream that it surprised her how much she still understood when she spoke with Adam's attending physician.

His room was spacious and light, looking more like a hotel suite than a hospital room. Flowers and cards were everywhere. Adam was relaxed, reading a book, looking as though he was on vacation. She stood at the door and watched him. He was dying, she could tell. It was inevitable. The gray hands of death were closing in.

"I hope that is one of my letters that you intend to answer," she said quietly, moving fully into view. Adam looked at her from sunken eyes and for a moment she was not sure he even recognized her. A single tear rolled down his face. Andrea's heart felt the jolt of the full force of love that she had always felt for this man. Even in his condition, he was the most handsome man she had ever seen. She moved over to the bed and rested her face against his cheek. He moved an arm hampered by IV tubes around her shoulder.

"I'm home," she said softly, her tears mixing with his.

"I knew you would come," he said quietly, "you are the love of my life and the love of my death—my eternity."

"Please don't talk like that," Andrea pleaded, "We are going to get through this together." He wished he could believe her.

"How long will you be here, Andrea?" he said, not sure if he wanted to hear the answer.

"For as long as you want me here," she said, as every other responsibility vanished from her thoughts.

"Move over, darling," she said, "I want to get into bed with you".

"The nurses won't like that, you know, apart from the fact that they want to keep my blood pressure down, they are all in love with me and will be very jealous."

"Since when have I ever had to worry about other women? Our love was made in heaven. What God has joined together let no woman put asunder," she smiled. "Anyway you may not know this, but when I make up my mind about something, it is as good as done, and you, my pet, are spoken for."

Adam smiled wearily. "No one could ever have taken your place," he said softly.

"And no one has ever taken yours," Andrea said, resting her head on his shoulder. "I love you," she whispered, and the tears came flooding down her face.

Raymond watched them from the doorway, knowing they had forgotten he was there. He had never seen a love so strong. To have endured so many years of pain and so many disappointments. He was glad Andrea had come. Now his brother would rest in peace.

Andrea had another bed put in Adam's room and moved into the hospital. Everything she had learned about nursing in the Stougborough Infirmary came back to her. Once a nurse always a nurse, she thought. And no matter what it took, she was determined to be Adam's only nurse. Her well-known single-minded stubbornness prevailed. Her home in New York, her brilliant successes, her business maneuvers, Jacobson's Industry itself, all were forgotten. She was a nurse now. And she was nursing the only man she had ever loved.

It was the beginning of March, a beautiful day in Jamaica, and instead of reading the book in her lap, she found herself staring out the window. It was a perfect day for lovers to stroll hand in hand, giggling and proclaiming their undying love. She longed to share another day like this doing those things with Adam. Although she tried so hard to deny it, the knowledge of his illness kept rearing its ugly head. She glanced over at Adam. He was sleeping peacefully, his chest moving up and down in perfect rhythm. Brilliant sunlight bathed him in its healing glow. Today his skin had lost its gray tinge, his complexion was much healthier than it had been. Since her arrival, Adam's spirits improved daily, but much as he tried to be jovial and mischievous, Andrea could not avoid the fact that he was gravely ill. She moved her chair closer to his bed, wanting to feel his warm breath on her face. It was a sensation that comforted her.

"Ms. Jacobson," the nurse came into the room, "Dr. Jones would like to speak with you."

Noiselessly, Andrea gathered the progress chart and her notes on Adam. She flinched as the bushes outside Adam's window rustled. She could have sworn she saw someone. Ah, she shrugged, tiredness. Quickly she recollected her nerves and followed the nurse, walking briskly down the long corridor. The nurse's freshly starched white uniform, stiff cap and peppy walk, brought back some good memories of her school years in England, years that now seemed a millennia away.

"Good afternoon, Ms. Jacobson," Dr. Jones greeted her from behind his modest desk, standing as she entered the room. They shook hands as he continued, "I am so glad to finally meet you. I've been away for the last few days, but I'm sure Dr. Roberts has filled you in on Mr. Stern's condition."

"Yes he has, and I must add that he has done a wonderful job of taking care of Adam, doctor, but I've been thinking. The Mayo Clinic specializes in the condition that affects Adam. I spoke with Dr. Shiperio in Minnesota this morning and he feels that an esophageal bypass should help. What do you think about transferring him there?"

"I think it would be very risky to move him right now. He has lost a lot of blood. It would not be safe to transfer him."

"When will it be safe? He looks much better."

"I am not sure. Yes, he is making progress, but the slightest stress could cause another rupture. Why don't you start taking him on short daily walks? If he does well we can increase his activities until he is strong enough to travel."

"Very well, Dr. Jones," Andrea said, extending her hand, "Thank you. I'll keep you informed of his progress."

Each day at dusk, when the heat of the sun had subsided, Andrea and Adam went on short walks around the hospital compound. This was not easy to orchestrate because all the tubes leading from the portable IV had to be in concert with his movements. But they managed.

"Let's stay out a little while longer," Adam said, as Andrea prepared to return to the hospital room. "I look forward to these walks, you know. They make me feel that I am a part of the world again. I hate being cooped up as an invalid."

"Darling, you are not an invalid, but I don't think we should overdo it."

"Well, let's just sit outside and talk. It can't be any more dangerous than sitting in that bed waiting for my bedsores to start acting up."

"You exaggerate so much," Andrea kissed him on the cheek, "But you're right, it's too nice an evening to stay inside. So, Adam Stern, what do you want to talk about?"

"I want to talk about you. Tell me Andy, why is it that you never mention the years you spent in England?"

"What do you mean? I never talk about New York, either."

"That's true but your company is forever in the paper and from that I can at least guess what you are doing. I feel shut out of your time in England. Tell me, darling, about the missing years."

Andrea was naturally hesitant about discussing this topic with Adam. Since his horrible reaction so many years before over the men he had questioned her about, she was not sure it was a good idea to talk about this now.

"You have to promise to be objective about this," she

cautioned, "Remember what happened the last time we attempted this discussion."

"Scout's honor," he said, raising his hand, "Oh Andrea, I hope to God you have forgiven me for that night. I was insane with jealousy."

"When I left Jamaica, when the family moved to New York the first time," she said, "I was heartbroken. I couldn't sleep or eat. I could barely function. All I did was pray that somehow we would be reunited again soon. After six months of major depression, mother decided that traveling through Europe with my sister might be a good tonic. For a while that's exactly what I did, but when I got to England it felt so familiar because mother and father always told us stories of England where they had both gone to school, that I decided I would go to school there too. For the first six months in Stougborough I was very lonely, then I met this man. His smile reminded me of you. It seemed that I would only date men that reminded me of you, but, Adam, they could never be you, so one after the other they fell by the wayside. Adam, I spent two years trying to recreate what we had and couldn't. Finally, I just resigned myself to unhappiness."

Andrea stopped for a moment. She found that she could not tell him about Ralph. And she couldn't tell him about Helen. "I graduated from nursing school, and went back to New York, where I decided I wanted to get into business management instead of medicine, and finally I graduated from the Wharton School of Business. Remember, you told me I would be successful in business? Well, then I began working at Jacobson's Industry right out of college, and eventually I married Alex. The rest, as they say, is history."

"Did you love Alex?"

"I respected him. And yes, I loved him, but I felt no passion for him. He hired me because he believed in me and he taught me everything I know. I was happy with Alex. He allowed me to find a part of myself I didn't know existed." She told him of her progression to power and wealth after Alex died.

Adam listened, fascinated. His little girl had turned into a sophisticated and very wealthy woman. As much as he had agonized over their separation, he was positive now that he had done the right thing.

"And what about you, darling, did you ever replace me?" Andrea asked, raising her eyes to Adam.

He chuckled, his gaze fixed on the beautiful woman beside him, the woman who was once his protégée.

"I did replace you, Andy." Andrea's heart went numb. "But not with other women. I don't need to tell you with what," he said, "that's the reason I am here."

"Adam, that's enough. We're not going to talk about what should have been, nor are we going to talk anymore about the past," Andrea said firmly. "The only thing that matters now is the present and the future."

"Andrea," he said, turning her to face him, "there is no future." She began to protest but he put a finger to her lips.

"It is no use denying the inevitable, Andrea, and I don't want to spend what little time we have left concealing anything. I've done that all of my life.

"There is something important that I want to tell you. I have wanted to tell you for years but I never found the courage. I couldn't admit my failures. When I came back to Jamaica I left my wife and two infant children in Washington, DC." Shocked, Andrea started to say something, but preoccupied with his confession, Adam went on.

"I loved to drink. I went to my own wedding drunk. Drinking was fun, but I have no idea when it stopped being fun and became a necessity. When my father died I saw it as a chance to escape from my family; for a long time my wife did not even know where I was. I never told her about my father's death. I haven't seen my children since. I wanted to marry you, but marriage scared me. I could never tell you I was already a failure and a drunk when we met. Andrea, I loved you so much the only thing I could do for you was to let you go. You had your whole life before you and I knew that I had nothing to offer you. I am sorry, darling, for all the pain that I have caused you, but I think letting you go was the most unselfish thing I've ever done. Now I feel God has given me the opportunity to redeem myself in your eyes."

Dazed at his revelation, Andrea tightened her grip on his arm. Never would she have even dreamed that Adam had been married, let alone had children. It was impossible that they could have been so close yet not know everything about each other.

"I needed to say this Andy, I couldn't die with this on my conscience."

Catching her breath, she said quietly, "I'm glad you were finally able to share this with me."

"My first wish was granted. You're here," he continued sadly, "If God granted me another wish, I would ask to see my children, I would ask them to forgive me for not having been there for them, for not even wanting to be there," he said, "I chose to be selfish."

"My darling," Andrea said, closing her fingers around his, "don't be so hard on yourself. Your running away might have been selfish, but it was something you had to do, and if you had not, we would never have met. And Adam, our love was meant to be."

"Andrea, I can always count on you to understand."

"You know," she said, "I'm sure that God will grant you this wish. God listens. All you have to do is ask. Go ahead darling, Just close your eyes and ask."

Andrea watched as Adam looked up at the sky.

After awhile he said, "On the night that we met, the stars were in this exact arrangement. My wish came true then and I hope it comes true tonight. What do you wish for Andrea?"

Andrea's expression became more serious. "Adam, I too have a secret that I must tell you. More happened in England than I led you to believe. There were indeed the men but there is also more."

"Andrea, what do you mean?"

"If you have been a coward, then so have I," she said sadly, "I cannot judge you, my darling, for I have done the same. I left a child behind too. Our child, Adam. We have a daughter."

"My God, Andrea, why did you not tell me?"

"I was so young and so scared then. Oh Adam, I've spent thirteen years trying to forget this ever happened, but I can't sleep at night because of the guilt. Her name is Helen, and she lives somewhere in London with a woman called Maya who took her away at birth. I've never seen her. My only wish would be for her to be here today, to see her wonderful father and to know we both love her dearly."

Long ago Andrea had decided that the child was truly Adam's. And now she felt he had a right to know before it was too late.

"Dear Andrea," he said stroking her hair, "you should never have borne this pain alone. If only I had not failed our love, maybe you would have trusted me enough to tell me."

"It was not a matter of trust, Adam, keeping it secret was something I had to do." Andrea told him the story of Helen's birth, about Maya and the unusual circumstances that compelled her to leave the child in her care. She told him of her extraordinary metaphysical near-death experience, her voice breaking as she relived it, her tears flowing.

Holding her close, he murmured, "Oh my dear sweet Andrea, there is no need to cry. Every experience has a purpose, as you've said so often, and I can't tell you how happy I am that we have created a beautiful daughter, and through her we will live on together forever. It makes my death more acceptable.

"Tell me," he said, as though continuing a very ordinary conversation, "what is it like in the next dimension? Is it beautiful?"

"My darling, it's more splendid than anything you can imagine," Andrea said softly, leaning against his shoulder.

"You know Andy, I'm not scared of dying, I am just sad not to have lived my life better."

"Death is another opportunity," Andrea said kissing the back of his hand, sensing that he was tiring, "and you can be sure in your next reincarnation you will not make these mistakes again."

"Well, before I go there is one mistake I would like to rectify," Adam said, raising her hand to his lips, "Raymond tells me I am a divorced man. Andrea, will you marry me?"

Andrea smiled, "I thought you would never ask."

Light footsteps sounded behind them, almost as though some one were tip-toeing. The nurse coming to reprimand them, Andrea thought, turning to make her excuse. There was no one. It was eerie.

Chapter 24

The next day Andrea told Raymond of Adam's wish to see his children.

"I have kept in contact with them over the years," Raymond said, "and I can see if they want to come, but I don't know, Andrea, it has been a long time and there has been much pain."

"As soon as you know, I'll instruct my pilot to pick them up." Andrea Jacobson was asserting her power again. She wanted Adam to have his last wish.

Adam's two children arrived two days later. Andrea would never forget the pleasure on Adam's face when he saw them.

Dressed in immaculate white linen pants and a peach polo shirt, Adam looked so healthy and vibrant that the shadow of death seemed to have passed. He was again the handsome man she had always remembered.

"My boy," he said, turning to the eldest, "you are a Stern. My God, how much you look like me." He extended his arms and both men embraced each other. It was uncanny. Errol Stern was the exact replica of his father.

"Daddy, I've wished for this moment for a long, long time."

Just then Adam's daughter came into the room. She looked at her father and a mixture of sorrow and love played over her young face.

"Hello, Father," she said, "I have waited a lifetime for this day." She moved into the circle of his embrace and wept silently against his chest. "Mother sends her love," she said, pulling away to look at her father, "and she wants you to know that all has been forgiven."

Michelle Stern was beautiful. Andrea guessed she was about twenty-two and Errol twenty-three. Both of his children were tall and handsome. Andrea admired the girl's taste in clothes, recognizing that the belted navy blue suit accentuating her slender waist was a Vittadini. Andrea sat watching as the three stood with their arms around each other. For a brief moment time stood still and they were together again at last. She thought of the reunion as a beginning and an ending, as forgiveness and love, a true closure.

The children were patient, understanding and kind, and not for a moment did they make their father feel guilty for not being there during their childhood. It was obvious that they loved Adam and felt that their wish had also come true. Their mother had kept his memory alive in their minds. She too had loved Adam.

Andrea left Adam with his children. For the first time since her arrival, she left the hospital and was alone. She walked aimlessly, without purpose or destination, fully aware of the inevitable. She had kept herself so busy attending to Adam's needs and keeping bedside vigil at nights until she was sure he was asleep that she had blocked out the inevitable ordeal. Now, for the first time she was faced with the absolute finality of it all, and she found herself in great pain. Adam's memory had always been a tonic for her loneliness. When times were unbearable, Andrea envisioned the day they would be reunited and the thought would console her aching heart. What would she do without him? How could she go on living?

On the last night of Michelle and Errol's visit, Adam's hospital room was in chaos. Andrea had invited Adam's family and half a dozen close friends for a party. She had made a handsome endowment for the building of a new wing to be called the Adam Stern Pavilion, and so the hospital administration approved of anything she did. It was so fitting, she thought. It seemed so appropriate to celebrate death rather than to mourn it.

Andrea sat in the corner of the room and watched as Adam's strength began to leave him. He was pretending to be well, but she knew better, and she worried that the excitement was too much for him. Momentarily she wondered if having such a party might not have been a good idea, but then the satisfaction on his face throughout the evening told her it was the right thing to do.

At nine o'clock Adam kissed each of his children and said goodbye to his family and friends with tears of joy in his eyes. Andrea's love for this man had never been stronger. By his actions, Adam Stern was again teaching her something of immense value: She was impressed that this dying man seemed to have no fears, while she had lived her life hiding behind her impenetrable wall. In a burst of illumination, Scott Preston's theory about fear as a motivator began to make sense to her, and now the spiritual metaphysics that he had expounded seemed the thing that might give purpose to her life. She intended to find out just what that purpose was.

"My wish came true," Adam said, turning to Andrea. "Thank you, darling, my entire life was worth this moment." He brushed his lips against hers. Andrea rested her head on his shoulder and allowed herself to acknowledge her soul's emotional need.

"I love you," she said softly.

"Andrea," he said quietly, "I want to spend one last night with you in my arms. I want to make love to you."

"Oh my love," she said, clinging to him, "I want that so much, but it could not possibly be good for you, and my God not here."

"Fine," he said, "I am signing myself out of this hospital." He rang for the nurse and when she came into the room, Adam said, "Get me Dr. Jones so I can be discharged."

"But Mr. Stern I cannot—"

"I am not asking, my dear," he admonished, "I am telling you that I am leaving, with or without the doctor's permission. Now, please do as I say."

Andrea knew that Adam was wielding his formidable power and there was nothing she could do or say that would change his mind.

"Come now," he turned to her, "what are you waiting for?"

"I'm just waiting for you to lead the way. We can take my car."

"Let me," he said, taking the keys from her hand as they reached the car. Getting behind the wheel he spun the car out of the parking lot as though destiny called. Andrea knew instantly where they were going.

As they approached the old Victorian house the sweet smell of sugar cane filled the air and memories of their first conjugal explosion came rushing back. Andrea opened the door of the great mansion and stood for a moment letting the nostalgia of that first night come into focus. Nothing had changed. The gleaming brass lamp still cast it's shimmering golden light, illuminating the large tiled entrance. Andrea's fingers could not resist making rabbit ear shadows on the wall before she ran up the winding staircase. She stood at the top, waiting for Adam to join her.

Adam held on to the mahogany banister as he climbed slowly up the stairs and Andrea knew that he was very tired. She sat on the step, chattering happily as he made his way up to where she was.

"Come along, slowpoke," she teased, kissing him as he plopped down beside her.

"I would not want to negotiate these stairs daily," he replied, out of breath, "One would think I had climbed Mount Everest." They walked together hand in hand to the bedroom.

"Why don't we rest awhile?" Andrea said, falling on the bed.

"Soon," he answered, leading her to the adjoining sitting room. Looking through the stack of records by the stereo, he paused and pulled one out of its old jacket. Putting the disc on the turntable, he turned to her, "I would like to dance. Shall we?" He took her in his arms, held her very close to him, and looked deep into her eyes as the vocalist began singing.

"*...and the first time ever I lay with you, I felt your heart so close to mine, and I knew our joy would fill the earth and last till the end of time...my love.*"

"It's our song," she whispered softly, resting her face against his. Slowly they moved together to the rhapsody that was the symbol of their passion. By the time the song had ended, they were both emotionally rejuvenated.

"Come with me," he said, leading her back to the bedroom. He undressed her carefully, in return allowing her to undress him, and then they were loving each other as they always had. Andrea felt the familiar fervent hunger only Adam could evoke in her. I am home, she thought, I am finally home.

"I will always love you, Adam," Andrea said, still basking in the sweet ecstasy he had filled her body with. "And I look forward to the time our paths will cross again. Our love is eternal."

"If only I could truly express the love I feel for you," he replied, "but words will never be enough."

They were lying breathless in each other's arms, holding each other, loving each other as they were meant to and would never be able to do again in this life.

"Anyway I can't think of a better way to go out of this world," he said, kissing her eyelids. "To have just made love to the most wonderful woman, a woman who has made my dreams a reality and my life complete, is a happy ending."

"Ending? My dear, after that performance I will not let you go anywhere," Andrea said, rolling over to fit into the curve of his arms. She looked up at Adam more seriously now. "Are you scared, darling?"

"Right now I feel very fulfilled and if I were to die at this very moment it would be all right, but when the final moment arrives I may want to live."

"You know there is this theory that says one never dies," Andrea said, "they just pass on to a higher level of perfection and are reborn. We will be together again. I know it."

Kissing her lightly and suddenly sounding very tired, he said, "Andrea, thank you, my darling, for a lifetime of love, but I don't want you to try to find my replacement. We have a special love that can never be replicated, but it is not the only love that can be fulfilling. I want you to live life fully. I want you to find someone to love you and to be with you. Andrea, don't hold back your love," he continued, "share it with someone, and know that I will always be happy to have been loved by you. Come," he said, "move closer to me." His breathing was becoming labored, and the sound of it frightened her.

"Adam, it is time for us to get back to the hospital."

"I am not going back," he said, "I want to stay right here beside you until the end."

Andrea took him in her arms. And closing her eyes, her face on his chest, she listened to his difficult breathing and thanked God he was not afraid and neither was she.

"Darling," he murmured, "there is something I would like Helen to have. It is a picture hanging over the mantel in the living room, like the one I gave you years ago. I want her to know what her father looked like. Please find her and let her know that I—" His voice faltered.

Andrea took his hand. "I will, my love, I promise. Now rest." He squeezed her hand and looked deeply into her upturned eyes. Andrea could feel his endurance slipping away.

"Goodbye, love of my life," he said, "thank you—" His strength was fading, but he was not afraid. He had Andrea beside him, and he was not afraid.

"Please, darling," Andrea began to cry, "please don't leave me. I can't live without you, Adam," she held him tightly, "and Adam, you asked me to marry you."

"Repeat after me," he said with great effort, "I, Andrea—"

Tears streaming down her cheeks, she said the vows of matrimony with him, "I, Andrea, take you, Adam Reginald Stern, to be my husband, to love and to cherish, to honor and obey, in sickness and in health, until death do us part."

"And I," he said with his very last breath, "take you, Andrea to be my wife—" Then there was silence.

Andrea looked at the man she loved with all her heart and soul and kissed the lips that could no longer respond. Finally, she got out of bed and dialed the hospital.

Chapter 25

New York

Andrea had never hated New York more than she did the moment she landed at Kennedy Airport. The city was an absolute zoo. Andrea found that she had mixed emotions about the place, needing the bustle and excitement of New York, yet at the same time wishing she were almost anywhere else. She looked around with displeasure at the people busily hustling about, taking life for granted. She wondered whether any of them recognized the purpose of their lives. She was now convinced there was indeed a definite purpose to living. For the first time in her thirty-five years, she had come to appreciate life's fragility.

The night air was cold after Jamaica, but Andrea was too numb to feel it. She instinctively pulled her short jacket more closely around her and strode to the spot where her driver always picked her up. She looked around for her limousine, and only then remembered she had not notified anyone of her arrival. Elbowing her way through the crowd, she stepped into the street and hailed a yellow cab.

"Manhattan," she told the driver, "The Trump Towers."

Once inside the private elevator, Andrea slumped heavily against the doors, her body too weak to support itself, feeling that her world had ended. Finally she sat down on the cushioned bench and waited for the elevator to reach the twenty-fifth floor.

Andrea let herself into her apartment and walked around all thirty-eight rooms as though she were seeing them for the very first time. Suddenly the enormity of her wealth seemed too great a burden. For the first time she understood how alienating money could be. She would rather have a simpler life. The comfortable hospital room in which she had stayed with Adam had more warmth than this over-priced enormous apartment.

Over the years, she had accepted her wealth without question and she had been cognizant of the obsequious respect that it had brought her, yet no one really knew who she was on the inside. Her private self had been buried with Adam. And all the money in the world could not bring back the only man she had ever loved. Even after nineteen years their love had been so new and fresh and true. And now it was over. She wished she could feel. Adam had asked her to love again, but what love could ever live up to theirs? It could only happen once in a lifetime.

Andrea had not gone to the funeral. She had left immediately after Adam's death, wanting only to remember his smiling face and to keep him alive in her heart.

She unwrapped the picture she had taken from his house and hung it over her bed. She would give it to Helen when or if she ever saw her daughter. Andrea stared at the picture of Adam, tears rising in her eyes. She needed a drink.

Andrea went to the recessed liquor cabinet in her bedroom and poured herself a pony of brandy. She turned and raised her glass to the picture. "To eternity," she whispered. Adam Stern even in death was her soulmate. Tears drenched her cheeks. The unearthly primal screams were muffled behind the soundproof walls of her luxurious apartment as Andrea mourned.

Much later an exhausted Andrea refilled her glass with brandy and pressed the button to her answering machine.

"Hello Andrea, this is Maya." Andrea could not make herself listen to the message. She turned the switch off before the message had ended. "Not tonight," she said, "oh please, not tonight."

"There is so much to brief you on," Jonathan said as Andrea paced around her office. "Most of the news is good, but we do have a problem developing in Hong Kong."

"Fix it, Jonathan," Andrea was annoyed. "It is what I pay you for, is it not? Furthermore, I know you are capable." She continued, softening her sharp tone.

Andrea had never allowed Jonathan to act on her behalf when there were signs of trouble, but she was not up to any more negotiating. And what Jonathan considered a problem was quite insignificant to Andrea.

Jonathan Buckley was not in the least upset at the way his boss had spoken to him. The thought of handling the problems in Hong Kong pleased him. He was more than eager to show how well he could run Jacobson's Industry.

"Very well then, I'll let you know the outcome."

"You have exactly twenty-four hours to get back to me with a solution. And Jonathan, on your way out have Janice notify all the department heads to meet me in the big conference room tomorrow at three."

"Yes, Ms. Jacobson."

"Thank you," she said as he retreated from her office.

Already Jamaica seemed light years away, but not a minute went by that Andrea did not think of Adam. He was on her mind when the buzz of the intercom interrupted her reverie.

"Ms. Jacobson."

"Yes, Janice?"

"Dr. Preston is here to see you."

Andrea was annoyed. Scott Preston had a penchant for making her furious. How dare he presume he could just stop by her office unannounced and uninvited? His behavior reminded her of the past audaciousness of Ralph deHavalon and Saleem Shaheed. Was this presumption a characteristic possessed by most men? Blurred images of Scott Preston had begun to intrude themselves on her consciousness since Adam's death. Too frequently she had found herself curious about this man, and had vowed to keep from acting on her impulse to see him one more time. As much as she wanted to get even with Dr. Scott know-it-all Preston for his humiliation of her on national television, she had neither the energy nor the time to invest in a battle of wits with him. It had been five months since they had met.

"Tell Dr. Preston that I am in a meeting," Andrea said curtly, "and Janice, ask him to make an appointment the next time he would like to see me. No, wait, just tell him I will call him as soon as I possibly can." Andrea lit a cigarette and turned to look out the window. The nerve of the man.

"And what part does that cigarette play in the meeting?"

Andrea spun around at the familiar slurring voice and found to her shock that Scott Preston was leaning casually against her office door. He was a big man; his formidable physique blocked out the light from the outer office. Andrea's heart did a somersault before it regulated itself.

"Damn," she thought fleetingly, "he really is good looking."

"What are you doing in here? Didn't Janice tell you I was in a meeting, Dr. Preston?"

"Yes, she did, but from the look of things I gather that you are merely having conference with your cigarette."

"And on the other hand, I could have been in a very important meeting and your bursting into my office would have been entirely unforgivable."

Again Andrea found herself stubbing out the cigarette in the Baccarat ashtray on her desk, feeling stupidly compelled to intuit his implied command.

"I have tried to call you a dozen or more times," he said, entering the office and closing the door, "but your secretaries guard you with their lives. My hand 'accidentally' hit the intercom button when you were speaking. I was on my way to my publisher's office which happens to be on the twentieth floor of this building, so I made a detour. I only have a few minutes but I just wanted to see for myself that you were fine."

"Well, as you can see I am perfect, still mad, but perfect."

"You'll never forgive me for that will you?"

"Do you think you deserve forgiveness?"

"Absolutely," he grinned, "I've already forgiven you for not returning any of my calls. But to be honest, I was concerned."

"Concerned!" Andrea exclaimed, "for what reason?"

"Because you did not return my calls."

"Has it ever occurred to you that if a woman does not return your calls, it may mean she just doesn't want to be bothered?"

"Was that the reason?"

"No. I—I was out of the country."

"Thank goodness," Scott sighed with relief, "I was beginning to think I was going to have to go back to school to learn about human nature all over again."

"A class about tact may not be a bad idea."

"And all this time I thought your eyes reminded me of a tiger, and I was right, but it is your fangs that are most dangerous! Andrea, if I promise to retract everything I said, can we call a truce?"

"Maybe."

"In that case, Ms. Jacobson, I retract all statements implied or otherwise that you demonstrate signs of rich neurosis syndrome. And to show that we've buried the hatchet, I would like to invite you to a party at my home on Saturday," he continued, "I'm celebrating the publication of my fifth book, and I would like you to join us. Let's say eight o'clock. I will be happy to autograph a copy of the book just for you."

"Thank you for the invitation," Andrea replied, "but I must decline. As I said earlier, I've been away for the last three months, and there are projects that require my attention. I'm sorry, but I can't possibly take the time."

"A business trip?"

"It was—unplanned," Andrea went on, "and it was personal." She dared him to ask her to elaborate. Andrea could not understand why she was explaining her reasons for declining Scott's invitation, which to her ears was more like a command appearance. Incredibly, she found that she was stammering and sounding coy, "But I hope you will invite me again. Will I still qualify for an autographed copy of your book?"

"Most definitely."

"Thank you so much for stopping by, but I must get back to work. She held out her hand, indicating the end of the impromptu *tête-à-tête.*"

"Is everything really all right, Andrea?" Scott asked, sounding genuinely concerned, holding on to her hand longer than necessary. "From your tone I gather that your trip was not a pleasant experience. I am so sorry to have ignored the fact that you had reasons other than just ignoring me. Please forgive my insensitivity."

"Scott, everything is just fine. Thank you for asking."

"Well if you change your mind about joining us on Saturday, please call," he said, handing her his card, "and if not, then some other time."

By the time Andrea looked up from the card he was gone.

Andrea sat back in her chair and stared at the door. He had not even looked back. Scott Preston was dangerous. He made her feel like an awkward teenager. She was sorry she had been so abrupt with him, but Scott Preston seemed to have the ability to threaten her security and her tenuous hold on sanity. When she felt more composed, more in control of her emotions, perhaps she would invite him to dinner just to show that she too had buried the hatchet. She could not help but wonder what it might have been like had they met under different circumstances.

In the past six months, the exciting high of the giant merger and the devastating low of Adam's death had left her vulnerable to authoritative men like Scott Preston, it seemed. With her emotions raw and on edge, no good could come of a potentially volatile and explosive relationship. With that observation and the situation she now had to deal with, she pushed Scott Preston out of her thoughts.

She picked up the telephone receiver, dialed a number, and waited. There was no answer. Apprehension gripped at her stomach, but Andrea forced herself to focus on the stack of papers on her desk, knowing she would never be able to concentrate until this call and whatever it implied was behind her.

By Saturday, the night of Scott's party, prowling the apartment with nothing to do, to her surprise she realized she wanted to see him. Until her mind had settled down, work was not its usual panacea. She agonized over whether or not to call, and finally dialed the number on the card. On the first ring she put the receiver back in its cradle. Why was she acting like a silly schoolgirl? There was absolutely nothing wrong with changing her mind. After fifteen minutes of berating herself, she was able to dial the number again, praying there would be no answer. Scott picked up the phone on the first ring.

"Hello Scott, this is Andrea Jacobson, I'm hoping your invitation for tonight is still on. I got more work done than I expected, so I'm free after all."

"Andrea, this is wonderful!" Scott replied, sounding truly happy, "I can't tell you how much I hoped you would call. You have a standing invitation to my home," he continued, "with or without a party."

"Why, thank you," Andrea said, warmed by his enthusiasm. "I will most certainly remember that." Although he still sounded self-assured, tonight he did not seem so egotistical, and she found herself glad that she decided to go to his party.

"See you at about eight then."

"I'll give you directions," he said, "I am out in the Hamptons and somewhat hard to find, so write them down."

As Andrea dutifully began writing the directions he was giving her, she stared unbelievingly at the location of his house. She felt a shiver go through her body. Was this just a coincidence or was Scott Preston being funny? He probably knew all along that she owned the house next door.

Andrea had bought the house more than three years ago after falling in love with the airy old mansion the moment she had laid eyes on it. After Alex's death she had sold the more pretentious house in Southhampton preferring something smaller, a comfortable and peaceful place to which she could retreat from the city when it got to be too much.

Although she had not visited the house often, she welcomed the large open rooms where comfort and relaxation was the order of the day, rather than the ultraconservative decor of the Southhampton showpiece. The stone fireplace in the living room gave a soothing ambiance during the chilly winter months. Andrea had decorated the house with simple hand-crafted Early American furniture and bursts of vivid colors that warmed her cold heart. On summer days Andrea loved to walk through the French doors into the beautifully manicured garden, hidden from view behind ancient pine trees that lined the long driveway. It was a house she had always thought should be filled with the laughter of children, a house Helen would have liked.

She had never seen any of her neighbors, much less Scott Preston.

"Andrea," Scott was saying on the line, "are the directions clear enough?"

"Yes," Andrea replied, "I should be able to find it with no problem."

Chapter 26

Andrea tried on eight outfits before settling on a simple black chiffon Christian Dior dress which showed off her long legs to advantage. She pinned on a Mikimoto pearl and diamond brooch and clipped on matching earrings, the only jewelry she would wear. Sheer black stockings and Ferragamo black pumps completed the outfit. She brushed her hair back into a French braid, and after applying a touch of lip color, was satisfied with her appearance. She looked at her watch and found that it had taken her almost two hours to get dressed, but she rationalized that the extra care she took in dressing was because she needed an emotional boost, and as the owner of Jacobson's Industry, she always wanted to look her best. A small voice in the back of her head told her that she was lying to herself; she wanted to look good for Scott Preston.

At seven o'clock, she turned the key in her elevator door and pressed the button to the garage level. She would drive herself to the Hamptons. Andrea spun out of the garage and the Jaguar sped silently through the city streets to the Long Island Expressway.

She popped in her favorite Jerry Butler tape and turned the volume high.

Driving and loud music were two of Andrea's favorite pastimes. She loved driving fast and had often fantasized about being a race car driver. She loved the power she had over the car as it cruised at top speed. To her, the danger and risk of driving fast was synonymous with ultimate authority.

At eight-ten Andrea rang the doorbell. When no one answered the door she checked the house number to make sure she had come to the right address. She had. Impatiently she rang the bell again and this time Scott opened the door.

"Welcome," he said, throwing the door open so she could enter. "Come in, come in."

Andrea walked into the room and looked around in surprise. He must be married she thought. How stupid of her not to have guessed. A man such as Scott Preston could not possibly be single. She felt that she had misread his friendliness as sexual advances. The house was magnificent, yet so warmly decorated that only a woman could have done it, she decided.

"Hello, Scott. You have a beautiful home."

"I consider that an extraordinary compliment coming from a woman of such good taste. Later I'll show you my favorite rooms. Andrea, you look positively scintillating."

"Thank you. You look rather dapper yourself."

He escorted her to a glass enclosed patio where about twenty or so people were gathered. She waited to be introduced to his wife but the introduction never came.

It was an intimate party, a far cry from the lavish parties that she and Alex had given. Even their smaller parties had at least a hundred guests, most of whose faces were familiar to the public. Andrea knew no one here.

"Everyone, this is Andrea Jacobson," Scott announced. "Andrea does not believe in metaphysical hocus pocus so try not to bore her tonight," he laughed. She blushed. Scott seemed to be having a wonderful time embarrassing her, she thought.

"Come, I will get you a drink."

Andrea followed him to the bar at a corner of the patio.

"Andrea," he said leading her toward a handsome man standing by the bar, "This is Randy Levanthol. Randy, Andrea Jacobson."

"Hello Andrea, I've seen you many times in the building, but I have never been close enough to say hello. I did not know until your recent television interview that you were *the* Andrea Jacobson."

"The Andrea Jacobson? That sounds ominous."

"Not at all. It's admiration. I'm hoping one day you will let me publish your autobiography."

"I seriously doubt that, but if I do have a change of heart, I promise you will be the first to know. Tell me," she said changing the subject, "what made you publish Scott's book?"

"Habit. I published the four before this. I read his first manuscript because Angela twisted my arm. When I saw how good the material was, I smelled success. It's been a wonderful union," he said turning to Scott, "don't you think so, old boy?"

"I do indeed."

"What is the subject of the book?" Andrea asked.

"The evolution of the spirit to its rightful place, something like that," Levanthol shrugged and grinned.

"Never mind, Randy. Come, Andrea, let me introduce you to someone special. Her name is Shakti. She is a spiritual guide."

"Are all your guests metaphysical believers?" She asked when they were out of earshot of Randy Levanthol.

"All except Randy, but he may be finally coming around."

"But they all look so normal," Andrea said before she could stop herself.

He threw back his head and laughed. Again Andrea noticed

the perfect flash of white teeth and the way his face was transformed when he laughed.

"Shall we join the weirdoes? Shakti!" he called to a tall beautiful Indian woman, "I would like you to meet Andrea."

"Andreaaa," she said, rolling the 'a' over her tongue, "how wonderful it is to meet you at last. Scott speaks of you often."

"He does?" Andrea looked over at Scott who shrugged his shoulders.

Andrea liked Shakti immediately. She radiated a warm welcoming glow. Scott murmured that Shakti was a visiting professor of metaphysics at New York University.

"Come and meet the rest of the folks."

Andrea enjoyed the people at the party. The atmosphere was full of peaceful, friendly laughter. Except to Scott's publisher, tonight it did not matter at all who she was. The conversations centered mostly on the psychic and metaphysical aspects of life, and Andrea was intrigued by what she was hearing. The idea of soul mates and unconditional love she knew about because she had experienced it firsthand, but Andrea listened carefully.

"How are you holding up?" Scott asked.

"I'm having a wonderful time," Andrea said, and she was. She turned back to listen to another comment.

"Love is the only universal constant," Shakti was saying, "and all it requires is that we let go of the fears that prevent us from experiencing its full force. When we understand and accept love, only then can we find true happiness. Not to know that love always exists within us is what makes this world so chaotic."

Scott had been watching Andrea all night, happy that she had come. Tonight she seemed completely relaxed and quiet. She was so beautiful. He had to know what flame burned beneath the surface of this woman that made her so tough and worldly one minute and so modest and unassuming the next. He would marry Andrea Jacobson one day, of that he was sure.

By midnight most of the guests had said their goodbyes. "I should be leaving too," Andrea said, looking around for her coat.

"Please," he said, "stay a bit longer. You haven't seen the rest of the house. How about some coffee?" he asked.

"I wouldn't expect you to drink coffee."

"I don't, but I noticed that you did in the restaurant so I bought some Jamaican Blue Mountain just for you."

"You were that sure that I would accept your invitation?"

"If not tonight there would be other occasions."

Scott Preston, you are very sure of yourself, she thought, following him to the kitchen and watching as he adroitly juggled with a coffee grinder, boiling water and a Chemex pot.

"Let's go into the study," he suggested, carrying her coffee and his cup of tea on a silver tray. "It's my favorite room," he announced, ushering her in.

"I can certainly understand why," Andrea said.

Scott lit a match to the logs in the fireplace and turned the lights down low. He pushed a button on the wall revealing an entertainment center, and an unusually soothing music started playing.

"I love that sound," Andrea said closing her eyes and feeling the vibration of the music through her body, "Who is it?"

"Kitaro. He is Japanese," he answered, "he plays New Age music which uses a lot of crystal and water sounds. It is believed that crystals magnify energy and the notes match the vibration of the soul. I shall send you a tape tomorrow." He paused. "Did you have a good time tonight?"

"I did," Andrea said, "but I can't say that I understood a lot of what was said. I think I'm just too logical to believe much of it. But it's an interesting way of viewing life."

"It's a difficult concept," he said. "At first it is almost frightening to think of the implications, especially if one has been indoctrinated in traditional religions."

"How did you get involved in this New Age movement?" Andrea asked.

"My wife." Andrea was dying to know where his wife was, but Scott did not elaborate and she felt unable to ask.

Scott explained much of the archaic origin of New Age philosophy, and it was well after three o'clock before Andrea even stirred, surprised that she had sustained for so long a conversation that she was not dominating.

"It's all quite fascinating," Andrea said, "but I believe it takes a special person to deal with some of the concepts, especially the one about astral projection." Andrea understood that what she had experienced at the birth of her child was called astral projection or an out-of-body experience, but obviously she could not tell Scott about it. Also, she was not ready to accept all of this. It was just too strange. She wanted to maintain what she considered a normal existence.

"I guess in time I'll understand," she said rising, "but I must get ready to go home now."

"If you want to learn, I'll help you," he said, taking her hand and helping her to her feet.

"I'd like that," Andrea said, a rush of nearly forgotten feelings surfacing at the touch of his hand on hers.

"To self-discovery," he said quietly, holding her gaze, and still holding her hand, "and to a new beginning."

"It's late," Andrea said, withdrawing her hand from his. "I must start back."

"Please," he said, "stay here tonight. I would not be able to rest if I let you drive all that way home."

"I'll be fine," she insisted, "I love driving and it will give me more time to think about the evening."

"You must stay," he said firmly, "or I'll be forced to drive with you back to the city."

Scott was serious. And how could she tell him now that she

could easily sleep next door in her own house since she had not mentioned it all evening? She decided to go along with his adamant insistence.

He led her up the stairs and into a beautiful room with its own bathroom and a small sitting room. Andrea loved the room and wondered who it was decorated for, but she was too tired to think properly.

"You'll find everything you need, just poke around a bit."

She wondered what had happened to Scott's wife. He had not mentioned Angela again, but there was an unmistakable sadness in his voice when he had alluded to her.

Andrea washed her face, removed her clothes, donned a nightgown that she found in the dresser drawer, and climbed between crisp sheets. The bed was so comfortable. Just then there was a knock on the door. "Yes?" Andrea said pulling the covers up to her chin.

Scott opened the door a crack, "Is there anything you need?"

"No thank you, I'm just fine."

"Shall I have breakfast sent up for you in the morning, or do you just take coffee?"

"I doubt there will be time for breakfast. I have an early appointment and I must be back in the city by seven."

"Tomorrow is Sunday."

"I know that."

"Very well then, goodnight and have a good rest."

"Thank you," Andrea said, as he closed the door, "Goodnight."

Andrea set the alarm on the bedside clock for six, just two hours away, then rolled over and promptly fell asleep.

"Good morning, ma'am, I was knocking but I got no answer. Dr. Preston thought I should check on you. I have brought you some coffee."

"Thank you," Andrea said, eyeing the white haired woman. "What time is it?"

"It's eleven-thirty."

"Eleven-thirty! My God!"

Andrea jumped out of bed and headed for the bathroom. She dressed quickly and ran downstairs.

"Scott," she called out, "Are you here? I can't believe you let me oversleep. I must go," she called up the stairs, "but I can't find my purse."

Just then he appeared at the top of the steps wearing a bath towel wrapped around his waist. The strong muscles of his arms and chest made Andrea's body stir. It had been so long since she had felt even the slightest desire for any man except Adam.

"What's the hurry? You've already missed your appointment. But don't worry, I called your office and had your secretary cancel the meeting. How can you work on a Sunday anyway? I felt you needed the rest so I didn't wake you."

Andrea was furious. "How the bloody hell can you know what I need after one night of conversation? And who authorized you to call my office? For God's sake Scott, what did you tell Janice?" Scott was smiling. "And what in hell are you smiling about," she ranted, getting angrier by the minute.

"You are absolutely irresistible when you're angry. Let me change," he said. Ignoring her outrage completely, he disappeared from view.

"Well," he said, reappearing at the top of the stairs moments later, "now that you have a whole day free, why don't we have some breakfast?"

Andrea could not believe her fury was being so totally disregarded. She was used to people jumping when she spoke, but Scott Preston was either too stupid to understand who she really was—or he did not care. Andrea had a feeling it was the latter. Obediently she followed him to the kitchen.

"What did you say to Janice?"

"I asked her how important your appointment was and if she thought it was something that could be rescheduled without a hassle. I told her you were a little under the weather and I thought it would be best if you rested."

"And where did you tell her I was having this sudden attack of illness?"

"I told her that you came to a party at my home and got a little sick."

"I see lying does not bother you at all."

"What would you rather have had me tell her?"

"Absolutely nothing. I happen to call the shots at Jacobson's Industry. They would have waited until they heard from me."

"But was it necessary to have them sit around for five hours on a Sunday?"

"That was a decision you had no right to make."

"I'm sorry, Andrea, maybe I went too far, but you were the one who slept through the alarm. Was it really that important?"

"It was important enough, but I guess no harm will come if I reschedule for tomorrow. I must use the phone," she said, looking around the sunny white kitchen.

"There is one on the wall over here," he said," but if you need privacy there's one in the library, first door on the right, remember?"

The library was just as impressive in daylight as it was at night. With dark leather-covered furniture and an ornate desk, unlike the simplicity of the other rooms, it had a more masculine, somber look. The walls were covered with books, some, she noticed, were by Scott himself. This was the room of a scholar and a very well-read man.

Andrea picked up the phone and dialed her secretary's number.

"Janice, I want to remind you that as long as you work for Jacobson's your orders come from me and me alone. Please apologize to Jonathan for me."

"Yes, Ms. Jacobson."

As she hung up, Andrea thought she heard a muffled giggle but then Janice could have been nervous. Andrea made her way back to the kitchen and found Scott buttering toast. He handed her a cup of coffee which she accepted gladly while thinking, what the hell am I doing here?

"I'll bet if today had been Monday you would have gotten me up so you could get to work."

"No, I might just have taken a day off."

"How is it that you can just take a day off whenever you feel like it?" Andrea asked.

"I have to answer to no one, and I am neither obsessive nor compulsive."

"Implying that I am?" Andrea said, recalling her initial dislike for his pomposity.

"Obviously not," he said "you're here, are you not?"

She was indeed. Knowing she should walk out the door, she wanted to stay. She would probably have to go into deep therapy to find out why.

"But I'm hardly dressed for a day in the country."

"How about a pair of my sweats? I believe they would actually look great on you. What color? I have several."

Andrea smiled in spite of herself. "I like peach."

"Then peach it is."

"Then I give up," she relented, "but I need to make a call out of the country. May I use your phone again?"

As Andrea's fingers dialed the number in England they seemed almost disconnected from her brain. Waiting, she shifted nervously from one foot to the other, and was about to hang up on the sixth ring when the phone was answered.

"Hello," the very British-accented voice said.

"Hello, this is Andrea Jacobson, I would like to speak with Maya, please."

"This is Maya, Andrea. I expected you to return my call before now. I tried to reach you again yesterday," she said.

"I was out of the country," Andrea said, "Maya, is Helen all right?"

"Helen is wonderful. She is in school."

Helen. Andrea tried to picture her. She was going to be fourteen in a month. Andrea wondered if Helen knew about her, and if so, how had Maya explained her own relationship to Helen. Had Maya told Helen she adopted her? That her mother left her and ran off with the some stranger? What story had Maya told the child?

Maya was saying, "As you know, Helen will be fourteen next month. Would you like to be with her on her birthday?"

Andrea was speechless.

"Does she know about me?" Andrea asked, finally breaking the silence on the line.

"She knows you exist, but she does not know that you are Andrea Jacobson."

"Maya, does she hate me?"

"Not at all."

Andrea had never heard such kindness in Maya's voice before. Maybe she was being sweet before the kill. "Why, after all these years do I get to see my child now?"

"Because it is time now. We will expect you. I will contact you in London," she said, ringing off.

Andrea's knees felt weak and she sagged into the nearest chair. Sweet Jesus, she thought. How could she possibly face Helen? What would she say to her after all these years? Hello, darling, come to mommy. So sorry I deserted you, but it was just too complicated to explain you to the world.

Something was wrong, Andrea knew it. Maya did not just want her in England for Helen's fourteenth birthday. There was more to it than that.

She forced her analytic mind to break through and find a believable explanation for Maya's request. She paced back and forth in the library for fifteen minutes before the reason behind Maya's summons finally struck her. Blackmail! Why had it not occurred to her before? It made sense. With the announcement of the Southeast Asia deal, she was now publicly recognized as one of the wealthiest women in the world. Maya was ready to stake her claim to the Jacobson's fortune! The thought did not please her. Andrea moved toward the door with confidence, glad for the conclusion she had come to. Greed. It fell into the domain of controllable consequences, and this was something tangible she could understand. Fighting and winning was her forte and Andrea Jacobson never lost at anything. If Maya thought she could destroy her life this way she had better be prepared to battle to the bitter end.

"You look awful," Scott said, as Andrea walked into the kitchen. "What in the world is wrong?"

"No, everything is okay. I'm fine." Andrea said impatiently.

"You don't look fine to me. You look as though you've seen one of my spirit guides. Sit down, let me get you some more coffee. Do you want to talk about what's bothering you?"

"For God's sake, Scott, leave it alone. Do I seem to be a woman who is incapable of handling her own problems? I'm quite self-sufficient, thank you."

"I only asked because you looked distraught."

"I think you're one of those shrinks who can only respond to women in crisis. I've heard that some men can't get it up unless they're playing savior. Well get one thing straight, I take care of my own problems and they are none of your business."

"I think it's time to don our sweats," he said calmly, taking her

269

hand and leading her upstairs. Eventually he would find out what was going on in that pretty little head of Andrea Jacobson, but this was not the time.

At the entrance to his bedroom door, Andrea hesitated.

"You can't possibly find sweats standing there," Scott turned to look at her.

His bedroom was very masculine. Andrea remembered hearing you could tell a lot about a man by his bedroom. Like the rest of the house it was tastefully decorated, the king-size four poster bed neatly made, and everything in the room in its place. On the night stand was the picture of a very young and beautiful woman. Andrea guessed she must be Angela.

"My wife, Angela. She died several years ago," Scott volunteered at her questioning look.

Scott opened a chest of drawers that stood in one corner of the room and pulled out several sets of sweats. He held them up one by one and waited for her approval.

"Start over," Andrea said, as he came to the end of the second drawer.

"For goodness sake, Andrea, there are at least fifteen sweats here, one must grab your fancy."

"You promised me peach."

"Unfortunately I think that one must be at the cleaners," he chuckled.

"The white one then," she decided, "Yes, I think I like the white one."

"Good. Now go in there," he pointed to the large bathroom, "and change."

On her way to the bathroom, Andrea passed a study off the bedroom. She wanted to peek inside but was too shy to appear inquisitive. Inside the gargantuan bathroom Andrea dropped her black evening dress onto the slate floor. The air smelled of very expensive cologne and she wondered which one of the dozens on the dresser was Scott's favorite. Gray Flannel had to be it. She assumed that the rest were birthday or Christmas gifts from his romantic interests and tried to imagine what it would be like to take a bath with Scott in this handsome bathroom. Andrea turned to the mirrored wall, looked at her nude body and imagined Scott kissing her throat. She fantasized his hand moving down her body.

"Are you dead in there?" Scott shouted from the other side of the door.

"Of course not, I'm almost ready." Andrea snapped out of her daydream, hurriedly donned the white sweats and pulled her hair back into a pony tail. She emerged from the bathroom and turned in front of him slowly.

"What do you think?"

"Absolutely smashing. Much better than peach. And I have a great idea. If we hurry we can catch the two forty-five movie. Shall we go?"

As they walked to the car Andrea fell in step with Scott and the movement seemed to create a sweet familiarity between them. The walk to the car seemed to signify the beginning of something.

"It is good to see that you're patriotic," she joked, "you drive a good old American car. What is it anyway?"

"A Chrysler New Yorker."

"How appropriate."

"Would you rather take your car?"

"Oh of course not, I was just joking. What movie are we going to see?"

"*Back To The Future*." Scott laughed.

They were one of the few couples in the theater. They sat in the back row of the cinema, far apart from the others, and noisily ate popcorn and whispered loudly to each other through the entire movie.

"A totally unbelievable plot," Andrea said, as the movie ended, "but it was entertaining."

"It may not be as unbelievable as you think. If UFO's and men from outer space actually exist, and there is good evidence they do, then why can't man go into the future?"

"Hogwash. There is no such evidence."

"You are such a non-believer. It's time to get some food. Now that's reality, isn't it? I know this wonderful little restaurant not far from here."

"Sounds good to me."

In spite of Andrea's determination not to enjoy the day, she had to admit she was sorry when it had finally ended. They drove back to the house in silence. It was already eight o'clock.

"It's time for me to get going," Andrea said as they drove up the driveway, "I'll just run in and change."

"You don't have to, you can return my sweats the next time I see you. I will see you soon, won't I?"

"How about Saturday? My place for dinner?"

"Wonderful. I'll bring the wine."

"Listen, just bring yourself. The wine I must hand pick."

"So you think I have no class."

"Absolutely, and no tact either. Goodnight, Scott and thank you for a lovely day."

Chapter 27

The following Saturday Andrea announced, "Melissa I have invited Dr. Preston to dinner tonight." Melissa's eyebrows went up in surprise.

"Don't look at me like that, it was a moment of weakness."

"It is about time you had a moment of weakness," Melissa said raising her hands to the heavens. "It is about time we have some life in this place."

Since Alex's death no one had been invited to Andrea's home. The smaller apartment on the other side of Central Park was where she occasionally met the incidental men who supplied her with what she thought of as an uncomplicated sex life, a logical means of alleviating stress while giving her physical pleasure.

"Have the florist send arrangements of tulips, roses and orchids. Be sure to tell her what china and linen we are using so she can coordinate the vases."

"Which restaurant would you like to cater the dinner, Le Cirque, Petite Marmite, or the Four Seasons?" Melissa asked.

"We are not having it catered, Melissa, we're going to cook this meal from scratch."

"Dear God! have you gone crazy, child?"

"No I have not. Scott probably thinks I am a spoiled brat who's never cooked in her life before."

"And he will be right."

"But that's beside the point, I want to appear domesticated."

"Domesticated, eh, that sounds like a pet cat, dog or snake. Maybe you are falling in love."

"Absolutely not. I just need a diversion."

Melissa smiled knowingly. She was dying to meet this Scott Preston who had Andrea Jacobson in a tizzy. Cooking indeed. Melissa disappeared into the kitchen and returned with an apron for herself and one for Andrea.

"You will need this," she said tying on the apron. "What are we cooking, anyway?"

"I've ordered Coho salmon and lobsters from Zabar's, and from D'Agostino's, haricots verts, artichokes, wild rice and Granny Smith apples to make apple pie, oh, and Häagen Dazs. How much more American could I get? When the delivery comes make sure there is Blue Mountain coffee, Vittal water and tomato juice. And remove the candelabra from the table."

Andrea and Melissa spent the better part of the day preparing the meal because Andrea insisted that each recipe be followed exactly.

"Melissa," she shouted, "these lobsters don't look right! They aren't red!."

"*They* require cooking," Melissa replied placidly, peeling apples.

"Melissa!" Andrea exclaimed, "What if he is allergic to seafood? Why didn't I think to make a roast of beef or a duck?"

"Andrea, please, you are driving me crazy. If he does not eat seafood, then send out for pizza." Andrea gave Melissa a scornful look.

Everything was prepared as much as possible by three-thirty. Andrea surveyed the table setting. At the Duncan Phyfe crow-foot table that could easily seat forty people, Melissa had put them next to each other. She had thought of everything. Appliquéed napkins matching the linen place mats were tucked into porcelain holders. The blue and gold Carlyle pattern of Royal Doulton china was flanked by eighteen-carat gold flatware. Individual cut-glass salt and pepper shakers matched the Waterford stemware. The flower-filled vases were of the same rich blue and gold porcelain as the plates. Andrea looked at her watch. Scott was not due to arrive until six. She would shower and rest for a few minutes.

"You've done a marvelous job, Melissa. Are the other rooms in order? If they are, I'll go and lie down for a while."

"What wine did you say to chill?"

"A bottle of Curvee Rene Zalon champagne and the Mouton Rothchild Saviginon." Melissa nodded her approval.

"Melissa, I think I should meet him alone this time. But I'll tell him that you helped me prepare dinner. Is that fair? Would you do the final touches before you go? And make sure the maids know once dinner has been served they may leave. They can clean up tomorrow. Is that okay?"

"It is perfect, Andrea," Melissa said, kissing her on the cheek. "I am so glad that you are trying to be happy."

After a half hour of workout in the exercise room, Andrea took a shower and laid on a chaise longue to rest. She was sound asleep when the intercom buzzed. At the sound, Andrea jumped.

"Yes," she said sleepily.

"A Dr. Scott Preston to see you, Ms. Jacobson, shall I send him up?"

"Oh my God!" Andrea said, looking at her watch. She had overslept. "Yes—send him up, please."

Andrea panicked. Then her mind jumped into action. She

275

would leave a note on the door for him to come in if he dared to. She had never done a thing like this in her life, but it was fun and it could give her the time she needed to get dressed.

"This way," the porter led Scott to the gold doors of the elevator that was embossed with the JI logo. He turned a key in the slot and the doors slid open. "This will take you right to Mrs. Jacobson's apartment."

Impressive, Scott mused. The plush charcoal carpet with the JI logo was identical to the one in the lobby at Jacobson's Industry. Inside the elevator hung several pieces of African art. Very tasteful, he thought.

When the elevator doors opened again, Scott found himself in a huge black and white checked Italian marble foyer in which two Russian brass and crystal chandeliers were hung. A gilt-framed Italian mirror hung over a Duncan Phyfe table flanked by Louis XVI chairs. The walls were covered with off-white raw silk. Mahogany-framed glass doors separated the foyer from what appeared to be the living room. He saw a note with his name on it attached to the glass. Scott read the note and smiled.

He pushed the doors open and entered another large hallway separated from the living room by three sculptured Roman columns. The place was magnificent. He was truly amazed. Not because Andrea had such good taste, but because he had not imagined her home this way. Everywhere were memorabilia of her visits abroad, Eastern art and artifacts, huge Ming jars, and expensive Oriental rugs in exquisite pastel colors. Unlike the foyer, most of the living room furnishings were in white or off-white, beautiful, but sterile. Then he crossed the room to the fireplace and saw that on the Louis XV mantel were pictures of what appeared to be her family, surprised that Andrea would have placed them there. His attention was caught by an antique silver frame with no picture at all. He wondered what this mystery was all about. Above the mantel was a large oil painting of a man on a horse. The man looked very distinguished and seemed larger than life. The picture dominated the room. He wondered if it was Andrea's father. Although beautifully decorated, the room had no life, the energy was flat. Something traumatic had happened to this woman and he wondered what it could have been.

He had intended to hide from Andrea but he was so fascinated by the surroundings, especially the frame without a picture, that he lingered. He wanted to get a feel for the hidden Andrea and thought it would be there in her private world. Scott moved over to the window and looked down at the Queensborough Bridge and the East River. With no sound, it was like looking at another picture.

"There you are," Andrea said, as she walked towards him. "I hope you didn't mind the note."

Scott turned from the window and watched her as she crossed the room. She was breathtakingly beautiful. Their eyes met and held for a minute. It was Andrea who lowered her eyes first.

"What can I get you to drink? I did buy tomato juice." They both laughed.

"That sounds like just my kind of drink."

"Well are you dying of hunger or do you want to sit for a while?"

"I'm dying of hunger," he said.

"Very well then, dinner it is. I warn you, I'm no Julia Childs, but if you do get ill I have some basic nursing skills that may suffice until we get to the emergency room."

"I have something for you." he said, handing her a garment bag.

"My dress. Thank you. I'd forgotten all about it. I will fetch your sweats before you leave."

Andrea was in a jovial mood and Scott found being with her was more and more enjoyable.

The dining room was a splash of color. Either Andrea had

multiple personalities or she was trying to create a different feeling in each room of the house, Scott thought.

"I'm glad we're seated together. I could not have a conversation with you at the other end of this monstrous table," he said pulling out the chair for her.

"My husband and I entertained a lot."

Two maids in black uniforms with organdy aprons served dinner and then disappeared. Dinner turned out to be better than Andrea had expected.

"Let's take our dessert into the sitting room," Andrea said, leading the way, "we can have coffee, or tea if you like, and we can listen to some music." Andrea opened the double doors off the dining room and led the way down a long corridor.

"This is just one apartment?" Scott asked.

"Actually, we had three of them converted into one. We had to have a gym and a beauty parlor and an office and a swimming pool put in, you see."

"Do you get lost in here?"

"On occasion. But I like this part of the house better."

Andrea pressed a button in the wall and soft music filled the room.

"I've brought you something else," Scott said, reaching into his jacket and pulling out a flat square box. Andrea was delighted. She seldom received presents.

"Thank you so much, Scott," she said, opening the package. "Kitaro."

Andrea slipped the disc into the player that seemed to appear from nowhere. They sat together on the couch, listening to the Kitaro music. Andrea leaned back and closed her eyes, letting the music fill her being. The sound was so clear and precise and each note seem to teach a special message. She was startled when Scott spoke.

"Andrea, why do you have the empty picture frame on the

mantle?"

"Scott, do you ever stop being a psychiatrist? I told you before, if there is something I want you to know I'll tell you."

"I guess I listen better when I ask questions," Scott said, looking deep into her eyes. Andrea shuddered. His look was like the one she had seen in Maya's eyes when they first met at the dance in Stougborough, a look that penetrated her soul. He unnerved her. She hated the way he questioned her and she hated his curiosity. She should not have invited him here.

"Listen Andrea," he said, "I would like to help if I could."

"Help? I don't need your help," she said. "Stop trying to analyze me. I know your type, you cannot go out with anyone who is not close to a nervous breakdown, someone you can save and help to live a productive life. Well, Dr. Preston, you have the wrong person. As you can see, I'm a very successful woman. I take care of myself. I always have and I always will. And this is the last time I intend to have this conversation."

"I am not analyzing you, Andrea, and I'm sure that you are a woman of many resources. I'm just speaking as a friend."

"A day at the movies and a dinner does not qualify one as a friend. Be careful, you may be overstating your position."

"Andrea, be honest with yourself. You have to face whatever is bothering you," he said, ignoring her outburst, "or you will forever be tormented."

"There you go again," she said, "now you are making assumptions that I am tormented. What the hell do you even know about me?"

"I know you," he said, "I don't know how, but I know you." Couldn't we talk about it?"

"About what?"

"Tell me what made you cry out in your sleep."

"No," Andrea pleaded, "don't ask me anymore."

"Andrea, I am just trying to get to know you. I really want to get to know you," he said softly.

"I thought you already knew me," she said, repeating his earlier words.

"I recognize your soul," he said, "but I need to know what you have done with it in this lifetime."

Andrea laughed out loud, but the laugh was not filled with joy. She looked at Scott, wanting to trust him, feeling safe with him. Something deep in her psyche told her it was all right but her conscious mind kept screaming, Don't let him in! She had spent many years burying her past and now here he was dredging it up. She would go quite mad if she allowed the thoughts of Helen to come into focus. She shook her head trying to solidify the thin ice that her psyche was skating on, feeling her resistance dissolving.

"Scott," she said, "you want me in your bed and that makes you want to listen to my problems. When my problems get rough or I get too crazy to be with, you'll leave me—if I don't leave you first. I feel something for you that I have not felt for a long time, but I'm just not good at close relationships."

"I'm willing to take a chance if you are, to try to be there for you while you resolve your conflicts. Andrea, most emotional conflicts are in the imagination. It's fear."

"No one would call me fearful. Most men don't even see me as a woman; they see a castrating bitch and they're intimidated by me. At first they run to my beck and call. After a few days I end up tiring of them."

"Both you and those types of men have the same problem. You are each suffering from low self-esteem. They act out theirs by being submissive and you by being controlling. Andrea, what you need is total harmony to balance your energies."

"Tell that to Rachel Hersey. I promised her that when I found a man that was not intimidated by me I would let her know," Andrea interjected.

"Power and happiness cannot be found in material things," he continued. "That's only achieved with inner peace. True strength often comes when you give the unknown a chance."

Andrea said firmly, "I'm talking about reality, and there you go again with your hocus pocus stuff."

"It's not hocus pocus, Andrea, it is the essence of life. Knowing one's self is the only mystery, and mastering that knowledge is contentment. That's all New Age theory is, really Andrea that's it. I'd like you to start studying with me," he said, "I promise you, it will be worth it."

Andrea needed to smoke a cigarette, but she could never admit needing anything in front of Scott.

"I have a friend that you should talk with," he wrote on a notepad, "here is her phone number. Will you make an appointment to see her?" He put the paper on the coffee table and glanced at his watch. "It's already eleven o'clock. I really must go."

Andrea could think of no way of asking him to stay without seeming needy, and that admission was against her principles.

"I had a wonderful evening," he said, looking deep into her eyes.

"I enjoyed it too, Scott. Thank you for coming."

Andrea walked with him to the elevator door and watched him as he waited for it. When it arrived he went inside. She wanted him to come back, but she simply stood there.

"Andrea," he said, as the elevator door was closing, "Never forget that I am a man. And you are very much a woman, a very desirable woman, with brains and brawn and—tits." He smiled and the door closed.

What did he mean by that, she wondered? Her next thought was that she had not given him back his sweatsuit. She could dial the doorman and have Scott return, but she decided not to.

Chapter 28

Andrea sat quietly on the sofa, closed her eyes and thought over the evening with Scott. Scott Preston was undoubtedly an interesting, and dangerous, man. A vivid memory of him standing by the elevator, so handsome and so very self-assured, rose in her mind. She found his enigmatic smile irresistible and the tone of his voice comforting. Like it or not, she was forced to admit she had enjoyed his company immensely; and if she really wanted to be honest, she would guess she was falling in love. But of course she did not want to be honest.

Andrea tried to push Scott out of her mind with little or no success. "Damn you to hell, Scott," she whispered.

"You're scared, Andrea," she said to herself.

"Damn right," she replied, "Men like that can topple women's careers, turn them into pathetic fools with aprons and snot-nose children."

Her conversation with Laura in Paris sixteen years before

resounded in her head: I want to be different, I want to make my mark on the world. I want to eat caviar and wear Van Cleef & Arpels jewelry. I just can't settle for what most women want.

"God!" Andrea exclaimed, "Why are men allowed to make such fools out of women?" She had seen her material fantasy become a reality, and she would be damned if she would allow anyone to change that. Not ever. Not even Scott Preston. She had to maintain control over her own life!

"But," she renewed her introspection, "is it really Scott that makes me respond to him this way, or am I just trying to please Adam?"

"You must go on and love again, Andrea," he had said when he was dying. "Share the love that we have had for each other, experience the comfort of true love without the barriers. I want for you, most of all, to be loved the way you have loved me."

Could her subconscious mind be so powerful that she would invent love just to honor Adam's wish? Would Scott then just be Adam's replacement? She could not answer those questions.

But suspicion began to nag her. Somehow everything that had happened to her was just too coincidental: the interview with Rachel Hersey that brought Scott into her life with his New Age philosophy; the phone call from Maya, forcing her desperate need to forget Helen's birth to come into focus; and now the chance to meet her daughter after all these years; and finally Adam's death. If she did not know better, she would think there was a curse on her—or some unfathomable conspiracy was taking place.

"Beware those who claim loyalty and friendship," the old man had said. Andrea was suddenly chilled.

Her mind rambled on: What if there was any truth to those New Age theories? What exactly did this mean to her? And if it promised such peace and comfort, why was her awareness of it throwing her life into chaos? The recent events in her life certainly did not seem to be promoting a progression towards harmony, as the Buddhist fortune teller had said they would.

"Cleansing is necessary before perfection," Shakti had said. "Learning about life is like peeling an onion. We must shed our outer layers to get to the core, and along the way there will be many tears. As the cook learns to prevent the tears that peeling an onion causes by refrigerating it, so some people cheat themselves of life's experiences. This is called sublimation. And many people go through life denying pain, but denial is just delaying the inevitable. All of us will come to the light at some point in time. All of us will have to shed tears.

"Andrea, you are a special being. I know you don't understand this, but you will. Yes, I know that you are highly developed spiritually, but you are blocking the knowledge that you need in order to actualize your spirituality. Once you give yourself permission to know your creator and experience your oneness with the universe, life will be easier for you."

Was she really someone special as Melissa, Maya and Shakti told her, or was she caving in to the madness of loneliness? It was true that she felt strangely peaceful listening to Scott, but was it enough to continue exploring this theoretical metaphysical nonsense? Was it nonsense?

Then how could she explain Maya? She thought back to the night they had met at the Presley Hall party. Her resonance with Maya had been magnetic, uncontrollable, hypnotic; and that psychic allure continued to baffle her. What had she seen in those blue eyes? She had never found out.

Even though she was mentally and physically exhausted, she knew that sleep was not going to come easily, but she went through the motions and wearily climbed into bed.

The shrillness of the telephone ring made her jump as it jolted her mind back to the present. It must be Melissa, she thought.

Looking at her watch as she reached over to answer the phone, she saw that it was nearly one o'clock.

"Hi, darling. I know I should have called you, but it was getting late."

"Hi," Scott said cheerfully, "I hope that was intended for me. I love to be called darling. I thought you may be a little worried about my drive home, so I'm reporting that I got here safely."

"Oh! Scott. I'm sorry, I thought you were someone else."

"I can't say I am not disappointed, but don't be sorry because darling sounds wonderful to me. Use it any time."

"I am glad that you are home safely," Andrea said changing the direction of the conversation, "but I really didn't worry because, you see, I believe people can negotiate their own lives. And cars. But, it was thoughtful of you though to call, and—darling— goodnight."

"Call me that again."

"Not on your life."

"Then how about lunch tomorrow?"

"I can't. And if we don't find something else to do besides eat, I'm going to turn into a porker."

"How about tennis?"

"Sorry. I don't play tennis. Scott," Andrea said, "where is this psychic you mentioned?"

"Seventy-First and Riverside. Get a pen and I'll give you the address."

Andrea lay awake most of the night. Her mind would not stop mulling over the peculiar events that were happening to her.

"When you need the answers to your questions, the people who have them will be provided, Andrea, all you have to do is ask." Another piece of Scott's know-it-all wisdom.

The sky was light when Andrea finally turned off the lamp and drifted off to sleep.

On the third day Scott called again. She did not take his call. Over the past three days of speculation and rational thinking, she had decided it was too risky to continue seeing Scott. She had come very close to telling him about her past the night he came to dinner, and that scared her. After just two dates with a man who had called her neurotic on national television, she had felt disarmed enough to divulge to him a secret that could destroy her life in one fell swoop! She had to be crazy!

When Andrea decided to take a week off from Jacobson's Industry, the entire organization was in shock. She spent her days in the library reading about Eastern metaphysical research, looking through everything she could find on such foreign ideas as karma, mantras and chakras. The more she read, the more confused she became. Five days later she could still not fathom how any of the knowledge she was acquiring could be useful. But true to form, and as Scott had said, suddenly she was coming in contact with all kinds of crackpots spouting their beliefs. There seemed all of a sudden to be some sort of epidemic infecting those who were probably camouflaged as progressive Americans. "No!" she thought, "It's like buying a new car, once you own it, you begin to notice everyone else who has one!"

It was surprising, nevertheless, to observe those who were involved in New Age theory. Andrea had expected people with less control over their lives and little education to give in to what she considered brainwashing. On the contrary, what she found was that the affected group was made up almost exclusively of the intellectual elite. The highly educated were falling like flies into the "White Light."

If there was any purpose other than intellectual challenge to the massive movement of New Age theorists, Andrea was yet to find it. The last time she had seen quantum leaps was in her undergraduate physics class, which she almost failed miserably. Much as Andrea wanted to deny her growing interest, day by day she found herself becoming more curious. Finally she decided to take the next step. What the hell she thought, nothing else could go wrong in her life, so why not?

Andrea visualized the headlines if the media were to find out about her interest in metaphysics: "MULTIMILLIONAIRE ANDREA JACOBSON NEXT ACQUISITION MARS BY ASTRAL PROJECTION? Andrea laughed aloud, earning herself a cross glance from the stern-looking librarian assigned to a desk near the cubicle she occupied. She closed the book, donned her wide-brimmed hat, sun glasses and coat and walked inconspicuously to the exit.

Returning to work the following Monday, she spent hours simply staring into space. Nothing was getting better. Her agitation was even more pronounced. She noticed that her staff, even Janice, avoided her as much as possible.

It was useless trying to concentrate. She was losing her sense of reality and in danger of losing everything she had worked so hard for. In less than six months her life had completely changed: her work seemed unimportant; the only man she had ever loved was dead; Maya, the ghost from her past was trying to blackmail her; Scott Preston was pressing her to find her inner self; and in two weeks she would meet her daughter. Andrea felt a sense of impending doom, that her life was about to come crashing down around her. What the hell she thought, she might as well let them blame her fall on her belief in black magic. It would be better than reports that she had failed.

Andrea pushed the button that revealed her well-stocked bar and poured herself a brandy. She dialed her secretary.

"Janice, under no circumstances do I want to be disturbed for the rest of the day."

By the time Andrea was ready to leave her office late in the evening she was well on her way to being drunk. She called down to have David pull the car into the garage on the ground level of the building.

Inside the Towers, Andrea walked with her shoulders back trying hard to concentrate on the patterns in the carpet to help her balance. She continued drinking steadily through most of the night, but even with the amount of brandy she had consumed, sleep did not come easily

On Tuesday morning, Andrea slept until a concerned Melissa pulled the curtains in her bedroom. As she got out of bed she felt a wave of nausea that sent her flying into the bathroom.

"Andrea," Melissa said, noticing the empty bottle of brandy on the bedside table, "this drinking has got to stop. Child, I never interfere in your private life, but I will be damned if I will sit by and watch you destroy your life.

"Andrea, Adam is dead. Dead! Do you hear me? I suggest you pull yourself together. I have sent for Doctor Harding. He will give you something to help you sleep."

For the next four days, Melissa watched over Andrea like a mother hen. Andrea was up at seven, exercised until eight-thirty, ate breakfast, went for long walks with Melissa and read everything she could about God's intention.

On Saturday, a package arrived from Scott. It was an autographed copy of his book. It was entitled "Love, The Only Way To Self Mastery." With it was another book called "A Course In Miracles." Andrea decided she was not ready to deal with her thoughts of Scott or Scott's book. That night she began reading the other. God knew, if she needed anything it was a miracle.

Chapter 29

At four o'clock Sunday evening, Andrea, dressed in her oldest pair of jeans, dark glasses and a wide-brimmed hat, took the elevator to the garage and quickly made her way to the black BMW, looking around carefully to make sure she was not being followed. Since her interview on the Rachel Heresy show, reporters seemed to want to follow her everywhere. Andrea got into her car, the 325i BMW being the least conspicuous one she owned, drove out of the garage and headed toward the West Side, crossing Central Park at Fifty-Ninth Street. She flew up Broadway to Seventy-Second Street where she turned left to Riverside Drive.

After locating the number on one of the massive old buildings that faced the Hudson on Riverside at Seventy-First, she found a parking place nearby. "Psychic Readings" the small bronze sign over the door proclaimed. For a moment her preoccupation with this karma stuff seemed silly. What was she doing here? Other than a mild depression and some obstacles to overcome, there was nothing wrong with her. Her depression was certainly understandable. She was mourning the death of Adam. Andrea was about to turn around when the apartment door opened.

"Ah! Come in, please," a middle-aged woman said, "I am Madaline."

"I am Andrea Jacobson. I called yesterday morning." Andrea shook the woman's extended hand.

"I know quite well who you are, I read the papers, and I must admit I am especially addicted to the gossip magazines. You have had your share of publicity recently, eh?"

"Quite." Andrea replied.

"May I get you some tea or coffee?"

"I would like coffee, thank you," Andrea said, looking around the cavernous living room, which was neat and clean. Surprisingly, there was no incense burning nor was there a crystal ball on the table.

Madaline came back with her cup of coffee. "Please, be seated," she said, gesturing to an armchair.

"I am not a believer in psychic phenomena," Andrea began, as she and Madaline sat down, "but I was curious about some events I've been experiencing lately. I have done some preliminary reading, but I'm afraid I am more confused than I was before I started. I need some answers that can't wait."

"There is nothing to believe," Madaline said quietly. "Psychic phenomena is a part of your everyday life. Sometimes I think the names we give to learning scares people. What it should be called, really, is self-knowledge. For every skill there is a predetermined path to learning. Andrea, every idea you have is a psychic phenomenon. Even your idea to come here."

"No, that was Scott Preston's. He believes that you may convince me that I am God."

"If you develop your talents and rise to the perfection of your higher self then indeed you will be God. God is perfection and so can you be. It takes much dedication to find the truth, but most of all it takes faith in the unexplainable. Why do you seek my help?"

"Over the past five months several things have happened in my life that have forced me to do much soul-searching. I need explanations and maybe some solutions that will help me overcome the hurdles."

"You want to have all the information before you make decisions? Spoken like a true businesswoman."

"Well that's what I am," Andrea said impatiently.

"Yes, but one of the seven requirements for ultimate understanding is patience. You are growing Andrea, and growth takes time and patience. Life does not always go exactly as we think it should, but the direction it takes is necessary for our ascent. Even your pain and confusion is progress. So many times we create situations in our stagnant lives that will cause upheaval so that we can progress to a new level of consciousness. Mankind has resisted change since the beginning of time, but," she emphasized, "to enter into the white light of God one must embark on a quest of self-discovery, and only through self-mastery can we attain ultimate perfection. To find the answers you need you will have to spend time in self-discovery."

"I am not sure that I want to know all there is to know about myself, nor do I want to be God."

"My dear," Madaline said, refilling the coffee cups "you made this choice a long time ago. You have been preparing for your spiritual evolution since the age of thirteen. You are a highly developed soul and your self actualization will be an inspiration to many people. Your economic success is just a small part of your work. It has brought you worldwide recognition so that you can be heard by those who wish to hear, and it has also taken away the misconception that money can buy everything."

Andrea sat forward in her chair. "What do you mean, since the age of thirteen?"

"It will all be clear to you soon. Your soul mate has chosen to leave this world so you can get rid of the last crutch of dependency that you possess."

"But I am not a dependent person," Andrea said, annoyed.

"You are, and that is why you become so angry at people you perceive to be dependent on you. It brings your own imperfection too close into view. You will be taking a trip in two weeks that will bring you much peace and much torment. Your ability to transcend this obstacle will be the final test for your transition into a spiritual being."

Andrea slumped back in her chair. How could this woman know so much about her?

"I don't know any more about you than you know about yourself," she said as though reading her mind. "You already have all the answers you are searching for, if you care to listen."

"Listen to what?"

"Your inner voice. I think we have done enough," she said, seeing the strain in Andrea. "Be patient, in time you will know all that is necessary. I will give you the name of a master teacher. Call him. He will take you to the next level of consciousness. Just always remember my child, the road you must travel is not easy and the disappointments are many. Trust very few and always listen to your own intuitive voice."

Madaline walked Andrea to her car and waved goodbye as she got behind the wheel of the BMW. Andrea was deeply perturbed by their meeting. She should never have listened to Scott, it served her right. Andrea knew there had to be a rational explanation for all of this. There was a creepy suspicion that she was not actively directing her life but that it was being directed for her. She flipped the heater switch to full blast. She was cold...very cold, but it could not have been from the chill outside. It was summer. Andrea pressed on the accelerator and the car shot forward. Dependent person indeed!

She did not know where to go. She could not go back to her

apartment, she was too shaken to be alone, yet she did not want to burden Melissa who had been her savior over the last two weeks. She crossed the park at Seventy-Second Street and kept going until she reached the East Side Drive, where she turned north. She found herself on the Long Island Expressway, heading toward the Hamptons.

"Andrea," Scott said opening the door, "what a nice surprise. Have you been out of the country again?"

"I'm sorry," she began, "I should have called first."

"Nonsense," he said, "Didn't I tell you that you have a standing invitation to my home?"

"Well, here I am. Are you alone?"

"Yes, of course."

"Dr. Preston, I'm surprised. You don't have a Sunday girlfriend like most men?"

"What on earth is a Sunday girlfriend?"

"Oh come now, Scott. A Sunday girlfriend is the homey type of woman who acts as a surrogate wife to a man for as long as she is useful and not demanding. She usually cooks dinner and is never seen again until the following Sunday."

"Yuk! I don't think I would want a girl who cooks and cleans and obeys orders. I can always rent a robot. I prefer my women more challenging, terribly smart and super-confident, somewhat like you. I must admit, however, I like them to return my calls and stay in touch."

"I suppose I deserved that. So tell me," Andrea continued "what does a handsome man like you do on Sundays?"

"I meditate, I relax, I read the paper and sometimes I write. At this time there is no special woman in my life, but I have a feeling that is about to change."

"I see."

"Now, Andrea," he said coming back to the subject she had evaded from the moment she arrived, "tell me why you did not call me or return my calls?"

"I needed some time to think."

"Okay," he said, dropping the subject, "Then how about being my Sunday girl today? I am sure it will be punishment enough."

"I don't cook."

"That's not what I remember."

"Melissa did most of the dinner."

"Who is Melissa?"

"An old friend who takes care of me."

"All right then. You can be my Sunday girl who does not cook. And if you want you can be my Monday and Tuesday, et cetera, et cetera, girl as well."

"I saw that movie."

"What movie?"

"*The King and I.* Et cetera, et cetera, et cetera," she mimicked.

Scott chuckled. "Andrea, I'm glad you're here. Will you stay awhile?"

"If you want me to. But first explain this, not one woman in your life, Scott? Be honest."

"There was a time," he said, "when I could never seem to get enough of women. I got to be quite an expert at juggling women and my time. Then it all got very boring and none of them could measure up."

"Measure up to whom?"

"My wife. After Angela died, I tried to find someone who would bring me comfort, but I could never find anyone quite like her. Most women today want excitement and constant entertaining and I guess I'm looking for togetherness and growth."

"I am sorry about your wife, how long has it been?"

"Seven years in March. She had an aneurysm during her sixth month of pregnancy. They were forced to take the baby to try and save her life—but neither she nor the child survived."

"Oh Scott I'm so sorry, I didn't mean to..."

"It's all right, Andrea. I loved my wife very much and I would have loved the daughter she carried, but things happen for a reason. If I did not believe that, I'd have gone mad. That was when I became totally immersed in New Age theory. Angela had first introduced me to the concepts when we were in medical school together. Some scientists we were. After her death I was so angry with her for leaving me that I rejected those teachings. I became very self-destructive, choosing to be with women who were entirely unsuitable. I didn't realize that I was responsible for the choices I made.

"Then a good friend finally got me to see Madaline. As I began to heal I felt a power so new and so focused, I began fulfilling many of my dreams. Within eight months I had published my second book. I had been quite content with my own company—until I met you."

"Me? what do I have to do with it?"

"To be quite honest, I have fallen in love with you."

"Don't say that, Scott," Andrea said, taking a step toward him, "I can bring you nothing but pain."

"I love you. There is no pain in that for me."

"Please listen, Scott. I saw Madaline today."

"So that's why you are here, is it? And all this time I thought it was because you just had to see me," he smiled.

"Scott, I came to you because I needed to. After talking with Madaline I realize that I'm not capable of a relationship right now. I'm too mixed up. There are other commitments in my life at the moment that preclude a serious friendship and require so much attention."

"But Andrea, who is talking about a relationship?"

"I thought that was what you were leading up to."

"No," he said moving closer to her. "I was simply going to tell you that I wanted to kiss you and I want more than a relationship.

I want you to marry me."

Scott stepped forward and took her in his arms. Her head rested on his shoulders. He stroked her hair and cradled her until Andrea relaxed into the circle of his embrace. She felt her body begin to quiver.

"Scott—"

"Never mind," he whispered. Scott knew why Andrea had come. She was frightened at what was happening to her. His instincts told him she was ready to take a chance on life and discover the true meaning of love. That her search might exclude him was a possibility, but tonight he wanted her with him. He wanted her in his arms, and he desperately wanted her there for all time.

She was just a frightened child, a child who had learned to sublimate her disappointments in love. Yes indeed, a mere child that needed comforting. He held her close to him until she stopped shaking.

Scott moved his hand down the small of her back bringing it to rest momentarily on her buttocks. She eased her body into the natural curve of his, succumbing to his caress.

"I'm so frightened," she began, her voice uncertain. "It seems like my whole life is coming apart at the seams. Oh Scott," she sighed, "and I had been so careful all these years to sew it up so neatly. Everything may have a purpose and a reason but I don't know what this means, or why. All I know is that it frightens me."

"I wish I had a simple answer for you. Just don't worry about being distressed or confused, because out of confusion," he continued, "comes clarity. Darling, life is more than success and money. It's about love and friendships and family and children. How long does the pleasure of a new dress or a new deal last? Love is everlasting, and the fact that you are on the path of understanding that should comfort you—"

"Why are you being so good to me?" Andrea asked, "What is

it that you want from me?"

"I'm only being who I am. I want to know you totally. I want you to be my wife," he continued, "But I'm willing to wait until you trust me completely."

Something snapped in Andrea. Trust! Trust! What the fuck did he know about trust? She had trusted Adam and he had died and left her; she had trusted Maya and she had not even let her see her child at birth; she had trusted her father and Alex and each of them had left her. What did trust and love have to do with anything? She hated feeling out of control but worse than that, she hated to be treated like a child who knew nothing about living. It was more than she could tolerate. She had more life experiences than most people her age, and in spite of her losses, she had made something wonderful of her life. Each time she had turned her loss or failure into a win. She did know what it was like to love and be loved. Whose fault was it that circumstances beyond her control had prevented her happiness? Fuck them all. The faith and love that they were asking her to have had taken away her tranquillity.

Andrea detached herself from Scott's grip, began unbuttoning her blouse and allowed it to fall to the floor. Her firm breasts stood waiting for his touch.

"What part of me do you want to get to know first, Scott?" she said moving his hand over her breasts, "Spare me the monologue about trust and all that shit," she snarled. "Tell me why when men want to fuck you they always somehow find the right words and shortly after they're satisfied, the part of their brain responsible for such verbal tenderness seems removed by instant lobotomy? Why bother to act like some kind of saint? Just tell me that you want me in your bed. I have no problem with a good fuck. I like uncomplicated sex."

"Andrea, what has gotten into you?" I'm not interested in just getting to know your body," he said, "I want to get to know your soul too."

"Don't patronize me, Scott. I'm no fool."

A kind of madness had come over her. He wanted her soul, huh? Well, she would give it to him. Her outburst and lewdness had heightened her desire for Scott and now she wanted him inside her. All she wanted tonight was a warm body and the wild abandon of lust, not the deadly commitment of a relationship.

Andrea continued undressing. She unzipped her jeans, allowing them to fall around her ankles, lifting first one and then the other foot out of them. She stood before him completely naked.

"Do you want to make love to me, Scott," Andrea said tantalizingly, or do you just want to fuck?" Meanwhile her mind was screaming, what are you doing?

"Andrea," Scott began, "this behavior is entirely uncalled for and unnecessary."

"It's necessary to me," she said, wrapping her arms around his neck. "Let's get it straight right from the beginning. I find you terribly attractive and I don't mind having a roll in the sack with you. I'm sure it will be good for both of us."

"Andrea," he reprimanded, "put your clothes on and join me in the kitchen."

Ignoring Scott's order, she pushed him back onto the sofa and straddled him, arching her back so that her nipple was right over his mouth. "Taste them," she said enticingly, "I know you want me."

"Get up," Scott said angrily, pushing her aside so forcefully she fell to the floor. "Put your clothes on. Now! Or I'll throw you out of my house just as you are." Scott moved around the room picking up pieces of clothes strewn all over and threw them to her.

Her tall figure looked tiny as she sat on the floor, and Scott, although feeling he had been terribly hard on her, knew he had to do something drastic to bring her back to her senses. It was as if some devil had taken over Andrea's personality. He moved close to her, touching her shoulder. She was completely unresponsive.

"Believe me, Andrea," he said kindly, turning her face toward him, "I do want your body, but only if it comes with your heart." Andrea finally looked up at Scott, and even though his eyes expressed deep concern, there was no mistaking that he meant every word he had said about throwing her out.

"I'm so very sorry, Scott," Andrea said brokenly, lifting her mascara-stained, contorted face to him. "Scott," she repeated, "how can you ever forgive me?" She was horribly ashamed and confused.

"It's all right, Andrea," he said, gently putting her blouse around her shoulders, "I understand. It's a feeling of helplessness that sometimes makes us behave in ways we wouldn't normally. Get dressed and let's have some tea." He kissed her gently on the lips and stood waiting patiently until she was fully dressed. She followed him silently into the kitchen.

"Do you want some coffee?"

"Are you angry with me?"

"I'm not angry, Andrea. I know you're scared, darling, but trust me, it will be all right, you'll see."

"Oh Scott, I'm frightened of loving. If only you understood."

"If you were to tell me, I'd understand."

"Maybe one day—I'll be able to."

"Andrea, don't you want to be close to someone, to share with someone, to give to and to receive from someone, to trust someone?"

"I don't know if that's possible anymore. You see, everyone I've ever loved has been taken away from me and all that's left is the sadness, the emptiness, the pain. Scott, please don't ask me for what I cannot give, not now."

"It's been an emotional day for you, my dearest. Come and rest for awhile. I'll bring your coffee upstairs to you."

He led her to the bedroom where she had slept the night before. Again she admired the beauty and the simple elegance of the room. When she returned from the bathroom after washing her face and putting on the same nightgown she had worn before, she saw that Scott was turning the covers back for her.

"Scott," Andrea touched his hand, "please forgive me again. I've been under a lot of stress lately and as poor an excuse as it is, I guess it accounts for my behavior. Thank you for your patience and understanding."

"Remember that I'm a trained physician, my dear. I recognize symptoms of stress," he said, smiling.

"No matter what happens, Scott, will you be my friend?"

"I want to be more than a friend, I want you in my life. I haven't felt this much love for anyone since my wife died, but I want you to know that total commitment is all I will accept."

"I have no idea what the future will hold for us, Scott."

"When the time comes, and it will come, I won't accept less than all of you, Andrea, mind, body and soul. Now enough of this conversation, what do you say to that coffee?"

"I would rather you sit here with me until I have fallen asleep."

"Of course." Scott eased himself into the big Victorian armchair by the bed. He reached over to turn out the light, but Andrea stopped his hand. Moments later she was sound asleep.

Concerned about her, Scott sat watching Andrea's steady breathing, her rib cage pushing her shapely breasts up and down. He knew there was a mystery she was hiding, but what worried him was why she was so frightened. Whatever it was had devastated her so much that she had chosen to block it out. Feeling sleepy, Scott slid down in the chair, put his feet on the ottoman and switched off the light.

Andrea awoke drenched in perspiration, in tears. Her clothes were tightly wound around her body and she could hardly breath. Loosening the constricting grip of her nightgown, Andrea sat up still disoriented from the dream and in pitch darkness. She had no idea where she was.

"Oh God!" she screamed, fumbling frantically to find a light.

Scott jumped as the sound of breaking glass shattered his sleep.

"Andrea, Andrea, what is it?" he said, reaching for the lamp and turning on the light. He was beside her in a flash. Andrea's usually bright brown eyes were dulled with fear.

"My God, darling, what is it?"

Andrea looked around the room, slowly remembering the events of the evening.

"I had a nightmare," she said quietly, "that's all. Goodness, Scott, I've broken your lovely Baccarat vase. I'll clean it up and have a new one sent to you tomorrow."

Scott knelt beside the bed and took Andrea in his arms. "What is it that makes you so scared, Andrea?" he questioned her earnestly, ignoring the shattered vase.

"I don't know, I have the same dream night after night, but when I am awake I can never remember it. All I know is that it is a frightening nightmare and I always wake up feeling as though I'm suffocating. I'm all right now, but I would like some brandy, Scott, if you don't mind."

He said quietly, "I am going to make some tea. It will help you relax. Sometimes alcohol works as a stimulant."

Andrea sat up, rearranged the pillows propping herself against the headboard, grateful to be alone. She was still embarrassed from the earlier scene, but now with this new display of neurosis, she wanted to sink into the ground. Her mind drifted back to the evening and her appalling behavior. She had gone completely mad. Was she that frightened of falling in love? That was probably it, she decided. Love never goes the way it should, and 'happy ever after' never happens in real life. But could her fear be so great that she could make such a complete fool of herself?

She was lost in thought when Scott returned, a steaming cup in his hand.

"Am I about to get murdered?" he asked, handing her the cup.

"What do you mean?"

"That scowl on your face is kind of scary."

Andrea smiled, "I was just thinking."

"About what?"

"About life."

"There are so many things I don't know about you, Andrea. Are you ever going to trust me?"

"I don't know, Scott. That's the truth."

"Drink this," he ordered, "it's herbal tea." Scott swept up the broken glass and sat on the side of the bed. She was calmer now and even in her helpless state he wanted her more than he had ever wanted any woman.

"Move over, I'm getting in bed with you for the rest of the night," he said, removing his clothes as Andrea watched, not knowing what to expect. Andrea looked nervously at the clock. It was one in the morning. Although she was grateful that Scott was getting into bed with her, she was anxious about the hours until daylight. As she moved over to accommodate him, he put his arms around her and pulled her close. She did not resist.

"One day you will believe me," he said, kissing her forehead, "but for now you are safe here with me. Go back to sleep."

"Just so you don't turn into a werewolf before dawn," Andrea smiled, as she snuggled up to his warm hairy chest. "I must say Dr. Preston, I do feel very safe in your arms."

"You will always be safe with me," he said.

She moved more closely into his embrace and every fiber of her body told her that she was home. "Scott," she whispered, "be patient, darling."

"I will," he said kissing her tenderly on the lips. Before long she was asleep.

"Good morning, good-looking," Scott woke her with

breakfast on a silver tray. "I made bacon and eggs." He placed it on the bed table.

"Breakfast in bed, how nice. Do keep it warm until I return."

He lit a match.

"You are incredible, you idiot," she laughed, climbing out of bed and kissing him lightly. When Andrea returned from the bathroom, Scott kissed her and to her surprise, Andrea found herself instantly adrift in a sea of eroticism.

Scott held back the sheets and Andrea got back in bed. "You are beautiful," he said, sliding his hand inside her nightgown, caressing her thighs.

"I have wanted to touch you this way for so long," his hand continued upwards, his warm breath caressing her face.

"Is this what you consider breakfast in bed?" Andrea teased, removing her nightgown.

"It can be very filling," he said, kissing her, allowing his hand to slide over her belly, his fingers moving over her breasts. She felt her body contract.

"I want to make love to you Andrea," he said, climbing on top of her. "Do you want to love me back?"

"I think so," she said, in a little voice.

He cupped her face between his hands and kissed her tenderly. Andrea felt the room spin and she could not tell if it was from hunger or the kiss.

"Oh Scott," she moaned, "I need you very much."

His eyes were fixed on her face as she responded to his touch, but Scott could sense that she was not fully lubricated. He lowered her to the pillow. When she was fully accessible he buried his face inside her. Andrea's body convulsed in pleasure as his tongue darted over her, indulging her in forgotten fulfillment. Sounds of rapture escaped her lips and then suddenly she froze. She was fighting the memory of her past, slowly draining her of her desire. Scott moved his body up until he was directly over her and pushed himself slowly inside her. He was aware of the sudden stiffening of her body when he was only halfway inside her. He was allowed to go no further.

"What is it, Andrea?"

"I can't."

"Why not?"

"Because I just can't."

"How long has it been since you have made love to a man?"

"About six weeks. Before that, whenever I called one of my lovers."

"Lovers! You mean you keep them on call?

"Pretty much."

"And have you always stopped like this with them?"

"No."

"So this is the first time it's happened?"

"No. It first happened in England—after I came back from Surrey. It only happens with people I might fall in love with."

"Did you not sleep with your husband?"

"Our relationship was more or less platonic. Alex knew I was never in love with him. He didn't ask for much."

"What about the person in England when it first happened?"

"Ralph. He was my friend and I loved him, but we were never able to make love. I told you, Scott, I'm a basket case. I had a lover that left an indelible scar on my heart. To make love with someone else feels like betrayal. I have no problem with casual sex, only with sex that means caring from the heart. I *am* crazy aren't I?"

"Without question a true loon. Do you want me?"

"Yes, more than anything."

"Then let me in."

"I can't."

"Andrea, I want you to let me in right now."

"I can't, Scott, I can't."

"Andrea, I love you. Do you know that? What happened to you in Surrey?"

"Nothing, who said anything about Surrey?"

"You did a few moments ago."

"I had my daughter. She will be fourteen next month and I have never seen her since the day of her birth."

Scott looked at Andrea and for a moment wondered what he had gotten himself into, not sure if he should or could play doctor both in and out of bed.

"Andrea, you have to stop feeling guilty about what has happened in the past. Fourteen years is a long time to grieve. Don't push me away. Let me help you."

"You want to leave me now," she said, "I told you not to pry. If you hadn't been so nosy, you'd have had what you needed last night without complications. But no! You couldn't leave well enough alone, could you? And you wanted my soul! Christ, why did you have to be so insistent?"

"Who said I'm leaving you?"

"You've given up on me; I can tell by your eyes," she said. "You know they are the mirror of the soul."

"I am not going anywhere, but I think the time has come for you to trust me."

"I have never before come this close to being with another man because I wanted to be," Andrea began, "not since—" she allowed her sentence to trail off. "No one knows about Helen, no one except Maya and two others. No one else knows that I had her. I want you to forget what I have just said. Promise me."

"Who is Maya?"

"The one who helped me during my pregnancy—she took Helen away, and has taken care of her for the past fourteen years."

"That explains the empty frame then," he said. "Who is her father?"

"I will not tell you that."

305

"Do you love me?"

"I don't know."

He eased her back, his body pinning her on the bed.

"Say it, Andrea, say it."

This time he plunged deep into her forcing, her to yield.

"Andrea," he repeated, "I want to know if you love me."

"I don't know," she whispered again.

He pushed himself further into her and this time she could no longer resist. She wrapped her legs around his waist moving her body to the rhythm of his, thrusting herself up to meet his every move.

"Oh Scott, Scott," she pleaded, searching for his lips.

"Do you love me?" he repeated, sensing her passion reaching a climax.

"Yes, Scott," she finally answered, collapsing in tears. "Scott, oh Scott—I think I love you." She had not called him Adam.

"I will be there for you always, Andrea, always," he whispered, as she lay spent next to him. "I will be your friend and your lover and your husband."

Andrea turned to him, a feeling of vulnerability and fear clearly written on her face.

"Your secret is safe with me," he assured her.

The past month of restless nights and emotional turmoil had taken its toll on her. Andrea was exhausted. But for the first time since Helen's birth and her meeting with Adam, she felt guiltless. She fell asleep in his arms. For the first time in years she did not have a nightmare.

Andrea woke to find Scott smiling at her. Embarrassed about her earlier display of weakness, she jumped out of bed and headed for the bathroom. "I need a shower," she said.

"Towels are in the closet," he said, instinctively realizing she was going to pick a fight. She returned, a robe tightly belted around her waist.

"You don't play fair," she said, toweling her hair dry. "You've used your bullshit psychology to pry into my private affairs."

"Nothing about you is private anymore," he said putting, his hands under his head and winking at her, making no move to get out of bed. "Sorry, that wasn't meant to be funny," he said, realizing she thought he was talking about their lovemaking.

"Sex is sex," she said.

"Then why did you not let me love you without a struggle?"

"Scott!" she said, amazed that he would be so cruel.

"I pretended that you were my john," she said, dropping the robe to the floor. She pulled the sheets off his naked body and lowered herself on him. Both of them were swept away into an immediate, urgent passion. When it was all over she had a smug look of satisfaction on her face.

"There," she said, triumphantly, "sex is just a commodity."

"That was good," he said, "but you could have moved a bit more. I would only pay you about ten dollars for that performance."

Andrea slapped his shoulder.

"Tell me," he said seriously, catching her by the wrist and pulling her down against his chest, "who is the child's father?"

"It's a long story," she said "and I have to get to work."

"I called the office and told them you were not coming in."

"Scott, for God's sake. I don't know what my staff is going to think if you keep calling in sick for me."

"Who cares," he said, "you're the boss. Besides, they're probably happy to have a moment to breathe. Well look at the good side," he said, "now we have all day. And if your performance gets better in bed you could rack up a lot of money here."

Andrea threw her head back and laughed. She felt free.

"Now shut up," he said, "and start talking."

She started at the beginning, leaving little out except the cherished details of her love for Adam. Adam was sacred, and she did not want to share her memories of him, not even with Scott.

"I suppose now you want to leave me?" she said looking at him through lowered eyes after she had finished her story.

"Now do I look like a superficial person? Andrea, I have stories too you know, and I've heard some a lot worse than yours. Really, you've learned so much from your pain, and some of the stories have been downright funny, especially the bit about the camel," he said, laughing, "I love that!"

Andrea slapped him with the towel and went downstairs to the kitchen. She returned with two cups of coffee and some toast that she had managed not to burn. Andrea was happy even though she knew somehow that it was not going to last.

Tuesday morning at seven o'clock Andrea arrived at her office in a good mood. She pressed the buzzer and asked Janice to come in.

"I'm leaving for England for two weeks. I want you to transfer all calls to Jonathan."

"Yes, Ms. Jacobson," said the secretary, turning to leave.

"Janice, is that a new hairstyle?"

"Why, yes it is."

"It's very becoming," Andrea smiled at her.

"Thank you, Ms. Jacobson."

"Something is wrong with Ms. Jacobson," Janice said to Linda, Andrea's publicity director.

"Wrong? What is it, Janice?"

"She is in a great mood. I have never seen her like this before.

She told me to book a flight to England."

"England!" Linda said, shocked. Andrea never spoke of her days in England and she always said she would never go back.

On Sunday before her departure Andrea went to Long Island as she had done every night since their lovemaking.

Andrea said, as Scott massaged her temples to get rid of a raging headache, "I wish you would change your mind and come with me tomorrow."

"I told you I think you need to go to England alone. You should not have to be concerned about me when you meet Helen."

"I would feel so much safer if you were with me. Are you sure?"

"Yes darling. And Melissa will be there. You won't be entirely alone. But there is something I want to ask you before you go."

"What is it?"

"I want you to move in with me when you return from England."

"Scott, you know I can't do that."

"I don't know why not."

"I'm just not ready."

"But you love me," he said, "also, I need a Sunday girlfriend," he made a face.

"I can't," Andrea pleaded, "Scott, this is all new for us now. If it gets stale or tiring we both have the right to walk away."

"That is mere speculation, Andrea, and you are talking pure hogwash. It has something to do with this man in Jamaica doesn't it. I want to meet him."

"Don't be a fool," Andrea said, the argument was making her headache worse. "I don't want to argue," she said moving to the other side of the room.

"I want to meet him," he insisted.

"You can't," she said quietly, "he's dead."

"I'm sorry. Really sorry. But," he paused, "that makes it easier for you to say yes to me then."

"Scott, I have to go," Andrea reached for her purse.

"Always avoiding a confrontation, Andrea, aren't you?" his voice sizzled, "I can't always give to you without asking for anything back. I want a commitment. I want this love of ours to be based in reality."

"How dare you?" she screamed, "are you insinuating that my love for Adam was not real?"

"It was real enough, but you made more of it than it really was."

"I should have known better than to discuss Adam with you. And to think that I thought I could trust you."

"Andrea, you are living in fantasy land. Life is not perfect until you have worked for that perfection. I have no doubt that your love for Adam was divinely ordained, but his work is done and now you must let go. I'd like our love to be divinely ordained as well but the only thing divine about it right now is that you are a heavenly pain in the ass."

"Listen, Scott," she said angrily, "you knew what you were getting into. You can just fucking leave this relationship right now."

"That is what you would like, isn't it? To make our love another fantasy."

Getting her coat from the closet, Andrea said furiously, "I don't have to stand here and listen to this."

"And I am not going to stand here and have you abuse my feelings either," Scott said, getting angry. "I happen to love you. If you choose to belittle what we have had then just do it out there." With that he opened the door and pushed her out.

She heard the door being bolted from the inside. When she pounded on it there was no answer. Finally she got in her car and headed home. Damn him, she cursed all the way back to

Manhattan. What was it with him anyway, throwing people out of his house.

That night Andrea could not sleep. She had not slept apart from Scott for two weeks and tonight she missed him more than she could bear. She dialed his number, but before it rang she hung up. What did he expect from her? They barely knew each other. They were having a passionate affair, but that did not mean it would last. She could not give up everything and move in with him. Scott was expecting too much of her. Andrea knew she had to end the relationship before all the disagreements turned into hatred. But tomorrow she would be off to England; she needed the time to think. England. She shuddered and pulled the covers over her head.

Chapter 30

Andrea had been in England for two days, and so much had happened in that short time. She had spent a whole night with Ralph. He had been so happy, and now she had to break his heart again. It was sad. Things had not worked out for them, but she realized things might never again work out for her with any man. Scott had come closest to her ideal. He had a mind of his own. He was so sure of himself and the direction of his life that she could not fathom why he would be attracted to someone as confused as she was.

With him, she had felt secure. If only he had not pressured her, she could have been his lover and friend, roles that were not good enough for him. He wanted too much. If only he had not asked her to make a commitment.

Andrea looked down at Ralph, a whispered sound of contentment escaped his lips. He stirred at her movements and peered at her though half-closed eyes.

"Andrea," he said, raising up on his elbow, "why are you

dressed so early?"

"I have a very busy day today and I must get an early start. I'm going with Jacques to a party tonight and I have to be fitted for the dress he has made for me. Ralph, I don't believe we will see each other before I leave England," she said sadly, "I'm leaving day after tomorrow and there is no time.

"But darling—" Ralph began. She put a finger to his lips to silence him.

"My dearest Ralph, let's not speak of this anymore. Let's be thankful that we had the opportunity to finish what we started so many years ago."

"Let me take you back to the hotel," he said, getting up from the bed.

"No Ralph, the cab is waiting."

He watched her leave him for the second time in twelve years. He knew he would never forget his beautiful nymph as long as he lived, his beautiful heart-breaking *Chocolát.*

Back at the hotel, Andrea stepped in the hot shower and soaped herself thoroughly. For years she had not had more than casual sex with a man and here in a few months she had slept with the three men that had been most significant in her life. How ironic, she thought, as she toweled her body dry.

She dressed casually and decided it was time to confront her feelings about meeting Helen. Tomorrow was the child's birthday and Maya had not contacted her to see if she was in England. Surely Maya had read of her arrival in the paper. Perhaps not. Knowing Maya, they would probably be off in some mountain cottage without even running water, much less television or newspapers. She picked up the phone and dialed the number Maya had given her.

"Hello," a tiny English-accented voice answered, "this is

Helen, who is ringing?" Andrea was speechless. She was actually hearing her own daughter's voice for the first time, a lovely British accent that belonged to her daughter. She was unable to speak.

"Hello," the voice repeated, "is anybody there?" Andrea wanted to call her by name. She wanted to tell her how much she had missed her and how much she loved her.

"Hello? Hello?"

"Hello," Andrea was finally able to articulate, "May I speak with Maya."

"Who is calling please?" Helen sounded so bright, so happy and so young.

"It is a surprise. I would rather not say. Is she there?" Helen went to fetch Maya. Andrea could hear her shouting in the background.

"Nan, there is some strange lady on the phone who wants to surprise you." Andrea smiled, just like a child, she thought. Her daughter sounded cheerful. Andrea was not sure whether to be happy or sad.

"Hello," Maya said, "I am glad you called."

"I've been here for two days but I needed the time to get myself together before I called."

"I know. I read of your arrival in the Times." So much for the mountain cabin bit, Andrea thought.

"Well, what do I do from here?"

"Tomorrow I would like you to come as a guest. The party will begin at six o'clock.

"Will Helen know who I am?"

"That is entirely up to you. I will not introduce you as her mother, but—"

"Nan," Helen said, coming into the room, "what time are we going shopping?"

"Helen dear, I am on the telephone. Can you please wait until I am off the line?"

"Very well, but do hurry Nan, will you?"

"Helen," Maya called after her, "close the door when you leave, and dear, do remember to knock before you enter a room with the door closed."

"Right, Nan, remember though, the stores will open soon."

"She sounds very fond of you, Maya," Andrea said jealously.

"Yes, she is. Now I have to give you directions. Do you have a pen and paper?"

Andrea wrote the directions carefully and said goodbye. She sat on the bed and tried to picture her daughter. She could not help feeling envious of Maya.

She was still apprehensive about meeting her child, but she picked up the phone and dialed Jacques. The least she could do was look stunning.

"*Chéri*, where have you been? I have been trying to reach you for a whole day and night."

"I spent the night away with some friends and now here I am. What time do you want me?"

"I want you all the time," he said, half jokingly, "but for your fitting, as soon as you can get here. I don't believe there will be too much alteration, but do get here quickly would you? Shall I send a car?"

"No, thank you, my driver will bring me. See you soon."

Andrea arrived in exactly a half an hour. The awe-stricken receptionist flapped about Andrea for a full minute before she disappeared to find Jacques. She was used to the names of Jacques' clients but most of their fittings were done in their homes, very few came to the studio. She was delighted to meet a celebrity.

Jacques came into the room looking particularly dashing. "*Dahling*, I am glad you made it here so quickly."

Andrea, as usual, loved everything in her fall collection. "Jacques, I want to wear the green and blue tunic tomorrow instead of the red dress."

"But *dahling*, that is not evening wear."

"Who cares—*dahling*," she mimicked, "I did not tell you it was an evening affair, did I?"

Jacques rolled his eyes as he flitted here and there and pinning things just so.

"What time are you picking me up tonight? I must warn you that I will not stay out late tonight."

"We are expected for dinner at eight."

The party was entertaining but Andrea was too preoccupied about meeting Helen to enjoy herself. By midnight Jacques had taken her back to the hotel and again she did not invite him up. He was disappointed. Things were not going as he had planned.

Andrea paced around her suite in circles for fifteen minutes. She wanted to call Scott. He would be able to console her, but if she called him now, she would seem too dependent. She dialed the number anyway. It was only seven-thirty in the evening at home.

"Scott, I'm so glad you're there," Andrea said, when he answered the phone.

"I suspected you would call tonight."

"So you came home just for me?"

"I predicted you would need to talk before seeing Helen tomorrow. See, I was right. Are the arrangements complete?"

"Yes. I meet them tomorrow evening at six. Maya has not told Helen I'm her mother, I am just to be one of the guests, one of Maya's old friends. Scott, I'm not sure what to do."

"Will you tell her that you are her mother?"

"I don't know. Maya said it was entirely up to me. Helen answered the phone this morning when I called. Scott, she sounds happy and contented. I don't know that I have the right to disturb her life now."

"Darling, you are her mother, you have every right. What you

316

have to decide is whether you want to know your daughter in spite of Jacobson's Industry."

"That's not fair, Scott. You know Jacobson's Industry has nothing to do with this. I made a bargain with Maya under duress. How could you be so cruel? You must still be very angry with me to make such an insensitive remark."

"I am not mad, and you know that. But Andrea, if you did not want to claim your daughter, then why did you go to England?"

"So I could see what she looks like," and to be sure whose child she is, she wanted to add. Instead she said, "I assure you I will decide something by tomorrow night."

"Whatever you decide I hope it will be the best for all concerned. This is your test to go past denial and blame."

"What do you mean by that?"

"I mean that you handle problems by pretending they don't exist, or you run away or blame someone else for them."

"I should have known that calling you would be a mistake, and to think I felt you would console me."

"I told you from the moment we met that I will not aid you in your denial."

"I don't think we have anything further to talk about."

"By the way have you given any thought to what I asked you before you left?"

"You are unbelievable. Scott, I would not consider you as a husband if you were the last man on earth."

"When you get back I want an answer. A yes or a no," he continued.

"Scott Preston, you are neither deaf nor stupid!" Andrea said angrily, "My answer is, absolutely no!"

"Good luck tomorrow," she heard him say as she slammed the receiver down.

"Bastard."

317

Andrea dressed painstakingly, wanting to be beautiful for her daughter. She was so nervous that she had to repair her makeup three times before even leaving the hotel. On her way to the car Andrea downed a glass of brandy to calm her racing nerves and took Adam's wrapped portrait from the closet.

Andrea gave Peter, her driver, the address as she stepped in the car. It is in Hampshire. Are you familiar with it?"

"Yes Ma'am. I know exactly where it is. It is a very popular address in London."

"What exactly do you mean?" Andrea asked, curious.

"A woman who lives there is said to be an advisor to the royal family, Ma'am."

"What kind of advisor?"

"They say, Ma'am, that she can predict the future and that she is a medium."

"What else do you know?"

"Nothing Ma'am, except she has a little girl they say her inspiration comes from." Andrea was sick. She wanted to walk into the house and strangle Maya. She could not believe Maya was bringing her daughter up in such an environment, using her for financial gain. But who could she blame for this other than herself? She could have fought to have her daughter if she had really wanted to.

For all the years that Andrea tried to visualize Helen, at that moment she could not bring that vision into focus. As the car pulled up to a splendid Tudor house, she felt relieved.

"Wait here for me, Peter," she instructed her driver, "I am not sure how long I will be."

Andrea's palms were sweating as she rang the doorbell. She had to wipe them quickly on her handkerchief. How she wished Adam could have been with her at this moment. Andrea shifted nervously from one foot to the other, but just as she decided it had been a mistake to come, the door opened. Andrea gasped and tears threatened to well up in her eyes.

"Thank God," she said, under her breath, "Thank God." A most beautiful child with the darkest brown eyes she had ever seen, set beneath long black lashes was standing there. Her skin was smooth and her thick black hair fell in ringlets around her delicate ears. Her olive bronze complexion was the exact color as Andrea's, and she was the image of her father. Andrea's instincts were confirmed. There was no mistaking the father of this child. Thank God she had told Adam about his daughter.

Again Andrea felt the tears sting her eyelids. She wanted to hold her child and never again let her go, to speak softly to her, to tell her of the love she felt, and to claim her as she should have done years before.

"Who are you?" the clear youthful voice asked. "I have never seen you around before. My, you must be a model or a movie star! You are so beautiful! Oh my, " she opened the door wider, "I am so sorry," she said moving aside, "Please do come in."

Andrea was impressed with the child's honest curiosity. She had been the same way. Andrea marveled at her daughter's openness and her gestures, which were a replica of Adam's. Genetics go far beyond the obvious.

"Thank you," Andrea heard herself saying. "I am delighted that a beautiful girl like you would find me so attractive. I am Andrea Jacobson and I am...a very old friend of Maya's. We met many years ago in Stougborough. And you must be the Helen of this fourteenth birthday extravaganza."

"That I am," she said. "Follow me and I will fetch Maya. She is around somewhere."

Andrea followed her daughter into a room full of people who looked as if they were from all over the world. Many of them wore their traditional national attire. Andrea wondered why so many people were invited to a fourteen-year-old's party.

"Nan, I have a surprise for you," she heard Helen say.

"There is a very beautiful woman here who said she is a friend of yours from Stougborough."

Maya spun around and her gaze fastened on Andrea. Andrea again found herself looking into the familiar crystal blue eyes. Maya looked very distinguished, not at all like the nurse she had known at Stougborough—or at Surrey. She had not expected Maya to look at all like this.

"Andrea," she said, "it is so good of you to come." Both women stared at each other, remembering a past that only they knew. "Please let me introduce you."

Andrea needed no introduction. Already a small group was forming around her. She moved through the evening in a dream state. Her gaze went often to the happy child that was her daughter, hers and Adam's. His eternity had truly lived on.

Helen found herself watching Andrea. She could not explain why she was so drawn to her but she found it difficult to avert her eyes. She wanted to get to know this woman called Andrea Jacobson.

"Well," Helen said, approaching Andrea, "It seems that you are well-known. Did I guess right that you were an actress?"

"Oh, I don't do anything quite that glamorous. I am just an overworked business woman. I was in London and I wanted to see Maya. We were rather good friends back in Stougborough."

"I would like to hear about that. Why not walk with me in the garden and tell me about yourself? I get very tired of these parties. They are more for Nan than they are for me. I always feel like a spectacle."

"Why is that?"

"Well, you see, I have quite extraordinary powers and people always want me to read their fortune or something corny like that."

"What do you mean, extraordinary powers?"

"Oh, I am able to see and predict things and sometimes make things happen."

"How do you know this?" Andrea asked, trying to keep the disbelief out of her voice.

"I just do. I was born with it. I guess the same way some children are born being left-handed. Nan told me that I got it from my mother and my grandmother."

"And you've used your powers?"

"Yes. That is how all this nonsense started. And ever since one of the royals contacted Nan, it has been an absolute zoo. That is why I had to go away to boarding school in Switzerland. I will only be home for five days. But that's enough about me. Tell me about yourself."

Andrea did not want to appear overly inquisitive so she talked about the parts of her life that she could disclose to Helen. As Andrea spoke, Helen's eyes became wider and wider.

"I would like to have a life like yours someday," she said, when Andrea concluded.

"I believe you will," Andrea said, taking hold of her daughter's hand. She wanted to remain like this holding the soft hand forever. "Now it is your turn again to tell me more about yourself. Apart from your powers, you seem to be a lucky girl with a very nice life."

"I suppose one could say so. I was adopted by Maya at birth." Andrea noticed that for the first time Helen did not call her Nan. "I don't know my parents at all. Maya gives me everything possible, but she never wants to talk about my parents. All she ever tells me is that my mother wanted the best for me. She said it was best for me to not dwell on that but to concentrate on developing my powers and continue the work my mother was supposed to do. If my mother is alive, I am going to do everything I can to find her. But I don't know where to begin to use my powers. You see, I don't even have a family keepsake. Maya says I should develop my powers to their fullest as a tribute to my mother. Nan has been good to me, but I would just like to know where I am really from. Everyone should know their roots and their history."

Andrea bit her lips to stop them from trembling. She put her arms around her daughter and pulled her close to her.

"Sometimes," Andrea said softly, "it is so hard to understand why people do what they do. I am sure there is a good explanation for your mother's absence. One thing I am sure of though, is that your mother would be very proud of you today."

"I hope so," Helen said thoughtfully, her eyes downcast. But she quickly regained her cheerfulness. "Actually," she said, "since I don't know my family history I can invent it, can't I? I can make believe my mother is someone like you, then one day perhaps I will be like you."

Andrea felt tears sting behind her eyelids.

"I would like that, but Helen, you are going to be a far better person than I am." For a long moment she placed her palm on Helen's flushed cheek. "Now," she said, "I think it's time we get back inside so you can cut your birthday cake."

"Good idea," said Helen, linking her arm through Andrea's. Looking into her striped brown eyes, she said, "You have the eyes of a tiger."

Andrea laughed, "I promise not to devour you if you hurry on inside." They moved toward the house together.

"I like having you as a pretend mother. Will you come and visit me again?"

"I would love to, but I leave for New York tomorrow afternoon. But what would you say to visiting me in New York sometime?"

"Oh!" Helen squealed, delighted, "I would love that!"

"You would love what?" Maya said, looking from Andrea to Helen as they entered the room.

"Ms. Jacobson has invited me to come and visit her in New

York. Oh please, Nan, may I go."

"I am sure we will be able to arrange it one of these days. Now come along," Maya said kindly, placing her hand protectively on Helen's shoulder, "it is time to cut your cake and open your gifts."

Helen skipped happily off behind Maya. "Please come with us, Ms. Jacobson," she beckoned, when Andrea made no attempt to follow her.

"I'll join you in a moment. I have to fetch something from the car for a very special girl."

Andrea watched Helen disappear into the parlor. If only Adam had lived to see how beautiful Helen was, she mused. And Maya had done a wonderful job of raising her, she had to admit that. She slowly walked to the car to get the emerald and sapphire brooch, the painting of Adam, and a camera. Pleased with their meeting and glad she had come, Andrea planned to take a picture of her daughter to fill the empty silver frame, and then she would leave. If only she could find the courage to tell Helen she was her mother, she fretted.

Helen had opened the last of her gifts and most of the guests had left when Andrea rejoined the party. "Thank you all so very much," Helen began, her pretty face beaming.

"Not so fast. Here is something else for you," Andrea said, handing her two wrapped gifts.

Helen eagerly tore the wrapper off the smaller gift, and shrieked as she opened the small velvet box. "Nan, look! Isn't this the most exquisite brooch? Thank you so much," she hugged Andrea, "It is simply lovely and I will cherish it always. When I arrive in New York I will be wearing it."

""But you must try it on now," Andrea insisted, "It goes so well with your lovely dress." As Helen pinned on the brooch, she said, "Now smile so I can take a picture."

Helen obliged her with a warm smile, but moments later was

tugging at the wrapping on the other gift that leaned against the wall. "What else have you brought for me?"

"Helen!" Maya scolded.

"Maya, it's all right," Andrea interjected, cross that Maya had interrupted their special moment.

"Look and see," Andrea said kindly, "Shall I help you?"

"Yes, please."

When mother and daughter had finished tearing off the wrapping paper, Helen stared at the picture, transfixed. It was an oil painting of a man on a horse. The handsome man looked familiar, but she could not recall ever having met him. Then she looked more closely at the picture and saw that the eyes that looked back at her were her own. They seemed to call to her.

"Who is this man?" she asked Andrea, her eyes pleading, "Is it someone special? I feel as if I have seen him before."

"Oh yes, he is a very special person—to the painter," Andrea kept her voice light in order not to give away the truth. "It was done by one of my favorite painters," she added hurriedly, "and when I saw it in Jamaica a few weeks ago, I felt that you might like it. Maya told me you love to ride."

"I do," the girl said, turning away to hide her disappointed face and the teardrops that were collecting in her eyes, "It's just that," she said, her voice quivering, "well, the man in the picture has my eyes and I was hoping—"

"I know," Andrea kissed her daughter's cheek, tasting the salty wetness. "But you can make him a pretend father," she whispered, "Just think, Helen, then you would know both your make-believe parents." At that Helen perked up, but only slightly.

Chapter 31

That night Helen hung the picture over her bed, unable to look away from the somehow familiar face, especially the eloquent brown eyes that tried to speak to her. "Oh," she sobbed into her pillow, "if only they could have been my parents, my dream would have come true."

For years she had daydreamed of having real parents like Andrea and the man in the picture. She had seen herself shopping with her mother, then coming home and showing her purchases to an adoring father; had seen herself dancing in the ballet as her parents beamed with pride; or playing the piano in the parlor while her father puffed on his pipe and her mother embroidered a cushion. For the first time, Helen realized her childhood dreams would never come true, and she felt lonelier than she had ever been in her life. She hugged her pillow and rolled over to avoid looking at the picture, knowing that something strange had happened to her tonight after meeting Andrea Jacobson. Now she could never again be contented without her parents. She had to find them.

Helen cried herself to sleep.

Maya heard the sobs through the solid walls separating their rooms, and felt completely helpless. What could she possibly say that would make the sadness go away? She stayed awake until the sobs had quieted down, until Helen had finally fallen asleep.

At two-thirty in the morning, Helen awoke from a bizarre nightmare. She had dreamed she was being born to a terrified young woman, hearing blood-curdling screams as she was pushed and pulled from the warm womb, through the narrow canal, and into the cold world of a bright room. As soon as she was in the doctor's hands, her mother's body went limp and lifeless, and her voice was silent. Helen reached out to her mother, but the nurse carried her quickly away before she could see her mother's face.

Helen lay back on her pillow, drenched in perspiration. She turned on the light. "It's been a very busy day," she told herself, "by tomorrow things will be all right." Her dream had been more vivid tonight than it had ever been before, but she knew why. In addition to everything else, she was going through puberty and a girl needs her mother at a time like that, she thought; and no matter how much Maya loved her, there was nothing like a real mother's love.

She sighed as she drifted back to sleep. Had Helen seen the minute inscription Andrea had written on the back of the picture, that would have given her the answers she searched for: "To my beautiful daughter Helen with love—Daddy."

Andrea tried to quiet the thoughts that kept her awake. She wanted to tell Helen the truth, but what right had she to catapult her daughter's life into an uproar? She reflected on her own happy childhood and thought how different it had been from Helen's. Even as a youngster, she had known her roots from generations before. She was from a close-knit family, so close they sometimes tended to stifle each other.

Lila Francis had won after all. Much as Andrea had fought for her independence, she was just beginning to realize how much she had conformed to her mother's expectations. In the Francis family, excellence was expected. Mediocrity, carelessness and failures were never tolerated. Andrea had approached most of her life with the discipline of her family in mind, except once—when she become pregnant. She had never been able to face the consequences of her failure until today.

Andrea thought how wonderful her own father would have been with Helen. Tonight she wanted to tell him about his granddaughter, but it was too late. He had been gone for ten years now, but she still missed him terribly. If only Andrew Francis were still alive. If only she could only curl up in his sheltering arms, she would have no reason to be afraid. He would have understood. Why had she not known that before? Only now did she realize that she had deprived him of his grandchild.

Taking a last sip of brandy from the glass on the bedside table, Andrea switched off the light, curled her body into a fetal position, and waited for sleep to come or for dawn to break, whichever came first.

Arriving at the hotel dining room at eight the next morning, Andrea waited at the table for Maya to arrive. A commotion at the entrance signaled the arrival of someone very important. Andrea looked up to see that the dignitary was Maya who was being escorted to her. Maya looked every inch a distinguished woman in her yellow Louis Féraud suit studded with black pearl buttons. She wore simple black pearl earrings and her hair, pulled back in a becoming chignon, had a silver streak, making her look slightly older than her thirty-eight years. It dawned on Andrea that this meeting would have nothing to do with money.

"Hello Andrea," Maya said in her crisp British accent, "I am so glad you agreed to meet me." The maître d' seated her opposite Andrea. When she removed the expensive Jean-Claude sun-glasses, the crystal clear blue eyes forced Andrea to look away. Although much had changed about Maya, and she was not the young girl Andrea had met years before, there was no mistaking those eyes.

"Well," she said, "what did you think of your daughter?"

"She is beautiful, charming, bright and polite. You've done a wonderful job and I am deeply indebted to you for that. Thank you."

"Yes, Andrea, she is a wonderful and special child."

"Which, I'm sure, brings us to the point of our meeting. Before we begin though, Maya, I must tell you this. When I received your call a few months ago, I was convinced that your motive was blackmail. I hope I'm not offending you," she went on, noticing the slight arch of Maya's brow, "but for a woman in my position such a thought is an everyday occurrence. Now I know I was wrong. So please, just tell me the real reason I'm here."

"Very simply, Andrea, it is time for your work to begin."

"What work?" Andrea was puzzled.

"Your spiritual work."

"Oh my God, not you too. What is happening? It's as if I'm supposed to save the world, another Messiah. Well, I'm not the Second Coming, but I've never seen so many people interested in converting me into a beam of light. I don't even go to church."

"This has nothing to do with churches. Andrea, you were born a special person. You have demonstrated an enormous capacity for unconditional love, as well as the determination and discipline to succeed in life. You have a desire for understanding. And you have courage. It took courage first to have your baby and then to give her up, not knowing if it was best for her. Why does the thought of being spiritually privileged scare you so? So many seemingly 'normal' people are advanced souls."

"Like?"

"Ghandi, J.F.Kennedy, Martin Luther King, even Michael Jackson. These people elevated the consciousness of masses just by realizing fully the lives chosen for them. It's a driving force from within and Andrea, you have it. You are an advanced soul whose time has come to speak out to the world."

Andrea's head was spinning.

"Listen," she shouted angrily, lowering her voice as various patrons turned to stare, "I can tell you right now, I have no intention of becoming involved in any black magic, white magic or any other kind of magic. Damn it, Maya, what do you really want?"

"Andrea," Maya said calmly, "I have no knowledge of magic. To be gifted only forces you to internalize the meaning of life. It has nothing to do with witchcraft or magic. People like us find each other. All I know was that you chose me to guide your life."

"Now wait a damn minute, Maya. You've been nothing in my life but a barrier between my child and me. You were the one who stalked me in nursing school and made your eyes do all kinds of weird things. How can you sit there and act like all you have ever done for me were favors?"

"Let me try to help you," Maya continued patiently, "Your mother was also a chosen one who had many special qualities characteristic of a higher being, but she lacked discipline. She was far too pampered as an only child and that hampered her spiritual development. In England she missed her opportunity to connect with her mentor and lost the opportunity to continue her spiritual journey. When she was approached by her teacher, she became so angry and in a struggle, her guide fell backward down some stairs. The fall damaged her spine so badly that she never walked again."

Andrea stared at Maya in disbelief, "My mother? Who told you this?"

"That spiritual guide was my mother."

"So you are here to avenge your mother! Well if she was so psychic, why didn't she predict her own fate?"

"There is nothing to avenge Andrea, my mother was just the casualty of an unfortunate accident. Sometimes things simply happen. When a person of latent psychic powers is in the presence of another person, intense feelings of establishing contact and to guide them just happens. Just like it happened to you when we first met. Only if you had latent powers would you have recognized my effect on you. There was nothing intentional about your mother's action. Her fear heightened her hidden powers and they were operating in spite of her. Andrea, I am not angry, nor was my mother. We do not operate under the same laws as most people. We are advanced souls."

"Then why didn't one of you become the new Messiah?"

"That was not the chosen path of my higher being."

Andrea shook her head trying desperately to clear her dazed mind. Meeting Helen, too much brandy and too little sleep, had been more than she could handle. She was obviously delirious.

"Andrea," Maya began again, "as a mere child you experienced the greatest love that anyone could have for another person. This uncontrollable desire was a good example of how one person, by mere thought, can cast a spell on another Many called it nothing but a childish fantasy, yet you recognized it as a true and worthwhile love. Your lover, just like you, had no idea of the reason for that love. He was an instrument of your destiny. His recent death concluded his role in your life so you could learn to move on. Although his love was a test, it gave you the strength to be all that you have become today. Andrea, sometimes we have to let go in order to grow. Helen was your first lesson in letting go and Adam's death was the second."

"How do you know about Adam and what does Helen have to do with this?" Andrea said warily.

"Helen was a love child. Every time you looked at her you

would have been forced to remember that, and you might have decided to tell Adam. Such an action would have altered your learning and stifled Helen's own abilities. It was more important to your destiny for you to become Andrea Jacobson, credited with intellect, widely known and well-respected, rather than Mrs. Adam Stern. I guess I took advantage of your fear of disappointing your mother. As for Adam, I have known about him for a long time."

"Why me?" Andrea asked weakly, "Shirley MacLaine has already done this."

"Yes, and she has done a fine job, but she was the first celebrity to openly discuss the metaphysical experience, and since the entertainment field is often fraught with charlatans, many people can justify their non-belief based on the fact that she is an actress. As more and more successful and respected people become involved, the world will have to sit up and take notice. When *you* begin to proclaim your belief, people will be more inclined to heed our theories."

Andrea sat very still, not capable of uttering a word. Her mind was screaming but her lips could not move. She, a chosen disciple? Ha! She wanted to laugh, to stand up and tell everyone in the restaurant that she was having breakfast with a crazy person. A fruit loop. Most of all, she wanted to get up and walk away, but she was immobilized. She had never discussed Adam with Maya. How could she know? Was there really some truth in all of this?

Finally Andrea heard her own voice say, hardly above a whisper, "What am I to do about Helen?"

"I believe Helen has the right to know who you are now. She was very upset last night after you gave her the picture of her father. However, I think you should wait a while before you tell her, perhaps when she comes to New York to visit you."

Andrea looked at her watch. It was time for her to leave. She motioned to the waiter to bring the bill, which she signed hurriedly.

"I have to go," she said, standing up. She looked squarely into

Maya's clear blue eyes, and for the first time she did not feel the need to look away.

"I am perplexed that you know of Adam, and some of what you've said makes sense. I can't say that I believe a lot of it, but I will certainly give it some thought. Right now I have no intention of changing my life, but time will tell. I'll be in touch soon," she said, sounding more composed than she felt.

Maya took Andrea's extended hand between both of hers.

"Andrea, I have no reason to hurt you. I could have taken your child away where you would never have found her. Be patient. Patience is the seventh and final quality of true understanding. We are pleased with the six you have already learned."

With that Andrea turned on her heels and walked away without a backward glance. She went quickly to her suite where she found the huge stack of Ginka luggage in the foyer awaiting a porter.

"I have packed everything," Melissa said, "so there is no need to check every drawer. She knew Andrea had an irrational fear of leaving something behind. "Is everything okay?"

"Everything is fine, except that we have a change of plans. You will fly back today without me. And take all the luggage."

"Andrea—?"

"Please, Mel, just do as I ask. I need to make a couple of quick calls." Melissa left the room.

"Ms. Jacobson's office."

"Janice, this is Andrea. I have had a change of plans and will not be home today. I'd like you to have my jet pick me up at nine tomorrow morning at Heathrow. I'll call again when my plans are finalized. And Janice, I want no one to know of this change, and I mean no one. Is that clear?"

"Absolutely, Ms. Jacobson."

When Andrea hung up, Melissa poked her head into the room.

"The porter is here, Andrea, and I should get going too," Melissa said.

"Mel, wait a couple of minutes, will you?" Melissa nodded and left.

"Jacques, this is Andrea. I've had a change in schedule which requires me to be in England for another day. If my fall wardrobe is completed I might as well have you make arrangements to transport it with me."

"Yes everything is completed. There is something, though, that I would like to discuss with you, Andrea. I had planned to deliver your wardrobe to New York personally and would have waited until then, but if you have time for lunch, I would just as soon discuss it now."

"Sounds ominous, but I'm definitely curious. See you in an hour then?"

"Until then, *ma chérie.*"

Andrea walked into the sitting room, "Melissa, have a great flight, dear, and I'll see you soon." Andrea kissed Melissa affectionately. "Please call once you are home, and Melissa, don't discuss anything with Scott." Andrea again hugged Melissa and suddenly felt very alone as she watched Melissa walk the short distance to the elevator.

Much as Andrea knew her secret would be safe with Melissa, she could not bring herself to discuss Helen with her. She was getting old and she did not need to shoulder any more of Andrea's burdens. But Andrea needed a friend, someone who would understand. The bottom was falling out of her life into a place she had no desire to go, and she was frightened.

There was only one such person in the world. Andrea picked up the phone and dialed.

"Helloooo," the voice on the other end said, "identify yourself."

"Hello," Andrea said, smiling at her friend's consistently jovial attitude.

"Ah, Andrea! Darling, I know you're not going to believe this, but just today I was thinking of ringing you. For some reason you've been on my mind a great deal lately. Maybe it's because we haven't talked in quite some time."

"I must say I find it frightfully neglectful of you that I seem to be the one entrusted with maintaining this friendship."

"Duckie, don't scold. Darling, why do you sound so terrible? Isn't everything going well there in America?"

"Maria, I am not in America, I'm in England."

"Oh bloody hell, then something must really be wrong."

Andrea replied quietly, "My life is falling apart."

"I'll fly out immediately!"

"I have a better idea. My plane will be here tonight. Why don't I pick you up in Zurich tomorrow and then we can fly to my villa in Monaco? It is your turn to visit, you know."

"Wonderful! Ring me when you're close to the airport and I will have my driver bring me out. Take the car phone number in case you have to change runways or something. Oh," Maria squealed, "I will be so glad to see you."

"Shouldn't you check with Archibald?"

"Archibald who, darling? Oh you mean my husband," she said, laughing at Andrea's gasp, "he's on some business trip or other, thank God. He was beginning to get on my nerves. And the children will not be out of boarding school for another three weeks, so I'm all yours."

Andrea chuckled at Maria's casual attitude. She had not changed a bit. Andrea felt a twinge of jealousy. Maria had it all. She had married an older man, a wealthy diamond merchant whom she loved very much, and they had two adorable children. She wished her life were as straightforward and uncomplicated as Maria's.

Ah well, she told herself, no use crying over spilled milk. She had to make one more call before she met Jacques.

"Hello? Helen speaking."

"Helen, this is Andrea Jacobson. I'm leaving England shortly and I just wanted to let you know that I had a wonderful time at your party. I enjoyed our talk in the garden. I wish we could do that more often," Andrea found herself rambling on but was unable to stop, "and I hope that you can get Maya to let you visit me in the States very soon. I would really like that."

"I promise I will keep asking Nan until she says yes. She will, you know, if I ask enough times. Maybe next year for the entire summer. What do you say?"

"Darling, I would love it."

Helen liked the sound of Andrea calling her darling. "Andrea—may I call you that?"

"Of course you may."

"I just want you to know how much I love the painting. I will cherish it always. I would love to meet the man in the picture, if for no other reason, because he is so handsome."

"Yes," Andrea said sadly, "Helen, I must go now, but I'll give you my address and phone number. Call me anytime, collect."

"I will, so you will not forget me. I love you, my pretend mom."

Andrea wiped her moist eyes with the back of her hand.

Exactly at one o'clock, Andrea rang the buzzer to the secluded door of his office and was greeted by Jacques himself.

"Hello, *chèrie*," he kissed her lightly, "do you want to see your new wardrobe or shall I have it sent directly to the airport?"

"I am hardly in the mood for dresses today, so send them on to the airport. My plane will be there by eleven tonight and we leave promptly at nine tomorrow morning." Andrea signed all the pertinent customs documents and returned them to Jacques.

He sighed with relief, "now that all this is done let us have lunch."

"After you, Madame," Jacques said, opening the door of the navy blue Rolls Corniche. He maneuvered the car expertly out of London's traffic jam at the busiest time of day. "I hate to drive at this time of day; but for you, Andrea, I would subject myself to anything."

"That's what you say when you are about to raise the price of my dresses, is this what this little chat is all about?"

"My dear you have a tongue like a sharp pair of scissors."

"But am I right or not?" Andrea insisted.

"No, you are not. In fact, you can have all your dresses free—if you would only consent to marry me."

For a moment Andrea was speechless. Trying to avoid another confrontation, she said, "Jacques, why do you always have to joke? What is it that you really want to talk about?"

"I am not joking, Andrea. You must know after all these years how I feel about you."

"Jacques, I don't know what to say."

"You could say yes. I can make you happy, Andrea. No matter how successful a woman becomes she needs a man in her life. I am the man for you, Andrea. I know you and I love you. You will have all the freedom you need, because I would never ask you to give up anything, just as I am sure you would not ask me to alter my lifestyle. We are both busy people and our careers are important to us, but when we do have the time, I can think of no one I would rather spend it with than you. For you, I would relocate to New York, but keep my offices in Paris and London. This could be a perfect merger. Marriage is based on more than love, but if love is what you need I have more than enough for both of us. *Ma Chère*," he continued, "I want you in my life."

"Dear, dear Jacques," Andrea touched his cheek, "I appreciate your offer as well as your honesty, but I have so many things to sort out. So many things have occurred recently—they've altered my life, things I cannot discuss. How flattered I am that you want to marry me, but, you're right, I'm not in love with you and I won't allow you of all people to become a casualty of my emotional problems. Your friendship means so much to me." Andrea leaned over and kissed him gently. "Much more than I can ever express."

"If you ever change your mind, *ma Chère*, I will be waiting. Jacques had done all he could. He would not pursue the subject further. Much as he loved Andrea, his Frenchman's pride would not allow him to grovel. That damnable Scott Preston, he was sure, had a lot to do with whatever had altered her life.

Lunch was subdued, but wonderful, and Andrea felt a twinge of regret as she said goodbye to Jacques.

"See you in a few months," she said lightly, "My spring wardrobe will be calling out for help. Until then," she blew him a kiss, "*au revoir*."

Chapter 32

In the three years since Andrea had last seen Maria, almost nothing about her had changed.

"I can't understand it," Andrea proclaimed, kissing her long-time friend, "I thought blondes showed age lines earlier than anyone else, but you seem to look younger all the time. It isn't fair! Even being a year younger than you and black, I have crow's feet."

"Darling, a year—you make it sound like an eternity. And if my memory serves me right, you're only eleven months my junior. Honestly though, dear, you do look positively awful."

Andrea opened her mouth to protest.

"Well," Maria continued hurriedly at the shocked look on Andrea's face, "I should qualify that. What I meant was, to those who don't know you as well as I do, you would look absolutely ravishing." Maria returned her friend's kiss, and both women laughed as they embraced each other. "Now tell me what's wrong?"

"I am working on having a nervous breakdown."

"Then what are we waiting for? Let's get on board. Monte

Carlo awaits us, and if there's any place on earth that can delay a nervous breakdown, it's Monaco."

Shortly after they boarded the Lear jet, the pilot announced, "We're ready for take off when you are, Ms. Jacobson."

"Anytime."

"Okay, ma'am, we'll be on our way as soon as we have clearance. That should be momentarily."

The women fastened their seatbelts.

"What will you have to drink?" the attendant asked when they had reached cruising altitude.

"Never mind, duckie," Maria said, "you go and take a nap or something, Andrea and I will fend for ourselves."

The attendant looked questioningly at Andrea who nodded.

"Now what do you want to drink?" Maria said, clinking ice cubes at the bar. "No don't answer that. Brandy. Ah, we have fruit and cheese! This will prevent us from getting tipsy." Maria filled two plates with exotic mangoes, kiwi, oranges, apples, strawberries, and an assortment of cheeses.

Andrea pushed her plate away, "I would just like brandy on the rocks."

"It doesn't matter what you want dear, this is good for you. You might consider cutting down on the brandy and increasing the fruits. That might delay the aging process," Maria joked.

"Did I ever tell you how much I hate your sense of humor?"

"That too, does not matter," Maria replied eating happily as Andrea made a face.

"Now," Maria said, pausing between bites, "tell me what the hell brought you back to England."

"I came to my daughter's fourteenth birthday party."

Maria's choked on her apple and spluttered, "You did what?"

"You heard me all right."

"But, my dear, was that a wise decision?"

"I'm not sure. But Maria, I had to see what she looked like.

For fourteen years I have been tormented with the guilt of giving up my child, and to not have a face to put on your own child is...well, I just had to come. She is so beautiful, Maria, and I'm so glad I saw her."

Maria saw the pain in her friend's eyes. She remembered how much Andrea had suffered for months on end after the birth of her child. She had seen Andrea go from a fun-loving girl to a broken woman. She had been unable to comfort her dearest friend, and had thanked God when Ralph came along, but she had always known that Andrea's pain was far too deep for time to heal the wounds.

"Why are you causing yourself more suffering, Andrea?" Maria asked.

"More! For God's sake Maria the pain has never left me. I've tried to cover up my torment with hard work, but the time came when I had to face all the deep dark secrets lurking in my subconscious. I'm still petrified to go to sleep at nights because I know the dreams will come and I can never remember what they are about, but they drain my strength. I know they have something to do with Helen, though, so when Maya called, I decided it was time to face the past. Then Adam died—and Helen is all I have left of him. But when I saw her, I couldn't bring myself to tell her who I was. Maria, she looks exactly like Adam."

"My God!" Maria exclaimed, "Oh, Andrea, I had no idea. When did Adam die? Oh darling, darling," she said putting her arm around her friend, "I'm so sorry."

"Adam died several months ago. He drank himself to death. I should never have left him. It's all my fault."

"Darling, you cannot blame yourself for Adam's behavior. He did what he wanted to and he paid the price. It's the law of nature, Andy, we reap what we sow."

"Then what price will I have to pay for being a coward? I didn't have the courage to tell my daughter that I am her mother.

Maria, it's hard to face the fact that I've been spineless all my life. I feel like such a failure."

"Stop it, Andrea, it's so out of character for you to feel sorry for yourself. How can you use the word failure to describe a woman of your magnetism and *chutzpah*?"

"Then why do I feel so dead inside? Oh, Maria, I don't know what to do. I have a problem that I can't begin to understand, much less to solve." Tears glistened on the long dark lashes and her eyes had a vacant glassy look.

"Andrea, please don't cry," Maria begged, "Things happen for a reason, only sometimes we can't see the meaning right away. I think you've been very brave to carry this burden alone for so long. Please darling, let me just hold you."

"You know, I said those very words to Adam the night he died."

"Tell me all about it," Maria said, after Andrea had wiped the tears from her mascara-streaked face.

"It's a long story, but to put it all in a nutshell—"

"Andrea, please, you have me for two weeks. We don't have to rush, and of course you do remember that I am a great if not positively fantastic listener. Will it take more than two weeks to tell?"

Andrea smiled at her friend who was trying to lighten the mood. Maria knew how to take the edge off morbidity.

"When I returned from a business trip to Hong Kong about five months ago, I had a message on my answering machine from Maya. It was too late to return the call. I couldn't imagine why she was calling because all I ever got from Maya were brief notes every few months saying that Helen was fine. I tried calling her the next morning and there was no answer. That same day I got a telegram from Raymond, Adam's twin, about Adam's condition, and I flew to Jamaica immediately and spent three months with Adam before he died.

"I called Maya as soon as I got back to New York, and she asked me if I wanted to come to Helen's birthday party! Imagine my shock. At first I was convinced that she had seen all the publicity about me and that her motive was blackmail, everyone knows now that I'm worth millions, but after meeting her at breakfast yesterday morning and seeing the kind way she treated Helen, I don't think it's that.

"Anyway, she proceeded to tell me that I am a spiritual disciple or some such nonsense and that she was my 'guide.' She told me she had to take Helen so I would have the chance to gain world-wide recognition in order to champion the cause of the New Age, whatever that means. I still haven't figured out what the hell she is talking about or what her motive could be, but I promise you that I will. Maria, if she ever tries any weird voodoo stuff on me, I'll crush her beyond recognition."

"Spoken like a true Andrea," Maria said.

"There seems to be something strange surrounding me," Andrea continued, "because Maya is not the first person to speak this baloney to me. It all seems so contrived, but everyone I've met lately thinks I have a mission, and they're all involved one way or the other with this New Age business. I believe someone is trying to drive me crazy. What do you think?"

"What kind of shit do they tell you?" Maria said curiously.

"It started when I met this perfectly arrogant jackass of a psychiatrist. You remember, the kind that we used to meet on psych rotations, who always seemed to have something stuck up their asses. Well this one has a whole goddamn coconut up his ass and I should have given him an enema the first time I slept with him! It was after I got back from Jamaica—somehow I needed to have a warm body next to me. I might have made a mistake, but I have to admit I loved spending time with him; and since he seems to understand my neurotic, psychotic and other craziness, I guess it made him more appealing. God, I seem to be so vulnerable, Maria!

"He wants more than I am willing to give at this time, but to be honest, I think I might be falling in love with him, Maria, something I simply must not do."

"And why not?"

"Because I am a curse. First there were all the men I hurt who loved me and just wanted me to care, and then there was Graham who killed himself over me, and don't forget Ralph, whose heart I have just broken again. And Adam is dead because of me. I tell you, I'm a curse. But the worst thing about it, Maria, is that with Adam, I had the best love that a woman could ever hope for, yet it has caused both of us so much pain that I don't know if my love was a blessing or a curse. When I fall in love, I guess I turn into an absolute fool."

"You're talking poppycock. You love me and I haven't come to any ill fate."

"But that's different Maria, you're a friend, not a lover."

"For one night, Andrea, I was a lover. Don't forget that."

"Maria, one night of being stoned out of our minds and doing what came naturally does not constitute being lovers, for God's sake."

"Well," Maria said, getting up to bring some more drinks, "Let us drink to a perfectly fucked-up year and to a perfectly fucked-up man, if you get what I mean."

Raising her glass, Andrea laughed aloud, "I must admit that he was a perfect fuck and he didn't cost me a dime."

"Well I couldn't think of anything more devastating than an arrogant shrink with a coconut stuck in certain places who was a lousy fuck and cost money too!" Both women roared with laughter.

"Then, my friend, a toast is in order. To the unfortunate act of falling in love with a man who has a foreign object up his posterior, namely a coconut, and yet is a perfect fuck. My dear I would marry this man."

Maria's big blue eyes were dancing with mischief. Andrea kicked her legs in the air and began howling. The thought of Mr. know-it-all walking around New York in such a state was the funniest thing she had heard in months. Both women looked at each other and laughed until tears were rolling down their faces, tears of sadness had turned into tears of joy. Andrea looked at Maria and felt the totality of her love for her long-suffering, oldest friend.

"I'm so glad you are here," Andrea said taking Maria's hand.

"Let's toast," Maria said, between gasps of laughter, "to the perfectly fucked-up year that brought us back together. By the time this plane has reached Monaco we may have to be taken by ambulance to the alcoholic unit of the hospital, but my dear, let's get drunk. Or drunker." And they were both perfectly drunk when the plane touched down.

Andrea and Maria spent their first day together catching up on the last three years. Not only had Andrea told and retold every detail of her life over the past five months, but she heard what had happened in Maria's. They shopped during the day, lounged in the evenings at Club Dauphin, and gambled at the casino, or danced at Jimmy'z until dawn. Andrea had not felt this carefree in years. Time went far too swiftly.

"Thank you so much for this time," Andrea said, as they walked toward the jet that would take Maria home.

"I needed this as much as you did," Maria said, "I know there's a lot for you to sort out in your life, but don't let your fear and pride get in the way of this promising love affair.

"There is something else, though. About spirituality. I can tell you now. Last year I almost lost Archibald to a coronary and I was never so scared in my life. I couldn't imagine what I would do without him. As much as he and the children drive me insane at times, without them my life would be incomplete. I watched him get worse day after day until finally the doctors decided to do a triple bypass. His health was so poor the doctors told me it increased the risk of surgery. For three weeks after the operation, Archibald barely held on to life. He just didn't have the will to live because he refused to be an invalid when he finally came home. I was watching him waste away. As a last resort I decided to join a support group of women who were experiencing the same fears I had. The fear of being alone. Every night for two months I met with these people who taught me self-reliance, how to stop holding on to Archibald for my own selfish reasons and how to have faith that if I were to let go, God would take over. By God, Andrea, you can imagine my surprise at this theory, but I did what they asked anyway. Soon, as though a miracle had happened, Archibald's desire to live began to grow. I've studied with a spiritual leader ever since and my life has never been better. Andrea, there is truth to metaphysics. I know this. Even though it seems weird, my friend, just try to follow through."

"Maria!"

"Adam," Maria continued, wanting to say all she had to, "must have recognized your purpose in life, and he fulfilled his role in it. He told you to share the love that he had given you. Scott is no doubt ready to take up where Adam left off. I know you must be shocked at what I'm saying, and I know that I should have told you before. Dear Andrea," Maria continued touching her friend's face, "I have never been more at peace in my life. To understand your higher self is true wealth. Archibald is twenty-four years older than I, and his heart could stop at any moment, but now that we both understand the purpose of our union, and our own separateness, we can fully serve our love before he dies."

Andrea stared at Maria as she talked, a stark realization crystallizing in her mind. Was she going mad or was everyone in her life succumbing to the 'mystical dawning'? Suddenly it all became very clear to Andrea. They were all involved in a conspiracy! But Maria, her dearest and oldest friend? She could never be a part of this scheme, could she? Andrea shook her head, refusing to believe it. But Maria was the only one who knew everything there was to know about her, the only one who could have orchestrated it all. That had to be it. Maria had betrayed their friendship and she could not fathom why. She looked at Maria sadly, and all she could think was, *et tu, Brute?*

Chapter 33

Andrea had been back in New York for two weeks. She was completely immobilized by Maria's revelation. Her mind felt as though it would explode from all the unanswered questions. What was it that they wanted from her? Was this all happening or was this a new symptom of her extreme stress and discontent. She knew that greed for money had made otherwise rational people do terrible things, Maya, maybe, but Maria! She could not believe that of Maria and it made no sense since Maria had as much money as any woman could want. Andrea suddenly thought of the negative repercussions of her past. If Maria were to leak to the press that she had a child, or if she told of their one-night physical relationship! Andrea could not bear the thought. Everything she had worked for would be over. There would be no Jacobson's Industry and no hope of ever reconciling with her child or getting her family to understand. Suddenly her apartment seemed too confining. She was not functioning well. She needed to go some place where she could have a staff to take care of her basic needs and more space to fill with her grief.

Even getting out of bed the past two weeks, Andrea found difficult. Because of her non-existent appetite she had already lost eight pounds from her already lean frame. Andrea had never been lonelier in her life. She needed to get away, but where? Going to her home in the Hamptons was not an option because she ran the risk of seeing Scott who, she thought painfully, must be a part of the conspiracy. No wonder he had sent her to a psychic that no doubt had been briefed by the conspirators.

Not even her work was of any comfort. She had not gone into her office for over a week, nevertheless, to keep up her image she called in every day. Andrea had given Janice strict instructions to tell Scott nothing of her return to the U.S.

"Tell him that I am still out of the country."

Andrea could not decide where to go. She supposed she could buy a house in Connecticut but she was not up to choosing furnishings and planning decor and she certainly was not up to interviewing a staff. She needed to be completely alone. But in New York she could never really be alone.

Scott was worried sick about Andrea. He had called her office every day since the time she should have returned from England only to be told that she was still out of the country. In desperation he telephoned Claridge's in London, but the concierge replied, "Ms. Jacobson checked out four weeks ago." Several times he had gone to her apartment in the Trump Towers where he had been informed that she was not there. Eventually he became furious because of Andrea's inconsiderate behavior. He had never before been involved with such an unpredictable woman, and he hated it. On one hand, Andrea was self-assured and headstrong, while on the other, she was like a betrayed child, afraid to allow anyone to get close to her.

Her negative reaction to his suggestion that they live together had left him a little frightened at her inability to let go. By asking her to make a commitment, he supposed, she felt he had broken some kind of trust. But how could he have known she would be so inordinately upset at his proposal?

In the few months they had known each other, they had shared a deep emotional and physical experience. But there were still areas of her life that he was shut out of completely. In spite of the problems that could arise from marrying someone he knew so little about, he had felt compelled to have Andrea in his life permanently.

Trying to find understandable reasons for her behavior, he decided perhaps things had not gone well at her meeting with Helen, and then, instead of feeling angry at her thoughtlessness, his heart began to ache for her. If only she had trusted him enough to come to him for support, he thought. But Andrea was too fiercely independent to seek comfort in another human being. To her such a display of need would be a sign of weakness.

Over the next few weeks, Scott's concern vacillated between empathy and anger. Why he should be surprised at Andrea's behavior baffled him. He had realized from the moment they met that Andrea Jacobson was a stubborn, hot-tempered woman who was used to control and certainly not used to having her decisions questioned. Andrea was the most alluring woman he had ever laid eyes on in his life, not so much because she was a raving beauty, but because her manner was so decisive. On seeing her in person for the first time, he knew television had not done her justice. The cameras had not captured the flawlessness of the olive skin, the long shapely legs, the inviting red lips that sometimes pursed with disapproval, the regal presence, or the light that danced behind the piercing striped brown eyes, the eyes of a tiger. If nothing else, her appearance should have warned him that falling in love with her would be like riding a roller-coaster at an amusement park, an experience that used to leave him disoriented and ready to throw up. Would he ever be able to get off such a ride? He would know the answer to that once he found her again.

Andrea Jacobson needed to be taught a lesson, and he would show her that he was not a man she could control, not even with love.

Andrea packed hurriedly. No one, not even Melissa, would know exactly where she was going. She contacted her pilot and arranged a for a flight to Chamonix in France. Why the thought had not occurred to her before only attested to her confusion. Her chalet in the mountains of Chamonix, far away from civilization, was where she needed to be.

First Andrea called Lance Spenser, the master teacher whose name she had been given by the psychic Madaline. She explained her needs and found that he was agreeable to her plan and would make himself available to her in Chamonix for a couple of months. She liked his mellow voice. Then she phoned the caretakers, Philipe and Brigit Junot, to make sure the house was well-stocked and staffed, to have them arrange for a masseuse and a nutritionist, and to tell them she would be arriving at seven the following evening. Andrea also asked that the Junots arrange rooms in the west wing for the guru. She felt absurd about having a spiritual teacher on call, but if there was anything to this hocus pocus business she had to find out once and for all.

For a moment Andrea was excited about her pending trip, but the elation evaporated quickly. The thought of being away from Jacobson's Industry indefinitely bothered her since she had already been gone, on and off, for more than two months. Never before for any extended period had she left Jacobson's to be run by her staff, yet somehow doing it made her feel free. Besides, she needed a vacation after what she had gone through in London and Monaco, and Chamonix would have beautiful new snow in November, unlike the slushy grime in the streets of New York.

Chapter 34

In the mountains of Chamonix, Andrea finally found peace. Every morning at seven she had a massage and beauty treatment before joining her athletic instructor to go jogging. By eight-fifteen she settled for a light breakfast of strawberries, cottage cheese, a slice of toast, and orange juice. She added the toast because Scott used to insist she needed the fiber.

Andrea's thoughts returned again and again to Scott, who might have betrayed her. Never again would she fall in love. She developed a needed routine: after breakfast Andrea would read the *New York Times* and the *Wall Street Journal*, and then call her office to make sure things were under control. The rest of the morning she spent in her studio completely engrossed in doing colorful oil paintings. With paint smudged all over her smock and under her fingernails, she felt like a child again.

The paparazzi should get my picture now, she laughed, how in vogue my appearance would be. Sweats, no makeup, unpolished nails, unruly hair and paint smudges? It would be a front page

Enquirer story.

Andrea delayed her first meeting with the celestial being who was living in a remote wing of her chalet. She agonized over her resolve to delve into things she was not sure she wanted to know. But if she actually had some kind of supernatural powers as Maya had suggested, it would be the only way to fight the conspirators who were trying to tumble her world. She could just zap them to hell, she thought triumphantly a smile creeping to her lips. Evil begets evil; she twitched her nose like the witch she had seen as a child on some TV show.

Andrea shuddered at her desecration of her religious upbringing. Although she had not set foot inside a church since she was sixteen, she had been raised as a Christian. The product of an all girls' Catholic boarding school, Andrea never again wanted to attend another mass. For seven years she had gone to mass every morning at six and could recite it in both Latin and English without really understanding a word. She had only pretended to conform to Catholicism, making a mockery of the Hail Marys, her penance after confessions. Maybe that was why God was punishing her excruciatingly before accepting her back into the fold. At the thought, Andrea laughed nervously.

At the beginning of her fifth week in Chamonix, Andrea finally got up the courage to send a message to her spiritual teacher inviting him to join her for breakfast.

To her amazement, instead of a wizened old man in flowing robes, here was a handsome tall lean man in his early thirties. He had striking jet black eyes that were shadowed by long lashes and his dark brown hair was fashionably cut. Andrea wondered if he used mousse since not one strand of hair was out of place. She stifled a smile as she watched him approach, wondering if God would approve of such vanity.

He wore comfortable baggy Middle Eastern pants and a white gauze shirt. Andrea first noticed his strong hands and his long tapered fingers, but then as her astonished gaze moved down all six feet three inches of the man her glance stopped on the most enormous feet she had ever seen. He wore no shoes.

"Do you have to have your shoes custom made?" Andrea asked, looking at his feet as he crossed the room.

"You bet," he said smiling, "In fact by the time I was seven my mom forced me to take a paper route to pay for my own shoes."

"I'm sorry, I didn't mean to be rude."

"Who said you were rude?"

"I always seem to say the wrong things."

"Nothing is ever wrong or right, it just depends on the way the world interprets it. The universe does not make a judgment, it just picks up vibrations, and to me your vibrations are good enough for a laugh." His smile broadened and Andrea waited to get a glimpse of his teeth, which of course had to be perfect.

"What kind of vibrations do you get from me?" he asked.

Andrea wondered what the hell he was talking about. It sounded like he was speaking a foreign language. What she got from this gorgeous hunk was not just a vibration, it was a full-blown earthquake.

"You have a great sense of humor," she murmured.

"I think we are going to get along famously, Andrea. For a while there I thought I was going to be banished to the west wing forever and I can't stay here indefinitely. I'm glad you decided to begin your metaphysical work."

"Then I guess we should get started."

"Today we'll get to know each other, but after that we keep to a schedule. We'll meet every afternoon at two, well after lunch because I need all your blood in your head not your stomach."

"Planning to use your fangs on me? Very well," Andrea stated, getting up from the table, "but I'm warning you, Lance, if you plan to use any mind control or other unorthodox ways of getting me to think like you people, you'll be permanently erased.

Poof! Just like that," she said making an offhand gesture.

"The first thing you have to do, Andrea, is to put down your defenses. I'm not here to battle. I know how frightening change can be but it's inevitable—if we want to be in charge of our own lives."

"You seem to have the ability to make me apologize. I'm sorry."

"Let's put all hostile feelings aside—and then there will be no need to apologize."

"I will. I promise."

"Before we begin our studies in spiritual progress, there is one principle that I want you to keep in mind always. The universe as it exists is totally supportive of anything you desire, even an idea that will destroy you. As a woman who has enjoyed the material success of power, you can appreciate how power works. Just think, if you could allow that power to govern your spiritual life as well as your material life, then nothing would be impossible. Your transformation as a spiritual being depends entirely upon you and your willingness to become totally aware of who you really are and for what purpose you have been put on this earth. Finding that truth is entirely up to you. You must never deny your strengths or cover your weaknesses. Spiritual growth is simply allowing oneself to become totally exposed to one's desires and fears, no matter how painful such a disclosure may be."

"I believed that my life was complete," Andrea began. "Until a few weeks ago, I was content with the way things were. And then everything changed. Now there seems to be an evil conspiracy of some sort to convert me to another way of thinking about myself. I have to find out if I do have unusual powers—in order to fight evil with evil."

"Andrea, there is only one way to fight evil and that is with love."

"But they don't love me."

"Things sometimes are not as they appear. Even if there were such a conspiracy, and I must warn you it is not uncommon for such thoughts at a time like this, you must have attracted these changes to your life. Nothing happens without a reason. A few weeks ago you thought you were content, but there must have been a big void in your life or something you need to resolve for you to have attracted upheaval and chaos. These experiences may become the vehicle for the most powerful growth you will experience. Understand that to resist change is to resist God and to resist God means to resist yourself. Since the basis of all spirituality is God, and God is love, your only weapon is love. When you understand unconditional love you will become one with God. Therefore, Andrea, you cannot fight evil with evil."

"That's taking it too far," Andrea said, feeling very uncomfortable with the notion of being one with God. "If you are God, why did you not give yourself smaller feet? You would not have needed a paper route to support your shoes, surely you could have foreseen that?"

Lance smiled, "Had I given myself permission to have smaller feet, you and I might never be having this conversation, but most importantly, I would never have met my own spiritual teacher. You see, he was one of my paper route customers."

Andrea decided she liked Lance. She liked his easy attitude and the peaceful sense of tranquilly she felt emanating from him. She admired his intellect, having found most men to be ruled by their genitals rather that the logic they were supposed to be famous for. Lance was different. He was supremely confident, but in a quiet, commanding way that often reminded her of Scott. For the first time she was with a man without feeling the need to be in control, a man over whom she had no power, sexual or otherwise. Their close relationship was refreshingly unique and relaxing without the sexual edge she had always anticipated and received from other men.

With Lance's guidance and encouragement, Andrea investigated the concept and premises of New Age theory. The scientific and spiritual support for the philosophy that Lance used were amazingly intelligent and logical, a far cry from the mumbo jumbo Andrea had expected.

Andrea felt intellectually stimulated. Lance's knowledge of physics, chemistry, biology, mathematics, psychology, as well as various religions was astounding. He was also adept at playing several musical instruments, including the sitar. Andrea was impressed with this gentle man who made her feel comfort and curiosity, around whom she could let her guard down.

Soon Andrea was fairly well-versed in spiritual or metaphysical terminology. New Age theory had a language of its own, and karma, chakra, white light, Kundalini, higher self, vibration and aura were words that gradually became a part of her daily vocabulary. Their meanings became clearer by usage than they were from her own earlier reading.

After a month of discussions Lance began introducing Andrea to techniques that would help her appreciate the fact her life was in her own hands. She learned to bring her body to a state of complete relaxation through meditation, began to see how creative visualization could bring about the future she wanted, but most intriguing to Andrea was learning the technique of dream induction and interpretation to help solve difficult problems that the conscious mind could not handle.

One day as they sat on the balcony still in their ski parkas sipping herbal tea, Andrea asked, "You really believe I'm attracting all the upheaval in my life for a particular reason then?"

"Without question," Lance answered. "Each of us has what is known as a divine plan. It's like a blueprint of your life. At a very early age you experienced a comforting love, that love has been a foundation for your financial success, now it is time for you to come face to face with your spiritual responsibilities. You have much work to do and your unconscious mind knew it was time, so it created events that would force you to search deeper for the meaning of your life."

"Can a person who is *special* have negative powers?"

"I really don't believe in *special* powers. I suppose though, as there are positive forces in the world so are there negative ones; these forces can be exhibited by anyone, not just gifted people. New Age theory, Andrea, does not fall into the arena of evil. It is simply one theory that seems to work for some people when they reach a spiritual level that forces them to look for the deeper meaning of life. Its effect is no different from Christianity, only it's premise.

There were times when Andrea was tempted to talk to Lance about Helen, to confide in him, to ask how psychic powers would work in her case, but if Lance was part of the conspiracy she felt surrounded her, what would that kind of trust accomplish? After all he was recommended by Madaline, who was referred to her by Scott. She had come a long way in her growth and she felt in some ways transformed. More at peace but she still couldn't shake that these people could have hidden motives. "Beware those who call themselves loyal," she recalled the words of the old guru in Hong Kong.

On the sixth week of study and her eleventh week away from New York, Andrea said, "It's time for me to go home now, Lance. I've learned so much from you, I feel a new person is evolving inside me. But I'm insulated here and I have to get back to the real world. As a businesswoman, my search would be considered ridiculous and would subject my company to negative repercussions, so I have to request your silence about all this."

"In time your belief will be your greatest asset, but Andrea, you must go at your own speed. If you still find yourself trying to control every situation, remember to let go. Give yourself permission to relax."

"Where will you go from here?" Andrea asked, incredulous that three months had passed so quickly.

"I go to Los Angeles at the end of March for a conference. I was getting a little concerned that I would have had to leave before you decided to see me. I'm presenting a paper. When I'm back in New York I'll come to visit you. My work with you is done for now but it's only the beginning of your growth. You'll continue to meet all the people that are necessary to help you go further. You know the adage, 'When the student is ready the teacher will come.' In fact, you've already met several."

"Who?"

"Me for one."

Andrea did not push for an answer because she got the same eerie feeling that there was a conspiracy going on. How was it that everyone seemed to know so much about her life? Was Lance involved, she wondered?

Chapter 35

Maya pulled on her gloves and was waiting for the chauffeur to buzz that her car was there when the phone began ringing. When it continued to ring, she remembered she had given the maids the night off, and moved hurriedly to pick it up.

"Hello, this is Maya."

"Maya, this is Maria, I'll be in England next week and I think we should talk. Say Tuesday for lunch."

"That will be fine," Maya said, "I will meet you at one o'clock at the Bistro."

Andrea returned to New York from Chamonix feeling more in control of her emotions. Many of her problems still remained but she felt certain that the answers would come in time. Although not completely convinced about the concepts of New Age theory, she had learned some very valuable relaxation techniques, and was in excellent physical and mental shape. After scolding her thoroughly for disappearing without a word, nothing but a scribbled note that she would be away for a while, Melissa hugged Andrea as though she would never again let her out of her sight.

With a twinge of disappointment, Andrea discovered that nothing had gone even slightly wrong at Jacobson's Industry without her. She would have felt more necessary if she had returned to find the business in chaos. Of course, she consoled herself, she had hand-picked and trained the staff to handle any emergencies. The staff were already there by the time Andrea emerged from the elevator at eight-thirty.

"Good morning, Ms. Jacobson," Janice came hurrying toward her. "It is so good to have you back."

"Thank you, Janice, it's good to be back. I'll have some coffee and then you can bring me up to date on everything. Please tell Linda and Jonathan to join us in my office."

"In your office?" Janice looked surprised. She was not in the habit of questioning her boss, but Andrea rarely had meetings in her office. It was her private space and she wanted no one to invade it.

"Yes, Janice, right here. And have the cafeteria send up some doughnuts and fresh fruit."

As Andrea walked jauntily into the outer office to greet her employees, the satisfying chorus of good mornings and hellos made her feel glad to be back in her element.

Linda, Jonathan and Janice conducted an informative, superbly organized meeting. Andrea was so impressed that she made a note to give each of them an enormous bonus in their next paycheck. And Janice had done such a great job she deserved to be promoted. Andrea was proud of all of them. Janice lingered after everyone had left the office.

"Is something wrong, Janice?"

"I know this is probably a terrible time to bring this up, Ms. Jacobson, but Dr. Preston has been trying to reach you every day for the past three months. He is frantic, and I am running out of excuses."

"Thank you, I'll call him," Andrea replied coolly, "And by the way, I want you to have the workmen double the size of your office. You can furnish it anyway you want. I'm also giving you your own assistant."

Janice smiled and thanked her, grateful to have her services appreciated. She was glad to have her boss back and making decisions. Everything had gone well at Jacobson's, but without Andrea the atmosphere was entirely different and not to her liking.

Andrea did not know what she was going to say to Scott, but she decided whatever would be said, was best done in person. She would drive out to his house later that day. She hoped he had forgotten about asking her to live with him and now that she thought he was a part of a conspiracy against her, she would never, never in a million years consider doing that! When it was a matter of Andrea Jacobson against the world, there was no question that Andrea Jacobson would win. Of course she had embraced some of the New Age philosophy because it had confirmed what she had known since the age of seven. Her destiny was in her own hands. Yes indeed, she was glad to have studied with Lance, but she was no fool.

She left the city at nine o'clock that night, hoping that Scott would be home by then. Unsure about staying with him, she planned to spend the night at her house next door, depending on how things went. Andrea rang his doorbell at ten-twenty.

When he opened the door, she said defensively, "Now Scott, if you intend to scream at me and behave in an irrational manner I'll just leave."

For a moment Scott entertained an impulse to wring her beautiful long neck, and Andrea was aware of a dangerous gleam of fury in his eyes.

"Hello there, Andrea," he responded, his voice registering

none of the anger, "Are you sure you have the right address? Don't you want the house next door?"

"For God's sake, Scott don't be sarcastic. And as I said, if you behave irrationally I most certainly will go next door."

"I am not being sarcastic, Andrea, I am simply stating the way I feel. You have been grossly inconsiderate and I'm used to people being more thoughtful of other people's feelings, especially if they profess to care about them."

"And I am not used to people who profess to love someone when they have ulterior motives."

"Just exactly what are you talking about, Andrea?"

Andrea ignored his question and said levely, "After I met Helen, I needed to have some space and time to think. I'm sorry, but I have to do things my own way. I came here to tell you that I can't see you any more. There is too much unfinished business I have to attend to, and any relationship I could have at this time would only suffer."

"Are you speaking for me as well? Don't I have any say in this decision?"

"The only decision that can be made must come from me."

"Andrea," he said firmly, "stop making excuses for your behavior. Stop justifying yourself when you're simply running away from facing things again."

Being so close to Scott made Andrea feel weak. All she could think of was how much she wanted just to rest her head against his broad shoulder and be held in his strong arms. She was in love with Scott Preston. But she was unsure about his motives for wanting her. She choked back the tears as she began speaking.

"Scott, I wanted the wonderful part of our relationship to last forever, but it had no chance, right from the beginning. Please forgive me," she said, moving backwards towards the door. "but I must say goodbye."

"If you walk out this door, Andrea, you will never come

through it again. I can understand the turmoil that you are going through. I can also understand your desire for space to think through all that has happened, but that's no reason for you to push our relationship over a precipice. You're scared, but I can help you, Andrea. Why do you find it so difficult to believe I love you? Give up the need to control, Andrea, and let me help." Scott caught hold of Andrea's arm.

She felt her adrenalin flow. "Don't touch me," Andrea hissed as she tore her arm out of his grip. "I don't need your kindness or your martyrdom," she said, stepping dangerously close to him, her arm raised. For a moment Scott thought she was going to hit him, but her hand came down, her fist clutched tightly against her side. "I'm warning you, Scott Preston, if you ever do anything to hurt me I'll kill you."

Scott pulled Andrea to him, his face close to hers, his dark eyes flashing anger.

"You—"

"Careful Scott, God does not swear, and if I remember correctly, you, along with all your other cronies, are God. What do you want from me?" she snapped.

"I only want to love you," he said quietly.

Scott walked toward the stairs, then turned around to face her. "You know, even though I almost went crazy over the last three months wondering what had happened to you, when I opened the door and saw you I was more happy than angry. I don't know what you are insinuating by your comments about hurting you and my 'cronies', but I see you came here to fight. For the last time, if you walk out that door, you'll never come back. Far from the strong woman you represent to the world, Andrea, you are a coward."

Andrea was shaking with anger and hurt. She could not bear to hear what he was saying. The word coward resounded in her mind until she had to put her hands over her ears. Scott's attack was too close to the truth.

"You cannot fight evil with evil," she heard Lance's voice resonate in her mind, "Love is your only weapon."

"Scott, listen," Andrea said, abruptly changing her tone, unable to allow him to continue with her psychological deficiencies, "I think there are better ways to get rid of our anger. There's no reason to argue. We've just missed our closeness, you know?" she said, smiling suggestively knowing that seduction was as efficient a defense as anger.

"If you are insinuating that I should make love to you, I can tell you right now I have no interest in doing that. Sex does not take the place of communication. And you can go to hell."

"But darling, I have interest enough for both of us and we have the rest of the night to talk. I've missed you, Scott," Andrea said, moving to close the gap between them. "Darling, please understand. I needed to have some answers that only I could supply, so I went to Chamonix. Now was that so bad?"

"But you could have called."

"I know," she said sweetly, moving closer to him.

"Christ, Andrea," he said, "do you think you can solve every problem by either seduction or—?"

"Yes," she breathed, brushing her lips against his. "Darling, I'm trying to make it up to you."

Scott looked at Andrea curiously, thinking she must have been drinking, but all he smelled was the familiar sexy fragrance of her Joy perfume. He wanted her so much that his loins ached, but he could not allow her to manipulate him this way.

Sensing his resistance, Andrea immediately changed her tactics once again.

"How about offering me a drink, Scott? All this arguing is making me thirsty."

"I have no alcohol."

"You're certain I was asking for alcohol?"

"What would you like?" Scott said, flabbergasted at Andrea's ease in changing a situation.

"Well how about tomato juice?"

"Very well," he said, heading toward the kitchen.

"I'll meet you in the study," she said.

Andrea walked to the den where she kicked off her shoes and removed her coat. She switched on the stereo and turned down the lights, then slid out of her tunic and her underwear and lay down on the chaise where she waited for Scott to return.

When he came into the room, she rose gracefully and walked barefoot towards him. She took the two glass of tomato juice from his hand and set them down on the cocktail table.

Feeling an uncomfortable rise in his pants, Scott knew she had won again.

"I have truly missed you," Andrea said, putting her arms around his neck. I hope you've missed me too." She moved sensuously against him and kissed him, allowing her tongue to dart quickly over his lips until her mouth was locked on his.

Scott was helpless. He was like a man addicted. He simply could not resist this maddening woman, and his firm decision to keep her out of his bed disappeared completely.

"Andrea, I was crazy with worry," Scott said, burying his face in her soft neck, "my darling, please don't ever do that to me again."

"I won't, darling, at least not tonight." She kissed him searchingly again, removing the last vestige of his resistance.

"I can't imagine why I let you do this to me," Scott began.

"Shush, don't say another word. We have all the time in the world for talking later, but for now just hold me and love me."

"Andrea," he said, covering her lips, "God, I love you so much."

"Oh Scott," Andrea whispered, "I don't ever want to be without you again." Not until tomorrow at least, she thought.

"Darling, does that mean—"

"Yes, it does." Two could play this game, Andrea thought. Eventually he would have to confess about the conspiracy he was a part of if he was deeply in love with her—and if she married him.

In spite of Andrea's caution, the next few days were bewitching for her. They spent hours packing and sorting her things as Andrea prepared to move into Scott's house. As she looked around her apartment, now stripped of her personal belongings, she suddenly felt an overwhelming allegiance to Manhattan. For the first time, Andrea realized just how much a New Yorker she had become. She would miss the things she had taken for granted: Nathan's hot dogs, the acrid smell of roasting chestnuts, Madison Avenue galleries, Broadway theaters, fabulous restaurants, Central Park, Macy's windows, the crush at Bloomingdale's. From the sublime to the mundane, these could only be found in New York and nowhere else in the world. But she had to live with Scott to keep an eye on him.

Andrea settled into Southampton. Jacobson's was running smoothly without her. She became devoted to Scott and adopted his tranquil lifestyle. Many nights she sat reading peacefully while Scott finished another book; she had even been in the audience at one of his television appearances. In spite of her suspicions, she wondered how anyone could be as loving and kind as Scott, yet be scheming at the same time. Try as she might, she could find no proof that Scott was part of a conspiracy against her; worse yet, she was no longer sure if she cared. Because she had fallen hopelessly and ridiculously in love with him.

Southampton, although serene, was not entirely Andrea's cup of tea for any extended length of time. Now and then she and Scott would venture into New York. She had not sold her apartment, and they would spent a night or two there occasionally, shopping all day before returning home to get ready for a night on the town.

One night, after seeing *Phantom Of The Opera*, Andrea and Scott were strolling back to the apartment when he said, "When are you going to give up this huge apartment? We're hardly ever here and I'd really rather we get a smaller, cozier one."

Scott knew that Andrea had kept the *pied-à-terre* as a security blanket, but he hated the pretentious atmosphere of the Trump apartment; it no longer reflected the woman he now felt he knew. She had grown so warm, loving and thoughtful that he sometimes had to look twice to make sure she was the same person.

It had been over a year since they had begun living together, and Andrea knew that what she was experiencing with Scott was real and powerful. He was like no man she had ever met, strong but gentle, commanding and kind, all at the same time. She was happier than she had ever been in her life. Without question she had loved Adam, but with Scott it was a different kind of love. Even though choosing to live with Scott had been motivated by suspicion, her growing love for him was a far cry from her abject adoration of Adam. That love had left a permanent imprint on her heart. Never for a moment would she forget Adam, but she was ready to be a mature and complete woman with Scott.

With Scott she had run the gamut of emotions: anger, hate, uncertainty, frustration, love, passion, friendship and trust. They had fought, sometimes it seemed without possible reconciliation, when they were establishing their individual boundaries. But their love had been strong enough to weather even Andrea's acid tongue and Scott's pompous authority, and she had found happiness with him. For how long she was not sure, but she would risk taking a chance. She whispered a silent thank you to Adam for telling her that love was meant to be shared, and she had begun to share it with Scott, glad that she could finally put away the feelings of pain and loss. When she slept snugly beside him her nightmares never occurred. Yet there was still a vestige of uncertainty.

Andrea looked at Scott as he lay sleeping beside her, his face the sculpture of a Roman god. She could not believe that all this joy had happened in such a short time. Most of the turmoil of the past year had somehow sorted itself out. She had phoned Helen to remind her of her invitation to visit, but was disappointed when Helen said she would not be able to come that year because of summer classes. Andrea sighed and eased her body closer to Scott, who stirred slightly at her movement.

From the age of three she had learned to control and manipulate almost any person or situation, and as she adapted to her role as head of Jacobson's Industry, she had grown accustomed to using her power and money to alter the very essence of people's lives. This very power she was now willing to relinquish to the man who lay beside her. She felt as though she had been given a new beginning.

In the morning Andrea awoke before Scott and hurried into the kitchen to make breakfast. As she entered the bedroom carrying a tray holding soft boiled eggs, toast and orange juice, complete with a rose and the morning paper, she wished she were a better cook. Everyone has some limitations, she shrugged. Putting the tray down, she became aware that Scott was watching her behind half-closed eyes.

"Ready or not, here I come," she said, jumping into bed. "I know you're not asleep," she said, lifting his eyelids with her fingers. "Peek-a-boo. I have breakfast for you."

Scott rolled over, pinning her under him.

"Poison?" he made a face.

"Cyanide. Now eat."

"Andrea," he began, "it has been over a year since we have been bedmates and I don't want to start taking you for granted as my Sunday girlfriend. You know how much I love you. Wouldn't you say that there are a few things we should discuss?"

"Can't it wait?" Andrea said, shifting her body from under him.

"No, it cannot."

369

"But your eggs are getting cold."

"Andrea, I thought you were finished with your avoidance behavior."

"I am not avoiding anything, Scott. Don't you understand the importance of this occasion?" Puzzled, he shook his head. "It's the first time I've ever made you breakfast. And with this kind of gratitude, it will be the last time."

"Well," he said getting up from the bed, "then let's eat."

Wiping his mouth with the napkin, Scott smiled, "Thank you, darling. That was delicious. Now let's get back to the subject."

"Scott, you're impossible. What's so urgent?"

"I want you to marry me, Andrea, not next year, next month. Before you say yes or no, though, I must tell you my conditions. One, I am never ever going to defend my manhood, so if for one moment you mistake my love for you as weakness, I will leave without looking back. Two, I will not play your jungle fighting games. I expect to be treated with courtesy and respect. Three..."

"Darling," Andrea interrupted him, "do you have to enumerate?"

"Yes. Now where was I? Ah yes, three. I know that for most of your life you've been used to control. That control has made you the woman you are, the woman I happen to love, but I want this relationship to move into one of equal partnership. You must know by now that I can't be controlled or bought. Together our life has endless possibilities, but only under these conditions."

She had gone to the trouble of making this pompous ass breakfast and all he had done was lecture her about how she could become his wife! Andrea could feel the old but familiar reaction of fight or flight. The hair on the back of her neck bristled and she knew she was about to fight. But Lance had taught her how to manage her anger and remembering this, she closed her eyes and willed her mind to go blank.

Since she did not respond immediately, Scott thought perhaps he had gone too far, but he meant what he said.

After a few moments Andrea spoke, "Well Scott, that's quite a list of demands. Do I respond or does equality begin and end with you? Please understand when I say I have no desire to change who I am, because I happen to like myself this way. Here's what I hate more than anything: One, I don't like losing. If I lose it's because I choose to. Two, if you can live with the woman I am, then I want to be your wife. Three, I'm trusting you with my life, and if ever you hurt me, even unintentionally, I will never again be able to—"

Scott lips covered her mouth before she was able to finish her statement.

"Scott," Andrea said, gasping for breath.

"Yes, darling?"

"I wasn't finished."

"There's just one thing left to say. Tell me you'll marry me."

"Yes. I'll marry you."

Much later, Andrea said as they lay spent next to each other, "Scott, you've never asked me what happened in England. Don't you want to know about Helen?"

"Only if you want to tell me."

"I want to tell you," she said, breathing unevenly as she grew more passionate under his touch, "but you're distracting me again."

Scott smiled and kissed her again. He could not get enough of her. Andrea slid closer into his arms as he fondled her firm nipples.

"Darling?" she said between kisses.

"What is it now?"

"What you said about me on the Rachel Hersey show was true?"

"Of course, or I wouldn't have said it."

"I was so angry I considered having you murdered."

"If you had me done away with," he said, kissing the lobe of her ear, "you'd have been doomed to a lonely old age. They say that there are only two truly compatible mates possible in anyone's lifetime, a soul mate and a twin flame."

"And you are the fire, I'm sure. I hope you don't burn too hot," Andrea said languidly.

Chapter 36

It was a sunny April day with not a spring shower in sight when Andrea and Scott were married in front of the arbor in his English garden. Andrea wore a satin and lace St. Pierre bridal gown which had been designed specially for her by Jacques once he had gotten over the shock of her decision to marry Scott Preston. Scott's wedding gift to her, a pearl and diamond necklace with matching earrings, completed Andrea's look of radiance.

"*Ma chérie*," Jacques had said, as he fitted her dress, "I could cry. But I only cry for my own loss. You are so happy that I must be happy for you." She hugged him.

The wedding was small and private. Besides Andrea's family and a beaming Melissa, and Scott's mother and sister, only a few close friends were invited.

"Darling, I don't see any crow's feet today," Maria said, kissing her. I'm so happy that you have finally found love, Andrea." Leaning closer she said, "we'll have to toast to the perfect...man." Her eyes twinkled.

Maria turned to Scott, kissed him on the cheek, and whispered something in his ear. Andrea saw them exchange smiles.

"Good morning, my beloved husband," Andrea said the next day as Scott stirred from his sleep,"I can't imagine for the life of me what you have been up to that makes you so tired." Andrea popped some toast into her mouth and opened the newspaper.

"Andrea Jacobson, multimillionaire businesswoman, has wed the prominent author/psychiatrist, Dr. Scott Preston, who once called her a neurotic overachiever on national television," Andrea read aloud. "Well, darling, we made the front page, not the society page, the front page." She tossed the paper into the trash.

Andrea spent most of the first three months after her marriage looking for an apartment in the city that was more to Scott's liking. Finally she found the ideal apartment in a quiet, posh neighborhood on East 86th Street. Leaving the realtor standing in stunned amazement, she ran from the apartment, "Don't leave," she said to her,"I'll be back in half an hour."

"Scott," Andrea said, whirling into his office unannounced, "darling, I have found the most perfect apartment in New York!" Scott looked up from his desk and grinned at her. She looked like a teenager, windblown and flushed with excitement.

"Wonderful, darling. When can I see it?"

"Right now," she said, "I have the realtor waiting in the apartment. The car is outside. Come on, darling, do hurry."

The apartment really was splendid. It had tall floor-through ceilings, and what seemed like miles and miles of windows which gave the apartment a bright ambiance.

"I'll have it completely livable within a month or two," Andrea beamed. She wanted to decorate it herself. "We will take it, won't we, darling?"

"Yes dear, we certainly will."

Andrea left Scott to work out the details of the contract with the delighted realtor, and then spent the rest of the day in Manhattan shopping. By the time she arrived back in Southampton she was exhausted.

"How was the remainder of your day?" Scott beamed at her, handing her a frosted glass of lemonade.

"Wonderful, but exhausting, I almost fainted in Tiffany's." At Scott's worried look, she said, "Well it was almost ninety degrees outside, you know, and walking into that refrigerator I guess was too much for me. I can't understand why they keep it so cold in there."

That night as Andrea climbed into bed she said, "Darling, I'm so very happy with you, do you suppose anything could go wrong for us?"

"Not a chance." he said, pulling her close to him. "Want to play?"

"Honey, I don't feel quite up to par yet. But you can hold me very tight," she said, snuggling against him.

"By the way, you haven't forgotten that we have a publisher's party to go to tomorrow night, have you?" Scott reminded her.

"Of course not, darling."

Andrea was so tired the next morning she could hardly get out of bed. She rang for the maid. "I'd like just some tea with lemon this morning, please. Nothing to eat. I'm am not going into the city today, so would you call and have the stores send me some catalogs and fabric samples?" By late afternoon Andrea felt back to normal and decided that tea and lemon would cure anything.

That night Andrea dressed carefully. It was her first public appearance as Mrs. Scott Preston.

"Scott!" Andrea shouted from her dressing room, "Would you come in here?"

"What is it, Andrea?"

"I can't get the damn zipper up. I think it's stuck."

Scott took a look. "It's not stuck, dear, the dress is just too tight."

"Scott, stop playing around, we are already running late."

Andrea, dear, this dress *is* too tight."

"I'm going back to work, Scott. This lazy life is fun, but I have no intention of turning into a porker. I'll have to wear something else."

Andrea felt herself perspiring at the party. Even at night the July weather was hot, and the suffocating crush of people surrounding her did not help the air conditioning.

"Hello, Ms. Jacobson." Andrea frowned. "I'm sorry, it's Mrs. Preston now, isn't it?"

"Ah yes, you again. I suppose you'd like to invite me back on your show. I told you once that when I found a man who was not intimidated by me, I'd tell your viewers."

"I would love to," Rachel Hersey began, "after all I did kind of introduce you two."

"It would be a cold day in hell when you interview me again. It was only fate that saved you from being fired."

Andrea turned on her heel and walked away. More than anything, Rachel hated to be snubbed. She determined to fix that Jacobson bitch once and for all.

Scott heard the thump. "Andrea, what happened?" Scott said, rushing into the bathroom. He found his wife sprawled on the floor.

"I think I must have passed out," she said, trying to get to her feet.

"No darling, don't move." Scott lifted Andrea in his arms and carried her to the bed, then dialed her doctor and told him to come right away.

"No need to be alarmed," said Dr. Riley, "Your wife is going to be fine. She has a touch of what we'll call pending motherhood." Scott's body stiffened.

"Doctor, are you sure?"

"I can't be positive until I have the test results, but I would say it is a good bet. I'll call you as soon as I know more."

Scott walked the doctor to the door. When he returned he was silent and looked morose.

Andrea swung her feet over the side of the bed and sat next to her husband. "It will be all right, darling," Andrea said, resting her head against his shoulder. Intuitively, she knew he was thinking of Angela, his first wife who had died in childbirth.

"I don't know if I can stand it," he said covering his face with his hands. "If I lose you, Andrea, I will die. Promise me you'll never leave me."

"I won't," she said softly, "I won't."

Andrea was as healthy as an ox. By the time she was almost eight months pregnant, Scott had finally got used to the idea that she would be fine. He had been so overprotective that Andrea had felt stifled. She was glad when he left for work in the mornings although he called her at least a dozen times a day.

"Darling, I might deliver early if I have to get up to take so many calls from you. How about cutting them down to three a day?"

"Okay, darling, I will."

But he did not, and understanding his worry, Andrea indulged him.

One Monday morning, at the end of Andrea's eighth month of pregnancy, she awoke feeling more than usually energetic. She had decided it was time for them to sell her apartment in the Trump which she had kept even after finding and furnishing the new place. The compulsive need to hold on to her own apartment was gone. With the baby coming and her absolute love for her husband, she could find no reason to want to go back to her former sterile existence. And in two years of being with him, she had not found one reason to suspect Scott of joining in a conspiracy against her with anyone. She had abandoned her investigation—for the time being.

Andrea called the realtor and made arrangements to meet her at the apartment. She felt so energetic that although it was a cool February morning she decided a brisk walk through Central Park would be good exercise.

"Let me out here," she instructed the driver.

"But Mrs. Preston, Dr. Preston has told me to be with you every minute while you are out."

"James, Dr. Preston is overreacting. I feel like walking today and I will meet you at Trump Towers in half an hour or so."

Andrea heaved herself out of the car, not used to being so clumsy. As she moved, the baby suddenly landed a blow to her stomach, reminding her to be more careful.

"Stop it, you bugger," she said gently, touching her stomach lightly. It had been such a different experience from being pregnant with Helen. She wished she could have shared this pleasant, carefree life with her first child. If only she could have given her daughter the family she so badly wanted. Well, she couldn't, not yet. They had made headway though, Andrea consoled herself, Helen was finally going to come to the States this summer for three weeks. It had taken two years, but the girl had gotten Maya to consent this time. Although Andrea was a bit nervous about the timing of her visit because of the responsibilities of the new baby, she would be glad for Helen's company.

The baby was due the third week in March, which would give her enough time to prepare for Helen's arrival. Andrea sang as she walked along. She felt definitely a part of New York today.

As Andrea passed a news stand, a headline in the *Star Press* stopped her in her tracks. She picked up the paper and read the bold print.

"ANDREA JACOBSON SECRET LOVE REVEALED!"

Andrea pulled her hat down to cover her eyes and paid for the tabloid. She wanted to read the article immediately but she forced herself to wait until she reached a secluded bench where she could sit down. The paper shook in her trembling fingers as she began reading.

"Andrea Jacobson, the multimillionaire owner of Jacobson's Industry and wife of the prominent psychiatrist Scott Preston has had a secret lover since the age of thirteen, according to *Star* sources. The ongoing affair ended less than two years ago only because wealthy Jamaican Adam Reginald Stern died of complications caused by alcoholism. Twenty years her senior, and the father of her illegitimate child, the *Star* has been told that Stern was the only love of Andrea Jacobson's life. She was with him when he died."

A photograph of the two of them together highlighted the front page. Andrea could read no further. Motionless, she stared at the paper as though she could not comprehend the words. She was sweating profusely in the middle of a chilly February day. Suddenly she stood up, screamed and collapsed on the ground, crying out again as an excruciating pain shot through her. A gush of water poured from between her legs, signaling the onslaught of labor.

"My God, they have ruined me," was her last bleak thought as she slid into unconsciousness.

"Dr. Preston this is Lenox Hill Hospital. Your wife has just been brought into the emergency room. She is premature labor and we have contacted Dr. Riley," a voice on the telephone told him. Scott Preston sank to his chair. He pleaded with tears in his eyes, "Not again, oh please God, not again."

By the time he had reached the hospital, Scott was wild-eyed and frantic.

"Where is she?" he demanded, "I want to see my wife."

A nurse took him to the room. Andrea was lying very still, an oxygen mask on her face, an IV dripping blood in her arm.

"Darling," Scott said, "please speak to me. Andrea please don't die. I can't live without you."

"She will be fine, Dr. Preston. Apparently she had a scare in the park. Thank God some Good Samaritan called 911. But she's gone into labor and I cannot stop it. We've sedated her because she was hysterical and semi-conscious when the paramedics brought her in. I realize the baby is a month early, but we had no choice."

"Listen doctor, take the baby if you have to, but please save my wife."

"She is in no danger of dying."

"Are you sure?"

"Yes, of course. She'll be fine and so will the baby. We've taken the P/L ratio and the baby's lungs have matured enough to survive outside the uterus. Naturally it will have to be in an incubator for about two weeks. I imagine your wife will be in hard labor in a couple of hours or so, but until then I feel it is best for her to rest under mild sedation. By the way, she was clutching this paper when she came in."

"Thank you Doctor, I will stay here with her. Scott sat beside his wife stroking her black hair that was wet with perspiration. He did not look at the paper.

Andrea opened her eyes slowly and looked around. "Oh Scott, I can't believe they would want to hurt me like this."

"Who, darling, who?"

"They want to take my baby away again, I know it."

"Andrea, who is trying to take the baby?"

"Are you a part of it too, Scott?"

Andrea doubled over in pain as a contraction stabbed, "Oh Scott, the baby's coming, please, please don't let them take it—Scott," Andrea screamed at the onslaught of another contraction, "I can't stand it. Please make them stop it."

"They can't, darling, the baby is coming early and they can't give you anything more. Breathe, darling, just like they told you." Andrea began panting rapidly. "Look at the wall over there," he pointed, "and breathe." Scott rang for the nurse.

"How did they know about him?" Andrea sobbed. As the pain became excruciating, she felt her consciousness began to alter and she fought it. No! No out-of-body experience this time, she thought. She would not let them take this baby away.

"Don't let them take her. I want to keep her. Please Scott, don't let them take our baby."

The nurse hurried into the room and pulled the cover back. "Wheel her in, she's crowning."

"Push, Andrea," Dr. Riley said.

"I am pushing," Andrea said, between clenched teeth.

"Scalpel, I have to cut her." Dr. Riley cut into the old incision and wondered again why Andrea had never told him that she had given birth before. He had wanted to ask her many times during her visits to him but he dared not. He had treated her as a multiple birth case nevertheless.

"You have a son," the doctor announced. The baby started crying. Andrea held out her arms and the nurse placed her son on her breast. She held the tiny warm slippery body so close their heartbeats blended, and tears of relief and joy flooded unchecked down her face.

"Thank you, my darling, you're wonderful. And so is our son," Scott said behind his surgical mask. Andrea allowed the nurse to take the baby to wash and weigh him, and then, exhausted, she fell asleep in Scott's arms with a contented feeling of pride in her accomplishment.

"I would like to name him Reginald, darling, if that's all right with you," Andrea said, watching from a chair in her hospital suite as Scott packed her things. He smiled and nodded his approval.

"Why are you packing, dear, where is Melissa?"

"She is at home getting everything ready and interviewing women for a nanny position."

"But I—"

"Never mind, sweetheart, you are going to have help whether you think you need it or not. Melissa will hire the right person, you know."

"Very well, Herr Hitler. He is such a beautiful baby, Scott, and he looks just like you," she said, kissing her husband. Cards, flowers, and gifts filled the room.

In all the excitement Scott did not notice the tabloid stuffed in his pocket until he returned home the next day for a change of clothes. After reading it, he was furious at the *Star* for this slanderous attack. Once Andrea was strong again he had every intention of suing them, but he did not want to bring the topic up with her just now.

The nanny Melissa chose was so competent that at first Andrea felt like an outsider rather than the mother of the child. Soon, however, she realized that the nanny was well-trained and good with the baby, and each began to value and appreciate the other's role. Andrea was glad for the time to rest, but by the end of four weeks she was ready to get to the bottom of the puzzle she had to solve.

Andrea dialed the *Star*.

"I want to speak to the publisher."

"Who is calling?" the receptionist asked.

"Andrea Jacobson-Preston."

There was a perceptible pause.

"Hold please."

Moments later he came on the phone.

"Good morning, Mrs. Jacobson. How may I help?"

"You may begin by calling me Mrs. Preston. I want to know where you got the garbage you printed in that trashy magazine of yours, and I want names."

"I can't divulge sources, Mrs. Preston, that's journalistic policy. I'm sorry."

"I can assure you that you will soon be much sorrier." She cut off the connection and dialed another number.

"Harold, Andrea Jacobson. I want you to get in touch with Anthony and buy the *Star Press.*

"Is it for sale?"

"Everything is for sale at the right price, Harold, and I want this execution over fast." To Andrea, lawyers and accountants were two of the most irritating professions. She paid them too much for them to ask stupid questions.

Within two days Harold called to inform her that she owned the *Star Press.*

Andrea squeezed into her Chanel suit. It did not fit comfortably.

"Melissa!" she screamed.

"What is the matter with you?"

"I can't fit into this damn suit. Call Sak's and have them send me one just like it, one size larger," she snapped, throwing the suit onto the bed. "And Melissa, tell them it must be here by seven tomorrow morning."

"Andrea, you are most impatient. You have just had a baby, and if you waited another few weeks you would fit perfectly into that suit."

"That is not the point, Mel. I want to wear it tomorrow."

Tomorrow she wanted to command attention without saying a word and she had always found the austere suit sobering to her employees. They called it her shake-up suit, because whenever she wore it heads rolled.

At eight a.m., Andrea pushed through the revolving door of the *Star* building, pressed the elevator button for the fourth floor and waited impatiently for the car to ascend. Andrea walked into the large reception area, surveying the newest addition to her empire. It was handsomely furnished. The company was making money from all the trash it printed. After she had accomplished what she wanted, she would obliterate the publication as though it had never existed.

"We don't see anyone until eight-thirty," the receptionist said, not bothering to look up from the splashy tabloid.

"I don't need an appointment," Andrea said, "I am Andrea Jacobson-Preston. I own this place. Gather the entire news staff at once."

Sneaking a startled peek at the elusive Andrea Jacobson, the girl scurried away.

Once the staff had gathered, Andrea entered the board room. Everyone stood waiting in shocked silence. The deal was so freshly inked that not even the editor-in-chief had known of the change of ownership. Andrea threw the ownership papers on the table and looked dispassionately at the sorry appearance of the employees. Not a bunch she would have hired, but she had never owned a publication before and she supposed their dress code was different. Andrea did not speak for a full two minutes.

"Who is the editor-in-chief?" Andrea asked when the tension became almost unbearable.

"I am," a middle-aged, chunky, balding man came forward.

"I want the file on the story that was printed about me. I want it all, including the sources and the details. I want it in under a minute. And, by the way, don't bother to contact your union representative, because at the end of the day this paper and your job will cease to exist."

Andrea had not told Scott of her acquisition. Not only would he have found some altruistic reasons to discourage her, but she had to find out if Scott had anything to do with this latest attempt to destroy her. Was it really part of a conspiracy?

Her fingers were shaking as she opened the file. She took a deep breath, wanting to close it and shred it. If her husband was implicated, she knew she would never recover—but she would survive.

Chapter 37

London

Helen read the article over and over again, her eyes going from it to the picture. Unbelievable as it was, the man beside Andrea Jacobson in the photo was the man on the horse in the painting over her bed. Andrea Jacobson was the mother who had abandoned her. And Adam Stern was her father, an alcoholic, and he too had abandoned her. She was the daughter of one of the richest women in the world, and she supposed she should feel happy, but what she felt was anger, loathing and betrayal. No wonder she had felt so touched by Andrea. No wonder the man in the picture looked familiar. Helen walked over to the bed and took the picture down, leaning it against the wall in front of the mirror. She looked from the picture to her face and back again. Why had she not realized it? Her eyes and nose were exactly like that of her father's. That explained why Andrea had said he was special.

Helen picked up the bottle of Joy she had bought because it was what Andrea had worn when they met. She had spent days in

Harrod's smelling various perfumes just to find out what scent Andrea was wearing the night of her birthday. Helen threw the bottle at the mirror smashing both into pieces of jagged glass. They would pay for leaving her. She would show them that she could be just as cruel as they were. Well, she could not hurt her father, because he was dead, but she would make her mother pay dearly for both of them. How could Andrea have lied to her?

"Helen," Maya pleaded outside the door when she heard glass shattering.

"Go away. I don't want to see you ever again. You are as bad as they were. How could you deprive me of my own parents?"

"I can explain everything, Helen, if you would just listen for a moment."

"It's too late. You cannot stop me from being angry. I have a right to be!" Helen shouted, as Maya tried to reason with her. "How dare you? I will never forgive you for this. Not any of you."

"Helen, darling, you must listen to me."

Helen's tone was acrid as Maya tried to reason with her, "I will never forgive you. Not any of you."

Maya opened the door.

"Get away from me, just get out" Helen said evenly. The look in her eyes was cold fire.

New York

Andrea flipped through the folder. It was all there, every sordid detail, every name. Still, she heaved a sigh of relief. There was no mention of Scott or Maria.

She closed the folder, slumping back in her chair. Having seen the name of Hersey's main source of information, she was disappointed but not surprised. But Jonathan, how could he? She had trusted Jonathan to run Jacobson's in her absence, but the slimy viper had been the *spy*. No wonder he had pushed so hard for the television appearance. It had nothing to do with Jacobson's Industry, just pillow talk for Hersey's sexual favors. She was nauseated at the idea of the two of them copulating like rabbits. The damn fool. To trash his career for a two-bit hussy. He would be fired in the morning only because it was beneath Andrea's dignity to kill the bastard. And this time sleazy Rachel Hersey had investigated the wrong story. It would be her last. Andrea was thankful she had never told Scott of her suspicions about him. What a fool she was to ever think Maria would betray her. But to put all the missing pieces together she still had to find out exactly why Maya had wanted her to meet Helen.

Scott looked up as she entered their bedroom.

"Hello, darling. I was wondering where you were. Come," he said gently, "tell me about your day." Andrea sat next to her husband and rested her head on his shoulder.

"Darling we now own the *Star Press*. I just bought it."

Scott did not need to be told why. "And what did you find out?"

"Rachel Hersey, through one of my vice presidents, was the source of information about Adam. Can you believe they even had me followed to Jamaica and eavesdropped on all my private conversations? I would never have believed that of Jonathan. I suppose lust and passion will always destroy logic. I just wonder why she didn't publish it herself, but I guess she was planning to dig further and continue on where they left off. If I have my way she will never sell another article or do another interview again. And Jonathan has a surprise coming in the morning."

The phone rang.

"Hello," Scott answered, "Yes. Who is calling?"

"Darling, it's Maya."

Andrea's eyebrows went up.

"Yes, Maya?" she said, as calmly as she could, knowing the

article was why she was calling.

"Helen has disappeared, Andrea, and I don't know where she is. When I got up this morning she was nowhere to be found. She read the article in the *Star Press* and was quite distressed. Hopefully, she will return here, but I thought you should know."

"Thank you, Maya, I'm glad you called."

"Andrea, you must understand that Helen was so upset that I am worried about what she might do. Andrea, she has certain powers that are most uncommon, and if she is angry enough she could lose control."

"Maya, that's utter nonsense. No matter what, I *am* her mother. What exactly are you saying?"

"Her sixth sense is highly developed. Under my supervision she learned to use her powers positively, and she is not aware that she could be destructive because she has never had to use them in defense; but anger heightens one's powers adversely. Andrea, she may come to you in New York. Please call me if you hear from her and I will do the same."

Was Maya deliberately planting fear in her? If so, she had succeeded. What was her motive for this maneuver?

"Who else knows about Helen? Who could she possibly go to?" Andrea asked, her voice revealing nothing of what she felt.

"Maria. I told her after the child was born because she was so concerned about you. I had to explain why we took the child or she would have caused a scandal. Maria and I had lunch just after you left England. She has kept in touch with me over the years. I wish she had mentioned it when you met in Monte Carlo, but I presume she did not want to make you any more suspicious than you were. When we met, she was very concerned that my loyalty to you had changed. She loves you Andrea. She is a dear friend."

"But I never told Maria that it was you."

"She suspected and I had to admit it, but I swore her to secrecy. Andrea, in order to deal with Helen if a confrontation arises, you may have to call on your own special strengths."

"Of course. Thank you. Maya, I have just one more question. why did you invite me to Helen's party after all those years?"

"Because I wanted you to see that being a special child was not negative. I was hoping that you would tell Helen that you were her mother. She would have insisted on returning with you to the States. Andrea, you would have trusted your child more than anyone in the world and with her help you would have recognized our good intentions and your own powers. There is strength in numbers and there is a greater and greater need for spiritual awakening. We could not take the chance of losing again as we did with both you and your mother. Worldly exposure has a way of altering divinity. I only hope that you can forgive me. I did what I thought was best."

Oh Maria, Andrea thought, how could I have doubted you?

Scott was waiting for Andrea to explain the conversation, but she could not talk. She went into the bathroom to try to think for a moment and the tears came. No one, not even her husband could help her. Wearily, Andrea undressed and got ready for bed. It had been a very long day. All this time Maria had known about Helen and Maya. Of course, she nodded with recognition of her friend's loyalty. Keeping her secret all these years had been the only common thread that made it seem like a conspiracy. When she came out of the bathroom she went to the nursery to see Reginald, her second love child. She hoped she could do a better job with him than she had done with her firstborn. She wondered if Reginald had extraordinary powers. It was all too far-fetched for Andrea to believe or to grasp, but there was still one person who might be able to explain some things to her. Andrea used the phone in Reginald's nursery.

"Mother," she said quietly, "I need to see you."

"I know, Andy, I know," was the steadying reply.

"Andrea," Scott said when she came back into the bedroom, "I want to know what happened on the phone."

"Not now, darling," Andrea said, getting into bed. "I can't talk about it right now."

"Andrea, I am your husband. I can tell that you are withdrawing from facing problems again. They will not go away until they are solved. Let me help."

"Next week," she stated, "I'm going back to Jacobson's. I need to be the master of my own domain again. Tomorrow," Andrea said, suddenly feeling very tired, "I will tell you everything."

Scott sensed Andrea's underlying despair. He held his wife in his arms until she was asleep. Work was her way of sublimation. Such a stubborn woman, he thought. Scott could not sleep so he decided to go downstairs to the study and read awhile. He had been reading for about two hours when he heard a blood curdling scream coming from the bedroom. Scott dashed up the stairs and threw open the door.

"Andrea!" he cried, turning on the light. His wife was sitting on the floor in a corner of the bedroom, legs drawn up to her chest, tears flowing down her face. She looked disheveled, almost deranged. Postpartum depression, he diagnosed.

Scott knelt beside his wife, who clung to him fiercely. "What is it, darling? Please, Andrea, what is it?"

"My dream," she said, "I can finally remember my dream. Oh Scott," she whispered almost inaudibly, "she was demented."

"Who, Andrea?"

"Helen."

"Darling, it was just a bad dream. It has been a difficult past few months, and after your day today your nightmare is completely understandable."

"I was in labor. The pain was unbearable. I begged them to

stop it, but they said the baby was prolonging my labor and that it would not allow them to hurry. I sensed danger, and I knew I had to get away from what was happening or I would die. That was when I lost consciousness, and when I came to I was floating above my body. I was terrified. Then I looked down and saw the most beautiful baby being born. But Scott, oh God, she was laughing! And her eyes—her eyes flashed at me like fire, and her lips formed words I could not hear, hateful words. I begged her to stop laughing at me, that I was her mother and I loved her. But they were already taking her away and I was crying for them to give her back to me. Scott," Andrea said, "I need to find Helen. I have to understand what this is all about."

"Andrea it was just a dream. None of that is real. The guilt you feel about Helen is causing you much pain. It is not uncommon to have terrible dreams under the circumstances. Darling, get hold of yourself. Tomorrow everything will be fine, and I'll take you away for a long rest."

"It's real, Scott," Andrea insisted. "That's why Maya called tonight. Helen is gone. She may come here and Maya insinuated that she could be dangerous because she has powers. Tomorrow I am going to see my mother. She may have the answers I'm looking for. I want to know what is so special about us, my mother and me—and Helen."

"Why don't you talk with a therapist? It may help you to sort out your confusion and your fear."

"No," Andrea said, "I must do this my way. The way that has been chosen for me." She turned to look at her husband. "I'm so glad I have you, darling, God knows I'll need you through all of this, but I hope you love me enough to let me find my way." Whatever had to be done was something only she could do. Hopefully, tomorrow the missing piece of the puzzle would fall in place.

"I must find a way to help my child," Andrea continued, "and

392

understanding my own powers may be the only way, according to Maya."

"Now Andrea, after all we have studied. You have no powers other than faith and love. If Helen comes to us we will welcome her as we should have done two years ago. If she has occult ability, we'll deal with it then. Now darling let's go to bed."

London/Jamaica

Helen slammed the door and bolted it. From the closet, she snatched the matching luggage she had carefully stashed away pending her visit to New York that summer. At sixteen, having graduated at the top of her class, but still undecided about her future, a year in New York with Andrea had been an exciting option. With that option now impossible, her direction was more uncertain than ever. The stab of betrayal turned it's bloody tip in her heart and she felt as though she were hemorrhaging to death. How could Andrea have deceived her this way after she had confided in her the pain of not knowing her parents? Her anger grew. Andrea Jacobson must be made to feel the agony of loss. Hurriedly she threw in enough clothes to fill the two suitcases on the bed. She retrieved her passport and the bank book with the three thousand pounds she would have taken on her trip to America. She hastily packed, then looked solemnly around. This was all she had in the world now. Helen wiped the back of her hand across her eyes. No need for tears; tears could not help her. She was on her own. Until she found work she could manage in a cheap flat, she calmed herself. She picked up the telephone and punched the number of City Cab.

"Yes, send the cab at exactly nine." Maya, would be out until ten p.m.

At five to nine, Helen descended the steps of the gracious

house. One hour was enough time to go halfway across England. At the bottom of the staircase she cast her eyes upwards and shuddered. There was no remorse, not even a shred of sadness. She had never liked this house. And with it, she was determined to leave behind the charade of her so-called powers.

"Tilt your head a little to the right, yes that's it. Now just let those straps fall casually over your shoulders. Good, good. More, give me more. Perfect." The camera clicked continuously as Emanual spoke. He was challenged and his adrenalin was high. It had been a long time since he shot a model whose beauty he could not enhance with the camera. Helen was a mixture of intrigue and mysticism and even with his expert eye he was incapable of capturing her essence with his lens. With so many angles to her face and body however, he would never tire of photographing her. There was that part of her, he accepted defeat, that would always remain untouched and unexposed to her public.

"I am so tired, Manu," she preferred to call him. "Can't we call it a day and do the rest of the shoot tomorrow?"

"Jacques wants the proofs on his desk by tomorrow morning. We may have to work all night. I am not sure why he is so protective of your career. Never seen anything like it. He wants your spread to hit the circuit in September."

"That's three months away!"

"You are right. Hardly enough time to perfect our art."

"Then, my sweets, I suggest you give him what you have done already because I am bushed." With that Helen donned the silk robe on the chair next to her, pulled it closely and walked off the set.

It had been only four months since she had come to the agency. After months of rejections for jobs, because of her age, she felt desperate. Her funds were dwindling and although she was not yet starving, she felt a sense of urgency. The bright idea of modeling dawned on her as she read her *Seventeen* magazine from cover to cover. She could be on the front of one of those glossies. She was certainly beautiful enough. The olive bronze complexion had deepened. The dark brown eyes had a new depth. Her tall slender body had filled to perfection and her raven hair shone as though brushed a thousand times. The curved pouty lips were now blood red from the application of Jacque's new line of cosmetics. That's what she was going to become: the top teenage model for his line of cosmetics and young fashions. She was convinced she was prettier without all the gook.

Still, though all the agencies wanted her, they required her to put together a portfolio at her own expense and she was on her last ray of hope by the time she entered the St. Pierre offices. Jacques St. Pierre took an immediate liking to her. Within hours he had arranged for her to begin work. Though the pay was beyond her expectations, Helen found the whole business of modeling not only phony but very rigorous and demanding. Up at five, shoot until eight, and then the publicity began. With increasing frequency, she had to be on the arm of Jacques St. Pierre at high visibility gala affairs.

"It is called priming *chère*," he had said when she protested about being tired. "These are the people we are interested in. They, *ma chère*, are the ultimate in superficial beings. *Ma* Helen, surely you can see it's important that they can brag how long they knew you before you become famous. When your face is on every magazine cover from here to Nairobi, they will be the first to claim you as a personal friend and they set the fashion trends here in London. Trust me Helen, I know what I am doing."

She had indulged him. After all he did rescue her from the near squalor she was living. The boarding house in London, although not seedy or dirty, was a far cry from the comfortable flat in which she now lived. Certainly a situation more befitting to the heir to the Jacobson's fortune. Yes, she intended to have every penny of the Jacobson's fortune!

"What's this about quitting early from your shoot?" Helen spun around to see Jacques framing the door of her dressing room.

"I am out of energy. I can't do another turn. Not tonight," her voice was pleading.

"All right, all right. But tomorrow we must get back on schedule." As if it mattered. If she presented the same problem tomorrow, Jacques would have given in completely. She had him, hook, line and sinker, in her spell.

"How about just a quiet dinner tonight? Let's leave the plastic smiles behind, eh *chère.*"

"OK, just as long as you take me straight home afterwards."

"A deal, as they would say." He approached her. "Wear the pale yellow chiffon dress tonight, chère." He backed away when he realized what his intentions were. He was old enough to be her father, even her grandfather. Damn, she was beautiful. But more than just beautiful, she had him mesmerized. What was it about her that was so familiar? In his lifetime he had only felt the need to be domesticated twice. Both with *femmes exotique*. If he stretched his imagination, he would say this child, so tender, so voluptuous, with the dark brown mysterious eyes reminded him of his first love, Andrea Francis. No, Andrea Preston. He had to accept that. Andrea was now married. She had been so happy until the scandal had rocked the world. He had not seen her in months.

"Just two tonight, John. We would like a private room."

He led them back to an area off the main dining area, set for two. Helen was not comfortable with the privacy of the room, for as handsome and famous as Jacques St. Pierre was, he was merely her ticket to the small fortune she would need to carry out her plan. A transitional phase, she called it.

"You are especially beautiful tonight, *ma chère*. The yellow softens your hair and brings glitter to your smile." Helen's eyes brightened, with an intransigent stare that was as filled with ambiguity as it was with real annoyance.

"Thank you, Jacques"

"Tonight you look so much like my very first love."

"Really? What happened?"

"She loved someone else."

"I'm sorry."

"Don't be. We are still very good friends. Like you, she was a woman of great beauty and mystery. I met her on the streets of Paris. I wanted her to become a model for me as I knew she would hasten my path to fame and fortune, but alas she had no interest. I never saw her again until years later— and only then did I realize she had become the one and only Andrea Jacobson."

Helen stiffened, but Jacques, engrossed in his memory never noticed.

"You mean Andrea Jacobson of the Jacobson's fortune?"

"Yes, that's who you remind me of. It's almost *déjà vu.*"

Helen could not believe her luck. Here in the palm of her hand, was an instrument to her destiny. She had intended to accumulate income from Jacques, but never had she dreamed he would know her mother. How life had a way of going full circle. She toyed with the idea of leading him on but finally abandoned it. Time was of the essence and she did not have much of it. She let the subject drop and concentrated on the menu. Jacques was more valuable than ever.

Over the course of three months and just before her spread was to become a reality, Helen had every detail she could garner, without suspicion from Jacques and others who knew anything about Andrea Jacobson. The time had come to move on. Once her face hit the magazines, Maya would have the bloodhounds out and Jacques, she felt a twinge of regret, would be disappointed to loose his protégée. But she shrugged, *c'est la vie* in the big world.

"What may I get you to drink?"

"Tea please," Helen replied folding the article she was reading in half. She was glad to have a row of airline seats all to herself. The article, and subsequent ones had given her enough details about Andrea and Adam Stern to make her trip worthwhile. She had a small fortune in her pocket and she would stay in Jamaica as long as it took to get what she needed.

"You want a car, miss?"

"Pardon?"

"You want a car?"

"I am sorry, I don't understand."

"Would you like a cab to take you to your destination, miss?"

"Oh yes, thank you." Helen smiled.

The cab driver's English was now almost as British as hers but his lilting voice had been at the very core of her beginning. She was in a country where she should have been all her life. She was unsure if she would have been able to stand the heat, she mused, as she pulled her cotton cardigan off.

"I would like to be taken to the Stern's estate. Well no, first you should take me to a hotel nearby and later to the estate. I want to freshen up," she said quickly, allaying any suspicions her curiosity may have caused. "Do you know of a good hotel within walking distance of the estate?"

"Not much in the way of hotels there, mon. They own damn near the whole place. Its like a private part of the island. I know a beautiful cottage that you could rent though. It comes with a maid and a yardboy and you could have me as your personal driver."

"How far is it from the Sterns?"

"Not very far, mon. But what difference does that make? I take you where ever you want to go. What business you have with the Sterns anyway?"

Helen was amused by the straightforwardness of the driver. He wouldn't care if she were the Queen of England. She soon found out this was a culture thing. The self-appreciation and superego of the Jamaicans was like nothing she had ever seen.

"Well I am a friend of a friend and I promised to deliver a gift to them for her."

"That is nice. They are nice people but they are still in mourning after the loss of their son. It's been almost three years but the women still wear black in this hot sun. "

Again Helen laughed at the nonchalant attitude of the driver.

"Do you know much about them, eh...what is your name?"

"Cecil. As much as everyone else knows. They have their own workers that live on the estate but they are my friends. Everyone know the Sterns."

Good, Helen decided. This was going to be easier than she thought.

By the time Cecil deposited her at the cottage, she was nearly prostrate from the heat. The car had no air conditioning and as it climbed the hill on which the cottage was set, it sounded as though it were on its last leg. Thank goodness the cottage had a cooling system. Helen looked around the spacious two bedroom house shaped in a circle and built around its own private swimming pool. Tropical flowers hid all passersby from view and the place was elegantly furnished with a mixture of rattan and mahogany. A woman with the complexion of midnight hurried in to give her a drink. How was she ever going to afford this place?

"Welcome to Lover's Cove. A welcome drink for you."

Helen gratefully took a long swig of the reddish drink topped generously with ice. Only after it was almost gone did she realize it was rum punch. Well the worst it could do was relax her. And relax her it did. She slept until dawn the next morning. Although it was only six o'clock, all the staff were already up and about. She quickly changed into her swimsuit and noticed that a table was already set for breakfast.

"You want your coffee now, miss?" A voice startled Helen.

She spun around and the woman of the night before was right behind her with a steaming cup of coffee. It was the best she had ever tasted.

"Do you want anything special for breakfast or would you like something Jamaican?"

"Something Jamaican. I feel adventurous."   The woman disappeared as quickly as she came.

"Miss Helen, I want to know what you have planned for today," Cecil's lilting voice had taken on its familiar accent as he sauntered onto the patio. "I am going to the airport to pick up a few people on the early flight and will be back before ten. But if you need me all day I will wait around for you."

"Cecil, what is all this luxury costing me? And how do you think I am going to afford it?"

"Miss, if you know the Sterns you can afford this measly old place. It's not going to cost you much.   One hundred and fifty US dollars per day. The maid and yardboy get 40 dollar a day and I take what you give me. My usual fee for private transportation is sixty dollars a day. That's about," he cocked his head to the side and did a quick calculation, "two hundred and fifty US dollars. Not much eh? "

Helen laughed loudly. "You are such a con, Cecil, but it's fine." After all, she had a quite a stash from her short career as a fashion model. It was all going to be worth it in more ways than one and Cecil was proving to be a valuable resource.

"Want to have a cup of coffee?"

"If you like." His eyes, hidden behind dark glasses, observed the perfect figure of this striking beauty he had picked up the night before. "So I take it I am to forget going to the airport?"

"Yes, I would prefer if you just spent your time driving me around. I want to see all the island."

"All the island? Miss, how long will you be here?"

"As long as necessary—ah, for complete relaxation," she added hurriedly.

The sun was just now coming up over the trees. This, Helen decided, had to be paradise. She should never have been deprived of her roots so callously. Instead of growing up in this warm country where the people seemed even warmer and the scenery out of a postcard, she had been abandoned by her mother and had wasted her valuable time playing fortune teller. How she longed for revenge for this cruelty. No doubt she had powers, but it was like anything else: once you have it, it's old hat. She hated those stupid psychic improvement sessions Maya forced her to attend, as though her gift were something more precious than it really was. She breathed a sigh of relief; this was life, she held her face to the rising sun and smiled at Cecil.

"Now fill me in about the Sterns. I don't want to go there totally ignorant."

Cecil was under a spell. He could not stop talking. He proceeded to tell her everything he knew about the Sterns. And if she didn't stop looking at him that way and smiling with those white teeth, he would have to invent a few stories just to keep on being close to her. She had a strange effect on him.

Indeed Helen had a peculiar effect on anyone she wanted to control. She didn't mean it intentionally but when her emotions were high, her psychic powers were acute.

Helen spent a week talking with anyone who could add to the Stern's emerging picture. She even met a woman who knew of the

Francis family. Once her image of the family was completed she prepared her next step.

She looked at the picture of her mother and father, and again the pain was acute. After just a week in Jamaica she felt more fully the deprivation of her childhood. Her father it seemed, had been a man of great charm and being the product of a wealthy family, was prone to excesses. After her mother left Jamaica it appeared he became more and more involved with the bottle but he was apparently loved by all. She was unable to find out much about his funeral. Cecil informed her it had been a very private service on the family's own property. Tonight, she planned to visit the nightclub that the Stern's owned.

"Cecil, will you collect me at eight o'clock? I am going to dance at the Coconut Grove. I hear it's lots of fun."

"I wouldn't know. The club only caters to the elites."

"Are you kidding?"

"Am I laughing?"

Cecil was daft about Helen. He never left her side unless she told him to. He was annoyed that she would choose to hob nob with the socialites. It only meant she would find him quite common after this. Tonight she wanted to go to the Coconut Grove without him. Not even as much as an invitation. He was a fool to think he was anything but the hired hand. He was to pick her up there three hours later. How he would have loved to enter the club on the arm of this beauty. Normally, only upper crust islanders with membership could go to the Coconut Grove. He would never be able to afford the membership, much less get the attention of a woman like Helen. Observing her over the past week, at their usual breakfast, lunch and dinner gab sessions on the patio, he noticed she had developed a natural ability to mimic his lingo and a taste for anything Jamaican. Her interest in the Sterns was consuming and he could not help but wonder if she had roots in Jamaica, or was somehow connected to the family. When he asked her however, she said no. She was born in England and studied in Switzerland. The thought of the cold weather made him shiver. It also froze his curiosity.

Helen was as nervous as a kitten. She climbed the narrow stairs and followed the sound of merriment. The club was dimly lit. Off to one side was a private dining room with a few dinner guests. Just beyond, one entered a smoky room filled with patrons sitting at tables or at the bar drinking and eating gaily. A band on stage drummed out the deep hypnotic beat of reggae music. Several couples were dancing rhythmically to the soulful music and immediately she felt lighter. She loved to dance. Helen moved gracefully into the room. For a moment the room was quiet and eyes turned towards her. She continued to the bar and ordered a brandy. No one seemed to care if she was old enough to drink.

Raymond Stern noticed the woman immediately. What a beauty. She seemed familiar but he could not place her. He approached her.

"You are new in town?" It was more a statement than a question.

"Yes, I am." Helen turned to greet her admirer. She gasped as the face of the man came into focus. It was the face of her father.

"I *am* sorry," she bent down to pick up the glass that had slipped from her hand and splattered his immaculate white linen suit.

"No, I am sorry. I did not mean to startle you."

She reached for some napkins.

"It's OK. Really. It happens all the time. I have this effect on women." His smile was warm.

She was furious at herself. Her first blunder. But this man was entirely unexpected. She had heard her father had a twin but this was far too eerie.

"I will be happy to take care of the cleaning bill."

"Fine." He brushed her offer aside. "What were you drinking?" he signaled the bartender. "Would you care to join me at my table ah, miss...?"

"Helen Stenson," she lied.

"I am Raymond Stern."

Raymond collected her glass and led the way to the table. Although everyone was polite, Helen could tell that a particular woman dressed in black was not especially happy.

"This is my sister Josephine," he introduced the woman. Josephine, still attractive, had to have been a striking beauty in her day. Too much life it seemed had happened to her.

"Doesn't she remind you of someone?" Raymond asked his sister.

"Yes," she said quietly, "she does. "

Helen was disturbed by the turn of events. She had to find a way to break through the barrier of Josephine Stern. She had obviously been very close to her brother Adam. The two matching pair of eyes met. Both jet black and each filled with their own remorse.

"I have often been told that I have an unusual face. It's uncanny that you both think I remind you of someone," Helen said, without moving her gaze from Josephine's. "I imagine everyone has a twin somewhere."

"I had a twin," Raymond offered, "My brother Adam."

"Oh how nice. Where is he tonight?"

Everyone at the table shifted uncomfortably. Helen ignored the unease. She couldn't let on that the reason she was in Jamaica was because of the very man they referred to.

"Are you new to the island or are you just new to these parts?"

Raymond asked.

"I have been here a week. I just graduated from high school and I wanted to do a bit of traveling before college."

"Why Jamaica?"

"My mother was from here. I was born and raised in England. Both my parents died tragically when I was young and I can't help but wonder if I still have roots here. I was adopted when I was two years old. Somehow it feels right to know where one is really from. My mother it seemed never talked much about the island although Nana said she missed it desperately. My father was British. She was ostracized from her family when she married my father. She kept in contact with a sister, but I guess Nana could not find the sister after my parents died."

"What was your mother's name?"

"My mother's name was Stephanie Stenson. Her maiden name was Francis."

"Francis? Were they from these parts?"

"I believe so. From the letters I could find, my mother used to write to a sister of hers in New York and they often reminisced about a place with this name. Her sister's name is Andrea Francis. I tried to send a letter to the address on the letters, but as Nana predicted, they all came back. I came here in hopes that some of my relatives still remain and that I might find the other half of my roots."

"This is most curious," Josephine looked at Helen, but quickly the steely gaze softened. "We knew some Francises once. The entire family moved to New York some twenty or so years ago. We never saw them again until Andrea showed up when my brother Adam became desperately ill. She has a sister named Stephanie."

"My goodness!" Helen exclaimed, I wonder if they could be the same people?"

"I am pretty sure, if they are from these parts. Only one set of

Francises here. If you are interested why not let me take you to their old family house? I think they still own it. There may be a couple of servants there you could talk to. My brother was very much in love with your Aunt Andrea. He died with her at his bedside. Extraordinary really, their love. Come to the house tomorrow for lunch and I will tell you what I know about your family."

"Oh thank you," Helen said sadly, "I would love to if it's not too much trouble. I can't believe my luck. I didn't dream my search might be so easy. I would be so grateful for your help, Miss Stern. Maybe after this trip and knowing about my family I can go on and continue my schooling. I just had to know."

"Please call me Josephine. I am glad to help. Your Aunt Andrea was a real comfort to Adam and my family admires her greatly. She lives in New York and is now Mrs. Scott Preston. She is the Andrea Jacobson of Jacobson's Industry. I suppose it would have been hard to trace her not knowing her name had changed. Raymond is in contact with her, aren't you dear."

"Yes I will give her a ring tomorrow and let her know you are here."

"Oh please, no. I would so much like to surprise her. I will plan to visit her before I return to England. I hope you will let me at least have that wish. For so long I have prayed for a family of my own and now I can't believe I will actually have one."

"Of course my dear, as you wish."

"Thank you so much for everything tonight. I am so relieved that I think I will go now but, if you give me directions, I will arrive tomorrow. What time would be convenient?"

"Noon. And we will send a driver to get you."

With that Helen scribbled the address of Lover's Cove on a napkin. She wished the damn place had another name. It was not complementary to her innocence. Her goal was now accomplished. She would find Andrea Francis-Jacobson-Preston's

Achilles heel and she would make her a nobody, begging in the streets.

New York

Andrea beeped the horn at the gate of her family's home in Roslyn. It was still beautiful, but now with her father and her grandmother gone, and all the sisters grown up with lives of their own, it was so quiet. The front door opened as Andrea approached.

"Hello, Mother."

"My darling," her mother kissed her cheek, "come inside."

It was unusual for the two women to embrace warmly, but Andrea was very glad to be in her mother's arms.

"Why, Mother?" she pleaded, "Why me?"

"Andrea, yours was a difficult pregnancy and a hard birth for me. From the beginning you seemed determined to exercise your individuality. You were the happiest child, always laughing. Then when you were only two you almost died from a fever so high that only the gods could have saved you. But you refused to let go. As I sat holding you, grief-stricken, I suddenly felt a surge of confidence inside of me. Immediately, I knew you would live. I had given you my will. I have felt very close to you since then and have protected you always. No one else noticed the change in me, not your father, not even the nurses. I knew for sure then that you were *special*, that your purpose on earth was beyond the ordinary. And darling, it has all been true, just look at your successful life and the gift of wealth and happiness that you have given to so many."

"Like whom, Mother?"

"Andrea! Jacobson's Industry employs thousands of people. You have affected each and every one of their lives."

"Do you think I have 'powers,' mother, extraordinary

powers?"

"Yes, after your illness, I knew you had inherited the same powers that I possess. You were my only child to have received this gift. Since the age of six I was aware that I possessed innate powers. I had been successful at controlling them until an unfortunate incident in England.

"Andrea, I hoped you would never find out how special you are. I'm sorry, darling. Perhaps if I had told you, I could have spared you some misery, but I wanted you to have a normal life. But don't be alarmed by your gift. There are many in the world just like us who have gone through life without really knowing the true value of their powers. Nevertheless, I was always overprotective because I was afraid for you. What you perceived as anger from me was fear. I did not want to leave you when I went to England, but your father insisted.

"Since the incident in England I have never used my powers. When you were with Adam, I wanted to, but I never did."

"Mother, I must tell you. I had a daughter while I was in England. She too has these powers and I am afraid she may use them to hurt me. Her guardian Maya, is the daughter of the woman to whom that unintentional accident occurred. For generations, mother, they have wanted us in their fold."

"I know of your child."

"Mother, what are you saying?"

"I woke up on the night you gave birth with severe pains in my abdomen, cramps just as I had at your birth. I had called Stougborough weeks before and was told you had taken a leave of absence for four months. Instinctively, I knew why."

"What do I do now, Mother?"

"Now that you are forced to acknowledge your specialness, you must spend time understanding the depth of your powers even though you may never have to use them. Helen has had more practice than you, but as your offspring, her powers can never be greater than yours, just as yours can never be greater than mine. My child, I can help you. Many people have special qualities and their only difference from others is their deep and profound need for self-understanding. It is the prerequisite for understanding one's special powers."

When Andrea returned from seeing her mother, she was a different person, one Scott had never seen before. The woman that he had come to know and love had become a shadow of her former self. Scott watched as Andrea retreated deeper and deeper into herself. There was nothing he could do about it. He wanted her to get help for what he thought was serious postpartum depression but it was to no avail. To Andrea, he did not seem to exist. She was so distant that even when they made love he no longer felt close to her. Scott was angry not so much for his own anguish, but because Andrea's way for coping with her pain was to block out the rest of the world, a world which included their son.

"Scott," Andrea said one night as they got ready for bed, "I'm going away for awhile. I would like to go to France with my mother for a month or two. I'll take Reginald and his nanny unless you want them here with you."

"Andrea, running away is not the solution. You are still running away from a problem you should have faced seventeen years ago. I am not going to let you go."

"Since when do you have the authority to tell me when to come and go? I thought this was a marriage of equality. I should have known better. Men are all alike."

"That is quite enough, Andrea. I am not the one who has shut you out of my life. For God's sake, I am your husband. I want to be with you, but Andrea if you continue to hide away every time you can't cope with a problem, I am not sure this marriage can make it."

"Well, you finally said it," Andrea snorted, "You're just like the rest, when things don't go the way you want, you're ready to call it quits. Why does going away have to mean denial? All I wanted to do was find some answers. You are the one who got me into this in the first place. If you can't understand that, then the damage to this marriage has already been done and you can leave whenever you want to."

"You would like that, I'm sure."

"Scott, I told you a long time ago that I was *jinxed* as far as relationships are concerned. You're the one who wanted to get married. I agreed to marry you so you would never betray me."

"Betray you? Whatever do you mean?"

"In my paranoia, I believed that you were part of a conspiracy against me. You have proven that our love is important to you and believe me I feel the same way, but *please* Scott, allow me this; don't threaten my future. I have to do this on my own."

"I want what's best for you Andrea, but going to France is not the answer. Your place is here with Reginald and me. All the help you need is right here. Andrea before we both say things we will regret, let's talk about this further when we are both calm."

"Well, can't you call on your higher self for the strength to be calm?" Andrea said condescendingly, but feeling the last wind go out of her fight.

Scott had had enough. He walked over to his wife and took her by the arm, squeezing it so tightly that she felt her circulation stop.

"Sit down," Scott commanded, forcing her to the edge of the bed. He hovered over her unemotionally, like an eagle ready to strike.

"You will not go to France, Andrea. This is not an order, as you wish to think, it is a very strong request. There is somewhere I would like to take you and I will not take no for an answer. Once and for all you must understand the true meaning of spiritual awakening. Andrea, I love you. I want to share your happiness as much as I want to be there for you in your times of uncertainty. But I feel so helpless. You are forcing me out of your life, and I can't just sit by and let you destroy us. Tomorrow night there is meeting that I would like you to attend with me. There will be a special guest speaker I think you will find interesting."

Scott understood Andrea's isolation. After his first wife died he had gone down the same path when he confronted his loss, coming so close he remembered, to giving up. He was forever grateful to the people who forced him, inspite of his resistance to find his inner peace. It had been hard work. Now, he was convinced, his purpose in Andrea's life was to help her to find inner tranquillity. He loved Andrea so much. If only she knew how much.

"Very well, Scott," she said with resignation, "I'll go." It was time for her to help herself, to bring her external and internal being into harmony, to learn to love from a position of strength rather than weakness. The strain and guilt over how she had lived her life, and now the realization of her spiritual responsibilities were too much for her. She no longer look forward to each new day. With her real life challenge now clearly before her, the tremendous success she had made of Jacobson's Industry paled in comparison. Her dynasty could not bring her peace. And her son, she shuddered, would suffer as much as her daughter if she did not pull herself together. She owed her healing to Reginald, to Helen, to Adam, to Scott, but mostly to herself.

Andrea sat in the back row of the church just in case she had to make her escape. She nodded to everyone who acknowledged her, but made no effort to become involved in conversation.

411

Andrea was lost in thought when the speaker began.

"The need to live with purpose and meaning is greater than the need to conform," the voice stated, "and all of us want to live. But it takes courage to live." Andrea looked up. Lance! How glad she was to see him. The familiar voice was comforting as always.

"There is no oppression but in the mind. Oppression, condemnation, anger and hatred are only disguises for fear. Fear that prevents us all from the search for harmony in our lives. If we want harmony in our lives we can have it, but I tell you tonight, it will probably be the hardest work you have ever done. But you might say to me, why have our riches, power, wife, husband, children not made us happy? Because my friends. No one can give it to you. Not your work. Not your husband, brother or child. Not your riches or your power. You and *only* you can give it to yourself. But why, you might ask, must we first experience such pain, such disharmony to be happy? To get rid of fear and anger and guilt creates the disharmony that is sometimes the catalyst for change. Only very few of us are willing to do the work necessary for attaining spiritual harmony. That is why there is so much pain and suffering in the world. And when we attain such harmony, we must continue to challenge ourselves to grow and to help others. The reason for our growth will then be positive and we will have found the perfection that is intended for all mankind. You will no longer have fears and since fear is what brings disharmony, you will be free."

"Oh Lance," Andrea choked back the tears. "You have appeared just when I needed you. When the student is ready, she whispered, the teacher will come." Andrea felt a tremendous pain in her heart, a pain she could not share with her husband or her mother or her son. A pain that was created out of the bondage of love and of hate and of guilt. Stripped of all trappings of wealth and fame, she was empty. Her love for Scott, although real and profound was only a temporary bandage for her wounds. In her life, because she had not understood, she had failed Adam, she had failed Helen, she had failed Ralph and Graham, and Laura. She would put that all behind her now. She would not fail her husband, but most of all she would not fail herself.

It all made sense for the very first time. *Love*, the simple power to love *oneself* was what she had struggled to find for so long. So much pain; so many disappointments; so many fears; so many, many years. And all the time she had spent in search of love, she finally acknowledged, was nothing more than the search for herself. Yes, ah yes, she breathed a sigh of relief. Love was indeed one's only shield. Liberation, strength, love. She would find it all.

Andrea, armed with new understanding, and finally realizing she would no longer fail herself was ready for the challenge that only few could face. After all, winning was her forte. It fell, as always, in the realm of controllable consequences.

Chapter 38

New York

Andrea, took off her glasses, not the chic gilt-framed Ferres, but her bifocals. She was satisfied. She was delighted. She was complete. All her plans were made.

Today was her fortieth birthday, and to Andrea it signified the beginning of a new life. She had finally conquered and vanquished the ghosts of her past. In this, her mother and Lance had proved invaluable. And Scott, dear, dear Scott. She would never choose to do without him. She understood the magnitude of their love as well as their separateness.

"Darling, I am taking you to lunch today. Will you meet me at the office? I want to wish you a happy birthday," he kissed her. "And, I want to remind you just how much I love you."

"Where are you going?"

"Un Deux Trois, of course." His eyes twinkled. "It means one...."

Andrea made a murderous face, "Insult me at your own risk!" She puckered her lips to be kissed.

"Goodbye, love. Don't be late." He walked towards the door.

"I'll hurry with my packing." she called after him.

With Reggie close to school age, she had thought it best that they have a new home, not Scott's house on Long Island. She felt that house belonged to the past and contained too much of his life with Angela. She had sold the apartment in the Trump and her house next door to Scott's. They would keep the apartment on 86th Street for New York excursions. They were building a permanent home, one that would be just theirs.

Andrea had grown so close to Scott over the years that she could not remember what life had been like before him or imagine it without him.

With the house near completion, she took a last look to make sure there were no last-minute changes to the plans. In three months they would move into their new home.

In front of the Plaza Hotel, Helen stepped off the curb and into the street to flag a taxi.

"Lady," the cab driver said as he screeched to a stop, "that was a dangerous stunt. If I were you I'd learn how to whistle. Where to?"

"Southampton."

"That's a good hour-and-a-half away, maybe even two."

Helen handed the driver two one hundred-dollar bills. "That should ease your mind," she said. He took the money along with the hint that she was not in the mood for small talk.

The doorbell rang.

"Mommy, Mommy, there's someone here to see you!"

Reginald bounced up the stairs. "She says she's my sister. Do I have a sister, Mommy? Do I?"

"Reginald dear, it is time for nursery school." She caught her son as he hurled himself against her leg. "Go and find Melissa and David and be off before you are late. Don't forget your lunch," she called after her little tyke, already halfway down the stairs.

"OK, Mom, but please, can my sister stay until I get back?"

Andrea headed downstairs immediately. She had been expecting Helen to appear for four years and although she was surprised, how appropriate it was on *this day* of all days. At the top of the stairs she paused to look over the banister. No one was there. Who would play such a practical joke? She reached the foyer and still saw no one. Reggie was already in the car.

"Melissa? Melissa, where are you? Reginald said someone was here." Taking a deep breath Andrea walked toward the front door.

"Hello, Mother," a cool voice behind her spoke, "I am home."

Andrea spun around. There was no mistaking that face. She was four years older, but it was Helen. And as promised, she was wearing her birthday brooch.

Their eyes met and held. Andrea's stripped tiger eyes locked with the dark eyes of her daughter. Helen smiled, but Andrea was sure she saw fire flash behind the translucent irises before they embraced. It was beginning.

THE END